by

Dirk Walvoord

"ARC" is a work of fiction. Characters and situations arise from the fevered imagination of the author and any resemblance to people living or dead is purely coincidental.

ISBN-13: 978-1-950547-25-8

Cover design by Robin Ludwig Design Inc.
www.gobookcoverdesign.com

"It is that hunger to be moved that elevates us. It is that need to immerse ourselves in a story like this that redeems us."

Kees DeWet
Jan. 7, 2181

CHAPTER ONE

The ruddy glow of the engine housing gradually fades to black. The artless, ungainly *Scavenger* glides through space toward a scattered cluster of eleven power cell cylinders, each cell five meters diameter by seventy meters length. As the distance closes, bow thrusters ignite to synchronize the *Scavenger*'s pace to that of the cluster.

Kees DeWet eases into the worn captain's chair. His first mate, Dahlia Cutter, glances up in quick recognition and returns her attention to her sensor readouts. Kees peers at the LCD display and feels the adrenaline surge.

"Radiation?"

The radiation sensor already has Cutter's full attention. "Six hundred R."

"Back us off to eight klak."

Cutter eases the navigation sliders down. "Eight klak, aye sir."

The cells recede. Kees' fingers fly over the keypad in the arm of the chair. The display zooms in, 2X, then 4X, then 8X. The Steenmeyer logo is unmistakable.

The Steenmeyer J-26 has always had a unique operating

signature. You can pick it out from background noise as far away as sixty thousand klak. Over the eighty-some years since the *ARC*'s disappearance, hundreds of scavengers have combed this debris field, looking for that signature. You find the Steenmeyers—you find the *ARC*.

And here, in this God-forsaken corner of space, is a cluster of eleven Steenmeyer J-26s. There should be twelve. There's no signature because they were powered down before being jettisoned. Why are non-operating power cells giving off radiation, and where's the twelfth one?

"You count eleven?"

"Aye sir."

At Kees' keystrokes, the monitor displays a schematic of the *ARC*—a massive ship, at the stern of which is an array of cylinders. He has dreamt of this day for years—studied her configuration a hundred times. Just to be sure, he marches his finger around the schematic display and counts to twelve.

He rotates the display toward Cutter and watches his first mate for any sign of reaction. "What take you, mister?"

She gives the display a long look. "Promising, captain."

Efficient and cool, as always. No hint of excitement—no clues of any kind from her hard, trim body. Not that a woman can afford body language on a ship like this. If the men around you are hammerheads, no matter what message is sent, all they get is, "I'm a nail."

She stares at him and waits ...

"Affix our claim flag and set a course along their trajectory."

"Aye, sir."

#

An iris opens in the belly of the *Scavenger* and a spacesuit muscles a torpedo out into the void. The iris closes, the torpedo's propulsion unit lights up and it heads toward the cluster of power cells.

Talons close on one of the cylinders. A flagstaff unfolds from the torpedo housing, a claim flag mechanically unfurls into the

2

eternal, windless night and the tip of the staff blinks red.

The *Scavenger*'s propulsion fires up and she accelerates sharply.

#

The *ARC*'s Observation Deck is lined on three sides with bookshelves. A transparent hemisphere dominates the fourth wall.

A desiccated man sits erect before a large monitor, beyond which his hollow sockets "gaze" at the starfield creeping toward him. An open book rests in his lap and his arm is propped so that in death he still seems about to click the mouse.

Into the starfield creeps the bow of the *Scavenger*—very close.

#

Kees steps over the clutter of projects half-finished on the floor of the *Scavenger*'s launch bay. He examines the docking port of the utilitarian shuttlecraft.

Cutter seals her gloves to the sleeve ring of her space suit. "You going to board her?"

"Shouldn't I?"

"This no Ishwaddi long-hauler." She pauses. "Peacekeepers find you out, they'll take everything."

"And why would the Peacekeepers find me out? Why this time?" Of course she has already given that answer: *This no Ishwaddi long-hauler.* "No one is to follow me until I order it so."

He climbs into the cramped pilot's seat and closes the canopy, feels the excitement rising. In a universe where space travel has become steadily more mundane and tedious, there's a small handful of ships that continue to stoke the curiosity of the masses. And the *ARC* is the queen of that domain. When launched back in 2091, she represented the hopes of a Terran world that had lost all hope. All of Earth's dreams and aspirations were projected onto this vessel and the passengers who shipped out on her. In every corner of the galaxy where her name is known, the question lingers, "What happened to her?" And now, if every indication is true, the *ARC* is drifting less than two klak off the *Scavenger*'s port bow and Kees DeWet is about to become the only person able to

3

answer that burning question.

Cutter twists the bubble helmet onto the collar ring, gets a thumbs-up from the captain and initiates a noisy purge of the atmosphere in the bay.

The iris opens. She flips a switch on her boots, checks the now-active magnetism, then shuts down artificial gravity in the bay. Unsecured items drift slightly. She walks laboriously to the shuttle, lifts it a few centimeters and muscles it toward open space—watches as it disappears behind the closing iris.

Kees peers out the canopy as the exterior of the massive, ghostly "flying Dutchman" glides past. She's over ten klak in length. When the *ARC* was built, they probably still used miles. Kees runs the conversion in his head. Seven miles long, three-and-a-half wide and over a mile high. If there's a derelict out there with more mass, more steel tonnage, he's never heard of it.

The sight of all this scrap should be generating visions of bare-breasted wait-girls arriving at the lanai of some luxury suite on Velkaa VII, late in the morning, their trays laden with exotic fruits and foaming mugs. For each ton of steel delivered to the scrappers, a man can buy two or three days of every imaginable delight. And there's not millions of tons of steel, there's tens of millions of tons of steel. All that's needed is for Cutter to fire up the plasma torch and start in.

Cutter has a first name—it's Dahlia—but no one calls her that, and with good reason. When she's on the torch, every piece of hull-plate is within a few centimeters of OHD (Optimum Hauler Dimensions). She never spills ores or rare earths—there's never any tailings or uncollectables. When she's finished, nothing's left behind.

But Cutter's not on the torch. She's on the *Scavenger's* bridge, watching Kees skim the derelict's exterior.

As klak after klak of her hull slides by, the shroud of mystery remains opaque. No blast marks; no breaches. Ninety years in open space is hard on a ship's exterior. Yet her basic structure is sound.

Kees inspects the massive engine. There are no cracks in the mounts and the blast chamber is as it should be for an engine properly shut down. For some reason her captain decided to interrupt the journey. Why?

Jury-rigged scaffolding extends several hundred meters from the stern. The twelfth power cell is there, cobbled onto the far end. A rigid human figure drifts near where the two connect.

Only a fool boards a derelict. If a ship was abandoned by her crew, whatever is inside wasn't worth taking. If she wasn't abandoned . . .

Gruesome tales are retold around the "scavengers' campfire" to remind everyone of the price oft exacted upon the curious—tales of scavengers infected or ravaged by some alien life form, microbial or otherwise, secreting itself on board.

But this is not "some derelict," this is the *ARC*. If ever there was reason to take that risk . . .

From the time space became littered with enough scrap to make scavenging a viable occupation, "trash-pickers" have dreamt of finding her. What place will there be in scavenger lore for the man who stole their dreams, if he comes to market with a hold full of scrap and no story to tell?

Kees nuzzles the shuttle to the *ARC*'s docking hatch. Puffs of dust as the long-unused latches engage. If the *ARC*'s sensors and servos are powered up, he should get a readout. He waits.

One green light. The seal integrity falls within acceptable parameters. A second green light and while the terminology on his cockpit display is antiquated, the iris in the *ARC*'s hull appears to have retracted.

Every working brain cell tells him that holding his breath is useless. He takes a deep breath anyway and then activates the shuttle's iris.

He stifles a quick image of the canary dead in the bottom of the cage and, despite his lung-full, sniffs the now-mingled air.

It's a little stale.

He unbuckles from his seat, snakes his way forward, squeezes through the narrow docking hatch and drops onto the floor of the *ARC*'s pressure lock.

He has seen all these vintage control mechanisms before—just never in this kind of pristine condition.

What a collector couldn't do with these!

But that would require an Alliance-issued Salvage License rather than a simple scavenger permit.

"Task at hand, Kees, task at hand."

He peers into the dark hallway, then turns back toward the empty shuttle. After a moment he keys in commands for the *ARC*'s iris to spool shut. He's in, and he's in to stay.

The conduit from the power cell is patched through the ship's hull in what must be engineering. That would be to his right.

Ahead is a faint glow. The room itself is unlit, but for some reason the power-usage display has its monitor set to "permanent on." He stares at the schematic and gets his bearings. The only light left on is on the "front porch."

Kees makes his way through the labyrinth of corridors to the Observation Deck.

He pauses in the entryway to take in the scene. Sitting in the chair, the mummified man stares through the portal at the *Scavenger*.

Kees thumbs the safety of his weapon, advances cautiously. Upon closer investigation, he secures his weapon and looks closely at the book, open to its first page.

"Call me Ishmael."

#

The desiccated hand, propped just so, insists that the mouse be clicked. Kees DeWet stands here today because in situations like this one he analyzes first, leaps second.

The figure wears a robe—homespun, of simple construction. This was no vain man preserving his splendor. No, he had some other goal in mind. In dying, what pains had he taken to assure that he would sit erect, head up, arm propped just so? Personal vanity could hardly drive a man to do that.

Kees once saw a holo of the *ARC*'s captain, Edward Timms III—a large man and proud, by the look of him. History paints him a small-minded man, disinclined to this sort of flair for the dramatic.

No, the man in this chair is some prophet, some guardian of secrets, some steward of . . . what? There is only one way to tell: click the mouse.

A crackle of static and the monitor comes to life. On screen, the head and shoulders of an old man, almost certainly the soul seated here in the Observation Deck.

"Call me Ishmael, for that is in fact my given name." His voice is deep and resonant, his brown eyes gaze directly into the camera. "Like my fictional namesake, I am the sole survivor, the final chronicler of the events aboard this great ship." Ishmael sounds like a genial old friend, but with undercurrents of pathos and drama behind the engaging affability.

His onscreen image fades to newsreel and promotional footage of the construction of the great ship in an orbiting assembly platform.

"The saga began before I was born, in the Terran calendar year, 2084."

Scenes roll by of dignitaries, leaders and shakers junketed into space to observe progress.

"News of the Andromeda Expedition's discovery of a pristine planet fired the imagination of Earth's inhabitants. When the heartbreaking news finally reached back to Earth that those pioneers' hopes had been despoiled by the unforeseen sterilizing effect of long-term cryo-sleep, it only stoked humanity's passion for planetary colonization."

Kees knows of the Andromeda Expedition, though only in general terms. Details of Earth's early attempts to colonize habitable planets never were particularly forthcoming. Interstellar travel was brand new and none of those first colonizing efforts went as planned. Little wonder that the companies responsible for them discouraged in-depth reporting.

"And so was born the Andromeda Repopulation Consortium,

whose acronym—A, R, C—is of course the name with which this ship was christened." A shot of the logo atop a massive headquarters building—ANDROMEDA REPOPULATION CONSORTIUM—is followed by corporate promotional footage of an obviously wealthy, sophisticated couple beaming as their mid-twenties son and blue-blood daughter-in-law hold up a giant certificate of acceptance.

"Within eighteen months, funding was assured and the first girders of the great ship's keel were laid. Earth was to send her brightest and best, pioneers whose grandchildren and great grandchildren, born aboard this ship, would one day walk in paradise. The ARCans, or so we called ourselves, were selected for their intelligence, physical superiority and emotional stability, but also screened for potential genetic flaws."

Newsreel footage shows a riot outside an ARC screening facility. "Competition for the one thousand berths was intense. Violence erupted at many ARC recruiting facilities, fueled by allegations of bribes, corruption and favoritism."

A cold weariness settles over Ishmael's voice as he narrates the events from that dark period in Earth's history.

On screen: Manhattan Island under ten meters of water. "The climatic upheaval of 2087 and the subsequent world-wide economic collapse threatened to derail the project."

The wealthy parental couple reappears on screen, only this time the tearful wife surrenders items of jewelry to an ARC collector. Kees whistles low at the absolutely pristine '85 Toozy, from which the husband retrieves and hands over the fob. "But additional fund-raising," Ishmael's voice-over continues, "and stringent cost-cutting made it possible for the ARCans to finally board the ship on January seventeenth, in the year of our Lord twenty ninety-one."

The *ARC* fires its maneuvering thrusters and eases away from the orbiting construction dock. Celestial-scale fireworks.

"A magnificent departure, it was."

The last of the massive fireworks display fades on the screen. Ishmael's narrative pauses for a dramatic second then resumes with a dark and somber tone.

"Twenty-seven months into the voyage, it was discovered that the cowls of the Steenmeyer J-26 fuel cells were defective—the unhappy result of cost-cutting by the Consortium."

A maintenance pod creeps a few feet above one of the power cells. It splays a fan of laser light across the exterior skin.

The scene shifts to the engineering section, where workers line one wall of the ship's interior with lead panels.

"Shielding, though helpful, proved to be inadequate. The ovulation and menstrual cycles of the women had already become erratic by the time the cause was discovered. Shortly thereafter, they ceased altogether."

A plain, homely woman stands before the assembly of beautiful people. Her body language says fear, but there is defiance in her eyes.

" . . . except for Hagar, a servant to the ship-master's consort who, as punishment for her insolence, had been banished to the forward hold of the ship—farthest from the fuel cells."

Insolence? Kees turns from the screen, stares out the portal at the *Scavenger*, hanging in space a few klak away.

What sort of ship was this that there were servants, where insolence was sufficient cause for banishment? The ARCans on the screen are as beautiful, as perfect as the legends describe them. Could it be that this olive-skinned, exotic soul was now the only fertile woman on board?

" Even if..." Ishmael's image stutters and the audio blanks out. After a few seconds of white noise: "... fifteen years before . . . likelihood of the Consortium . . . rescue mission . . . zero . . . no financial incentive."

Kees stares at the screen as Ishmael's trailer degenerates into broken images and unintelligible syllables. The image clears briefly and a spacewalker executes a spot-weld on the scaffolding, the immediate vicinity littered with his floating comrades, rigid in death. The audio spits out "fuel cells" and "jettisoned" before falling completely silent. The screen's last visual is of a golden wheat field, its beards nodding in a steady rain. The image freezes with droplets hanging in the air.

Kees clicks the mouse, only to have the screen go dark. He strides to the portal and gazes into the starfield that was Ishmael's last sight. "Why?" he intones to no one.

Melodrama is not a trait one normally associates with scavengers and yet Kees turns his attention back to Ishmael and sweeps his arm toward all the elements of the carefully staged scene. "Why all of . . . this?"

Something about the bookshelves arrests his attention. In all the rows upon rows of book spines, each meticulously aligned dead flush with its neighbor, one tome protrudes. He pulls out *Raise the Titanic*, its cover art depicting the great ship breaking the ocean surface one last time. He runs his fingers over the raised printing, his mind a million miles and two hundred years away. If he remembers the story right, some fictional oceanographer refloated the great lady, towed her into New York harbor, restored her . . .

"Nah," he mutters to the empty room and then returns the book to the shelf, flush. Upon further reflection, he eases it an inch out of line, as it was when first he saw it.

Suddenly energized by the concept blossoming in his imagination, he charges into the darkened hallway and makes his way toward engineering.

CHAPTER TWO

Edward Timms III flicks a mote of lint off his lapel. *We do have to keep up appearances.* Funny, there wasn't a single course at the Academy on maintaining appearances. He'd taken all those classes on motivation, leadership, command, and decision-making. When was the last time he'd used anything from his Academy curriculum?

He steps out onto the bridge's starboard wing and peers at the dock, now thirty yards away. Leontine makes subtle adjustments to rudder and thrusters. She's the best he's had in years. It never occurs to him to order any kind of "ahead, one quarter," or "right full rudder." What could ensue except distraction and confusion?

A passenger waves from the promenade deck. He returns the greeting with a benevolent smile. That poor soul thinks Captain Timms is somehow responsible for docking smoothly. In truth, the only thing he's responsible for is accepting the blame if anything gets fouled up.

A few stars manage to penetrate the haze and a full moon hangs low above the horizon. Lake Michigan is dead calm, but then when they're "at sea" the lake is always dead calm.

He glances up. *"Space, the final frontier,"* except not for Edward

Timms. Who would have thought that the son of Edward Timms II, the grandson of the prodigiously decorated Edward Timms, would fail to get a Federation commission upon graduating from the Academy? *All right, maybe I wasn't head of the class,* but how had the strings not been pulled? How had the back room deals not been struck?

Movement across the face of the moon interrupts his reverie. The *ARC* is up there, nearly complete, and at seven miles long and three wide, plainly visible. He retrieves the binoculars from their wall-mounted case and dials the magnification up to max. If he can trust his eye, it looks like they've finally gotten all the power cells attached.

He rubs his hand across his face—tries to wipe away the boredom and nagging frustration. In another two months it will be twenty years. How does time fly so fast when the hours crawl so slowly?

Leontine shuts down the thrusters. "All secure, captain."

"Very good, mister."

"Permission to leave the bridge, sir?"

"Granted. Good night, Leontine."

"Good night captain. See you tomorrow."

Tomorrow, yes. Tomorrow morning Edward has an appointment. Uncle Rastus called today—called in person rather than have his secretary do it. Why?

Edward steps back onto the starboard wing. The last of the passengers make their way down the gangplank. *Smile and wave, Edward, it makes them feel good about the voyage.*

\#

The receptionist ushers Edward into the luxurious office. Uncle Rastus rises crisply from his massive desk. "Ah, Edward, so good to see you. Thank you for making time this morning." His handshake is rock-solid as always and his firm clasp on Edward's shoulder delivers just the right feel of familial affection. "Sit down, sit down."

Rastus wears his seventy-two years well. The shocks of gray at his temples give a certain *gravitas* to his still-youthful face. His suit follows his every movement—looks like the tailor cut and stitched it specifically for whatever pose Rastus happens to strike. Edward entertains a fanciful vision: his uncle in a headstand and the suit still drapes perfectly.

"How's my favorite nephew?"

"I'm well, thank you uncle." Somehow the "favorite nephew" ritual doesn't get stale. Uncle Rastus doesn't have any other nephews. The banter is lighthearted, yet there's a feeling of closeness in sharing it, a feeling that comes so naturally one wants to ignore the calculated purposefulness behind it. It's hard to think of anything Uncle Rastus does that doesn't have that calculated purposefulness behind it.

He likes his uncle, likes being with him. It's not adrenaline— more a feeling of "I'm really alive." And this morning, Rastus has something up his sleeve

"So, uncle, what's on the agenda this morning?"

"Well Edward, you've had a long and distinguished career at Endora—twenty years now, right?"

"In about six weeks."

"Ah yes. And yet I seem to recall when you came out of the Academy, you hoped there might be a commission in the space fleet." He pauses for effect. "And I was just wondering if the opportunity came up now, whether you would still be interested?"

That dream has been stifled for so long, can there be any life left in it? Apparently so. His pulse quickens. "Is there some opportunity that has come up now?"

"Have you been following the Andromeda Repopulation Consortium project?"

"They've announced a firm launch date, if I remember right?"

"They have."

"Is this related to the opportunity?"

"If you had a chance to command the *ARC*, would that be of interest to you?"

Would that be of interest to me?

What could Uncle Rastus be thinking? What does he want me

to say? What's his agenda? How is it possible that the prodigious honor of leading the expedition is available to me? Where's the catch?

Edward edges forward in his chair. "I . . . hadn't realized . . . How is it possible that the position is not already filled?"

"Their original choice has backed out."

"Because . . . ?"

"Well, Edward, everyone who ships out on the *ARC* will die there long before the journey is complete. Their children almost certainly will as well. It takes a significant leap of faith to commit to all of that in hopes that the third and fourth generations will reach some promised Garden of Eden. He apparently decided he was not ready to make that leap."

Talk about one's whole world being suddenly turned upside down. How does a plum like this, command of mankind's greatest venture, suddenly fall into the lap of a cardboard mock-up of a captain, a man currently shepherding a sluggish cruise ship through its paces on a lake? "Why me, uncle?"

"You're a Timms."

"And that's enough?"

"I assure you, Edward, the search committee and the vetting process have been most rigorous. They asked me to feel you out because your name is in the very highest bracket of those deemed suitable for the venture. You are in many ways exactly what they are looking for."

"I don't know what to say."

"They realize the magnitude of this decision and will give you or whoever else they have contacted as much time as they can."

"And the projected launch date?"

"A little over three months. One hundred seven days, to be precise."

"And they really want me?"

"If you say yes, especially if you decide quickly, I believe the position is yours. Will you consider it?"

"Consider it? I'll take it."

Even in the best of times, this was a dicey part of town. Over the last months it has become downright dangerous. Of the eight lampposts on the block, only three have a functional bulb. Edward's pulse races—his hand shakes as he looks at the scrap of paper: "5724 W." That's across the street and two houses down.

Something moves in the shadows.

Edward dashes across the street, up the stairs and rings the bell.

. . . and waits.

The house is totally dark. *If there's no power, the bell won't work.* He knocks.

The small glass pane above the door flickers dimly, as though a candle or flashlight were behind it. The peephole darkens. First one, then a second locking device; the chain on the third one rattles. The door opens a crack.

"You Edward Timms?"

"Yes. Are you Xander?"

"Come in."

Edward sidles through the narrow gap allowed by his host. The chain rattles through its hasp and the deadbolts slide home. "Follow me."

Xander is a large man, and powerful. There is a grace to his movement, a sense of solid balance and good coordination.

They descend the stairs to what must at one time have been a separate apartment. Xander sets the stubby candle in the middle of the kitchen table. Its flickering light reflects off the glass panes of the empty kitchen cabinets. "You bring the money?"

Edward slides one hand into his breast pocket and slowly removes the envelope. "Right here."

Xander takes it. "Drink?"

"Uh, yes please."

"Have a seat." Edward's host fetches a handsome bottle from the upper cabinet and a pair of old-fashioned glasses. "Neat?"

"Please." The scotch warms Edward's throat on the way down. It's good scotch—a significant step up from the fare aboard ship. *Who is this man who lives in a rat hole and pours a lovely aged scotch?*

Xander settles wearily into the chair opposite Edward. "I'm sorry about the money. They froze my accounts."

"I understand."

"Do you?"

Of course Edward does not understand. That's why he's here, because there is so much to not understand. "I will be grateful for whatever you can say to enlighten me."

"How much do you know?"

"I know that until eight days ago you were the chief engineer of the *ARC*. Beyond that, my questions to those in charge have been stonewalled at every turn."

Xander is mildly amused by that. "I'm surprised."

"That they're secretive?"

"That after eight days they still haven't settled on their cover story."

"The official announcement, what there was of it, cited 'family issues,' but there have been several 'leaks' from 'undisclosed persons close to the project.'"

"Let me guess—psychological instability? Maybe they've mentioned substance abuse?"

"Yes to both."

"That's more like 'em."

"If those are lies, why not refute them?"

"Do you think I would be living in this hole, asking you to give me money, if I didn't believe they aim to kill me as soon as they can find a way?"

Edward waves off the notion. "Kill you? I hardly think . . ."

"These are not nice people, Edward."

Edward swills the scotch in his glass. So many strange twists in the last weeks and now this seemingly sane person voices what nags at Edward more and more. *These are not nice people.* "Is that why you quit?"

Xander rises thoughtfully, refills his glass and freshens Edward's as well. "I suppose it contributed to the decision. What kind of society will it be aboard that ship when you neither trust nor respect those who have set the selection criteria?"

"How is that a concern, engineering-wise?"

"Originally, the constituent elements of the ship's population were highly engineered."

"I don't understand."

"There are two ways the voyage can fail. There can be a breakdown involving the ship's mechanics, or there can be a breakdown involving the ship's population. To think that those persons who can afford passage at these elevated prices will also fall within the desired psycho-social parameters is unrealistic."

"Surely that's not the reason you resigned, because rich people won't fit into the population?"

"In planning a venture of this magnitude, failure to factor in the possibility of mutiny is folly."

"But the ship itself is mechanically sound?"

Xander's eyes twinkle. "Did I say that? If so, I misspoke."

Edward is less amused. "If you would be so kind . . . "

The chair squeaks as Xander settles back onto it. "Following the cataclysm, the Consortium offered to 'cut regulations' and 'eliminate red tape'. They pressured their suppliers to find creative cost-cutting measures."

"What sort of cost-cutting measures are those?"

"Inferior materials, parts machined to tolerances outside original specifications, reduced shielding, elimination of redundant systems."

"So the ship is not space worthy?"

"If it was just me, my own personal safety, I might still ship aboard. But to risk my family, my good name—my father's good name—that I should be remembered for eternity as 'the chief engineer of the *Titanic*,' those are risks I am not willing to take."

#

Was a time when Solange would breeze through the revolving door and hail a cab. Was a time when there were cabs to be hailed, when litter didn't swirl in the corners of the buildings, when the trendy shops were open rather than boarded up. She pauses at the curb of the once-busy street, waits for the two cars to pass and then crosses to the tram stop.

She had been so above it all—so separated from the masses. How did it never occur to her that the bubble might burst? Does every little girl think her daddy can do no wrong, that even if his world is turned upside down he will still land on his feet?

A number forty-nine tram pulls up to the stop, loaded with people. Six get off and the first six at the head of the queue take their places. Seventeen people are ahead of her in line. She counts the minutes that will be lost waiting. Eight minutes between trams and perhaps five trams until she can board—that would be ...

Solange was never very good with numbers.

Not very good at anything, so it seems. The job interviewer must have mentioned ten things about which she knew nothing—zip—nada. Some things a girl is offered because she's pretty. For others, you need to actually have some skill.

The man in the line three ahead of her feigns interest in what is displayed on his screen. Every time Solange glances his way, she catches him staring at her. A year ago she might have toyed with him—given him flirtatious smiles. Back then she could "practice" on a man like this, a man standing in the line for the forty-nine tram, and then when his hopes were up, leave him ... standing. A cab would arrive or her father's car would pull up and whisk her away and the poor soul would board his tram. That night he could go to bed saying, "A pretty girl flirted with me today."

That was then, when life seemed so much more playful. But today, there's a good chance she and this stranger will share a tram ride, no doubt jammed in. He will position himself so that his body presses against hers. Flirting is a thing to be done at a distance. Somehow it loses its charm when forced intimacy follows closely on its heels.

The next tram arrives and a crowd of people exits, gesturing and yammering in some foreign language. The man three spaces ahead hesitates a moment. *Will he board or will he play the gallant gentleman and offer the lady behind him the last spot?* He shows his practical side and boards, leaving Solange to wait for the next one.

"Catalpa," the mechanized voice announces. In all the years Solange lived just up the hill, she never knew this was a tram stop. No one she knew ever took the tram—well, no one but Hagar.

It was three years ago that Hagar came to that house for the interview. Her mother asked the strange little woman her litany of questions. Solange peered over the railing as Hagar was about to leave.

"No thank you, ma'am, I can catch a tram."

She watched Hagar trudge down the hill, stand at the corner and, when the tram stopped for her, step on.

I wonder if the people who bought our house ever take the tram? Do they even know it stops here? The tram doesn't stop at Catalpa Lane today. No one is waiting to get on and there's no reason for Solange to get off.

Solange's mother greets her at the door to the weary little apartment they now call home, the "lifestyle" section of the local newspaper in hand. "Look at this! There's one more opening on the *ARC* and you get to be the wife of the captain!"

The offer doesn't actually use the word "wife," though the wording cleverly describes a mutually respectful, potentially loving relationship. "Who's to say," her mother offers defensively, "that an arrangement of convenience can't turn into a loving relationship?"

Every few hours there's some new rationale. "A captain has responsibility. What are they going to do, assign it to some shirker? They are not! This man is going to be cosmopolitan, educated, capable," and then with a wink, "worldly-wise." It's almost as if she wants to interview for the opportunity herself.

If her mother married for love, she stayed out of loyalty—some might say out of practicality. She never said it in so many words but the message is clear. *Love between a man and a woman? It's not all it's cracked up to be.* She has said, more than once, in so many words, "It's a generational ship, for goodness sake. You'll have children. Do you think a woman deserves more love than that?"

It's her most persuasive argument and she knows it. Solange has wanted to be a mother since as far back as she can remember. As an only child, Solange would spend endless hours mothering her baby dolls.

Eventually her father joins in. Whether the two of them convince her or she just wants the pressure to stop, Solange submits her application. The interview is scheduled for the very next day.

#

Condescension oozes across from the massive desk. The Consortium screener is a homely woman with brutish, angular features. Her tailored suit screams, "I wish I was a man, I wish I was a man." Her name will not be on the *ARC*'s passenger manifest—she is clearly not going on the voyage—she is clearly not going anywhere. Twenty years from now, she will retire from behind this massive desk with a barely serviceable pension, and that will be that.

How can a bitter woman not be condescending? After all, she is going to ask a delicious question of this stunning beauty. The question is couched in polite terms, but at its heart she asks, "How will you deal with being the captain's whore?"

Solange responds with the same polite code words, but the heart of her answer is as dark as the heart of the question. "If it means I can escape the hopeless depression that engulfs our world, and if it means my grandchildren and great grandchildren will be part of the Andromeda Repopulation, I will be whore to the devil himself and be glad of it."

Is the massive mirror on one wall a viewport? Is the captain actually behind the mirror, or is it only cameras?

"I see you have changed address several times."

"Yes."

"That area on Catalpa is beautiful."

20

"Yes, very nice."

"Why did you move?"

The mouse never actually escapes the cat. "My father's business collapsed after the cataclysm."

"Ah, the cataclysm."

And so the screener lords it over her subject, unspoken of course. "Oh the poor helpless fellow's business collapsed after the cataclysm? Always the lame-ass cataclysm excuse. Maybe he was just an idiot. Maybe he should have seen it coming. The Consortium saw it coming and now you don't see our business collapsing after the 'cataclysm.' We're about to launch humanity's most impressive undertaking since - - - the FLOOD."

Stop it, Solange! Projecting your own evil thoughts on this woman is not going to help. "We moved to conserve financial resources."

"It must have been painful to part with such an expensive house in the midst of the real estate collapse." The screener proves herself to be as ugly on the inside as she is on the outside.

"I'm sure my father would have preferred to sell into a stronger market."

The screener says nothing.

Well, Solange, do you have to take this? Or do you have the sand to stand up to her? "It's right that the Consortium had to take a significant write-off in divesting its real estate arm, yes?" *Let the bitch chew on that one and see how she likes it.*

And if the captain finds me too abrasive, he can choose someone else to be his whore.

A light flashes on the screener's desk. There's new loathing in her eye as she looks up. "That will be all the questions for today."

#

In better times, the hookers would be cruising, offering their services in the rolling seclusion of a back seat. But these are not better times. They stroll the sidewalks or pose in the doorways of the shabby tenements, their pimps never far away.

A tram pulls up at the end of the block and Hagar steps off. She

21

makes her way to her sister's tenement. The threatening low-lifes on the stoop part to allow her to pass. The elevator door stands slightly ajar. The car, seen dimly through the slit, is several inches below floor level. She makes her way to the stairwell.

A john descends from the top floor, tucking in his shirt and zipping his fly as he makes his way toward her. He's a big man— but then, relative to Hagar all men are pretty big.

As they pass he grabs her arm, twists it behind her back and grabs hold of her neck.

"How 'bout it you little fox? You want to see what a really big...?

She tugs his hand away from her throat. He slaps it across her mouth. *Big mistake!* She twists her head, opens her mouth and his middle finger comes into harm's way. She closes on the errant digit—hard—and shakes her head like a shark in a feeding frenzy. She tastes the blood—feels her teeth scrape the bone.

He bellows and lets loose the hand he had pinned behind her back. *Second big mistake.* He tries to beat her about the head but she's too quick for him and deflects the blows with the hand he just freed up. He will win out eventually, but she's not going down without a fight and the finger has to be . . .

"Bo!" Her sister's voice echoes from the landing at the top floor. "You ever want come here again, you let go my sister."

He stops trying to strike Hagar's head. After a second, she releases her bite on his finger. The bone shows white in the ragged gash. He takes out a filthy handkerchief and wraps it—squeezes it to slow the bleeding, and stumbles down the stairs.

Her sister looks down, bemused. "Feisty as ever, I see."

"Yours?" Hagar asks.

"Oh yeah, he one of mine." She closes the robe over her nakedness, ties the sash. "Come on, I fix you cup of tea."

Hagar makes her way up the stairs, shaking a little as the adrenaline in her system backs off.

The apartment is a shabby, beat-up place, saved by a few of Naomi's softer touches—a reproduction of a Monet landscape and a torchière with simple yet elegant design. Naomi boils water.

Hagar fingers the sticky blood on her chin. "Bloody bastard!"

Naomi wets a cloth in the sink and hands it to her. "I thought you bitin' it all the way off. Here."

"I spoil something for you?"

Naomi doesn't smile often but her sister's question elicits just the hint of one. "His finger heal up, he come back."

Hagar wipes the blood off her chin and neck, rinses the cloth in the sink.

"What bring you, little sister?" Naomi asks.

"You remember Solange?"

"The rich little girl?"

"That one. She be . . . "

Naomi interrupts. "Not so rich any more."

"No."

"She want you back?"

"Not exact."

Naomi sets the packet of tea leaves aside, focuses. "Do tell."

"*ARC* captain pick her for consort."

The teapot whistles. Naomi turns off the heat without making tea. "She goin'?"

Hagar nods.

"She take you?"

"She ask." So now it's out—at least the first half.

Naomi dances a little step. "Little sister go the *ARC*, sister Hagar go the *ARC*."

The other half of what Hagar came here to tell hangs in the air; Naomi stops the playful chanting and dancing.

"Little sister *do* go the *ARC*."

Naomi pours a cup of tea and waits. And Hagar makes her wait: sips the tea, takes in the Monet landscape, the torchière, the grimy window looking out onto a brick wall less than a meter away, the faucet with its drip, drip, drip . . .

"This?! For this you give up *ARC*? Oh no girl."

"Yes for this! What in *ARC* for me?"

"What here for you, girl?"

23

"A place of my own. A life of my own."

Naomi rises, angrily paces and gestures. "You call this a place? You like my place? Here, take my place—I take your place!"

"It yours, at least."

"It not mine. You know what I got do for this place? Landlord come here twice a week. When he busy, he send a friend."

Twice a week? "For the rent money?"

Naomi laughs—not a funny laugh. "Rent money? Who got money?" She pulls open her robe. "This! This pay rent." She picks up the gas-fired teapot. "This buy gas." She throws open the sparsely filled pantry. "This get food."

Hagar reaches down and takes a handful of her own crotch. "And this get nothin'!"

That stops Naomi in her tracks. "Men not all they cracked up to be. And besides, there be men on *ARC*."

"I'm slave woman to the captain's whore. There be no man for me. There be no child for me."

There—it's out.

"And then I die. Alone. No man to love me. No child to love me."

"Mm-hmm. How many men on *ARC*?"

"Five hundred."

Naomi is amused by the number. "Five hundred men and you want a child? And because of science they all gonna say no."

"Even if it happen, what kind of life that child got? What kind of world she grow up in?"

"Better than here."

"I don't know that."

"Exact—you don't know. On *ARC*, maybe something bad happen, maybe something good. You don't know, but stay here and you do know. You got to take the chance."

#

Edward's hands shake as he pours himself another shot. *God, this is second-rate swill!*

I know, I'm drunk already. He keeps pouring.

Why shouldn't I get drunk? The salvation of my career, the resurrection of my hopes to be a real captain—all that dangled in front of me a week ago by Uncle Rastus. Now all that jerked away by Xander's revelations.

How had he said it? ". . . to risk my father's good name because I will be for eternity 'the chief engineer of the Titanic,' *that's a risk I am not willing to take." As if anyone gave a flying fart about Xander's good name. What is Xander's name? Not Timms, that's for sure. And who gives a damn about the ARC's engineer? It's her captain who is ultimately responsible for the welfare of her voyagers.*

That would be me—captain of the ARC.

If I stay here, live out my professional life on the bridge of this gaudy monstrosity, my stone will read, "Here lies Edward Timms, III" . . . and then what? Nothing. No one will have anything to say about Edward Timms, III. My branch on the family tree will be nothing more than a withered twig—a footnote without so much as an asterisk to bring attention to it. At family gatherings it will be, "Neddy had the chance to be captain of the ARC but decided to turn it down. Pity."

Stay here, and night after night I'll play the host at the captain's table, chatting up the wealthiest patrons, stroking their inflated egos, making small talk with their dazzling trophy wives or mistresses as the shoreline drifts by.

How different it would be aboard the ARC. There my arm will be graced by God's own creation of female perfection. At the ARC's captain's table, men will be looking at me with envy in their eyes, looking at Solange with lust in their hearts. And when I retire for the night, it will be Solange waiting for me in the bed, eager to please me, appreciative of the favors I've bestowed upon her. And then she will bear me a son, Edward Timms IV. And that son will sire a child of his own and that child another, so that when the ship arrives at her destination, a Timms will lead the way, a Timms will be the founding father of the new Eden. No withered twig on that family tree. Edward Timms III will be the progenitor, the sturdy trunk from which all the noble branches rise.

No, Xander, I don't give a damn that you won't risk it—I will!

And what if Xander's fears are founded, if the ship is flawed? Who is to say that disaster will follow as night the day? After all, haven't adventurers always faced hardships? Is that not what boldness is all about, daring the hardships and dealing with them? Is her captain's reputation not enhanced if something does go wrong with the great vessel and he leads the ARCans in overcoming the challenge? In that light a man could almost wish for obstacles to be hurdled, catastrophes to be averted, disasters to be anticipated and thwarted.

Xander thinks me a fool to go, but this is no fool's errand—it is a Hero's quest.

Edward pours again. *And the scotch will be better, too—better even than yours!*

Despite Edward's blood chemistry, a sobering thought intrudes. What if Xander's evidence leaks? What if his concerns bollix up the final stages of construction? What if the *ARC* never launches? So much for being the bole of a noble family tree. So much for the breathtaking consort at his table and in his bed. So much for the excellent scotch.

Xander's evidence must remain hidden. Yes, the Consortium froze his accounts, but it's baseless paranoia to suggest they want to kill him. Surely a price can be found to buy his silence.

But how—exactly?

If ever a soul knew how to get this sort of thing done, it's Uncle Rastus. Edward dials.

#

The next morning at 8:15, Edward pokes his head into the waiting area of his uncle's office. The earpiece and microphone lie neatly aligned on the desk, awaiting the arrival of the receptionist.

"Hello?"

Barely a second goes by before Rastus opens the door to his inner office. "Edward—come in."

No favorite nephew jokes this morning. Rastus looks tired as he closes and locks the office door. "Let's get straight to it. I would rather we finish this before Lilly gets in."

Edward sits. "I appreciate you making time for me, uncle."

No magnanimous waving off of Edward's gratitude. There's nothing in Rastus' mien this morning to invite chitchat. "Please," he offers.

Edward explains his meeting with Xander and his concern.

"You met with him in person?"

"Yes."

"And how did you find him?"

"Uh, a little shabby. He was . . ."

"Not his state of being—his location?"

"Oh. He found me, actually. I was researching him and he popped up on the screen."

"I see." He waits for Edward to continue.

"He asked me for money."

"And he told you where to go to meet him?"

"He told me where he was going to leave a piece of paper with directions. I guess he didn't want to give away his location electronically."

"Of course. So you gathered the money, went where he instructed and followed the piece of paper to the actual meeting place."

"Yes."

"And where was the actual meeting place?"

Edward takes the scrap of paper from his wallet—unfolds it carefully, "Fifty-seven twenty-four west Dixon."

"Hmm. Way over on the southwest side?"

"I guess so. Yeah, southwest."

It's as though a light was turned on. Suddenly Rastus seems a different man—congenial, relaxed and confident. "You were right to come to me with this, Edward. Now it's important how you deport yourself—how you respond to the questions you are sure to face."

"Questions? From reporters?"

"The media in general, yes. But more than that, the discretion you exercise with everyone throughout the coming weeks."

Edward shifts in his seat. "Discretion?" he asks. *Isn't the Consortium going to pay Xander off, give him some kind of new identity and send him somewhere he won't be found? That's why I came here, for Uncle Rastus to take care of that. Why will there be questions and why do I have to be "discreet"?*

"You managed to track Xander down—it would be naïve to think others will not be able to do the same. If that happens, you will be assumed to have been complicit in the cover-up. Do I make myself clear?"

Crystal comes to mind but with better judgment, Edward says, "Yes uncle, very clear."

CHAPTER THREE

Kees traces the serpentine cable from where it penetrates engineering's outer hull to where it plugs in to the main power panel. He unlimbers his communicator. "This is Kees."

A crackle and Cutter's voice from the device. "Aye, captain?"

"I require a four septa power module."

"Aye sir." A pause. "Captain?"

"Problem?"

"Yours be the only working shuttle."

"Sling it to a jitney bug. I shall open a service bay." He studies the insertion point. "The connector will require a Steenmeyer eight-pin adapter."

Cutter whistles at the outdated request.

"After I have switched over power, use the laser cutter to detach the defective cell. Drain its energy and tag it for later salvage."

"Aye, sir."

"Call me when you are ready to send the power unit. Over."

#

Cutter senses Roman Pollack standing behind her—closer than

she would like.

"Switched over power?" Roman slithers to her side. He is serpentine, silver of tongue and not to be trusted. "What does he mean, switched over power?"

"Captain request a four septa power module with a Steenmeyer eight-pin adapter. I assume he intend to bring her to full power."

Roman leaves a hand on the armrest as he circles in front of her. His voice is smooth and oily with uninvited intimacy. "Have you ever heard of a scavenger repowering a derelict, Cutter?"

"This be no ordinary derelict."

He puts an unwelcome hand on her shoulder, rotates the monitor to give himself a view of the *ARC*. "No?"

She stares at the hand, pans slowly to his face. People seldom stand up to Roman, but she is not people. "No."

He backs out of her space. "And what are we, Cutter, salvagers?"

"We be scavengers."

"Ah yes, and what is our goal, out here in God-forsaken space?"

"To profit from what we find."

"To profit from whatEVER we find, not so?"

"Your words."

Suddenly the silky smooth snake turns threatening. "No, mister Cutter, not my words—words of the contract!"

"Whatever."

The cleverness of that takes Roman completely by surprise.

She smiles innocently. *He thinks me a fool. But then, he is so proud of his own cleverness, he thinks everyone a fool by comparison. And just as well to let him.*

"Scavengers are a hard lot, Cutter. Our only protection from each other lies in obeying the contract."

"Contract says Kees be captain."

"Yes it does, but it is we who made him so. Even the captain is not above the contract."

"Think you this be grounds?" she asks.

Roman uses his sleeve to blot the little beads of sweat that have popped up on his forehead. "Deposing a captain in mid-voyage is not a matter to be taken lightly."

"No, sir."

He weighs for a moment.

He's unequal to the task—breaks eye contact—turns to leave. *The spine of a snake.* Yet also the venom of a snake. It's a fool who turns her back on him, and Cutter is no fool.

"It is in the end only four septa of power. I will have Ugg bring the module to the shuttle bay. A Steenmeyer eight-pin, you said?"

"Aye, sir."

#

Roman waits for the passing crewman to get out of sight, then enters his quarters and locks the door. It would be unfortunate for someone to learn of Imogene's presence in his safe.

He keys in the security code and sets her on his desk. She's a pretty little thing of elegant design—simple to operate, reliable, and more powerful than one would ever suspect to look at her. Image Extended Network. Image E.N.—Imogene.

But her power is also her Achilles heel. If she were plugged directly into the grid, she would set off every alarm on the ship. She's that hungry.

Which is Cappy's *raison d'être.* He's an ugly thing of brutish design—hard to control and prone to gremlins. And yet, without Cappy, Imogene would be useless, impossible to deploy without detection. Roman plugs Cappy's output cable into Imogene's power port—beauty and the beast, conjoined.

While Imogene spends her days idling in Roman's safe, Cappy crouches under his worktable, suckling off the grid. Day after day he stockpiles his meager three quarms of energy, undetected by anyone. Then, when Imogene must be employed, Cappy delivers his pent-up load—releases into her the great spasm of power she demands. If the arrangement is inelegant, it is at least serviceable.

Recent events warrant calling upon Imogene's services, even though the next scheduled packet is not until Friday.

Cappy's gauge reads 71 percent. While that's plenty for today's task, Roman raises the input rate from three quarms to four. The risk of detection is significantly higher at that level but it's a risk he will have to take. If he's right, Imogene is likely to be much more active in the days ahead.

He sets her controls to "capture" mode, sits down before her scanner and closes his eyes. After a moment, she splays a fan of laser light from head to shoulders. A soft chime sounds and the status light turns green.

"This is Roman Pollack aboard the *Scavenger*. We have come upon a massive vessel that by its age, mass and design seems likely to be the *ARC*. For reasons unknown, Captain Kees DeWet appears ready to repower the ship. I require specific instructions how I am to proceed. End of transmission."

He leans forward, touches "stop," then "compress" and then "send." Cappy's discharge meter gutters all the way left. The red bar fills every pixel of the field. After a few seconds the gauge returns to neutral.

Roman will never be smart enough to understand the physics behind how Imogene works. That is the purview of the quirky genius who invented her. Sometime later today, the reply will have filtered into Imogene's passive receptors and she will be ready to display the hologram of his supervisor's instructions. He can only hope those instructions are clear and comprehensive. With Cappy now at twenty-three percent, it will be three days before Roman can follow up for clarification.

In the meantime, there's the matter of the power module he promised to Cutter.

#

Kees holsters his communicator. It will be half an hour before Cutter can deliver the power module. Wasting that time is not an option. There's a world of things to recon and no time like the present to get started on it.

Once he leaves engineering, he'll need light. But then, the ARCans must have faced the same challenge.

Sure enough, next to the doorway is a makeshift rack of rechargeable light wands, six of which are nestled in their slots. A seventh has been laid out diagonally across the top of the rack as though wanting to be more noticed than the rest. He picks it up and twists the handle, happy to see the lighting element respond. He dials the switch to its lowest level and steps into the dimly lit hallway.

Engineering is near the stern, as are the manufacture and fabrication areas, raw material storage, mechanical equipment, forges, smelters and the like. As a scavenger, he should be focused here, on commodities with immediate value. Yet his interest lies in the other direction. One ton of taconite is no different from another. But the residences aboard the *ARC*—the recreation areas, the entertainment venues and places of worship—these things are unique. It's those places and the stories embedded in them that set this ship apart from what Cutter quite rightly called, "No Ishwaddi long-hauler." But for the moment, though his heart calls him to the left, he maintains his scavenger discipline and turns right.

The narrow hallway runs for about a half klak. He slows as the echo from his footsteps changes timbre. The light from the wand, which until now had been reflecting off the walls and ceiling, suddenly reflects off nothing at all. He takes a cautious step or two, then dials the light up to full power.

Even at that intensity, it doesn't reach the farthest corners. The space is a klak-and-a-half in diameter—maybe two. You could fire a small cannon in here and not reach the far side. Vertically, it is nearly as large, perhaps forty stories. Scattered around the circumference, makeshift ladders snake upward from one level to the next.

The motor pool is one level up and to his right. He powers the light wand back down to low, clips it to his belt and scales the nearby ladder.

The door slides open on overhead rails. Inside is a vast warehouse of vehicles, collectibles every one. Kees strolls among them, mentally catalogues what's here and tallies possible values.

Behind the rows of forklifts, haulers and jitneys is a sight to stop a man in his tracks.

Almost as if someone wanted to impress the first visitor, the dust cover has been pulled off the Broitaan 490. Across the galaxy, even now, seventy years after the last one was made, the Broitaan 490 is still the vehicle of choice when powerful political figures and captains of industry arrive at ceremonial occasions. From the day the first model rolled off the assembly line, the 490 has been a symbol of opulence—the absolute standard of luxury. Ordinary mortals seldom get this close, and the honor of it is not lost on Kees. He slides a hand along its velvet-smooth finish, pulls gently on the gleaming door handle. It opens smoothly and quietly. The interior seems none the worse for wear. Can a vehicle over a hundred years old really still smell new?

The tires still hold their air. If he slid into the driver's seat, would the grand dame start up? If time allowed . . .

Just behind it on the left stands a Toozebakker 85. The 85 was discontinued less than thirty years ago and there are constant rumors that Toozebakker might restart production. With its pro-induction matrix and pulse-boost quasar drive, the Toozy is without question the most powerful and sexiest vehicle ever made.

What sort of man or woman departs for a rustic, untrammeled world with a 490 and a Toozy in the hold? The *ARC* has roads, though not of the sort one would call "the open road." Did the owners of these classic vehicles mean to take the Broitaan out for a Sunday picnic in the hills? Did someone hope to arouse women and make husbands jealous by arriving at gala events in his über-sexy Toozy?

The questions pile one on top of the other as Kees rolls the heavy warehouse door shut. He climbed up here looking to tally the number of credits he might expect from scrapping the vehicles inside. Instead he comes out with a whole new set of mysteries about who these people were and what did they do? The answers may or may not reside somewhere on board. But before the mysteries can be plumbed, the first task is to restore power.

Resting on the floor of the *Scavenger*'s shuttle bay is a spidery transport device, the jitney bug. Cutter operates the touchpad on the jitney's "back" and it rises on its four support legs and simultaneously opens its four cradling legs.

Ugg muscles his way through the pressure lock, suitcase-sized power module in hand. He tucks his incongruous pigtails out of harm's way and slides the device under the jitney's belly. Cutter types commands. The jitney squats, captures the module in its cradling arms, then rises slightly with its load nestled beneath.

"This be foolishness," Ugg mutters under his breath.

She gives him a withering stare. "You be the fool who speaks so."

"Repowering be salvage, not scavenging."

That's not Ugg talking.

Ugg has his admirable traits—there's no one she would rather have at her side in a firefight. But the subtleties of semantics? Not included on anybody's list of his strengths. Someone else has put those words into his head.

"Shall I tell Captain DeWet that Ugg withholds the module?"

He stalks out—slams the hatch behind him.

"Thought not."

Kees eases down the ladder and turns the light wand up to full power for one last look at the vast chamber.

The security station, not so noticeable on the way in, catches his attention on the way out. The entranceway is surrounded by electrodes and on either side, draped over their hooks: flak jackets, riot helmets, truncheons, stun wands. This is no "show us your identification" desk; this is a full-scale security checkpoint.

In a normal world, where thieves or malefactors might be afoot, guarding the *ARC*'s resources with this level of force would be the order of the day. But every ARCan was surely vetted before boarding in the first place. Why is it that the *ARC*'s raw materials needed to be guarded, and from whom?

Cutter sits in the captain's chair, the jitney's controller in hand. The LCD screen displays the feed from the jitney bug's "eye." She thumbs the controls and the jitney bug glides through the iris, into open space. "Captain, two minutes."

"The service bay is port, stern, nine o'clock," Kees answers.

"Understood."

#

Roman has been patient all day—well, not actually patient but at least he waited all day. He closes the door behind him and locks it, takes Imogene from the safe and dials her controls to "display."

Imogene's projectors gradually generate the holographic image of Viktor Torquist: first, the dark shocks of hair and the stubby goatee, then the bushy eyebrows and penetrating jet-black eyes. As the rest of his features and the collar and epaulettes of his uniform solidify, he speaks.

"Agent Pollack, you did well to recognize these developments as worthy of our attention. Your record shall include a commendation for taking initiative. It is of the utmost importance that Captain DeWet be prevented from repowering the vessel. Under no circumstance should the ship be classified anything other than scavenging fare. Any attempts at salvage, any collecting or marketing of artifacts will not be permitted. I cannot stress enough the importance of this directive."

Imogene obediently complies with Roman's request to pause.

Viktor is not a man to repeat himself, yet he just now said the same thing three times over. Roman's original orders left no doubt that the Alliance was determined to find the *ARC*, but this focus on its destruction is a new twist.

Imogene invites Viktor to resume his transmission.

"You will be granted immunity from prosecution for any actions you undertake. In addition, the Alliance will match whatever share you have in the contract. This will be over and above the compensation previously agreed upon."

"Pause."

A scavenger signs the contract in his or her own name. No other agenda, no representation of outside groups is permitted. Viktor's suggestion that the Alliance is ready to cross that line—to inject itself into the dynamic of a scavenger crew is . . . disturbing.

Many's the scavenger been murdered or marooned for breaking the contract. If Roman is to play the Alliance's game, it must be done with care.

Not that he can walk away. Whether this is the *ARC* or not, it has massive financial potential. Every member of the *Scavenger*'s crew knew the minute the cells were sighted that their fortunes were multiplied many fold. If scrap rates are anywhere near what they were eighteen months ago, Roman will be a wealthy man in ninety-nine percent of the galaxy. And if the Alliance doubles his share he can go anywhere, do anything, for as long as he wants. It gives reason for pause.

"Resume."

"We are not insensitive to the consequences of your decision. Be advised, however, that failure to prevent Captain DeWet's salvage of the vessel will be most harshly dealt with."

Murdered by my crew if I'm found out spying for the Alliance, and murdered by the Alliance if I fail.

"You are to send a reply packet within one solar day confirming receipt of this message. End of transmission."

Viktor's image flutters away like so many pixels. The knot in Roman's stomach does not.

Somehow he will have to convince at least six of his crewmates that his opposition to salvaging the *ARC* is his own idea, that Kees is wrong and that scrapping her maximizes their profit. First he has to convince Cutter. She's the key.

#

Roman stands in the doorway of the mess hall. Cutter rises from her seat—reaches for the saltshaker. Her perfectly shaped, firm buttocks capture Roman's full attention. A man would have to be dead not to have any reaction to that sight. *Stay on target, Roman.*

He gets coffee from the urn and approaches her table, careful not to get into her personal space.

"Mind if I join you?"

"Help yourself."

Her tone is, as always, perfectly neutral. She doesn't want to share her space with him but has no interest in expending the energy to fend him off.

"Nice day," he says.

"Long's the weather doesn't change." And that's the standard, symbolic answer—the standard answer in a world where the temperature is always a few degrees above absolute zero, where there is no oxygen, no air, no light and a low-level background of deadly radiation. It's accepted tradition. If a person makes any answer to "nice day," they are willing to talk. If not, they're not.

"So he means to repower, eh?"

"Yes."

"He say why?"

"Did the captain explain to me his reasons for repowering the *ARC*? No. He doesn't normally."

So it is the ARC. "He say what's next?"

"The captain also is not in the habit of sharing his future plans unless I need to know."

That's two full sentences she has given. It's encouraging.

She goes on without prodding. "You could ask him when he returns."

"He's returning, then?"

She looks straight at him.

She doesn't know what to do with that question.

She glances around the mess hall to be absolutely sure they are alone. "If the captain were to remain on the *ARC* alone, that would be . . . a problem."

"What's he thinking?"

"I wish I knew," she answers.

"Everyone on board wishes they knew." *Now Roman, carefully,* "You're as close to him as anyone. You could find out."

She looks him in the eye, then shakes a little more salt on her food. "You flatter me."

"I speak the truth. You can learn the captain's plan and I say you owe it to your crewmates."

"To spy on the captain?"

"Not spy, simply observe."

"And do what with my observations, report them to you?"

"Now it is you who flatter me."

"I think not."

No, of course she is not flattering me. But she is talking to me—and she is listening. "We have rights under the contract. We also have responsibilities. If Kees defies the contract, we have a right to know. And if you know it, you have a responsibility to tell. Will you do it?"

She cuts a chunk of meat and chews on it before answering. "I signed the contract. I know my rights and my duties."

One seed planted. If it's not everything he wanted – and he knew going in he wasn't going to get everything he wanted – at least it wasn't a flat-out refusal.

#

Roman locks his cabin door and pulls the compact module from under his coat. He brings Cappy up from beneath the bench and connects him to the module's output cable. It's a huge risk, stealing power, but what else can he do? Viktor Torquist gave him one solar day to respond. He needs Imogene, and Cappy needs a "transfusion" before he's up to the task.

In a matter of seconds Cappy's gauge jumps to 100%. Roman plugs Cappy into Imogene and sits down.

"This is Roman Pollack aboard the *Scavenger*. I have received your packet and accept the duties, conditions and instructions described there. I will prevent the salvage of the *ARC* or die trying. End of transmission."

CHAPTER FOUR

Timms floats up into the restraining straps as the shuttle drops from the mother plane. The firing of the main thrusters drives him back and down, deep into the seat's padding.

The sky outside the window darkens quickly as the shuttle rises through the stratosphere.

Silence as the thrusters shut down. This time, the weightlessness is ongoing. Timms peers out the window, seeks any horizon on which to fix his eyes—settle his stomach. There, far above, the massive space dock lumbers in her orbit, her belly stretched to the limit by the *ARC*, now so near the end of its gestation.

Maneuvering thrusters fire and the shuttle climbs into the dock's orbital plane, waits to be overtaken. As the distance closes, the pilot makes lateral adjustments and the shuttle nuzzles up to the *ARC*'s docking port. *So many tons of bulk dancing in such close proximity.*

"Not so different from what you do, eh?" his uncle asks.

"Except in three dimensions."

"Ah yes."

A gentle impact and the sound of latches closing on their targets. *Leontine would be hard pressed to dock this well.*

Uncle Rastus takes Timms aside, away from the reporters. "They are hungry for any stumble, any statement they can elicit which might sensationalize their story."

The press has tried for days to make Xander's resignation a *cause célèbre.* With no smoking gun, their efforts have had little traction in the face of the Consortium's aggressive pre-launch advertising campaign.

Today, as they tour the massive ship, the reporters ask all the obvious questions. "Does the forest really create enough oxygen to keep the atmosphere in balance?" "How many bushels of wheat does this field generate in a year's time?" "Can the voyagers choose their own wall colors?" *Stupid questions. Why don't they ask, "Can the engine fire continuously for thirty years?" "What if there's an 'iceberg' along the way? Can you detect that in time and avoid it?"*

#

The crowd files into the grand hall, its tables strewn with sterling, crystal and delicate china. Course after course of gourmet delights follow upon each other. The President gives his welcoming address, followed by the Consortium's CEO, Augustus Pollack.

Pollack finishes his prepared address and, just when all should be sweetness and light, Kyra Mayford of Amalgamated Press comes to the microphone.

"Mister Chairman, we've just received a police report that Alexander McQueen's body was found on the city's southwest side. He apparently committed suicide. Do you have any comment?"

Timms observes the interplay at the podium as the CEO feigns shock at the news. *That son of a bitch already knew he was dead.*

The CEO finds his tongue, "Oh my! I can only hope that report is somehow inaccurate. Xander McQueen was a trusted colleague through all of the early phases of the project. He was truly an expert, a resource, and to many of us a good friend as well. Our thoughts and prayers go out to his lovely wife Rena and to his family."

41

No one was going to find Xander—he was too good. I couldn't find him, he had to find me. And then I told Uncle Rastus where he was.

Rastus gauges his nephew's reaction. He lays a symbolically restraining hand on Timms' knee. "Steady."

My God, what have I done?

#

The agent at the boarding gate looks up as Hagar steps onto the scale.

"No, with the bag."

It's almost surly, but not quite. He's a little out of practice. For days it's been nothing but ARCans, nary a one of whom has been accompanied by "help."

She steps off the scale, picks up her modest case and steps back on.

"That's all of it?" he asks.

"Yes. This is all."

He looks at the readout, puzzled.

He thinks I'm cheating or lying.

"Am I over the limit?"

He hesitates. "No." He stamps her paperwork but then keeps it in hand.

Hagar turns her back and makes eye contact with Solange, standing on the far side of the airlock. She waits until the point has been made, then returns her attention to him. "I'll take those." She holds out her hand.

It's a gamble, asserting herself like this, but today is the first of many days on which the gamble will have to be taken. The agent wants to give orders, not take them—especially not from her, and that's the point. *They only get power over you if you let them take it away.*

"Have a nice trip." He hands her the documents and she steps into the airlock.

One down—a thousand and some-odd to go.

Solange waits as the airlock completes its cycle. "Trouble?" she asks.

"No ma'am, no trouble. You want I get you something?"

"No thank you, I'm fine."

The point does not need to be made with Solange. She has always regarded Hagar as a person, not a thing. People are people and money is money and Solange understood that difference even before her father lost all of the latter.

Looking back, the agent locks up his post and retracts the gangway. Hagar catches her balance as the transport module eases away from the staging building. They stare at each other as the distance increases. The agent's surly persona, stifled these last days, washes back over him like a wave reclaiming its beach.

#

Timms stands in the *ARC*'s Observation Deck and stares out of the huge portal as the shuttle drifts away from the docking port. Yesterday it arrived with the last of the ARCans and today its first-class lounges are filled with departing political leaders and captains of industry. Its cargo hold has been fitted with temporary seating for the three hundred some-odd maids, busboys, chefs, waiters and maintenance workers for whom the time has come to depart. The shuttle drops into a parallel orbit from which those in the first-class lounges will witness the *ARC*'s departure.

The tin can has been sealed. What's inside the *ARC* will be inside forever and what's outside will be left behind—with one exception.

A pilot will execute the departure from space dock. At his signal Timms will say, "Maneuvering thrusters to one-quarter power," but in truth everything that occurs over the next four days will be the pilot's to command. At that point he will board his tiny shuttle and return to space dock and Timms will finally take the helm.

It has been a tightrope these last days. Soon, life will be a lot simpler. Good riddance to all the reporters and their never-ending questions.

Solange steps up next to him at the portal—nearly takes his

breath away. Her rich, lustrous brunette curls cascade over her shoulders. Her face is one to launch a thousand ships. If today it is but one, the *ARC* is after all a ship of a thousand souls. The markers he called in, the political capital he spent getting for Solange what she demanded? Right now it seems worth every minute and every penny. Hers is the last face he will see at night and the first face he will see in the morning. It's a face he will hold and caress, lips he will —

"Captain," she interrupts his reverie.

"I thought we agreed to call me Edward."

"Perhaps for today's launch 'Captain' is more appropriate." Her hand on his arm sends a thrill through every part of his body.

A voice over the intercom says, "Captain Timms to the bridge, please."

He offers Solange his arm. "My dear, would you care to accompany me? I believe it's time for us to depart."

Timms strides onto the bridge. The navigation officer announces, "Captain on the bridge."

As agreed, the crew stands to attention without saluting—except the pilot, of course, who remains seated at the helm.

"At ease."

Everything appears to be as rehearsed. Timms indicates to Solange where he expects her to stand. A flush of pride rises as he catches the bridge crew's surreptitious stares. He makes his way to the portal and feigns assessing the circumstances.

"Space dock reports ready to cast off," the pilot offers.

How should he respond? What will be his trademark order?—*Engage? Proceed? Make it so? So ordered?* He has thought about this moment for weeks and now that it's upon him, he's not quite ready. The pilot waits.

Or should it be *understood* or *permission granted?* Are they asking permission?

The pilot turns for Timms' order.

"Make it so."

"Aye sir," and then into his com mike, "Space dock, cast off all lines."

Timms feels the warm blood rise to his face. *What next? Is there something else I've forgotten?*

"We are clear of the space dock, captain."

"Understood." That comes out awkwardly. To his credit, the pilot keeps a perfectly straight face. After a moment he turns to the captain and gives a subtle nod.

"Maneuvering thrusters at one-quarter power." *Aaagh! That was supposed to be maneuvering thrusters TO one-quarter power. Idiot!*

"Aye sir, maneuvering thrusters are at one-quarter power."

"Take her out."

That one wasn't in the script but to Timms' ear, it came out just right.

Inertial dampers are supposed to completely offset thruster activity but he could swear he feels a shift as the *ARC* drops below and eases ahead of the arms of the space dock. He scans the faces of those around him on the bridge. *Did they feel that?* There's no visible reaction from any of them. Could it be this great, beautiful ship is speaking to him, just to him and no one else? People sometimes talk about the bond between a captain and his ship. *This must be what that feels like.*

It's as if all the pressure, all the stress of the last days and weeks is suddenly—what?—pixilated and sparkled away like the "Happy Birthday" text on some electronic greeting card. This is what was always supposed to —

Suddenly the sky is alight with a no-holds-barred, spare-no-expense fireworks display. If the Consortium cut corners in completing the ship, they certainly did not scrimp on the pageantry. When history records this day it will say:

"A magnificent departure, it was."

#

The last of the fireworks display fades. Hagar steps back from the small view-portal. The enormity of the situation settles like a stone on her chest. She is not going to cry—certainly not here where someone might see her. Weakness is not an option.

"You got to take the chance," Naomi had insisted. Now, Hagar peers down at the Earth. Will she, at her life's end, wish she had stayed?

But the Earth is way down there, far behind—and no way to go back. "This your lot, Hagar, and this last time you talk patois."

She takes several wrong turns on the way to the captain's suite. The ARCans she encounters stare, uncomprehending. Is this little woman a stowaway? Shouldn't she have gone back with the others?

Those "others" waited on the guests at the series of grand banquets, prepared their food and cleaned their dishes. Sheets had to be replaced and mints left on pillows right up until the last of the dignitaries departed. But none of those people are here any more. Just Hagar. She holds her head up and ignores the stares. If any ARCan thinks to challenge her, her steely demeanor discourages it.

Finally she comes upon the correct hallway, knocks softly on the apartment door.

"Come in." Solange unlocks the door. "Hagar! I was afraid we had lost you."

"No, I lost myself."

Solange smiles warmly. "That's funny, because I haven't met a single ARCan with the humility to admit they were lost, even when they clearly were." She points to the two beautiful dresses laid out on the bed. "Which do you think, the lavender or the gray one?"

Hagar tries to imagine any dress in which Solange would not be the belle of the ball. "The gray is good with your eyes, ma'am."

"I hoped you would say that. The lavender is just too day-timey. And what are you going to wear?"

"Beg pardon?"

"It's the departure banquet tonight. What are you going to wear?"

"I . . . I had not thought what to wear. I assumed if I were supposed to attend I would wear the uniform."

"Oh no. That's not appropriate for such a grand occasion. What else. . .?" Solange's voice trails off, but then, "Did you bring clothes of your own, clothes to dress up in?"

"I have the dress your mother gave me to wear for your birthday two years ago. I can still fit into that."

"You looked lovely in that. Yes, that will do. Perhaps we can spice it up with a little 'bling,' you think? Yes, I have just the necklace and bracelet to dress that up. Have you unpacked yet?"

"No. They said they would leave my bag at the loading dock."

"Your things weren't brought to your quarters?"

"No."

Hagar can't remember ever hearing Solange raise her voice in anger. "That's unforgivable. What sort of rudeness . . .?"

"It's all right, ma'am," Hagar answers quietly. "I went by the loading dock three times while I was lost. I can find my way now."

Hagar's self-deprecating humor takes the edge off Solange's stormy mood. "I'm sorry you have to."

"You want my help getting dressed?"

"No one has helped me dress in a long time. I'll be fine. You should hurry, we haven't a lot of time."

#

The grand ballroom sparkles—the mood is festive. Timms greets the arriving guests, decked out in their finery. All is goodness and light. The *ARC* is well underway, the pilot is steering and, for the time being, Timms is in his familiar role of making the guests feel at ease.

How young they look. He knew that's how it would be, but seeing them all together . . .

What kind of world is this, where every person is a student or recent alum at some college homecoming? And what's the proper role of the ship's captain in a world like that?

Uncle Rastus was, as always, a step ahead. This morning just before boarding the shuttle home he took his nephew aside. "Of the five hundred males aboard," he said, "four hundred ninety-six are age thirty or less. The doctor is unlikely to threaten your authority but Mayer and Kline will take as much of your power as you leave unguarded."

A commotion near the bar gets Timms' attention. Twenty or so young bucks are playing a game involving a ping pong ball and cups—and, of course, shots. It's boisterous, rowdy fun, perfect for the youthful participants and of no interest to their partners, their "wives." A few tables away, in what could be a tableau from a vaudeville show, the young beauties cluster around Phil Mayer. "Mayer will play the father figure," Uncle Rastus predicted, "a gambit that has significant promise. A certain percentage of the population will be starved for the wisdom, judgment and experience he will try to project." Sure enough, Mayer is busy creating the persona of patriarch or beloved uncle at a large family gathering. His paternalistic demeanor is a perfect foil to the childish behavior a few yards away. Equally clear is the success of his efforts.

Though Timms opposed bringing the Broitaan 490 aboard, he can't deny that the vehicle's arrival at the front doors makes an incomparable statement. Who, he wonders, did Arnold Kline persuade to wear the chauffeur's cap? WE ARE ALL EQUAL is the ARCan motto, but as the details sift out, some are already proving more equal than others.

Kline is staking out his turf, planting his flag, marking his territory. As he steps from the gleaming Broitaan, he exudes sexual power and virility. He personifies exactly what Rastus foresaw. "Arnold wants to be the bull male and he will clash horns with anybody who challenges him—you especially."

Timms looks over the vast banquet hall. Is there any way he can compete with Kline, his Broitaan 490 driven by some whelp who has already offered to play his chauffer? Can he compete with Mayer, surrounded by a circle of admirers, all of them hungry for a father figure? Was Xander right to be afraid of the *ARC*'s flawed socio-political engineering? *How young they look.*

For tonight, with all the "help" gone, one ARCan in five has "volunteered" to work the kitchen and wait tables. It's the last meal they will ever eat prepared by other hands. For one more day the kitchen is stocked with gourmet delights iced, vacuum-sealed or pre-roasted. The entrées will be plated, the main course will be heated and with the generous wine service to be poured, the banquet is sure to be well received.

Timms expected Solange to stand at his side as the guests arrived. How is it that she can't get here in a timely manner?

The clock in the great tower strikes its deep, melodious tones—seven of them, and the guests amble toward their places at the lavishly appointed tables. Timms gives one last survey of the entry area, grinds his teeth and turns to the Great Hall. It's a gauntlet, this long traverse to the captain's table at the far end of the room. His smile is forced and whatever magnanimous impression he projects, it is totally fake. Inside he roils and steams. *How can she be so careless?*

A ripple spreads across the hall. Heads turn, conversations interrupted as Solange sweeps through the doorway. She is without question the most beautiful woman in a room filled with the brightest and best. The dress highlights not just her eyes but compliments every one of her physical assets. She wends her way between the crowded tables. And a few steps behind, Hagar.

Timms can't take his eyes off her and apparently neither can the ARCans. It's not exactly a gasp, but there's hardly a better word to describe their reaction. The room is suddenly hushed, then quickly grows with urgent whispers.

Where Solange is perfection in every classical sense of the word, Hagar is the strange attractor. Where Solange is the apparition inhabiting dreams of sweetness and light, Hagar is the phantom in visions of a darker nature. What Solange inspires, Hagar stokes. The heights to which one climbs with this beauty in joyous daydreams is set off against the depths one plumbs in cold, sweaty imagination of fevered encounters.

As Solange reaches the table, a few of the ARCans clap—then a flood of applause rises as she steps up next to their captain.

"What is she doing here?" he demands in an angry whisper.

"She's here for the banquet." Solange looks at the table, all of whose chairs are filled. "Can we ask them to set an extra place?"

"No we cannot! She doesn't belong here."

"I invited her. This will be very embarrassing."

"Embarrassing!? To HER? What about me? You think this isn't embarrassing to me?"

"She's an ARCan, too."

He bellows, "An ARCan? She's no ARCan—she's a servant!" He turns to his master-at-arms. "Get her out of here!"

Jean-Marq rises obediently, lays a professional hand on her arm. Hagar stands her ground and stares at Timms.

Where his emotions are confused, hers are clear. Where his hatred is comingled with something even he doesn't dare identify, her defiance is unalloyed. The coldness of her disdain only serves to stoke the heat of his passion. "Now!"

She breaks her gaze with Timms and allows Jean-Marq to lead her toward the kitchen. The murmur from the crowd rises to a low thunder.

Timms roars above the din, "Take her to the forward hold and lock her in."

"Aye sir."

Timms steps onto the low platform and motions for the attention of the guests. It takes several moments.

"I'm sorry, ladies and gentlemen, there has been a misunderstanding. I have dealt with the matter and you can be assured it won't happen again. Let's not let this spoil the festive mood."

He raises his wineglass. "I would like to propose a toast. To the adventure ahead and to us, the boldest voyagers in the history of mankind. The ARCans!"

The audience rises and salutes, "To the ARCans!"

Solange rises with the rest, raises a half-hearted glass and takes the politically correct sip. She glares at Timms and looking out, reflects on the sea of young faces. She keeps all these things and ponders them in her heart.

\#

It is mid-morning by time Solange reaches the bridge. By then the crowd of onlookers has already begun to filter away.

"Initiate power-up sequence for cell number nine," Timms intones in his most authoritarian voice.

"Number nine is already up to full power and operating within nominal parameters, sir."

"Very good mister, initiate power-up sequence for cell number ten."

"Do you know where Hagar is?" Solange whispers urgently.

"I assume she's still in the forward hold."

"Nobody let her out?"

"This is neither the time, nor the place to discuss it." Timms turns away. Solange dashes from the bridge.

At the forward hold, Karl, one of the ship's sergeants-at-arms, stands guard. Solange storms toward him.

"Can I help you?"

"I'm here to get my handmaiden."

"I do not have authorization to release her to you."

"You don't have authorization to keep her here against my wishes."

"I'm sorry, I'm afraid I do."

She bristles. "Are we all equal?"

It's clear he doesn't think Solange is his equal, and certainly not Hagar, but he can't say no to the prime directive. He stands his ground without answering her question.

"Step aside—please."

He still stands his ground, though his eyes say he's looking for a face-saving way out. She's not about to let that happen.

"Are you sure you want to refuse my direct request? You might want to rethink that. A disciplinary demotion could last a long time and you know, there isn't someplace else you can go where they'll take you at your current rank."

Still he stands.

"Has she had food and water since last night?"

"No."

She stares him down. "You don't have a leg to stand on."

He opens the hatch and steps aside.

Inside, Hagar sits in the lotus position, composed and centered. Her eyelids rise smoothly.

"Are you all right?" Solange asks.

"Yes ma'am."

"Come, we'll get you some food."

Karl blocks the doorway.

Solange takes his measure. "You can let us both out or lock us both in."

Beaten, he steps aside.

#

Solange makes a face and sets her coffee cup down. The toast is burned, yet cold. Clearly the ARCans working the kitchen are in the steep part of the learning curve. On the plus side, it's important to keep her figure. With food like this, that should not be a problem.

"I can take those to the kitchen if you like," Hagar offers.

"I'll eat the last of it, thank you." She takes a bite. "What shall we do this morning?"

Hagar seems puzzled by that question. "I've been assigned to the stables," she says. "I really should . . ."

"You're serious? So have I. We'll be together."

"You've been assigned to tend the livestock, ma'am. I'm to work the stables."

Solange senses there's some qualitative difference between "tending livestock" and "working the stables," but she can't quite put a finger on it. "Shall we go take a look?" she asks brightly.

"I would like that."

#

The aroma of livestock reaches them long before they arrive at the pens. It's not a bad smell, just the normal processing of hay and grains. Hagar darts from cattle pen to sheep cote.

Solange is less enthusiastic. "Have you tended animals before?"

"No." Hagar shoos a hen off her nest, proudly holds up the egg. A young ARCan comes to the doorway. She is the epitome of "wrong" for her surroundings—dressed, made up and coiffed for a genteel brunch rather than for tending chickens. Hagar moves along the roost, distressed to find three eggs together in one of the nests. "These need to be collected daily."

"Oh, is that so?" The woman's tone establishes caste rather than questions the accuracy of Hagar's assertion.

"I don't mean you need to do it, but it must be done."

"Well then you can do it. You seem to know so much about it."

Hagar stares the woman down. "I will be by later today and if you haven't done it, I will have to."

The woman sniffs. "Well! That's settled then."

"For today at least."

The supercilious windbag wheels on her heel and stalks off.

The cows are restless and noisy. Hagar slips into the pen, wary of the beasts that tower over her. She approaches a distressed Guernsey from an angle where the cow can see her, gives the giant flank a pat, then reaches down to the swollen tits. She locates a milking pail and stool. She positions the pail then, with more than a little trepidation, grabs a pair of tits and squeezes.

At first only a few drops come, but after a half-dozen tries, she gets a generous stream of milk into the pail with each stroke.

"How do you know how to do this?" Solange asks, though over the last few minutes, more and more of the dots in her picture of "ARCan life" have been getting connected.

"I studied the video," Hagar answers. "But to be honest, I wasn't sure exactly how to squeeze to get milk."

"A video on milking cows?"

"In the materials for the training."

"I see," Solange answers as the picture gets clearer and clearer.

"If the cows aren't milked twice a day they will stop producing."

"I didn't know that." *And it seems I don't know any of the things I'm supposed to know. How did I buy into Edward's notion that I needn't "bother my pretty head about all those training materials," and not have alarm bells go off?*

Hagar squirts several more handfuls of milk into the pail

before responding. "These are living animals and they can't wait two weeks for their caretakers to get up to speed. I was afraid some of the ARCans wouldn't . . ." She opts not to finish.

"That's exactly what I've done." *How did I not understand that every ARCan has to learn the simple skills that we as a population will need when our grandchildren finally debark onto our rustic, totally unmechanized Eden? Worse, how did I assume that I should be exempt from that? That's beyond naïve, that's beyond stupid. That's—what's the word for it?*

"I'm sorry ma'am, I only meant . . . "

"Feckless!" First I was naïve and then I allowed myself to be stupid and now I've made myself feckless!

Hagar switches to another pair of tits and the fresh, aggressive streams ping off the sides of the galvanized pail. After a few moments she looks up at Solange. "Would you like to try?"

Despite her blossoming sense of duty and engagement, Solange hesitates. "Milking a cow? I . . . I don't know."

"Maybe the Holstein over there?"

"Holstein?"

"The black and white one."

The cows are restless. Solange minces her steps trying both to get where she must without brushing against them, and not step in anything. She gets a stool and pail, mimics Hagar's positioning and posture, then gingerly grabs a pair of tits. "Does it hurt?"

"To be milked? No. I think it's painful to be so over-full. I think the milking is actually a relief."

Solange gradually gets her technique in hand, enjoying the scent and warmth of the cow's hide so near her face. Soon both she and Hagar are persuading massive white squirts into their respective pails.

Look at me!

#

Solange sits up on the examining table, trying to find a bit of modesty in the skimpy hospital gown. A knock sounds on the door and a young woman enters without waiting to be invited. "Good morning. I'm Doctor Johanna Norris." *How many years could she have practiced medicine before signing on?* "And you are?" She looks down at her tablet. "Ah! You're Solange. I've looked forward to meeting you." *I wonder if everyone feels odd about having a doctor who isn't any older than they are?*

"Doctor Johanna" must be tired of that same questioning look. She projects a well-studied professional detachment as she executes the various elements of the cursory examination. "Any questions?" she asks, taking Solange's wrist for a pulse.

"What happens if a woman forgets?"

"To take her ovulation suppression meds? We won't allow that to happen. Anomalies involving the reproductive timetable mean the failure of our entire mission. Someone will come to your lodgings and verify that your daily dose has been taken. "

"I see."

"I'll leave so you can get dressed." She opens the door, then turns to look at Solange. "I will see you again in a month, unless of course you're part of my verification assignment, in which case I will see you every day, starting tomorrow."

For the next two years Dr. Johanna Norris, with her obstetrics and gynecology degree will "monitor reproductive health" and make daily rounds to fulfill her "verification assignment." To think that she will succeed, that every single woman on board will take her birth control medications every single day for somewhere around the next nine hundred days, seems arrogantly unrealistic.

At the end of that period, this doctor and a couple of her colleagues will be called upon to deal with five hundred simultaneous pregnancies, five hundred births and all the issues of motherhood and infant feeding. Add to that what's likely to be her own pregnancy and . . .

Was there even one woman in the Consortium's sub-group responsible for this schedule?

The cattle, on the other hand, are expected to reproduce on a carefully prescribed schedule throughout the voyage, the dairy herd in particular. Dairy cows that aren't impregnated stop giving milk.

And so it is that Solange stands at Hildy's head, stroking her flank and calming her as Hagar lubes her elbow-length rubber glove and retrieves an insemination straw from the quiver on her back. Early on, Hagar asked Solange to do the procedure a few times so that if something untoward happened at least one other person on board would know how. Hagar goes about the task today in her typical businesslike fashion.

The *ARC*'s cryogenic storage facility has what's estimated to be a two-hundred-year supply of frozen Holstein, Guernsey and Angus semen—hogs and sheep, the same story. No males were brought on board—well, except for some steers for butchering in the first two years of the voyage.

Solange can't help but wonder if the idea of launching the *ARC* with five hundred women and a hundred-year supply of frozen human male semen was ever considered.

Nah.

If the idea came up at all during the Consortium's sub-group meetings, it was surely quashed in the first thirty seconds of discussion.

CHAPTER FIVE

Kees traces his steps back to the engineering section. He opens a small panel cover. Inside is a graphic display—a narrow red band at the very left end, and below that an "available power" field showing 4 percent It's going to be close.

He keys in the command to send power to the service bay. The indicator light glows orange and the available power drops to 3 percent. After a second the service bay lights up green and the power drops to 2 percent. It's going to be very close.

The bay is fifty meters down a curving hallway, completely dark. His light stick gives a single chirp. Even if he can locate and retrieve the power module in a darkened service bay, when he gets it back here to engineering will he be able to work the *ARC*'s hundred-year-old controls by touch? Not likely.

On the bridge of the *Scavenger*, Cutter picks up the controller and activates the viewscreen. The port side of the *ARC*'s hull completely fills the jitney bug's camera field. A small clamshell door opens and she thumbs the controls to guide the vehicle into the service bay.

Once inside, the jitney bug rotates to view space beyond the open clamshell. The view jiggles as the jitney settles on the floor. She thumbs an increase in magnification on the clamshell's seam as it closes. "The seal appears to be sound, Captain."

"Well done, mister Cutter." Kees hold his light stick where he can read the gauge labeled Δ p as air whooshes into the pressure lock. He opens the hatch, strides in, and operates the touchpad on the jitney's back. The arms flex to set the power module gently on the floor. He whisks it away.

The light stick fades out just as he reaches engineering. He tries the six remaining sticks—they're all dead. He rotates the one illuminated monitor screen and in the dim light, examines the eight-pin adapter on the module. He unsnaps the clips on either side of the cable's plug. With one smooth motion, he two-hands the plug from its socket and, as everything goes completely dark, slides the adapter into the eight now-empty holes.

He gropes for the large toggle switch atop the module, flips it, and the room happily brightens up. He keys his communicator. "Power transfer was successful. Proceed with the salvage of the external cell."

"Damn!" Roman mutters. He peers through a small viewport as the *ARC*'s running lights come on. "Kees, Kees, why do you have to make my life so difficult?"

The contract governing the *Scavenger*'s crew has thirteen signers. Roman can count on Ugg's support and two others. That means before he can challenge Kees he will need three more. If he can persuade Cutter, she will bring at least two with her. But if she stays loyal to Kees, there really isn't any way to seven. Success is going to mean undermining Kees' plan—beating his offer, whatever the hell that is. "What are you up to, Kees? Why are you turning the lights on? Damn!"

Roman's not the only one peering at the grand dame as her

lights blink on. Cutter wouldn't normally indulge in reveries, but on this occasion she lets the thrill linger. A scavenger could go through half a dozen lifetimes and never come upon a treasure like this one. To actually face klak after klak of hull and strut and engine and mounts—who wouldn't have pause?

Admittedly, the logistics of carving her up and transporting her saleables to market will be a daunting task. But Kees has never been "daunted" by any task. So why? Much as she hates to admit it, Roman is right—there is no sense in powering up the *ARC*. "Kees, Kees. What's put a karflakk up your shadduck?"

Interior lights come on along the *ARC*'s starboard side as though someone were walking along, turning them on from one room to the next.

Kees threads his way through a warehouse of small farm equipment and slides open the huge door to the wheat field, now golden and totally dry. There's a smell, an autumnal smell to dried grasses that a man born and raised in space may have experienced only a handful of times in his life. "Hmm," he mutters to himself as he breathes in deeply. He shakes himself from his reverie, locates the climate control panel and throws the power switch. The "sun" expands to full power, bathes the five acres in light. He takes a grain beard, separates seed from chaff, and broadcasts the seed in the soil in front of him. He keys in a new instruction. First air from the long-idle nozzles, then rain.

The livestock pens are on his right—now empty. Kees imagines the scene is as it must have been: fat, healthy animals going noisily about the business of life. And then back to the barren reality.

Next is the recreation area: sports arenas, playing and practice fields, gymnasiums, weight rooms and exercise equipment. Sounds of a spirited handball game echo in the hallway, but when Kees opens the door, lights come on automatically in the now-silent handball court.

Townhomes and duplexes line the streets of the residence area. Leafless trees and dry lawns detract only slightly from the attractive and spacious dwellings.

Every door is closed, except for one. He pauses. His uncle Hoerke died on a booby-trapped derelict. Kees, fourteen at the time, made a promise never to forget that lesson. He stands out of harm's way beside the doorframe, reaches out and swings the door wide open.

Nothing.

He eases in, careful of any tripwires or triggers. On the floor to his left lie a pair of rustic sandals and from a peg on the wall hangs a work apron. A tight circular stairway rises to what must be living quarters above. On the far side, another door is slightly ajar. *It's as if every door ajar, every light left on, has been a signpost leading me through the ship.* Kees stands beside the frame and eases the door open.

Inside is a sculptor's studio. The chisels and mallets are lined up neatly on the worktable. The floor has been swept, but quickly, as a sculptor might in the midst of working—clean without being spotless.

And who is this?

The sculpture is lifelike in many ways and yet chiseled with an artist's eye. She's a mature beauty, perhaps in her fifties or sixties. He lays a hand on the smoothly polished marble. How does one craft a piece of stone at once so specific and yet so universal? What time this must have taken, what dedication.

But who was she and what did she mean to the sculptor?

"Captain?" from his communicator.

"Yes mister Cutter?"

"You should come back on board."

There's an urgency to her tone that sparks his attention. "Is there a problem?"

"Roman calls Parlay."

Kees knew from the start that repowering the *ARC* would raise questions; he just didn't think the pushback would come this soon and in a formal call for Parlay. He takes one last look at the sculpture. She's beautiful, shapely and seductive. The sonic pulverizers will render this to gravel in three tenths of a second—one man's life work converted in a heartbeat into another man's paving material.

There's no stalling now. Once called, Parlay won't wait. "I'll be there shortly."

That doesn't mean he has to retrace his steps back to the *ARC's* shuttle bay. He came here on the starboard side . . .

Most of the *ARC's* port side is environmental control mechanisms—water recapture and filtration, air quality and ventilation devices. But then, maybe two klak from the stern is another major security checkpoint.

The hairs rise on the back of his neck. The protective force field hums subtly now that power is restored. The sign above the doorway reads "firing control."

Merchant ships by tradition are unarmed, or at most armed with personal protection weapons. The approach of a pirate or privateer is very different if he thinks the prize might shoot back. Logically, the *ARC* should not have a weapons system, yet what else could "firing control" mean? Did the ARCans decide to arm themselves, and if so, why?

#

Roman looks over Cutter's shoulder at the *Scavenger's* bridge monitor screen and watches the shuttle disengage from the *ARC's* docking port. "Did he say anything?" he asks.

"Only that he will be aboard shortly."

If the "whispers in the fo'c'sle" are true that Cutter has a soft spot for the captain, then the answer she just gave might not be the whole truth. Fact is, the scavenger code to which Cutter agreed when she signed on specifically forbids a *liaison* between her and the captain. Question is, is she honoring the code? "You know what you have to do," he says.

"I know what you are asking me to do," she answers without turning.

"The crew deserves an answer."

"And the captain has the right to give it himself."

"But we need the truth."

She turns a cold, hard eye on him. "Shall I tell Kees that Roman Pollack calls him a liar?"

Nothing good will come of that and Roman knows it. "I only mean that the captain may have his own agenda."

"An agenda I am eager to hear."

"Because . . .?"

"Because after twenty years of doing this, he still owns his ship," she answers.

"To which the Alliance holds the mortgage."

Her expression turns a few degrees colder. "Be you the one to take it from him?"

"Only if he deserves to lose it."

#

The *Scavenger*'s forward hold is one of the few places where the entire crew can assemble. All twelve of them are already there when Kees arrives. He closes the hatch behind him, turns and slowly pans the room.

The twins are on his left, leaning on a shipping crate like a pair of matching bookends. Cookie and Scrounger are talkers. They've interrupted their conversation out of deference to the captain's arrival. If what he says keeps their attention all the way to the end, that's probably a bad sign. Sparks glances up from her screen and then holsters the device. She actually seems rather naked without it in her hand.

Roman Pollack. No matter what the surface looks like, you always figure there's something different going on underneath. Today he looks bright and eager—innocently curious. For whose benefit is that? Is he playing to his fellow crewmembers or to Kees?

Ugg looks sour, but then Kees can't remember a time when he looked sweet. He is heads to what Roman is tails. What you get from the surface of Ugg is what's deep inside. If he looks threatening, you should be on your guard. If he looks drunk, he's drunk—looks bored, he's bored. Today it's sour—sour and challenging.

Cutter stands next to him. She gets along with him well enough but the two are not normally in close proximity—even less likely when he's paired up with Roman. Is it just chance that she is next to them now? It's not like her to play cat-and-mouse games.

If he had it to do over again, Kees would probably not have signed on Melody and Trish. Trish is almost as good as Cutter with a torch and he's never seen anyone with more intuitive navigator skills than Melody, but he finds their incessant fondling a distraction. If they had their hands off each other and were paying attention, you'd have to figure mutiny was just around the corner.

"Prof" is what he is. It's a cruel nickname but in fact, he's so dense the insult sails over his head. And Gordo makes twelve. If he has more gray cells functioning than Prof, it's not obvious. But these two can exert more physical force on bulky, incorrigible objects than anyone Kees has ever seen. There may not be a better two-man wrecking crew anywhere. But they will think what they're told to think. The question is, who gets to do the telling?

"Captain?"

"Aye Roman. Be it you what called Parlay?"

The tradition of Parlay goes back as far as scavengers can remember. Though one may dispense with the ritual language as the meat of the issue comes up, to start a Parlay without the traditional call and response would be a breach of protocol.

"I did."

"What be the grounds?"

"Action taken not for profit."

"What action be that?" Kees asks.

"Repowering a derelict."

"I see. You be calling a vote?"

Little beads of sweat on Roman's forehead. "We ain't had Parlay yet."

So he doesn't have a majority. Roman is ambitious, Kees recognized that the day he showed up with Alliance certification and applied to be the ship's purser. Not that ambition is a bad thing. Only that one must guard his own status in the presence of an ambitious person. "All right," Kees says, "let Parlay begin. What be your question?"

Roman looks around the room, trying to establish a bond with the fence-sitters—get them to jump off on his side. He surely has Ugg's vote and Kees can imagine one or two others. It will take seven to overturn Kees' authority, and there's the rub. Calling Parlay before he is certain of victory is not Roman's style. A man behaving strangely is a dangerous man.

"We signed a contract that says every action taken is to maximize our profit. We want to know how repowering be maximizing?"

"You say 'we' want to know?"

"That be the question."

It's Kees's turn to pan the room. His next few sentences will be the captain speaking, the man they all chose at the signing to be their leader. The power is his to lose. If Roman already had the majority, he would not have proceeded this way.

"And a fair question it is. We all know that the great hulk off our port bow is maybe the biggest prize any scavenger has ever seen. You all can do the calculations. We cut her up for scrap and it be two years, maybe three of hard work. But after that, we take our shares and be wealthy by many's measure. The oldsters among us could quit the scavenging and be pretty comfortable at it. Them that wants to scavenge more will have the swag to broker up to richer shares on another crew."

Ugg interrupts. "And the four septa power's been pissed away."

"And the four septa power's been pissed away. If all we do is cut her up, Ugg is right, the power went for nothing because the pieces are just pieces."

Prof, emboldened by Ugg's interjection offers, one of his own. "Pieces are pieces."

"Exactly. And the whole is the whole."

Roman cuts off the direction Kees is trying to go. "Enough riddles, Captain. Back to facts."

"Fact is, when they built her, they took the pieces and made the whole and it was a great thing. Is it just the pieces floating out there, or is it the whole?"

Prof gets this one. "It's the whole."

"And if the whole was a great thing once, what's to say it's not still a great thing?"

As if on cue, Ugg responds. "We be scavengers, not salvagers."

"We be scavengers, true, but our contract says we maximize our profit. If salvaging her was more profitable than cutting her up, who's to say which way we go?"

It's Cutter who cuts to the chase. "Salvage her for what?"

He looks her in the eye. This is not a woman seeking to take over as captain—and if he were voted out, she would almost certainly be chosen captain. No, this is a woman asking an honest question.

"She's got a story to tell."

Roman mocks him. "The ship is going to tell us a story?" He plays to his audience, "Is it a bedtime story or a campfire story?" When that gets a laugh he goes on, "Shall we all get in our jammies and will we have milk and cookies?" He lets the levity play itself out a little longer but as it starts to fade he turns barracuda—all teeth and very scary. "And for that you waste four septa powering her back up."

"I spend four septa because it is the only way to answer Cutter's question."

Roman snorts. "Telling stories and answering questions—since when is that the business of a scavenger? I say the price is too dear."

"And I say this: the minute our torches breach her hull, we lose whatever she might have been whole. You say maximize our profit and I agree. And the way to do that is to find out her secrets before we cut her up."

"So you mean to cut her up in the end?" Roman asks.

"I mean to maximize our profit."

The captain has spoken, and to look around the room at the faces, he seems to have won. It is strange that Roman risks what leverage he still has. "I say it's a waste of time."

In the awkward moment that follows, it's Cutter who again finds the heart of the question. "How long, Captain?"

And so the scales swing back the other way. "Five days."

Roman says, "Five? One day is too long to wait."

Kees weighs his options. If he goes hard-nosed, he will win the day. If he caves in he seems weak—in fact, even if he compromises he will seem weak to some. But Cutter is the key. She is strong— she is smart—and as he looks at her, she is hot. And why that notion comes to him at a time like this is just another of the mysteries that have confounded him since they came upon the cluster of Steenmeyers. Before that, it was *I'm the captain of a scavenger crew and she's my first mate.* The logic of the rules about that have made sense to Kees his whole life long. He was born a scavenger, grew up a scavenger and right now, here in the forward hold, he needs to think like one and not like . . . something else.

He pans the room one last time. The twins, Cookie and Scrounger, who have not said a word, Sparks with nothing in her naked hands, Roman with his little beads of sweat, Ugg, vacillating perhaps in his support for Roman, Cutter, Melody and Trish, unentwined for once, and Gordo and the Prof, each counting the distance between five and one.

"Three."

Roman doesn't need to look at the others. He needs only to salvage something from his defeat. "I call Parlay after three days."

"And so it shall be."

Prof asks, "Are we done parlaying?"

"Yes, Prof, for today we're done parlaying."

#

Every space-going vessel has an exercise area. It's not a luxury but a necessity and daily utilization by the crew is not optional, it's mandatory.

The ball comes off the side wall of the *Scavenger's* handball court with a wicked spin. Kees barely gets a hand on it. He hops to get his balance as Cutter zeroes in on the fluttering lame duck

66

coming off the front wall. He might as well not even try. There's no chance he will get to the ball after she hits it.

He admires her sinewy grace, her power, her balance and coordination. He admires the ball as it skitters along the left wall.

"Twelve, eight."

The score could be a lot more lopsided. She never cuts him any slack, but somehow today her killer instinct has gone missing.

"You want to lose the ship?"

"No."

She gives him an easy serve. "Next time Roman ask you why, you talk about some story—they vote against you."

He handles the carom off the back wall. "He wants to scrap her now, that I understand. But why call Parlay? Somehow that doesn't add up."

"That true."

She puts the mustard on it and blows the ball right by him. "Thirteen, eight."

He fetches the ball from the corner and tosses it to her.

She serves. "Why fight him? What you see over there?"

"It's a long story."

The game is back to one easy volley after another. "Well, tell me a short story."

"The last man alive left a record of what happened to her."

She brushes against him going for the ball and leaves the scent of her sweat. "The ship's log?"

"No, the ship's log was erased."

She looks at him—misses the ball. He picks it up and serves. "Eight, thirteen?"

"Why erased?"

And why a weapon? But maybe this isn't the time to share that question, and maybe this is not a person to share it with.

"Every corner I turned was a new question," he answers.

Three volleys go by before she responds.

Am I that transparent? Does she know I'm keeping a secret?

"Questions make no profit," she finally answers.

"But sometimes a man's got to find the answer anyway."

"And after you find the answers, then what?"

He makes a simple miss-hit. "I don't know."

She ups the tempo of her game. The balls she's delivering have more velocity or more spin or better placement – fairly often all three at once. "Well know this," she spits. "Roman called Parlay and that doesn't make sense—not to you and not to me. He wants the *ARC* scrapped and he is taking risks to make that happen. He's got Ugg convinced, and when it comes to cutting up derelicts, Prof already understands the profit there. So do the twins and so does Gordo. That's six. Fourteen, eight." Her tank top clings as the sweaty blotches start to meld together.

"And you make seven?" he asks.

"Not if it means Roman gets captain."

"They'll make you captain."

"Don't want that either. Fifteen, eight."

"What do you want?"

She retrieves his missed ball from the corner and looks him in the eye. "I want you to convince me."

#

On Kees' first day back aboard the *ARC*, the clues lead to the story about ARCan society and the rift that developed soon after Ishmael's birth. The rift was apparently deep enough that some of the ARCans left the central housing area and moved into the ship's forest.

That's where Kees spends the second day. There, amidst all the rustic simplicity, he finds an extensive and sophisticated historical library. Why? They must have had to spend most of their days scrabbling for just their basic sustenance. Why did those who moved to the forest expend so much effort duplicating the ship's log? And then the question that always returns—who erased the ship's log in the first place, and why?

At every turn it feels like a thread they had spooled out so that Kees could find his way through the maze. Did the last survivors imagine how their ship would be discovered? Did they project what

Kees would think and feel? Did they leave clues to lead him around like a treasure hunter? Did they scheme and plot to distract the "Finder," as they call him, from his instincts to scrap the vessel and sell the commodities and artifacts?

How frayed had that thread become when the video Kees was meant to see in the Observation Deck failed for mechanical reasons? Kees had nearly turned away, nearly "lost the thread." But then, late on his second day aboard he finds in the forest library a backup copy. "Call me Ishmael," it begins and then the old man's story works its magic, casts its intended spell. All night long Kees awakens time and again, his subconscious mind piecing together what in real time hadn't quite made sense.

And now, on the third day, Kees is doing what Ishmael and the ARCans hoped he would do—chasing down their clues, following their lead to . . .

. . . a room labeled "firing control."

#

Aboard the *Scavenger,* Cutter increases the magnification. She watches in fascination as a tiny port opens just above the *ARC*'s bridge and a cylinder dollies out on a swivel base. What else can it be except the barrel of a weapon? Kees is the only person aboard the *ARC*. If indeed it is a weapon, he must be taking it through its paces to see if the aiming and firing controls are functional.

She zooms in further, only to find herself staring right down the barrel. *Is the weapon's sighting mechanism visual?* She steps right up close to the visual port. *You see Kees, it's me. You wouldn't shoot at me now, would you?*

She's surprised to find herself aroused by the idea of Kees looking at her, getting her in his crosshairs, sighting along the barrel of . . . The barrel swings around and gradually retracts.

Thought not.

The gun port closes.

Cutter zooms out and leans back in her chair. She now shares a crucial secret with Kees: there's a cannon aboard the *ARC*.

Roman would desperately like to know about the weapon. It

changes the playing field completely. A deposed captain spewed into the void aboard a small shuttle is no threat. A deposed captain aboard a massive, armed vessel is quite another matter.

But does it change the playing field for her? Until a few minutes ago, if Kees were deposed, what choice would she have but to side with Roman? But now . . .

"Anything new?" Roman asks.

She prides herself on being aware of her surroundings and is angry for letting him surprise her.

"No," she lies.

He stares out the portal as lights go on and off aboard the *ARC*. "What's he doing?"

"Don't know."

He watches the activity aboard the *ARC* a few seconds longer. "If you find out anything before Parlay starts, let me know. I'll be in my quarters."

"Aye sir."

Roman hates to sweat. It's the one physical manifestation that threatens to give him away. She was watching him—trying to read him. Did she notice the sweat? Is she that smart?

Right now, it is Viktor Torquist's most recent message that is making him sweat as he puts Imogene back in his safe. He mops his brow.

"Kill anyone who has that information." That's exactly the wording of Torquist's order. That means Kees and Cutter for sure. And what about the rest of the crew? *And what about me? I know it's the* ARC *that we've found. Does that mean I'm a dead man, too?*

Cutter turns from the viewport. Nothing new has happened on the *ARC*'s exterior in the last few minutes. What is Kees doing and why? But maybe more important, what is Roman doing and why? Someone has put him up to calling Parlay—someone is whispering in his ear.

As sure as God made ghyrfbats stupid, Roman Pollack is

70

communicating with the Alliance, and the only way that works is with Image E.N. From what Cutter has heard, he shouldn't be able to even have an Image E.N. transceptor aboard. It's a power hog that just can't be hidden. So the thing that can't be true must be true and it's up to her to find out which.

She may not have an ice cube's chance in hell of figuring out how to **send** on Image Extended Network. But receiving . . .

She fires up the ship's sensors and initiates a full-frequency sweep. A few minutes later, she gets a spike. It pegs the needle but lasts only a few seconds. That's enough to get the frequency, though not long enough to get any of the outgoing message.

Over the next few hours tiny wisps of data come filtering in. If she weren't looking on exactly that wavelength, she would never have recognized it. The message is more than halfway done before she figures out the algorithm for the input code.

Fortunately the one key piece of information is in that truncated last half. *Kill anyone who has that information.*

Any misplay of the cards in the next few days and both she and Kees are dead people.

CHAPTER SIX

Solange can feel the tension every day now. The two-year anniversary of the launch is only a week away and yet the first child will not be born for over a year. The stagnation of the perfect society is beginning to highlight the things that are less than perfect. There have been fifty-seven divorces, which in this case required fifty-seven partner changes. No one is allowed to be un-partnered. Eight of those are on their second partner exchange and two are on their third.

Having children will change things for the better—everyone believes that. To date the ARCans have been preserving what they brought with them. Not just the material things, but also the traditions, the practices, the society. Once there are children the focus will shift to what's ahead. She hopes.

It's not that the voyage's social architects were blind to the challenge. With the ARCans having so few childbearing years, they strove mightily to assure that the long intervening periods would still be satisfying. There is an extensive library of erotic practices and techniques. The sections on male anatomy, male arousal and gratification, male sexual fantasies—those extend for shelf after shelf.

In one small corner sit just a few materials on female arousal and satisfaction. The pages are well worn, almost exclusively by female fingers. What's good for the goose may or may not be good for the gander but it is, after all, good for the goose. If the men on board had a clue what was going on, the Council would no doubt create a panel to investigate. They have formed no less than eighty-one panels to date. Most of them report regularly on their findings and progress. If the engineers could harness all that "wind," the *ARC* would surely arrive at her destination several years ahead of schedule.

But a bitter woman is an unattractive woman, and being attractive has its perks. Solange exercises religiously, though with the heavy physical workload in animal husbandry, most of her workouts are simply for toning and tightening. She may have the strongest hands of any woman on the ship—second to Hagar's, of course.

She chuckles. Timms actually had the gall to complain of the calluses on her hands. You'd think he would appreciate the side benefits of her milking thirty-one cows a day. But appreciation is something he expects of her and seldom feels the need to demonstrate himself.

Solange still feels a pang as she approaches Hagar's quarters in the forward hold. They are farthest from every other thing on board the ship, and Hagar admits there's little heat at night. Not that she complains. She greets her mistress this morning with a smile. "Good morning, Solange."

It comes out easily and naturally now, "Solange." Solange chuckles, thinking of how Hagar so pointedly addresses Timms as "Captain Timms," always with a lilt that says the words begin with an upper case "C" and an upper case "T." Somehow she manages to be respectful and derisive, all in two words. It sets him on edge every time, and then when she calls Solange by name, Solange can almost hear him grinding his teeth.

Hagar's broad face turns serious. "Hildy's calf was still-born."

Hildy was one of the first cows Solange milked on that day so long ago. It's not just sad news, it's disturbing. Hildy is one of only two Friesians left. She was inseminated four times before conceiving and the gestation has been difficult.

"I think she'll be all right, but she lost a lot of blood."

There were forty milk cows when the trip began. The first calving was scheduled about six months in and several were born. All seemed well and so the oldest cows were butchered for their meat. At first the slaughters were almost unbearable for Solange but she toughened herself, as every animal husband must, to the reality that cattle are raised to provide milk and meat—not to provide love.

The fall-off in pregnancies in the last months has been alarming. All butchering has been halted as the herd now stands at thirty-seven, of whom thirty-one are producing milk. If it were exclusively a dairy cattle problem, it would be disappointing, but the beef cattle, sheep, goats and hogs are also not conceiving steadily and when they do, their miscarriage rate is outside the norms and rising. *How the men would whine if they lost their steaks and the* ARC *became vegetarian.* One could laugh, if it weren't so serious.

How can the Council assail deviant social behavior with one investigative panel after the next, but not stir themselves to address a problem of this magnitude? "The livestock issue," it's called. It's always on the agenda but when they get there, Arnold Kline moves to table discussion—"all in favor?"—"Aye."—"The motion is tabled and will be included on the agenda for the next session."

#

Solange and Hagar stroll together among the livestock pens, greeted by the few ARCans who are actually living up to their work obligations. The eggs are collected daily. They make their way to the kitchens, as they should. The animals are fed. Two women take care of that, for the most part. Solange does most of the milking, though there are a few others who have the skill if needed.

Hagar takes pride in keeping the pens clean. The lack of foot infections is the proof that the environment of the *ARC*, underfoot at least, is healthy. She fetches a shovel then pauses a moment in obvious discomfort before starting in.

"Are you all right?"

"Yes, thank you. Just a little cramping. It's my time."

It's my time. For twenty-three months and counting, only one woman on board the ship has said, "It's my time." The scientists, the men scientists, arranged it so. Do they have any idea how artificial this reality is? What kind of world is this where every single human female, every female . . .?

Solange staggers.

Hagar offers a steadying hand. "Are *you* all right?"

The animals' ovulation is abnormal. We're animals.

"No. But, yes, thank you."

For over seven hundred days the doctor has been good to her word. She arrives at Solange's quarters, observes her reproductive medication wheel, and confirms that Solange is following instructions and preventing ovulation, which in turn prevents the possibility of a pregnancy. *How would we know if humans are having issues with fertility? What if the lack of ovulation is no longer medication-induced?*

The next morning, Timms lies snoring in their bed. Solange rises, presses the tablet from her wheel and flushes it down the toilet. There are two steps to answering this "can I get pregnant" question and this first one, the flushing, was pretty easy. The second demands considerably more dedication to the ultimate outcome.

She brushes her teeth, primps her hair, changes to a lavender bra with extra under-wire support, gives herself a spritz of his favorite perfume, and slides back into the bed next to him.

#

Dr. Johanna's reaction is not at all what she expected. "You are not the first."

"What do you mean?" Solange asks. "Other women have also

stopped their medication?"

"You are the forty-third—that I know of."

"And not one got pregnant?"

"Three—so we think."

"But we've had no births."

"Those conceptions, if that's what they were, all occurred early in the voyage and none went past the first trimester without miscarrying."

"What about recently?" Solange asks.

The doctor's expression is deadly serious. "I'm not aware of any human ovulation within the last eight months."

Solange keeps her tongue. She needs to think about the implications of Hagar's ovulation before sharing it.

"No men know?"

"I suspect that a few of my medical colleagues are curious. In the non-medical male population, no, I'm pretty sure none of them even suspects."

"Shouldn't your colleagues be told?"

The doctor looks as if she's treading on eggshells. "It is the captain who will need to be convinced of the urgency of the situation and, forgive me, but his record in dealing effectively with problems leaves something to be desired."

Leaves something to be desired. That's the kindest evaluation of Timms' performance that Solange has ever heard.

"Perhaps you could be the one to convince him?" the doctor asks hopefully.

"If it falls to me to tell Captain Timms of this situation, I will do it. But I need some time to think first."

And so on Thursday, she invites herself into Hagar's quarters. "I have a secret I must share with you," Solange begins.

"What's happening with the animals is happening with the women too?"

Of course Hagar would have figured that out. She was always cynical about the ability of those in charge to stop the making of babies. "How did you know?" Solange asks.

"The medication makes your skin look ... unhealthy. I see many women with healthy-looking skin."

Solange just looks at her.

"You stopped about two months ago?" Hagar asks.

"Yes."

"And Timms been having his way with you but no baby?"

"No. I'm apparently not ovulating."

"Am I the only one?"

"It seems so."

"What they do?"

A chill runs down Solange's back. "I don't know." *And I don't want to think about what they'll do.*

"You tell the captain now?" Hagar asks.

"About the other women? Very soon. About you? I'm not sure when."

#

Timms' hands shake as he pours himself another shot. The frequency of these "pour yourself into a stupor" events has risen over the last several months, but he's still not ready to call himself a drunkard.

God knows there's good reason tonight. I thought it was going to be some sort of explanation for her mood swings but then no, it was a stab in the deepest heart of my being. The women on board, all of them, have somehow mysteriously stopped ovulating. And now I am supposed to fix that.

Is this what Xander knew? Was he privy to some finding that the ship or deep space travel was going to sterilize the women? What kind of real man lets five hundred women sail forth on a ship of his design knowing they would end up barren as a dry hole? And he played me the fool for letting me keep on as captain. If I'd known this, I would have resigned or at least demanded it be fixed before we set sail.

But what happens now? I've got to show leadership. I've got to have a solution already in hand before they find out. But if I announce it ... He downs the shot in hand and pours another.

The messenger of this news is going to be killed as the bearer of bad tidings—well, figuratively at least. No, not for me to report it.

Who then? Can I persuade one of the doctors—or the oby-gynie girls? It's their fault, right? And if I can't persuade them to do it, maybe . . .

Solange.

They can't blame her, she's as much a victim as anyone. She's well liked among both the men and the women. And if there's a backlash, what harm does it do her? She has no aspirations.

It's evil, but what about the little gnome? How perfect it would be to stick her with the task. It would never work, of course; no one would accept such news from her. But there she'd be, standing before the great assemblage, shaking, nipples all erect, probably creaming in her pants . . .

They'd stone her on the spot, if we let them have stones.

God, I'd like to get that little hobgoblin and . . . and Edward Timms III has no shame about what he thinks next—nor for the hard swelling knotting up his shorts.

#

The only other time Solange has been in Timms' ready room was the day he gave her the ship's tour. She is only a little surprised to be here today. "You want me to report this to the Council?" she asks.

"They'll take it much better from you."

"You're the captain of this ship. You want me to deliver the most significant news of the entire voyage?"

"I don't 'want' you to deliver it, I'm *ordering* you to deliver it. It's time for you to remember your station and the circumstances under which you were offered passage on this, the greatest voyage of all time."

She holds his gaze. "Soon to be the greatest disaster of all time."

"I hope you'll have the good sense not to use that kind of language when you stand before the Council."

"I'll use what good sense I have."

Her cold, hard stare gives him pause. It's what attracted him to

78

her in the first place, that day when he stood behind the mirror and she told the interviewer to stick the Consortium's fiscal balance sheet up her ass. But he is not attracted today—not now, at least. He's too angry to entertain thoughts of forcing her soft, full lips . . .

Control, Edward. "And we'll all be glad of however much good sense that is."

"Have you done anything about what the doctors suggested?"

"I've instructed maintenance crews to do a full analysis of the ship, and we have broadened the search parameters on the radiation sensors."

"They didn't question the order?"

"Are you implying my maintenance staff would not follow an order of mine?" Edward Timms restrains himself from hitting her again. "Get out!"

#

Every time the ship's company meets in the great banquet hall, Timms remembers that first night when he sent Hagar to be confined in the forward hold. He replays the infuriating scene in his head two or three nights a week. Sometimes he fantasizes revenge—going to the forward hold and punishing her himself.

So when Solange arrives at the banquet hall with Hagar in tow, his rage is more than he can control. "That woman does not belong here. Send her away!" More than a few in the room shift uneasily, clearly surprised by the anger in his outburst.

"Mister Chairman!" Solange calls out loudly, "What I have come to report today bears directly on Hagar. If you would sir, I would like your permission for her to stay."

Bears directly on Hagar? What is she talking about? This is not how he intended the meeting to go. But by rule, the chairman has authority over procedures in an assembly.

Mayer never lets a public display of his power slip by. "She will not be allowed to speak, but she may remain in the room." He bangs the gavel repeatedly for silence. "The meeting is called to order. We have only one item on the agenda. Solange, would you deliver your report, please."

And so it is that Solange takes Hagar by the hand and steps up on the podium.

"Fellow travelers all . . . " She intones the ritual opening sentence when addressing the full company. ". . . I come before you today with news of a most dire situation. Through the actions of a significant number of travelers, we have come to believe that our ability to generate viable eggs has been compromised."

One of the Council members leans to his neighbor and whispers, loud enough to be heard by everyone, "No eggs? Well as long as we've got bacon, I guess we'll get by." A ripple of laughter moves through the house until Solange says in a clear, firm voice, "There is evidence to suggest that every ARCan female is sterile."

The silence of stunned disbelief is quickly replaced with an uproar. Mayer stands at the podium like a wildebeest being disemboweled by a pack of dogs. He stares at his cold, impassive wife—pleading with his eyes for her to say it ain't so. She keeps sending, "It's so, kid," and when that finally sinks in, he whales away with the gavel, bellowing for order.

He's hoarse before there's any letup, but finally the need to know more outweighs the shock at what has already been reported. When he finally gets control, he sputters, "Women?! What women? Who are these women and what kind of proof do they have?"

"To date," Solange replies calmly, "fifty-six women have discontinued the ovulation-control medication and have failed to resume their normal monthly cycle."

"Fifty-six?! Is that all? And you come here to frighten all of us based on fifty-six women? Who are they? Let them stand up and be recognized." He glares out over the assembly, daring anyone to actually rise and be counted.

At first it's only a handful. They stand, fearful but determined. And as the seconds roll by, others rise up and join their sisters.

The next day, when the minutes of the meeting are posted, the record will show that two hundred eighty-one women rose to be counted. A footnote observes that two hundred nineteen remained seated.

Mayer says in a quiet voice, "Be seated, please."

"Hagar, would you stand please," Solange requests gently. She lets a full thirty seconds go by as, one by one around the room, ARCans, male and female alike, begin to suspect there is more to come. Solange sits down, leaving Hagar standing alone amongst the thousand.

She speaks from her chair. "Whether you noticed or not, when the chairman asked the women who believe themselves sterile to rise, she sat down. And if I were to ask the women who believe themselves fertile to rise, I can only wish there was someone to stand with Hagar." She waits as the audience cranes their necks in hopes that some woman, somewhere, will stand.

None does.

"I suggest to you that the dark cloud of this news has at least one silver lining. As long as Hagar continues to have her normal monthly cycle, there is hope that one or more of us may regain fertility. Even if that fails, one fecund woman is many-fold better than none."

Mayer raps again and again for order. "A committee will be formed to investigate —"

"Mister Chairman," Solange interrupts, "while I haven't much faith in committees, I agree that someone must oversee the search for the answer to this problem. My only demand—forgive me, my only request—is that the committee be comprised of no less than fifty-one percent women."

The roar rises anew. Mayer lets it run its course, then renews abusing the table with his gavel. As the crowd quiets, he hammers away, oblivious his own maniacal behavior, until his wife lays a hand on his forearm. He gives a few more lame raps, then takes in her meaning—a meaning not lost on the ARCans watching from every part of the hall as the silent drama unfolds.

Mayer clears his throat. "For reasons of parliamentary procedure, the committee will be sixty-one percent women."

#

Two days after Solange's report shook the ship's company, a maintenance crew sent to scan the exterior of the power cells reports to the infirmary with symptoms of radiation poisoning. Two members of that crew die the next day and the third lingers only a little longer.

Recalibration of the ship's sensors reveal that the energy has been leaking at an extremely long wavelength—below the sensor's bottom threshold. A footnote within the engineer's report mentions that the sensor thresholds were radically modified seven months before the ship was launched. The timing of that modification makes sense to only one person aboard the *ARC*—Edward Timms III.

The medical team orders cessation of ovulation suppression meds. The correlation between the medication and build-up of radioactivity in the ovaries cannot be ignored. Every woman on board puts two and two together. The doctors, to a man, deny culpability.

The oversight committee is impaneled, comprised of two-thirds women. They grapple with scenarios in which the goal of the voyage might be rescued. It is noted that the captain is one of only four men on board over the age of forty and that in general the ARCan males retain their potency and are in good health. If the leakage can be corrected, the life expectancy of the ship's company might be relatively normal, which is to say some would live into their seventies, eighties or beyond. If even a few women were to regain their fertility, a number of baby girls might be born. If so, the population might still be rebuilt to several hundred by time the ship arrives at its destination.

But it is the preservation of the gene pool that dominates their deliberations. All the genetic engineering principles that guided the original selection process were thrown in a cocked hat. Hagar's genetic profile had not even been analyzed, and now it would be the most significant factor in the ongoing pool. Long hours of heated committee debate are dedicated to the means by which the diversity of the gene pool can be maximized. For some it is a thinly veiled commitment to minimize the impact of Hagar's "obviously inferior" genetic makeup.

Consensus is reached, albeit grudgingly, that Hagar should be inseminated. Every scientific effort will be made to ensure that she conceives a girl. No contingency plan is created in case she refuses. That option will not be offered to her.

The doctors reject suggestions that she be allowed to return to her shipboard quarters. In fact, the interior of the forward hold, the place to which Hagar was banished that first night, is reconfigured and the three women with the best hope of restoring their ovulation, those who had conceived and miscarried, are billeted there in the slim hope that Hagar's living environment might induce a recovery.

And so begins the process of evaluating the genetic profiles of the five hundred ARCan males.

It falls to one of the "lesser ARCans" to donate his sperm for the salvation of the society as a whole. And this time it seemed that science had gotten it right. Adam Sidarus is a handsome, gregarious young man, well liked by everyone. He is stable, even-tempered, perceptive and hard working. Even those who are jealous have to admit, at least in public, that he is the perfect choice. His genetically superior semen will be manipulated to raise the likelihood of conceiving a girl to ninety-eight percent. When asked to donate, he agrees.

Finally it is time to inform Hagar of the committee's decision.

#

Timms waits in the committee room for her to be admitted—waits with a dark and resentful heart. It was four days ago he had made his most forceful case for the right to sire the *ARC*'s first child. He is, after all, captain of the vessel. Despite so little chance of winning, he deeply resents the women who refused him.

She enters—his little gnome, the hobgoblin of his nightly fantasies. How dare she pride herself in the other women's misfortune? Wasn't it he who sent her to the forward hold in the first place? Didn't the doctors conclude that the key factor in her ongoing fertility has been the distant proximity of her sleeping quarters from the radiation source? How the fates have twisted his fortunes—twisted the fortunes of all aboard. And of all those twisted souls, she is the only one to come out ahead—but not for long.

How will she react when the verdict is given? Will she try to wriggle out of her responsibility? Will she cry, will she strike back? She has no power against the committee. If she has to be tied down and forcibly penetrated, that is how it will have to be. How sweet it would be to watch her humiliation, she who mocks him with her singsong "Captain Timms," always with a capital "C" and a capital "T." Will she still be saucy when her belly is swollen and she waddles about like some overstuffed hippo?

Mayer's wife chairs the committee. She's as pompous a windbag as he—overbearing and arrogant. Oh, she's polite and deferential enough in public but in her heart of hearts she's constantly on the lookout for ways to promote her husband at the captain's expense. Now that she has real power for the first time, Timms can barely stomach her supercilious tone.

"Hagar, the committee have come to a decision," Mayer's wife intones to the assembly. "It is a grave matter and one that we do not take lightly. We trust that you will see the seriousness of it as well. Compliance with our finding is, I'm afraid, mandatory. What we're asking of you, what we expect of you, is in some ways a significant sacrifice but in other ways it is the highest honor a woman can have bestowed upon her. You will bear the *ARC*'s first child."

. . . have bestowed upon her. What a pompous, self-important ass. She's a servant girl to my consort. What sort pedestal shall we erect for her? I tell you what I'll erect for her, and I don't mean for her to stand on it!

Solange glances over, frowns at what she sees.

Mayer's wife continues. "You have permission to ask whatever questions you like and we will do our best to answer. Do you have any?"

84

"The child mine to raise?"

"Those details are still to be decided. Considering how important she will be to the ship's future, we want to assure that her upbringing is the best we can possibly provide. Of course you will be intimately involved. But no, one of the couples on board will be assigned to oversee her development. Surely you recognize the need for her to have a two-parent family."

"I do not." Hagar stares down each member of the committee in turn. To a woman, they avert their gaze.

#

And in that moment, Edward Timms hatches a scheme by which he might salvage his family honor, by which he might extend the family tree. He can't accomplish it alone, but he now knows how to enlist the ally he needs. Even the most insensitive lout couldn't miss the electricity in the room when it was announced that one ARCan couple would be designated "parents."

Five hundred women committed to this venture with the understanding that first and foremost, they were to be mothers. If the shipbuilders' criminal negligence has stolen from them the birthing element of that activity, they realize now that for one of them, the child-rearing part of motherhood is once again within reach.

He looks at his consort. For all her mysteries, one fact is crystal clear—she would do anything to be that woman. Until now he didn't have the leverage to persuade her to help him. But with this revelation . . .

#

Solange sits on the edge of their bed. "Of course I can't guarantee that we will be awarded custody." Timms stops his pacing and turns to her. "But this I can promise you. If you refuse to assist me in this, I will make certain that your name never even comes up for consideration."

Solange keeps her tongue. Her decision not to argue is the first positive sign of the last half hour. What she wouldn't listen to at first, she may be open to now. It's time for the final puzzle piece.

Now Edward, play to her empathy. That's the key. What she feels for Hagar makes her vulnerable.

"Think of it this way, Solange," he begins in his most earnest and thoughtful tone. "What will happen if you refuse and they impregnate Hagar with Adam Sidarus' sperm? She will bear a child and that child will be given to some other woman—some woman whose husband has influence with the committee. And how will that child be raised? Do you think those arrogant people, and I assure you it will be the most arrogant couple on board, do you think they will love that child? Do we really think they can hide their disdain for what Hagar is?"

"What is Hagar?" she asks angrily.

Bingo! It's so easy when you know what buttons to push. Careful, Edward, no victory lap yet – make it sound like you feel the same way she does.

"Hagar is a woman. But of all the people on board, you may be the only one who honestly considers her worthy. And the 'parents' of the baby? They will keep Hagar as far away as they can. Bad enough that the baby is 'soiled' with her genes. They will make sure the child is not further 'soiled' by Hagar's mothering, all the time believing that they are doing what's best for the ARCans."

"You disgust me!" Solange bolts for the door.

Oops! Think, Edward. "And yet you know I am more likely right than wrong."

She pauses with her hand on the knob. As much as she despises every word he's said, he actually is more likely right than wrong. She turns back.

OK Edward, we're so close! Go for the maternal instinct. Tell her what's best for the baby.

"But if you mother the babe, how different that will be. You will love her and care for her and raise her most admirably. And as she grows, she can also know and love Hagar as her biological mother. Instead of being a 'strangeling,' she will grow up loved by two mothers and she will love you back and she will love Hagar as well. Isn't that best for her? Isn't it best for everyone?"

And as all the pieces of the puzzle settle into place Solange asks, "What exactly do you intend to do?"

Convincing the doctors that Solange should perform the actual insemination was a challenge, until Hagar herself asked for the woman she trusted most. Nor had it been easy to quell Solange's feelings of guilt at betraying that trust. In the end, both issues were laid to rest and Solange waits in room B for Hagar and the doctor.

The doctor comes to the door. "I thought I said room C."

"Did I mix that up?" asks Solange. "Let me gather these things and we'll change rooms."

"Well no, there's no need to do that. This room will do as well."

It seems an innocent enough mistake and after all, the only real difference between room B and C is the two-way mirror. Actually, there's another difference.

A few minutes earlier, in room B, Timms ejaculated into the reservoir. It was easy—not only had he saved up for several days, he was aroused long before it was needed. He attached the reservoir to the dildo and hid it among the towels Solange had set out. Then he went to the other side of the mirror overlooking Room B, to watch.

An orderly delivers the official dildo to the doctor. Solange sets it atop the pile of towels.

"Any questions?" the doctor asks. When none is forthcoming, she leaves and closes the door behind her.

Hagar adjusts her pale blue hospital gown and lies back on the examination table.

The plan was for Solange to make the switch under the guise of lubricating the insemination dildo. Whether Hagar senses the dishonesty about to be perpetrated or is just curious, she props herself up.

"What are you doing, Solange?"

"Nothing. Just lubing this up." She approaches the table. Hagar looks her straight in the eye.

"What is that?"

"This is the device we're . . . "

Hagar points to the pile of towels where the official dildo is not quite completely hidden. "And what is that?"

Solange has nothing to say. She stands immobilized by her shame.

"Whose sperm is this?" Hagar asks in measured tones.

Solange is mute.

"It's Captain Timms', isn't it?" as always with the capital C and the capital T—only this time spat out in disgust. "You would impregnate me with that?"

The door to the observation room flies open and Timms fills the frame. Hagar snatches the dildo from Solange's hand, shakes it in Timms' face and throws it against the wall, smashing it and dribbling his spawn on the floor.

He grabs Solange by her collar, throws her into the observation room and slams the door, then clicks the lock shut.

She scrambles to the glass, horrified to watch Timms corner Hagar behind the examination table.

He's a soft man and not very agile, but he outweighs her by nearly a hundred pounds. Hagar has no hope of overpowering him, yet she launches, fists flying.

For a moment he is caught off guard, takes several punches and kicks—his rage roaring out of control with each one. Finally he gets a handful of her gown, twists it to pin her arms, draws back and cold cocks her with a devastating right cross.

She goes down like a sack of potatoes—out cold and limp.

He stands over her for a moment, triumphant as Solange pounds on the reinforced glass, a captive audience to a scene she's helpless to interrupt.

He lifts her limp body, drapes her over the examining table, spreads her legs . . .

Solange stares, numb to the horror she's being forced to observe. A wave of guilt and self-loathing washes over her as the truth presses itself on her consciousness. *If it wasn't for me, this would never have happened.* And she sinks to her knees, weeping without restraint.

CHAPTER SEVEN

Hagar awakens on the examining table, her left eye swollen shut. Solange sits in the chair next to her, weeping.

"Squirt that out," Hagar tells her, indicating the dildo whose reservoir still holds Adam Sidarus' sperm, "and lie about it if she asks." If Dr. Johanna believes that Hagar might still conceive a child and that the father might still be Adam Sidarus, she and the rest of the ARCans will leave her alone.

When she gets back to her quarters in the forward hold, she breaks down in a spasm of sobs. And it is morning and it is evening and the day has been consumed with rage, hatred, self-loathing, thoughts of suicide and tears enough to threaten dehydration.

And it is morning and it is evening and the second day is consumed with revenge, recrimination, scheming, morbid fantasizing and still some tears. She had put herself in the hands of the doctors and the woman she thought was her friend and this is what came of it. She is determined not to make that mistake again.

And on the morning of the third day Hagar has an epiphany and it is this:

In the history of mankind, be it factual or mythological, a

precious few women have been cast in the role Hagar is about to play. Gaia was mother not only to the gods but to the Titans as well, Mayadevi birthed Buddha, Fjörgyn was mother to Thor, Amina bore Muhammad and the Blessed Virgin Mary bore Christ.

On this morning, Hagar's paradigm shifts. No longer the scourge of the ARCans, she and the child growing inside her are their salvation. If the next few weeks bring death to everyone on board, so be it. But if survival is possible, her name will be whispered in the tales of this voyage in much the same way as all those other mothers.

Except each of them is known for the male child they bore. *How much greater the honor to be the mother of a girl who, in the fullness of time, will be the wellspring of all who come after her.*

And the malice and the rancor and the hatred seep out of Hagar's soul and she is made whole. Her appetite returns, and her vigor. She reenters her ARCan world, periodically granting audience to the doctors and the few others who seek her out.

Solange is not one of those. Not that Hagar has turned her away, rather that Solange did not request an audience. Hagar's anger has burned itself out, yet the hurt lingers over her friend, who was an accomplice to her violation.

In the months that follow, each new piece of bad news threatens to throw the whole ARCan society into chaos. In the face of the engineers' repeated failure to eliminate the radiation, they have clung to one phrase. *Hagar is with child.* As the power cells were shut down one by one, as the engineers were surprised to find that they still leaked energy even when shut down cold, as massive plates of lead reduced the levels of radiation only slightly, as the ship turned colder and darker in efforts to exist on the dwindling power resources, as the suicide count rose through the teens, in the face of all that, the ARCans clung to their mantra—*Hagar is with child.*

As Hagar's belly begins to swell, the trickle of visitors dries up completely. Most of the ARCans, as young as they are, have never had close contact with a woman in her third trimester and are understandably fearful. The doctors press ceaselessly for permission to take blood samples. Even more desperately they want to sample her amniotic fluid but she will have none of it—no blood, no fluid, no scans.

The futile exercise of sending a message back to Earth doesn't fool anyone. It was the Consortium that failed them. They can imagine the consternation among friends and families back home upon learning of the ARCans' distress. But as far as that consternation leading to any action that might save them, even the most optimistic of them knows better.

There are only two suicides during Hagar's ninth month. Call it curiosity if you will, but before checking out, they just have to know if the birth will go well.

Contractions start late in the afternoon. Shortly after nine in the evening Hagar reports to the infirmary, as she promised. She staunchly refuses any chemicals, monitors or interference. By ten-thirty she is fully dilated. At 11:04 PM the babe cries out for the first time and great is the rejoicing at the sound.

Then comes the news that it's a boy.

Within an hour, three hundred seventy-one people gather in the small docking bay on the ship's port side. An accomplice sweeps open the iris and blasts them into the cold void of space. He powers the iris closed again and hangs himself in the hallway.

At 2:30 AM the child is put in Hagar's arms and she is wheeled back to her quarters. She slides into her bunk with the baby. Ishmael nurses, then falls asleep at the breast.

#

The secrets surrounding his conception remain surprisingly well kept. But at some point it will become clear that Ishmael is genetically not the son of Adam Sidarus. The fabrication they agree upon is that a "laboratory accident" involving the treated semen meant that Timms had to step up at the last minute and that Hagar consented to it.

Weathering the storm of that disclosure forces Timms to call in every marker and even that isn't enough. Whereas before he was seen as a feckless blunderer, now the only thing standing between him and court martial is his authority over the MPs. They are bound by oath to obey the ship's captain and if they're unhappy about it, they honor that oath nonetheless. Timms barters away the last sliver of his soul to Mayer & Kline in exchange for remaining nominally captain of the ship. He will never be his own man again.

No one mourns his loss of power—least of all Hagar.

In truth, seeing Timms beaten is small comfort to her. His violation stole from her the chance to be the most important woman on board. In the moment of what should have been her greatest triumph, she was brought low. Many ARCans assumed that Ishmael's birth was her fault, that somehow her inferior genetics had spoiled everything. She had willfully defied nature and spawned a son when a daughter was needed. She was never worthy of being an ARCan and now Ishmael is the proof of it. The revelation of Timms' paternity does little to ameliorate their disdain—tends rather to confuse the issue.

The ship's engineers build a small robot to place the explosives on the struts of the Steenmeyer J-26's. Eleven of them are cut completely free. They gradually drift far enough astern so as to no longer be a radiation hazard. The twelfth remains tethered by its connector cable. It was chosen to be the ship's power source because deterioration of its cowling was much less severe than the others. Some aboard wonder why the oldest cell, the very first cell installed, the one which had provided internal power during the final year of construction, is somehow the only one to maintain even marginal integrity. Edward Timms III does not wonder why.

After the mass suicide of that first night a few ARCans intermittently opt for less dramatic ways to end it all. It seems there's a funeral every few days.

The lone remaining Steenmeyer cell, at first allowed to drift at the end of its tether, swings closer to the ship. Scaffolding will be required to fix its position as far from the hull as possible. Space suits will never offer enough protection from working in such close proximity to the cell and yet there is no shortage of volunteers. It is, for those unwilling to take their own lives, a perfect opportunity to depart honorably. And when the scaffold is complete, the population levels off. Three hundred seventeen voyagers opt to press on to whatever lies ahead as the *ARC* drifts through space, powerless.

#

Ishmael holds onto the edge of the crate, steadies himself on his wobbly legs. He'll be walking soon, and right away that's going to be a challenge. He has been a pistol from the start—alert and attentive at an early age, a barracuda at the breast, happy on his stomach or held facing outward but impatient with lying on his back or carried where he cannot see his surroundings.

By the time he's walking, Hagar will be hard pressed to keep up with him.

Through all her hard times, and there were plenty of those, he has been the joy of her life. Without him, she would be completely alone most days. The doctors came a few times in the first weeks but as soon as it was clear he was healthy and thriving, even they stopped.

She thought a few of her coworkers might remain friends. Perhaps "friends" has always been a misnomer. A couple did visit once but she could see how the sight of a mother and child just reinforced the sorrow of their own empty arms.

For the rest of the ARCans it is like Hagar and Ishmael never existed at all. Their "savior" will never save them. He will produce no eggs. More sperm, they don't need. He is the lightning rod for every flash of anger, the personification of their every desperation.

If she had any tears left, she would shed them now, watching him explore the world around him. He should have so much to look forward to, but the more he figures out his world and how he fits in, the more he will realize that in the ARCan world, he doesn't fit in at all. He's another mouth to feed, one more source of carbon dioxide, feces and urine to be processed on their limited power reserves.

Though most of the ARCans gave up all hope after Ishmael was born, Mayer and a few others argued that Hagar's ovaries should be extracted and "mined" for viable eggs. She refused, of course.

When Mayer threatened to force the issue, she found an ally in Dr. Emil Sanzari. Dr. Emil was the fourth "old guy" originally booked for passage. Someone on the planning committee had the foresight to suggest the ships company might need an "adult" psychologist. The *ARC*'s Charter gives the Surgeon General total authority over medical decisions. Mayer and Kline co-sponsored a petition to amend the Charter, hoping to get their way.

"I'm not a political animal and Mayer is," Dr. Emil explains as Hagar refills his teacup. "So many of us are disheartened, I'm afraid he could muck about with the Council and pass the amendment. Before I risk everything I need to know where you stand."

"I refuse the surgery," Hagar answers.

"I understand that and I will support you—insofar as I can. Is Ishmael still nursing?"

"Yes."

"And you've had no menstruation?"

"No."

"If you still have viable eggs, would you consider another pregnancy?"

"I should trust you?"

"I'm only asking if you would consider it?" When she doesn't answer he goes on. "Having a baby sister would change the dynamics for Ishmael."

Should she consider it? As it is, she has been left completely alone and there's no reason to think that will change if she refuses. Is it fair to Ishmael to make him the only baby? Would his life be better or worse if she bore another child?

"And of course, it would change the dynamics for all of us."

Part of her doesn't care about the "dynamics for all of us." Mayer and the others don't care about the "dynamics" for her as they insist on cutting out her ovaries. Timms only cared about his own "dynamics" when he raped her. And if she were to conceive a girl-child, what would the dynamics be then?

Dr. Emil watches quietly as these thoughts and questions roll along in her head. "I have an alternative that I would like you to consider. There are relatively non-invasive ways to determine the health of your ovaries. If we give ourselves that information, then we can pick which battles to fight and which to avoid."

When the results of the x-ray, ultrasound and magnetic-resonance tests have been read and evaluated, Dr. Emil sits down with Hagar again.

"I know the tests weren't easy for you but at least the results are conclusive. What I don't know is whether you will consider it good news or bad. It does simplify things going forward."

"I'm sterile?"

"Neither one of your ovaries has any eggs."

"Ishmael was the last?"

"It's hard to tell the influence of your hormones during pregnancy but yes, it appears he was your last viable egg."

"They give up now? We don't have to wean?"

"You should mother Ishmael exactly as you see fit."

Mother Ishmael exactly as I see fit. And how is that, how am I to raise Ishmael? What kind of boy will he be with no man to model himself after? She would rather see him dead than modeled after Timms, but Adam Sidarus? Ishmael could have benefitted from a father figure like that. How is he to learn to play? How to take responsibility? How to love someone—a woman or a man—without a man to show him the way?

But by what logic would Adam Sidarus take a paternal interest in Ishmael? He was cordial enough, the times he met with Hagar. If she had borne his child there might be a bond there. But she hadn't—she bore Edward Timms' child.

I am the oldest woman aboard. Even if I live a full life he will still be very young when I die. And what if I have an accident or get sick?

Who can he turn to?

When the committee insisted that her baby should be assigned to some other couple to raise, Hagar denied their logic. Now that she finds herself totally alone . . .

There is only one person likely to offer companionship and support to Hagar's child—there has always been only one person.

Solange.

#

Hagar eases into the pen, Ishmael asleep in the sling. She walks among the few remaining cows, strokes their sides, pats their faces. She senses Solange's presence without actually seeing her arrive. "Hello, Solange."

"Hello Hagar." The women are out of each other's sight—Hagar among the cows and Solange outside the rail fence. "It's sad how few are left."

"Yes, very sad."

The small talk part of the conversation comes to a quiet end. "You moved out?" Hagar asks.

"Yes."

"Long time ago?"

"About seven months."

Between people who have never been friends, the pause would seem uncomfortably long.

Solange moves to catch a glimpse of Ishmael. "How's the baby?"

"He's getting big."

"Is he still nursing?"

"Only when he's upset. He's got teeth now, so he wants food."

"Does it hurt?"

There's a catch in Hagar's throat. Her beautiful friend, a woman perfectly attuned to mothering, must learn what a baby's nursing feels like second-hand. "Only when he bites."

Hagar visits the livestock on and off over the next few weeks. When Solange is there, they chat. The topics go from feed supplies to milk production to the curious fact that the chickens and ducks have somehow maintained their fertility.

But then one day, Hagar says, "The tests all came out negative. He was the last one."

"It's a shame," Solange answers. "It would be so nice if he had someone to play with." She never reaches out to touch him, nor does she talk to him. She just stares, silent and absorbed. And he stares back.

"Would you like to visit?" Hagar asks.

"Visit you, in your quarters?"

"Yes. We could have some tea if you like."

Having tea is something friends do—women friends, at least.

Solange smiles. "I would love to. When were you thinking?"

"This afternoon?"

Ishmael plays with a few wooden spoons, a strainer and two pots. The ship's stores have every kind of toy. Hagar has brought a few of those for him but he is much more interested in the things he sees her use around the house. He is only briefly distracted by the soft knock at the door.

"Solange, come in please."

It is over a year since Solange has been inside. She takes it all in, walks over and touches the baby clothes hanging to dry. She breathes deep the smells of life, the earthy aromas of a small child who wets, sweats, drools and soils.

"It's not real tea." Hagar offers Solange a cup and saucer. "I have some ginger snaps. They're not very fresh."

"Yes, I'll have one please."

Hagar opens a tin, offers them to her. They sit down to a silence filled with portent.

"I'm . . ." Solange begins, "I'm so sorry about what happened. I *t* . . . There's never a day I don't regret what I did. I don't blame you for hating me."

"I don't hate you."

"You have every right."

"I only wonder why?"

"Of course." Solange's cadence is stiff and rote—not so much like she has rehearsed a speech for an audience, but more like she has tried over and over to formulate some words to express what she feels—to convince herself that she is not a monster. "He needed my help with switching the semen samples and he promised me if I did that, he would make them give the baby to me."

"I see."

"Even after he made you pregnant I didn't dare ..."

"After he raped me."

"Even after he ..." She can't say the word at first. "Even after he raped you I didn't want to stand up to him. I wanted the baby so much. It was foolish of me—and blind. He never had the power to make them give me the baby, but I ... I stayed because I wanted to believe it could be true."

"And now nobody wants to be the mother."

Solange looks over at Ishmael. "I do."

"With Captain Timms as father?"

"Never!"

There's palpable fury in Hagar's voice. "I never want that man to go near him."

"No, of course not."

It's as though Hagar's persona has morphed into some mystical seer enunciating an omen or curse. "He's going to try."

"Try what, to play the role of father? I can't imagine."

Hagar shakes her head. "That's why he did it."

"I beg pardon?"

"He wants power. That's all he ever wants. He's got no power over the others, so he takes power on me. And now that I won't give it to him, who is he going to get power over?" She pauses while her friend sorts out the answer.

"Ishmael?" Solange asks.

"Any man named 'the third' wants be sure he makes 'the fourth.' Having a son proves his power over every other man on board."

"Edward Timms the Fourth validates Edward Timms the Third."

"In his eyes."

Ishmael brings a wooden spoon to Solange. He holds out his hands to be picked up.

Hagar nods her assent.

Solange may have held less than five babies in her whole lifetime and for a moment, she's unsure. But her instincts are good and so are his. He settles into her lap, nuzzles her breast. But then, instead of rooting, he simply leans against it, looks up into her eyes.

Hagar takes in the sight. If her child and her friend bond like this, who is she to say no?

"He likes you."

"And I like him, too."

CHAPTER EIGHT

"Dithering" and Kees DeWet—words never spoken in the same breath. Even when the path hasn't been clear to him, he has always acted with imperfect knowledge, taken the risk. Until now he has always leapt, trusting that the net would appear.

Yet today he paces the *ARC*'s Observation Deck, distracted, agitated, frustrated with himself.

Parlay is a few hours away. He'll have maybe five minutes to convince twelve hardened souls to forgo immediate gratification, take the longer view, buy into a dream rather than grasp the brass ring so immediately at hand.

If he can't convince them he'll be deposed—forced to "walk the plank," face death in open space.

And after that, Cutter will fire up the torches and turn the *ARC* into scrap. Ishmael's story will never be heard, the ARCans will be forgotten and the name Kees DeWet will disappear from the universal consciousness forever.

"What have you done to me, brother Ishmael?"

Course de tar baby, she ain't sayin' nothin'.

Kees is stuck on the ARCans' story as sure as Brer Rabbit stuck himself on that tar baby.

He could have followed protocol and scrapped the *ARC* the minute they came upon her. But no, he had to punch that tar baby and board her.

And Roman Pollack, he lay low.

Kees could have simply returned to the *Scavenger* with some tiny memento to remember her by, kept Ishmael's story in his heart, cut up the *ARC* and been satisfied with being rich. But no, he had to kick that tar baby and repower her.

And Roman Pollack, he sauntered out from the bushes and he said, "Parlay."

Kees could have given in and saved himself as captain. But no, he had to wheedle three days out of them. He had to come back on board, find and watch all of Ishmael's trailer, immerse himself in the ARCans' story. He had to headbutt that tar baby and get himself totally stuck on the ARCans' dream—a dream they called ARC World.

And now, in a few hours "Brer Roman" will decide whether to roast Kees, or hang him, or skin him or drown him.

But that's a children's story, one that ends with Brer Rabbit getting away. If Kees lived in that fairy tale world, he might persuade Roman and the crew to maroon him aboard the *ARC*. He might trick them into "throwing him into that briar patch."

But this is the real world and Kees has to make the argument—make the argument and win it.

The ARCans, so prescient in everything else, don't seem to have left any hints. How could they not have foreseen that their first convert would face a world of skeptics? Where are the numbers, the profit margins, the revenue projections?

He turns to Ishmael again—more insistent this time. "You stuck me on this, now how am I supposed to sell it to my crew?" And the question echoes in the room.

He told me a story.

The story isn't just the treasure, it's also the tool. *I should have been the impossible nut to crack, the apostate never to be converted.*

Ishmael seduced me the only way he could, by telling me their story. The ARCans didn't leave me clues on how to do this, Ishmael showed me how it's done. And with no net in sight, Kees leaps.

When exiting a shuttle through its docking hatch, the procedure is, of necessity, a feet-first affair. But now, as Kees returns to the shuttle, he must wriggle headfirst into the narrow passageway. "Near the beginning of the twentieth century, Terran calendar years," he begins, "there was constructed a great ocean-going vessel, which rammed an iceberg on her maiden voyage and sank with nearly all hands."

He peers out the canopy as the *ARC's* docking latches disengage, feathers the directional thrusters and points the shuttle toward the *Scavenger*. "Great was the anguish when Terrans' prideful dream of the 'unsinkable ship' settled beneath the waves like so much misbegotten steel and glass."

He eases the throttle and coasts. "It was half a century before they had the technology to even locate the wreckage, but on that day arose dreams of precious artifacts, mementos, and personal effects all there for the salvage. There was even a fanciful imagining of how the ship might be refloated—the great lady brought up from . . ."

Cutter waits for him in the *Scavenger's* launch bay as he steps from the shuttle. She listens as he tells his tale. ". . . fanciful imagining of how the ship might be refloated—the great lady brought up from her watery grave. The tales of passengers' bravery and sacrifice were retold, the heroic songs were sung anew. The fate of that ship captured the imagination of generation after generation so that when a raconteur screened his vision of those events eighty years after the fact, millions indulged their fascination in dark theatres, in close quarters, over and over again."

"And you would be that raconteur?" she asks.

"Ishmael is the raconteur. The ship herself is the theatre."

"You're going to lose."

"Am I going to lose you?" he asks.

"It's not me you have to win."

He pauses a long time, stares at her, takes her measure. "Actually, it is."

Now it's her turn to stare—to take his measure and his meaning. "Because?"

"If I lose at Parlay, I'll take her myself."

"One man, alone aboard that great ship? What can you do alone?"

"I need a second. That's enough."

So that's her out.

If the message she intercepted earlier is true, then the Alliance has already marked them both for death. Even if Kees gives in at the Parlay, agrees to cut up the *ARC* for scrap, Roman must carry out his orders. However the "accidents" occur, first one of them will die and then the other. If she's to find any escape at all, it will be with him.

"I be second for you."

He looks her in the eye. "Done, then."

But Parlay is less than an hour away and they need a plan.

#

Kees spins his tale to the rapt attention of Prof, Gordo and the twins. The rest of the crew listens skeptically except for Roman, who listens with palpable hostility and disdain.

". . . indulged their fascination in dark theatres, in close quarters, over and over again. This is what the ARCans dreamed, that millions would come to hear their story . . . "

Roman interrupts, steps up with a swagger that doesn't fit him very well. "That's what you pissed four septa away on?" His laugh is forced. "And Ugg's going to take tickets and the twins here will make sure the rides keep working."

The only thing Prof gets is that Parlay isn't that serious any more. He joins in. "There's going to be rides?"

"Rides," Roman banters, "the fat lady, the two-headed donkey. That's what you're proposing, Captain? Surely you jest."

Gordo chuckles and pokes Prof's ribs, "He called the captain Shirley."

"Be this Parlay?" Kees asks.

The levity evaporates.

"This be Parlay and it be time to vote." Roman oozes confidence as he raises the lid on the small, rough-hewn ballot box. Inside, as per the age-old ritual, scraps of paper—black on one side and white on the other. The crew forms a circle, each member takes a ballot and stands at what would be their best imitation of attention.

"If any wants more Parlay, let him speak now." Roman waits the prescribed seconds as no one speaks up. "Then Parlay be over. We vote on the question and that be, do we side with the captain and salvage the derelict off our port bow or do we scavenge her and sell her parts for scrap?"

Each crewmember adjusts the paper in hand. They watch Roman and when he raises his, they each raise theirs. Every one of them can see every other vote in the room. Kees' is white and so is Prof's.

"You be with the captain wantin' to salvage her?" Roman asks.

Prof quickly drops his hand, switches the ballot and raises it again—black.

Kees looks long and hard at Cutter. There she stands, the black spot centered in her raised hand.

Twelve to one.

Roman tries to make it look like Cutter's blackball is exactly what he expected—without success. For several seconds he stares at her, his mind racing to find justification for the surprise.

Then he steps up to Kees, face-to-face and triumphant. "Deposed." Hands go down.

He looks around the room. "We need to choose a captain."

Some clearly saw this coming—others . . ."Kees isn't captain?" Prof asks.

"He's deposed." . . . *you simpleton.* Roman leaves the epithet unspoken.

Ugg speaks up—on cue, "I say Roman Pollack."

"Not Cutter?" Gordo asks.

That's the beautiful thing about idiots—you can't ever predict where they're coming from nor where they're going.

No one has ever accused Roman Pollack of being a slow thinker. "She's in with Kees."

"She black-balled him, just like the rest of us," Scrounger counters.

Of course. That's why she did it.

She may have anticipated the vote for a new captain but can't have foreseen what Roman says next. "She and Kees plan to steal our prize."

The pulse rate and blood pressure of every single crewmember is suddenly up by half at least. There isn't an un-tensed muscle anywhere.

"You got proof?" It's surprising how often the twins say exactly the same thing at the same time.

Roman moves his hand slowly, makes it clear he is reaching into his tunic for proof rather than for a weapon. He holds up a small electronic device. "Listen for yourselves. This was in the last hour." He presses a button.

If I lose at Parlay, I'll take her myself.
One man, alone aboard that great ship? What can you do alone?
I need a second. That's enough.
A pause and then, *I be second for you.*

"You deny it?"

There is no denying it—it clearly is their voices. With the odds at eleven to two, this is not the time to fight back.

"No," Kees answers.

"Take them both to the cargo hold."

With lesser prisoners, Ugg would grab them and muscle them from the room. But this is Cutter and Kees. It's a fool who steps within arm's reach of either one of them. He opens the door and waits for them to pass through.

"And put 'em in irons," Roman adds. "Anyone here vote for someone else as captain?" Even Gordo and Prof know better than to answer that.

#

Ugg points the ugly stub of a stun gun at his charges as he ushers them into the cargo hold. He hands Cutter a set of irons.

"Him first."

She binds Kees' hands and feet.

"Now you."

She turns, puts her hands together behind her back. Ugg slides the weapon into a hip pocket. He fastens her hands, then snakes the chain through Kees' manacled arms before locking it into her ankle irons. He tugs on them harshly—a bit more swagger now that they are no longer a threat. "You think you so smart now?"

No answer.

He gets right in Cutter's face. "Thought not." He slams the heavy door shut and activates the lock.

Cutter can't suppress the smile. If they had been chained separately, retrieving the pick would have been significantly more difficult. As it is, between the two of them, the irons are quietly eased onto the floor in less than a minute.

Before Roman can cut into the *ARC*'s hull he has to retrieve the power module and its four septa. They have to hope it takes him some time to figure out how to do that and who to send. For Kees' and Cutter's plan to work, they have to get to the shuttle bay before anybody else.

She's not called Cutter for nothing. She pulls on the goggles and fires up the torch with a well-practiced hand. The secret is to cut the deadbolt without melting either hasp.

Piece of cake.

A more experienced captain probably would have posted a guard outside the door—not so much to prevent escape as to raise the alarm when it happened. Roman has been captain for only about twelve minutes. He'll be "more experienced" next time.

The iris in the shuttle bay is a major obstacle. No one ever bothered to create a remote control, much less an automatic timer. One person in a space suit must operate the controls manually while the other is sealed in the shuttle's cockpit. The canopy can't be opened unless the pilot is in a full pressure suit, and if he is suited up, there's no more room inside for a second passenger.

That means somebody is going to have to piggyback, "wing-walk" the shuttle on the trip over. Cutter's space suit is the only one that's functional. The upside is that she's the only person in the last year to launch anything from the bay.

Time will be critical once they initiate the atmospheric purge and they have to hope whoever comes to investigate doesn't know how to reverse it—at least doesn't figure it out quickly. They have three-and-a-half minutes if they're lucky, two and change if they're not.

They've done this before, both of them. To be exact, they've done the first steps: 1) suit up and seal the cockpit, 2) purge the atmosphere, 3) open the iris, 4) push the shuttle out.

Normally, step 5) is "close the iris." Only this time, it's Cutter's job to leap after the shuttle, catch it in open space and then hang on while Kees pilots her toward the *ARC* using the maneuvering thrusters only.

Nothing scary about that.

Cutter twists the bubble helmet down 'til it locks. Kees gives the thumbs-up from the cockpit. One last visual check before she activates the atmospheric purge. Air rushes noisily into the pump intakes.

Standard procedure is to open the iris only after the purge is at 95 percent. The override becomes available at 85 percent. She has every intention of using it.

The ship's general quarters klaxon pulses. Somebody knows...Hell, everybody knows something's gone wrong. Seventy-two percent...77 percent...80 percent. The pumps are most efficient when there's lots of air to suck in. It's those last few percent that take forever. Eighty-two percent...

Sparks peers through the pressure lock. That's not good.

Kudos to Roman—he sent the most capable person. Cutter stares at her. Sparks' body language says she's torn. Her actions say she's not going to let her second thoughts slow her down.

If Sparks knew about the override, she could stop it in a heartbeat. But the heartbeat goes by, the vacuum reaches 85 percent and Cutter kicks in the override and activates the iris. Suddenly Sparks' face disappears from the pressure lock. She surely is at the control panel and will soon figure out what to do.

It takes less than a half-second for the vacuum to reach 100 percent. Deep space is always hungry for molecules of air. Cutter kills gravity in the bay. As the iris creeps open, she shuffles over to the shuttle and manhandles it toward the opening. She's good—with both timing and aim. There's less than six inches clearance on any side as the shuttle eases past the now nearly wide-open orifice. One meter away... three... six...

Ka-chunk!

OK, that's the iris moving to "close" mode. All she has to do is aim herself and ...

Suddenly she feels heavy. Gravity has been restored. The iris is down to a little over two meters open. She can do this.

The pull of artificial gravity declines sharply with distance. As a young track star, she cleared two meters in the high jump event. If she can get even half that much force in this bulky suit, she'll break free. She flexes—she jumps.

Nothing.

Shit!

She fumbles with the controls for the magnetic boots.

Off.

The iris is looking mighty small. She flexes her knees again and jumps.

Just before she's clear, the toe of her boot strikes the now nearly closed iris, spins her wildly. She's not going to break away. The gravity draws her back. At the last minute, she spreads her legs, avoids her foot sliding into a hole that would surely cut it off. Her heart pounds, adrenaline hammers away.

The suit is built to accommodate "moderately strenuous" physical activity. She passed that threshold a long time ago. The cold of space fogs her bubble helmet and the carbon dioxide warning beeps.

She can't clear the helmet—the fogging is on the inside. The shuttle must be "above" her as she stands on the now-closed iris.

Only not closed for long. The plates of the iris move beneath her feet. *Damn, that Sparks is good!* The hole beneath her starts as a small circle. Somehow it didn't seem to open this quickly when she was impatient for it.

What's the saying, "Leap and the net will appear?"

She can only hope after she leaps that the shuttle will appear— and that she can grab it before some sharp surface rips her suit.

. . . Two . . . Three . . . Jump!

#

She can't see the iris—she can't see anything, but if she didn't get spring enough to clear the pull of the bay's artificial gravity, the next thing she's going to feel is a thump onto the floor of the bay. By time her helmet clears, Sparks will have closed the iris and pressurized the bay. And then Roman will have Ugg kill her.

That's one possibility.

The other is that she did get enough spring. In that case, she's now drifting free in space and somewhere nearby is the shuttle. There's no motive device in the suit of any kind. Drifting is the one and only thing she can do. If she can't connect with something that does have motive power, in—she looks at the gauge on her air tank—one hour, thirteen minutes, the oxygen level in her suit will drop below threshold, she'll pass out and after a few more minutes, she'll die.

Calm is good. Her body uses more oxygen when she's under stress. She consciously slows her breathing, relaxes her leg muscles, then her arms, then her neck and head. The CO_2 sensor gives one final strangled chirp and falls silent. Eventually the small circulation fan will clear her helmet—it could be several minutes.

Her right arm is ever so gently pushed backward. There's only one thing that might cause that. The maneuvering thrusters on the shuttle release a tiny flow of energy when fired. If Kees has piloted the shuttle close to her, her arm must have been in the path of one of those pulses. What does he expect her to do? She surely is spinning—or was she spinning before and that pulse stopped her? He's good, but is anybody that good?

Abrupt movement is going to be a mistake but if he's trying to get close, she wants to make herself as large as she can. Gradually she extends her arms straight out and spread-eagles her legs.

It's her left boot that makes contact. Being able to see would be a major help but space is pitch dark. She moves the boot gently but there's little hope in that. Her boot would have moved away from, not toward whatever bumped it. *For every action there's an equal and opposite reaction.* There are times she hates physics the worst.

But then the left boot is bumped again. That could only happen if Kees somehow made the shuttle bump her boot this second time. Why not her hand? Why not . . .?

Oh Cutter, shame on you! Physics is your friend. She reaches down, slowly and smoothly and activates the magnetism in her boot. Right away it thunks down on something metallic. Right away it pulls.

When conditions are right for moisture to condense on the inside of a bubble helmet, it fogs up amazingly fast. When conditions are right for moisture in the helmet to be reabsorbed, the fog disappears as quickly. Thus Cutter is treated to the sight of *Scavenger's* hull whisking past her head less than a meter away. It must have been millimeters when Kees first pulsed the shuttle's thrusters.

She's not in position to "wing-walk." Her leg is blocking the starboard gimbal-correction port. Somehow Kees has gotten them clear of the *Scavenger* without it, but she's going to have to change her "grip" if they are to navigate their way over to the *ARC*.

She passes her hand across her throat in the universal "cut" gesture and immediately Kees kills all the thrust. She reaches down with one hand and grabs one of the external control shafts. With the other hand she turns off magnetism in her boots and the life-saving left foot floats free. Hand over hand she guides herself toward the canopy and grabs the narrow flange left and right. Her face is less than half a meter from Kees' through her helmet and his canopy. He smiles. He's got a good smile. She tightens her grip and gently raps her helmet on the canopy three times—*bonk, bonk, bonk.*

His hands move to the maneuvering throttles and they're on their way.

Her boots clank down. She watches the shuttle make its way to the *ARC*'s docking port. The heads-up display shows "oxygen" and a clock counting down—8:01, 8:00, 7:59 . . .

It's only another twenty meters but there's a limit to how much she can hurry. One foot does always have to be in contact with the *ARC*'s metal hull. Kees will board through the docking hatch as she trudges her way toward the service bay.

She arrives to find the clamshell still closed. Two minutes of oxygen.

Finally a crack of light and the welcome sight of the jitney bug on the bay's floor. They were concerned how she was going to climb in and the way the bay is constructed, it's more like a problem than a concern.

The CO_2 sensor chirps back to life—that won't be shutting down any time soon. Just one thing to do.

She turns off the boots and pushes off gently—floats past the gaping maw of the bay. If Kees isn't watching or if he doesn't get what to do, she'll float away.

"This would be a good time, Kees."

He turns the bay's gravity on just as she passes the midpoint. She's still conscious as she slides onto the floor. The cobwebs start forming on the edges of her vision as the clamshell closes. She folds her legs, hands on her knees, lotus position, and calms herself.

Then she passes out.

Roman watches the drama unfolding on the hull of the *ARC*. As the clamshell closes he dials the magnification back to 2X. For just an instant he's swept up by the grandeur of his massive prize. In that moment he can understand how Kees was seduced into his fateful decision. Understand it, but not agree. Before the hour is out her hull will be breached. Whether Cutter survived or not, in a few minutes it won't matter.

But the question nags at him. *Why did they board her?* Kees would have expected to be marooned—or maybe set adrift in a single-seater. People have survived that and if anybody could do it, it's Kees. Did they know he was ordered to kill them?

Too much thinking, Roman. Just cut her up and let's go.

Destroy the ship and kill them both at the same time. It's the simplest solution. *Easy peasy.* And of course this was his frame of mind when he had them in irons in the cargo hold, and look how that turned out.

"What's taking so long?" he snarls into the com link.

#

Cutter sees the concern in Kees' eyes.

"How long was I out?" she asks.

"About two minutes." He lays the bubble helmet next to her.

She runs a mental check on herself. Her arms and legs respond normally when she flexes them, the room is in clear focus, her equilibrium seems perfectly steady. She sits up with his help and the bay gives kind of a half-swirl and then settles down. "I'm OK."

He helps her to her feet. "I'll need you on the bridge."

"Aye aye sir."

"I'll get to firing control," and he dashes out.

The spacesuit will slow her down too much. Her wet jumpsuit clings to her as she strips off the bulky leggings and boots. By time she sprints to the bridge, there are a few dry patches and the exercise has warmed her up.

113

She steps onto the bridge and is stopped dead in her tracks, her breath taken away. She knew it was going to be impressive but she wasn't ready for the full scope of it. The *ARC* is ten times bigger than any ship she's ever seen and the grand lady stretches out before her now. The hull seems to go on forever. *They did know how to build 'em in the day.*

"Mister Cutter?" his voice booms over the intercom, rich and sonorous.

"Aye Captain."

"You're on the bridge?"

"Yes sir."

"Status?"

She curses herself under her breath. There's a job to do and instead she let herself be distracted. "He's got the cutter extension about half deployed."

"How far away?"

"Three klak, maybe four." A few days ago she would have been out of line to ask her captain's status. "What about you?" It feels right, but it is going to take some getting used to.

"The capacitors are at sixty percent. I've got targeting."

"You're going to fire on her?"

"Not if I can help it."

The proverbial shot across the bow? Roman's not likely to be deterred by that.

Kees' voice is cool and steady, "The last J-26 power cell, did you finish the extraction?"

"Yes sir, it's dry as a bone." *Of course.*

"We have to roll at least five degrees left before I can get a shot."

"Do you have helm control from where you are?" she asks.

"Negative that. You'll have to execute it from there."

"Aye aye, sir." And their lives depend on her figuring out helm controls designed seventy-five years before she was born. Then, when she executes the maneuver, mechanisms that haven't made a course correction in over thirty years will have to be functional.

And if all that works, this great cow, with all her inertia, will have to roll five degrees left before Roman can get the *Scavenger* close enough for Trish to fire her torch and make the first cut.

Cutter locates the area for helm control and swipes a finger over one of the thrusters.

Throughout the ship, structural pieces groan as the hull experiences g-forces for the first time in ages. The inertial dampers are slow to respond and things not fastened down shift to the right just a little. But respond she does. As the roll passes through one degree and then a second, the *ARC*'s position relative to the *Scavenger* changes.

"Hello *ARC*. Stand down your maneuver," Roman's voice booms.

"Steady as she goes, mister Cutter," Kees responds on the internal channel.

The first cut on a derelict, at least one with atmospheric pressure, is the most demanding. Rupturing the atmospheric containment on a ship of this size will create a massive blowout. If the cutting torch is in harm's way, the *Scavenger* will be thrown out of position at tremendous risk. Whether Roman knows that or Trish insisted, the *Scavenger* slows its approach and modifies its attitude.

"He's changed course, sir."

"I see it," Kees responds. "Capacitors at ninety-three percent."

At this pace it will take twelve minutes to recharge the capacitors for a second shot. Kees is taking a huge risk. If Roman is desperate enough, the destruction of the spent fuel cell won't scare him. If he orders Trish to make the first cut, there's nothing Kees can do to stop him.

Cutter watches a tiny spark flash from the *Scavenger*'s number one plasma torch. "The cutter extension is hot. Trish just fired it up." She knows from personal experience what Trish's adrenaline level must be.

"I've got a lock on the cylinder. Five more seconds to a full charge."

. . . Four . . . Three . . . Two . . . One.

She's never seen a weapon like the one aboard the *ARC*, but whoever designed it knew what he was doing. A small, red bead of energy forms at dead center of the Steenmeyer logo on the well-worn J-26. It blossoms quickly as wispy plasma filaments dance in a steady progression toward each end. Suddenly the entire casing ignites into a blazing flash and scraps of shrapnel blow out in a perfect sphere.

Whatever the force field was, it disappears like an old-fashioned candle under a snuffer.

"What the fuck?" It seems someone failed to turn off Roman's com mike. The connection is broken with a loud, angry click.

The cutting torch extinguishes and the extension retracts toward its sheath. Roman can't use the main engines with the extension even partially deployed. He does his best with evasive action using the *Scavenger*'s thruster.

"Roll right five degrees, mister Cutter."

"Aye aye sir, five degrees right." There's no way this tub can maneuver with the *Scavenger* but Kees wants Roman to think he may be lining up a second shot. Apparently it works.

"Don't shoot, DeWet."

Cutter remembers her queasy feeling looking down the barrel of the weapon and she assumes that Kees has lined up the *Scavenger*'s bridge in his crosshairs. She imagines Roman staring at it in full magnification, the sweat pouring off him into the captain's chair. She has seen it twice before—Roman sweating—and she almost wishes she could be on the *Scavenger*'s bridge to see it again.

"What are your terms?" They'll have to get a mop to clean up around Roman's chair.

Kees is only connected internally. Cutter shuts down the link to Roman. "Captain, he's asking your terms."

If a smile can be heard, she thinks there's one in Kees' voice. "Tell him leaving will suffice."

"Aye aye sir." She reopens ship-to-ship. "Roman Pollack, these are the terms offered by Kees DeWet, captain of the generational ship, *ARC*. You are to relinquish any and all claim to this vessel and leave the quadrant straightway. If you fail to comply within the next two minutes, you will be fired upon. We await your answer."

"Nicely done, mister." This time the smile in Kees' voice is unmistakable.

The sheath closes around the cutting extension and the *Scavenger* aligns herself in the direction she came. The main engine fires.

"I'll see you burn in hell, DeWet."

CHAPTER NINE

Everyone on board the *ARC* knew that when Raiff Ingermann took young Ishmael under his wing, it was a portent of doom for the thirteen-year-old Ishmael. Raiff was a ne'er-do-well, a "bad seed," a hooligan. His was the last name added to the ship's manifest before the launch. No one questioned whether his inclusion was the product of high-stakes favoritism or not.

It was.

Raiff's grandfather was at one time number three on the list of the world's wealthiest men. His son Rudi, Raiff's father, was a lawyer and a politician. With the family fortune to back him up, Rudi could buy favorable rulings in cases where his legal skills weren't up to the task. That's how all of Raiff's felony charges were overturned.

Six weeks before the *ARC*'s launch Raiff was involved in a prank that cost a seventeen-year-old girl her life. Suddenly Raiff was ushered aboard the last shuttle to the space dock.

The ARCans never particularly bought the cover story that Raiff was a "wunderkind," a programming genius of some kind, especially after the tech team had to show him how to operate the door locks in his quarters.

On the night of Ishmael's birth, it was originally reported that Raiff was a part of the group that committed mass suicide. Someone later discovered him passed out behind the chicken coop. He was not among the volunteers building the scaffolding. He was, as a rule, too drunk to be of any use at anything.

He did have one trait that served him well: he could unerringly spot the person most vulnerable to manipulation. As the population of the *ARC* declined and his cadre of cohorts and fellow travelers dwindled, he employed that skill in actively seeking replacements.

A few days after Ishmael's thirteenth birthday, Raiff arrived at Hagar's door and offered himself to Ishmael as a "big brother" (of twenty-three years age spread), a mentor, a soul mate.

And Ishmael bought it.

Raiff mentored him, all right. Never was a young man more thoroughly schooled in the use of recreational drugs and mind-altering chemicals. Long hours were committed to mastering all the levels of any number of video games. The "facts of life" were described, catalogued and visually portrayed in the most graphic and lurid of details. Every foolish risk was taken, every childish impulse indulged. They say the road to hell is paved with good intentions, which could not possibly be true in this case because, well, because no one has ever accused Raiff of having good intentions in any of his endeavors.

Hagar found herself on the horns of a dilemma. Does a mother tell her son that he must turn down the only person who has ever offered to be his friend? Is total isolation really preferable to contact with the real world, even when it's the seamiest, foulest underbelly of that world?

All of Hagar's soul-searching didn't matter much. At age thirteen, Ishmael was not about to buy anything his mother sold him.

It was a Tuesday when Ishmael announced that he and Raiff were going on a "road trip." They marched off into the farthest reaches of the ship—the forest, the deserted fields and the mineral storage areas. From time to time in the following weeks, one or the other of them would be spotted skulking about. Chickens began disappearing on a fairly regular schedule and food occasionally went missing from the kitchens overnight.

It went on night and day for over a month.

#

"You know, young man, these bottles are empty," Raiff slurs as he drains the last drops of bourbon into his cup. "If you were the man they claim you are, you could fill these up for us."

Not one to take such a challenge lying down, Ishmael stands up—on the second try. "And so I shall, sir, and so I shall." He manages to stuff the bottles into a gunnysack without breaking any and weaves his way toward what the two of them have officially designated "the booze locker." He has stood guard at the door many times while Raiff pilfers the ship's stores but never actually tapped the barrels himself. But he is a quick study and, in his current state of mind, unswervingly confident that he can handle the mechanics of the transfer.

The guard at the door is a surprise. Could it be that the bean counters have finally realized that their stores of fine libations are dwindling? Raiff regularly boasts that between the two of them, they are responsible for over 10 percent of the alcohol consumption aboard.

"Mister Churchill, you're drunk," Raiff so often intones in his funny, high-pitched woman's voice. He switches into his pompous windbag timbre and continues, *"Yes Madam, but you're ugly—and in the morning I'll be sober."* By time Raiff gets around to the ritual, they're so drunk they laugh their asses off—every time.

But the guard is no joke. He marches back and forth in front of the door. His visor is up but the chinstrap on his helmet is buckled and he's got mace containers on his belt and a stun stick in the holster. Ishmael has only seen two people stunned but he's pretty sure it's not something he wants to try.

What would Raiff do? How would he get by the guard?

It's not like he can go back and ask him—that would be

admitting that he can't get the bottles refilled by himself. And he can't make a distraction—that requires two people.

What Raiff would do is ask me.

Raiff may live his life outside the box, but his thinking is still very much stuck inside. It's to his credit that among his circle of "friends" he has always cultivated somebody who displays a creative streak. Currently, that's Ishmael.

Aboard the *ARC*, like any man-made environment, what appears to be one thing is pretty often something else as well. In this case, the floor of the booze locker is the ceiling of some other space. The ground isn't the ground, it's just another horizontal wall. And if gravity were turned off, "up" and "down" wouldn't mean much, neither would left or right. The "floor" could be a ceiling, the "ground" could be a divider wall. People think of walls having doors and windows but in fact on a ship like this, the floors and ceilings also have "doors." You just have to think that way.

Ishmael eases out of sight of the guard, frees the battens on a nearby hatch and drops into the level below. He pauses for a moment, recollects the direction and distance between him and the booze locker and heads off in that direction, counting his paces. When he gets where he believes is the right place, a fabric storeroom, he looks up. Sure enough, there's a hatch in the ceiling.

He climbs up on a stack of boxes and pulls himself through the hatch. *Which barrel?* The stain on the floor where a spigot has leaked smells like bourbon, or maybe some other whiskey. Ishmael fetches the first bottle and pours a little in. It's light brown. A swig confirms it—bourbon. It doesn't take long to fill the eight bottles.

Once safely below he reaches back up, eases the hatch shut and waits a minute or two, listening for any sign that the guard has raised an alarm. When all's quiet, he eases out of the room, gunnysack full of booze proudly in hand.

"Ah, my young apprentice returns," Raiff jokes. "Let me see the result of your quest." He makes a big to-do about opening the sack—holds up a bottle to admire it in the light. He pulls the stopper, draws a huge swig and jovially exclaims, "Ah, the golden elixir!"

And together they tie on a bender to vie with the best they've ever done.

And when all is blurry and warm and cozy—when they are on the verge of disconnecting with the dreary world of their makeshift encampment, Raiff suddenly comes to life with an idea.

"You know, young man,"—he always starts out that way when he's being dramatic—". . . we've been on this road trip for how many days? But we've yet to take to the road!"

Ishmael has been keeping pace with Raiff's drinking and he's no match for Raiff's capacity. He's sluggish and having real trouble focusing. "Uh, that's right."

"Come my fine young man, we are about to rectum-ize that deficiency!" Raiff drags himself to his feet, cutting a dashing figure as he helps Ishmael up. Off they proceed, the gallant Don Quixote leading the way on some heroic quest and his faithful Sancho Panza stumbling along behind.

And the quest leads to the motor pool and the object is no windmill to be jousted, but the Toozebakker 85. Raiff holds the door open.

Ishmael answers, "I can't drive this."

"And why not, my fine young man?"

"They'd lock me up for a year. This is Kline's."

"Kline, Schmine. You're the son of the captain. You can drive whatever you want."

"But this is the Toozy."

"Perceptive of you, as always, my fine young man. This is in fact a Toozy—the world's fastest vehicle. And you're asking yourself, will I crash it? Will I die a fiery death?"

"Uh, actually, yeah."

Raiff shows his disappointment as Ishmael refuses to cooperate in his levity. "What's the matter, you chicken?"

"Nobody calls me chicken."

Raiff makes manipulation look so easy. His playfulness restored, he gives a foppish bow as Ishmael slides behind the wheel.

"I'm gonna kill myself."

"You'll do nothing of the kind. You were born under a lucky star, young man, and as long as it shines, no harm will come to you. Take my word for it."

Ishmael sobers up a little as he looks over the controls. The start button is actually nice and clear. He presses it. The drives cough once and come to life with a low-pitched growl. Raiff is totally enchanted with the turn of events. "Hold on a second," he hollers and dashes over to move a forklift out of the way.

"Hit it!"

Ishmael takes a deep breath, stomps the pedal and the '85 lives up to its reputation. It takes less than three seconds for it to career into the protruding edge of the massive overhead door. Ishmael is thrown clear as the Toozy slews violently to the right and rolls over three times, pinning the forklift as it comes to rest. Raiff's maniacal laughter is replaced by screams of pain.

#

Ishmael eases up into a blurry, half-awake state. He tries to piece together what Dr. Emil is telling his mother.

"We'll be taking the pins out in a few days. It looks like he'll have full range of motion in both the arm and the leg. He's a very lucky young man."

I'm a lucky young man? Who is he kidding? The only person I ever called a friend is dead because of my jackass stunt. The few people who put up with me before despise me now. OK, I'm going to heal up, but then what? It's back to all alone with my mother. She's all, "Oh you poor boy," now, but pretty soon it's going to be the guilt trips and moralizing and, "How could you have been so stupid? What were you thinking? I never liked you hanging around with Raiff but he didn't deserve to die like that."

Everybody on this ship looks for a scapegoat when something goes wrong and with Raiff gone, it's all going to fall on . . .

Hagar sits at his bedside and watches as the painkillers take over and Ishmael drops back into a hazy, cotton-mouthed stupor.

The pain shoots through his shoulder as Ishmael reaches behind him for the handle of the resistance bands. "Ouch!"

"I'm sorry it hurts," Hagar answers, "but you have to do your rehab, else you won't get full use of your arm."

"Fuck my arm. I don't have . . ."

"I will not have you using that kind of language!"

"And I don't care what you'll have. I'll use whatever kind of fucking language I want and you can't stop me."

She's too fast for him—grabs him by the ear before he can avoid it. "You listen to me, young man."

Timms steps, unannounced, into the doorframe. Ishmael's shocked expression stops Hagar in mid-diatribe. She stares at Timms. Surprise rapidly morphs into loathing. "What do you want?" she spits.

"I came to see how he's doing."

"You came to see how he's doing." She has always suspected this day would arrive. Would Timms show up to "teach young Ishmael to throw a ball"? Would he offer to help with a third-grade science project or cheer from the stands at Ishmael's seventh-grade basketball team? *Of course not!* There wasn't any third-grade science project, and no seventh-grade anything at all.

This pompous, arrogant narcissist somehow got himself appointed captain of the ship. He has managed to piss that honor away through his incompetence and stupidity but now a new opportunity presents itself. Edward Timms III can lay claim to being the only "dad" in this entire population.

"Hello Captain," Ishmael offers.

Timms steps into the room, pauses.

Hagar suspected it was coming, dreaded the day, and now it's here, or so it seems. She storms past him, careful to avoid contact. "Look for yourself."

"How's the arm?" Timms asks.

"It hurts."

"I'll bet. You know, you don't have to obey your mother but it would be too bad to mess up your rehab just because she's the one telling you to do it. It may not seem like much now, but if the arm doesn't work so good when you get old you're going to wish you hadn't... Listen to me, telling you what to do. You're a man now, you can make up your own mind." He waits a second for that to sink in. "They leave any pins in there?"

"No. They took 'em out, oh, a month ago I guess."

"That's good."

Ishmael grabs the handle and works the shoulder-strengthening exercise.

"You miss Raiff, I guess."

"I miss him a lot."

"Road trip? I thought that was a great idea."

"Yeah, well it didn't end so good."

"Good ideas are like that sometimes." Timms straddles the bench press seat.

Ishmael does a few more reps, stops, looks Timms in the eye. "Why didn't they tell me when I was little?"

"Tell you?"

"That you're the one who, you know . . . "

"That I'm your biological father? I don't know, what did your mother say?"

"Nothing. Just that she, they thought, you know, wait 'til I was old enough."

"Hmm."

"Why didn't you tell me?"

"Well, as it turns out, I kind of wish I had but at the time it was like ..."

"I wasn't a girl."

"Things would have been a lot different if you had been."

"Tell me about it." Ishmael starts the exercise again, much angrier now.

"Lots of things probably should have been different. If I could go back I know I'd change what I did."

"Yeah, well, thanks." The sarcasm drips pretty heavy from that statement.

Timms takes it in stride. "There's no reason things couldn't be different going forward."

Ishmael sneers. "Oh, now you want to be my daddy?"

"I gave up the right to make that decision years ago. What I mean is, if you wanted to, you know, get to know each other better, I'm good with that."

"You don't need to appoint a committee for that?"

"Is that your mother or Solange?"

"A little of both, I guess. I'm sorry; that was pretty mean."

"They're angry—both of them. They had reason to be, I don't begrudge them that, but maybe it's time to let bygones be bygones."

"What do you mean, 'reason'?"

This is already like, five times as much conversation as Ishmael has ever had with Timms. There's just no history there to give him a clue why the response is so slow in coming.

"It's pretty complicated," Timms finally answers. "Probably better if you ask them. I don't know all their reasons—wouldn't want to give you a wrong impression."

"I've been under a wrong impression for thirteen years, why stop now?"

Timms smiles and gets to his feet. "Hey, I'll leave you to your rehab work. I just wanted to, you know, open the door. You know where I live. The captain's suite is always open. You want to talk to me, go tour the bridge, whatever, you're free to just come knock on the door and we'll do whatever you want."

Ishmael watches him go.

#

"Those are the throttles for the main engines?" Ishmael asks. He's part grown man and part wide-eyed kid as the bridge tour continues.

"Yeah," Timms answers, "somebody comes in and dusts them once a week."

"Do they still work?"

126

"The engines? Even if we had enough power to get them ignited, we probably shouldn't. Rebuilding the blast chambers was scheduled for, I think it was year one-oh-six."

"Huh?"

"We were still almost a year-and-a-half from MECO when the leaks were . . ."

"What's MECO?"

"Oh, main engine cut off. We had to shut the engines down prematurely, but they were only built to deliver power for fifty-one months. Then if things went the way they were supposed to, we were going to basically coast until we turned her around and fired 'em for braking."

"And the third generation was supposed to rebuild the blast chambers before they did that."

"That was the master plan—I think."

"You think?"

"I read every single word up to the point where I got too old and a new captain took over. It was going to be my grandson who executed those last steps, most likely. He'd be the one had to know all the details."

"So, I'd be captain next if it went like that?"

"They didn't make any hard and fast rules about succession to the captaincy, but I always kind of thought it would be my son who took over for me."

Ishmael takes that in for a second as he wanders the bridge, looking at the control surfaces. "So we're coasting now?"

"That's right."

"What if there was, like, something in the way?"

"Well, that's most of what we're doing now as far as piloting her. We power up the sensors for an hour each week and scan our trajectory for obstacles."

"What if they found one?"

"That would be a problem. We don't have the power to do more than make a tiny course adjustment. If we didn't start an evasive maneuver early enough, we'd run into whatever it was."

"Like the *Titanic*."

That one stabs Timms to the core. "Yes, a little like the *Titanic*."

"Except everybody on here is going to die anyway." The little kid in Ishmael takes over. "Crash, smash-o, crunch into some big ole moon."

"Well, maybe not that dramatic."

Ishmael is a little sheepish. "Sorry."

"No need to apologize. I tell you what, you want to see one of my favorite places onboard?"

"OK."

Ishmael thought he had been everywhere one could go on the great ship but when Timms leads him to the absolute forward hold and undogs the overhead hatch, it is in fact new territory. If he ever saw the ladder lying on the floor, it never piqued his curiosity. He's a little embarrassed that Timms has this secret place and he never found it.

They climb the ladder. A couple more roasted chickens and Timms wouldn't be able to fit through the narrow hatchway. Maybe those were the ones Ishmael and Raiff stole on their road trip. Whatever, Timms slides through and Ishmael follows close behind.

The room is small. That only makes the viewport that much more impressive. Its diameter is not nearly as large as the one in the observatory, nor the bridge's ports, but whoever designed it had a real flair. It's the shape of the port itself that is so unique. All the other places on the ship where you can look out are like a room—you stand in the room and look out the window. Here, the transparent aluminum has been blown into a cylinder with a rounded top. It's a little over a meter and a half in diameter and probably extends two-and-a-half meters up from the hull at its highest point. Ishmael is pretty sure it must look like a penis sticking straight up in the bow.

There's a tightly spiraled open-grate staircase that leads up to the meshwork "floor" of the viewport. Timms gets to the platform, steps aside so that Ishmael can squeeze in next to him. Ishmael navigates the last two steps and the vastness of space comes into view.

It's like they are standing on top of the hull, encased in a clear sheath, with the whole universe ahead and the massive expanse of the ship barreling along behind them.

"Pretty neat, huh?"

"Wow." A quiet *wow*, like a person too stunned to say anything louder.

"You're the first person I've ever shown this to, son."

"Wow."

"When I get depressed, when things get to feeling like too much, I just come here."

There's not a lot of room—hardly a way this could work at all if Timms didn't have his arm around the boy. "It's like, 'this is mine,' this is what I control. All those little people down there and I'm up here, and I feel like I can rule it all."

"This is so cool."

"You could have this. I mean, there's not going to be much of it to have any more, but it's not like it's nothing at all." He pauses a moment to let the view and the concept soak in. "You're a Timms, Ishmael. A Timms is supposed to be the captain of this ship. Right now that's me, but you could be in the future. How about it, is that something you would like?"

"Really? You could do that?"

"If you want me to, I will."

Ishmael looks up at him. "Thanks, Dad."

#

The ARCan Security Force didn't spring up overnight. It took nearly two years to lay the groundwork, several months to hammer out the wording of the ordinance and three separate votes to finally get approval. After all of that, the ASF became an everyday part of life aboard ship. As the ship's youngest recruit, Ishmael was in the first class of basic training. The undesired consequences of his self-indulgent youth melted away as his frame and musculature took a manly turn.

After years of living down to everyone's lowest expectations, Ishmael finally showed a few redeeming traits. He became an avid reader and his comprehension was excellent. One pass through a manual or textbook and its content was his to command. He proved good with his hands and a quick learner, so that within a few months after going to work in the forge, his older coworkers gave over to him the most demanding castings. He embraced their brawling ironworker personae and gladly accepted their camaraderie.

Without Raiff's leadership, the various factions of his "Wednesday club" drinking society splintered off into a handful of cliques. One of those was the construction, ironworker and manual-labor crowd. They were hard drinkers but seldom engaged in the rowdy, infantile risk-taking of their now-departed patron saint. Ishmael accepted their offer to be chieftain of the rambunctious, press-the-limits "tribe."

Timms took understandable pride in his son's blossoming influence and status. Ishmael's frequent drunkenness barely even registered with him, having excused it in himself all these years. The captain occasionally went "slumming with the boys" on the weekend. They would don their ASF uniforms and go for a drunken "midnight march" under the direction of their CIC.

Thanks to his father's politicking, when the Fellowship's fear-mongering about pirates finally persuaded the Council to authorize a "defensive" weapon, Ishmael was named supervisor of the project. He threw himself into the task with admirable animation and purpose.

The weapon was never fired, of course. A single shot would have taken nearly six percent of the remaining power. It was nonetheless a thing of beauty. Timms beamed with fatherly pride as Ishmael detailed its capabilities. The installation ceremony was the occasion for a meaningful uptick not only in his son's regard and reputation, but in his as well. It was also the occasion for an all-night bender.

The next day, noon had already eased past when Ishmael

awoke, sprawled across the bed. His head pounded and his mouth felt like cotton batting. He lay there for a second, getting his bearings, then stretched. His hand brushed a small cylinder. His brain very slowly formed, *what's that?* He pried his head up off the mattress and his eyes gradually focused on the object.

Even a person who has never played tennis knows what tennis balls are. The cylinder had three of them. Next to it was a note written by hand—Solange's hand.

"When you understand why this is here, I'll be waiting."

#

"Why the mystery?" Ishmael asks his mother.

"Because you're not a boy any more."

"Yeah, sure."

She looks at him for a moment. "Another slice?"

"I'll take another half." There hasn't been beef aboard the *ARC* for years but somehow Hagar's "meatloaf" brings back fond memories. She cuts a slice and splits it between her plate and his.

He puts some ketchup on and takes a big bite. "How do you do this?"

"How do I do what?"

"Make the meatloaf taste like meat?"

She's actually kind of cute when she puts on that Mona Lisa smile. "That's my little mystery."

No sense being angry with her—it never works. He can't keep it up any more. A few years back he could stay angry with her for months—could and did. Is that what she means when she says *you're not a boy any more?* What goes on in a man's mind that's different from a boy's mind?

"So she's being coy?" he asks.

"Do you think coy is attractive?"

Solange had been his "Aunt Soli" for so many years the idea that she might be attractive never - almost never - occurred to him. "Not really."

"Coy isn't exactly the right word," she says. "It implies the perpetrator is creating a false mystery. Life's full of mysterious

131

things without having to make them up."

"I hate mysteries."

"When you mount a piece of equipment with twelve millimeter bolts, there's no mystery that you need twelve millimeter nuts and washers."

"Exactly." It always takes him off guard when his mom talks mechanics and tools. She has a knack for . . . Actually, she has a gift for seeing how things work together and what to fix when they're broken. Did he get his aptitude for it from her?

"You dream of nuts and bolts?" she asks.

"Yeah. Just the other night there was this huge forty millimeter carriage bolt—coarse threaded . . ."

She smiles. "Your brain doesn't need to work on stuff where you already know everything about it. It's the mysteries that wake you up in the middle of the night."

He can't fight that logic. "You win. Mysteries are great."

"They drive you nuts and that's where their power lies."

"So which is it? Mysterious is good or mysterious drives you nuts?"

She just smiles.

"You're not going to tell me, are you?"

"I suspect she wants to wake you up in the night a few times."

He can imagine how that would go over with his rowdy friends. *Yeah, Solange can wake me up in the night any time she wants. Be my dream lover, baby. Wakey, wakey, shake and bakey.* In their eyes, Solange is the hottest thing on board. They know it makes him uncomfortable—maybe that's why they have so much fun doing it.

"We'll see if that wake-up thing happens," he says.

"Her note said, 'when you understand this,' right?"

"Yeah."

"She's willing to wait then, I guess."

Not the answer he hoped for. It's what used to piss him off the worst. A nice simple question and she's got this whole run-around deal with *maybe it's this* and *maybe it's that.* It's one of the reasons he moved out. Ask Dad a question and you get . . .

"Is this about Dad?"

It's never easy for Hagar to hear him say that word, as much as she tries to hide it. "I don't know. I'd be surprised if it was directly about him."

"Why does she hate him so much?"

Hagar simply holds her peace.

"Yeah, OK. Mysteries and more mysteries."

"If and when she wants you to know, I'm sure she'll tell you." She gathers the plates and silver and takes them to the sink.

"So what am I supposed to do?"

"They're tennis balls, right?"

Mysteries!

Even though many of his friends don't share the feeling, Ishmael likes being in the library. Today he's at the computer, sorting references to "tennis balls." He doesn't really think Solange wants him to take up the game. She might think he needs more exercise, but could she really want to play tennis with him, like, on a regular basis?

He looks up. Space, the final frontier, eases toward him on the other side of the huge portal. The Observation Deck was meant to be an inspiration for thousands of ARCans as they hurtled toward Eden. In truth, out there is a cold, dark vacuum that's going to suck the life out of everyone and then just go on like, like *the place thereof shall know it no more.*

Tennis balls. Lots and lots of predictable information—descriptions of the game and the history and how they are constructed. And then the oblique references. That's almost surely what she's challenging him to figure out. Knowing the kind of things that she's interested in, there's one that just keeps calling to him. It's Shakespeare, a really old Earth playwright.

To say Ishmael has taken to reading is not to say he is reading Shakespeare—there's just not enough action there. There may be drama, but first you've got to plow through that incredible antiquated language. He's not quite up to that task yet—maybe never will be. Does he need it if there's Bradbury, Rowling, Tolkien, Fleming, Dobie, Cussler and Scheer on the shelves?

The Shakespeare reference says the tennis balls were an insult to Henry IV. So if that's it, what is she saying? Does this mean she wants to insult me so I . . . so I do what.

Then again, it's always possible that she just wants to play tennis with me.

The livestock pens are really depressing now that all the cows are gone. With so little power, the ventilation doesn't really keep up with the smell of the chicken coop. Not that he minded the smell when he came in here in the night to light-finger a hen or steal a couple eggs. He can only imagine what this used to be like when his mother was here and there was all this horse shit and cow shit to shovel and Solange was . . .

"Hello Ishmael."

"Hi, Aunt Soli." The word feels funny even though he's called her that ever since he can remember. She's in her simple work togs; her hair tied back, no makeup, dirty hands. At some level he's aware why so many of his friends have sexual fantasies about her. Maybe that's why he feels funny.

"Looking for me?"

"You left me the tennis balls."

"And . . .?"

"You wanna play?"

She's disappointed and it shows. "I'd be happy to. How about tomorrow morning?"

"That's fine."

"Seven?"

Seven? AM? Who gets up at that ungodly hour? "OK, seven."

"Have you got shoes?"

"Shoes? Like official tennis shoes? No."

"Just asking."

#

He's not sure playing her in a tennis match is the right thing to do, but this he is sure of—he'd better at least know something about the game. She plays twice every week—doubles much of the time, or at least she used to when he lived at home and saw her more regularly. *OK, fifteen, thirty, forty-five, game point, love, advantage in, advantage out, game.* I've got that.

He will hit the ball. His eye-hand coordination is good and when he and Raiff were sober enough they used to play paddleball. She's going to beat him, that's a given, but if he brushes up a little more, at least he doesn't need to embarrass himself. He pours himself another shot and goes over the scoring again.

#

On further reflection, maybe those last couple shots were a bad idea. Maybe he's going to embarrass himself after all. It's only twenty minutes 'til seven and it takes twelve minutes to get there. In his lifetime Ishmael has seen six-thirty in the morning many times—most of those as the last minutes before he drops off to sleep. Today it's rise and shine, and he'll be lucky if he can handle just the "rise" part. He throws on shorts and a tank top and opens the box on his new pair of shoes.

He's proud of himself for that, at least. He tried to convince himself yesterday that his cross-trainers would be OK but after she made such a big deal out of it, he went to ship's stores and got himself a pair of real tennis shoes.

There's always something creepy about the warehouse. He goes there when he has to, but somehow seeing all those clothes that are never going to be used is, like, the saddest thing he ever has to do. At least now that he's wearing adult sizes he can skip the children's clothes.

#

Solange is already there when he arrives, dressed in her white tennis shorts and a tight-fitting top. He stands in the doorway catching his breath, unseen, as she warms up with the mechanical server. When the ship was built, the server was electric powered. He remembers the Christmas when his mom gave Solange the spring-loaded one. It has a big crank on the back and a spring-steel

135

band that drives the wheels and levers that she cannibalized from the old electric one. It was the first time Ishmael appreciated how good his mother was at mechanics. Solange gushed over that "wonderful present" all day long.

About every seven seconds the device spits out a ball and she volleys it back. Two things strike him.

First, he hasn't a chance. She may be the most physically fit person on board. Watching the power in both her forehand and backhand, he wonders if he'll win a single point.

And the second is like unto it. He's nineteen and she must have been at least eighteen when he was born. That means she must be . . . How does a woman in her mid-thirties look like this? What must Dad think every time he sees her and knows he'll never see her naked again?

That notion shakes him. For just a second he wonders what she must look like naked. She turns full front, a puzzled expression on her face for just a second, then his "Aunt Soli" smiles. "Good morning."

Then she's disappointed and all the warm flush gushes down the drain. He's so tired of having people disappointed in him and today, from her, it's the worst.

"You got the shoes."

"Yeah."

"No racket?"

Shit! "Uh, no. Forgot."

"There's a few in the rack over there."

He passes close to her on his way to the rack.

"Drunk?"

"Sobering up as we speak."

"Did you read it?"

"The Shakespeare thing? No."

She gathers her things, stops on her way to the exit. "You going to read it?"

"I will if you want me to."

"If you wait much longer, I'll be too old to play."

CHAPTER TEN

A leather chair, a good light over the left shoulder and a book in hand made of paper and ink. It's a hundred years since anyone got any real information from antiques like this, but in the last few weeks Ishmael is starting to appreciate why books and libraries haven't disappeared completely.

"*It's easy.*"

Until recently that expression was a prerequisite for him to attempt anything.

Stealing booze with Raiff? "It's easy. All you have to do is stand guard."—"OK, I'll stand guard."

Chickens? "It's easy. You snap your wrist this way and bingo—neck's broken."—"Like this?"

Build a weapon? "It's easy," his dad said, "well, easy for you. It's just a matter of reading the manuals."—"Oh, read manuals? Yeah, I can do that."

But lately the appeal of *easy* has lost its cachet. Lately words like "cachet" creep into his head at the most unexpected times. I mean, what's the upside to easy? If you try something easy and you do it right, who cares? It was easy. Anybody can do that.

But you fail at something easy, well what are you then? An idiot? A slacker? OK, you were already a slacker for trying something easy but to fail at it? That makes you a stupid slacker.

Your odds are much better with stuff that's hard. Fail at a hard thing and it's, "Oh that's too bad, but it was so hard and you made such a good effort at it." Does it hurt when they say that? NOT! And succeed at a hard task—what's that like? You're like a god—a genius—a . . .

The word sticks in his throat.

You're a savior.

But he'll never be a savior. He's not a girl.

Those kinds of negative thoughts intrude more and more often. He may someday reconcile what he's become with what he was meant to be, but not today.

Today there's a hard task to finish, because nobody calls reading Shakespeare easy. It feels good, though he's reading the passage for the third time.

First time through was just to get past the words. They say people really talked like that in his day. How often did they have to repeat themselves to be understood?

Second time through is for the cadence and flow. Tech manuals don't have a rhythm. Who knows what there is about it or why, but when you can read Shakespeare smoothly, there's something about the rolling of the words that's unstoppable.

Some of the speeches, the ones where the story turns somehow, those need a third read. They need a hard, thoughtful read where you can let your mind do that association thing. And the speech on the page in front of him now is a "third reader" if there ever was one. This passage may be what Solange meant when she said, *"When you understand why this is here."*

So far the parallels have been painfully obvious. The Prince Hal character has been jacking around with a bunch of ne'er-do-well's and with all the politics and shit going on, the country is in trouble and his dad is the king but he's not a very good king. So yeah, that's me and that's Timms and so I get it. And then the tennis balls are like, "you don't have balls" and that's what Solange was trying to say. Well, not exactly but close. And so Hal, who's going to be King Henry the Fourth is called up to be . . .

. . . he's supposed to be the "savior" of England and all its heritage and shit.

So he's with his buddies and they're like, "Hey Hal baby, c'mon have another drink," and they're thinking he's just going to get stoned again and let the good times roll. Shakespeare needs to show how he's changed, so he writes this scene where Hal like goes off and does a monologue. Seems that's how playwrights did it back then. *And now this is the third time reading it and I've got the words and I've got the cadence and lilt and let's see what happens now.*

HENRY, PRINCE OF WALES.

I know you all and will awhile uphold
The unyok'd humour of your idleness.
Yet herein will I imitate the Sun,
Who doth permit the base contagious clouds
To smother up his beauty from the world,
That, when he please again to be himself,
Being wanted, he may be more wonder'd at,
By breaking through the foul and ugly mists
Of vapours that did seem to strangle him.
If all the year were playing holidays,
To sport would be as tedious as to work;
But, when they seldom come, they wish'd-for come,
And nothing pleaseth but rare accidents.
So when this loose behaviour I throw off,
And pay the debt I never promised,
By how much better than my word I am,
By so much shall I falsify men's hopes;
And, like bright metal on a sullen ground,
My reformation, glitt'ring o'er my fault,
Shall show more goodly and attract more eyes
Than that which hath no foil to set it off.

I'll so offend to make offense a skill,
Redeeming time when men think least I will.

He sits for several minutes, thinking. He looks closely at the first pair of lines, covers the text with his hand. "I know you all and will awhile uphold the unyok'd humour of your idleness. Yet herein . . ." He takes his hand away and looks at the next pair. "Yet herein will I imitate the Sun . . . "

And twenty minutes later he starts with "I know you all," and ends with, "Redeeming time when men think least I will," and hasn't looked at the text nor missed a single word in between.

Hard is good.

\#

At two AM Ishmael doesn't really expect to find anyone playing tennis. He peers in just to be sure before throwing the huge switch to light the place up. The vapor lights spark once; then hum gently as their glow brightens. If anyone noticed when he wandered out of the apartment, they would assume he's out for a nightcap and perhaps a little carousing.

Tonight? They'd be wrong.

The first booze-free days were a significant challenge. Despite his youth, his cells had grown accustomed to their alcohol-soaked chemistry. Lately he's beginning to feel fresh, alert.

The court is littered with balls. Who would walk away without bothering to collect them? How did he not see the consequences for the next player? How did she convince herself she wasn't responsible?

"WE'RE ALL EQUAL," the ARCan motto, is in the end just gold plating atop the baser stuff of which her population was cast. Some never serve in the kitchens nor don a waiter's apron. A few hands haven't had so much as a mote of dust under their manicured nails. And a few tennis players will volley a hundred balls from the mechanical server without ever retrieving a one.

He straps a bag over his shoulder, fetches a retrieving stick and wades into the carpet of strays. The lighting continues to brighten.

He pours the balls into the server's bin and turns the crank. It has that old-fashioned *clackety-clack* of a ratchet.

As a young boy, he would rewind the server for Solange and then watch as the governor's brass balls whirled inside their mesh cage. It's only in the last year he finally learned enough physics to appreciate Hagar's ingenious mechanism. A spring-driven server tends to deliver high velocity volleys when tightly wound, but then lazy lobs as the spring tension declines. Not so with this little beauty.

He engages the spring, watches with youthful delight as the heavy metal balls rotate. As their speed increases, the brass arms flex, raising the lower sleeve until, when the governor has stored the right amount of energy, the sling engages and a tennis ball flies out the chute at exactly the calibrated velocity. He lets three balls go through the cycle before remembering that he's here to hit them instead of watch them launch. He gets his racket, jumps the net and fields the next ball—starts with forehand shots down the line. His shoulders are big, the work in the foundry tends to bulk them up, but over the last weeks they've gotten a little more sinewy with the repeated racket strokes. A good hard shot lands a couple inches from where he intended.

Of course showing up without even a racket, was only half of that first encounter's embarrassment. The other was his failure to read the Shakespeare play, which he just did for the fourth time. He can still recite from memory the whole "I know you all . . ." Prince Hal speech, but in yesterday's reading, it was the politics and Hal's leadership in the battle scenes that caught his attention.

The only warlike activity aboard the *ARC* is the "defensive" preparations for a possible pirate attack. Ishmael didn't know about the widespread discontent with the plan when the Council first proposed it—he didn't care, either. He was going to design the weapon and when it was done, he'd be a hero. And that all turned out to be true.

Nor did he care about ARCan politics when he enlisted in the ASF and went through the training. His mother's comments about how the ship's Council was just creating this "straw man" so that they could solidify their power went in one ear and then ... wherever. He figured it was her bitterness about Timms and the fact that he, Ishmael, was spending more time with his dad than with her.

He wishes now he'd listened a little more closely. Her political activism is a real burr under the saddle of the ship's Council. To a man, their response to her petitions is to impugn her standing— always with the innuendo that she didn't "qualify" as a passenger. A thirteen-year-old boy buys into that pretty easily, especially when his father is among those actively selling it. Lately he is beginning to appreciate how perceptive and just flat-out smart Hagar is.

He moves right and works his backhand. When he actually volleys with a live person, he's pretty sure he'll score more points with his backhand than his forehand. He smokes one off the top of the net and it drops in. That would be a point for sure.

What he's not sure of is where he fits in? If the parallels to Henry IV really apply, then the only person he could be is Hal. Was Solange's tennis invitation just a wake-up call, like "Grow up, kid," or does it go deeper?

Of the few things he's sure of, one stands out. If there are two political camps on board ship and Solange and Hagar are in one, then Timms and Mayer and Kline are in the other. Is that what Solange has in mind, that Ishmael should side with her and Hagar against his own dad?

The server fires a blank. Ishmael jumps the net, shuts it down, gathers up the strays and reloads.

Solange says yes to a rematch—actually seems eager. This time it's he who suggests seven o'clock AM. She's pleased at that as well.

She arrives at six-fifty and finds him waiting. He was here at six-thirty to turn on the lights and be sure the court was in order. Yesterday he went to the ship's stores for new tennis whites. This time he has his racket and a backup as well.

She makes no effort to disguise her delight that he's here and ready to play. She strips off her sweats and uses her racket in a well-practiced warm-up routine. Used to be he was embarrassed any time he had a sexual reaction to her. The last few times it has been easier—well, a little easier. He's not a bad man because he finds her attractive. He's just . . . a man.

If she's aware of his feelings, she makes nothing of it. A woman with her appeal could hardly function in life if she reacted to every telltale sign of her sexual attractiveness.

"Rumor has it you've been practicing," she says lightly.

"I am on the really steep part of the learning curve."

"You warmed up? Shall we play?"

"Sure. You care which side?"

"I'll take that side." She jogs onto the court and they volley for a full five minutes. Once in a while it's, "Nice shot," or "Sorry," but for the most part they're silent. His instincts and coordination stand him in good stead. The mechanical server can deliver many kinds of shots, but once it's calibrated there's no variety until you interrupt the session to recalibrate it. Where the machine prides itself on consistency, his live opponent strives for variety. That's how tennis fanatics can play several days a week and never tire of it.

She picks up the pace. The balls no longer come to his forehand or backhand for an easy volley. He runs more—a lot more—and she's got him off balance much more often than he'd like.

"How about it, wanna play?"

Scoring even a few points is going to be tough. "Sure. Volley for serve?" He lobs up an easy one and after three times over the net, she smokes him.

He's got more power. His points come when he can settle on the ball and follow through. It doesn't happen very often. There are only two ARCan men who play tennis, so she hasn't had much experience with serves coming from that height and that much power. Now if he could just get the first serve in more than about 20 percent of the time.

After an hour, he's won a total of two games, and each of those featured three successful first serves. "Another set?" he offers, though his legs feel like lead already.

144

"I'm surprised Eileen and Kelly aren't here yet. They play Thursday mornings."

The sweat makes her tennis outfit cling. Her skin is flushed with the exertion. There's no makeup to run. She is the beauty she appears to be.

"This was fun, thank you," she says.

He looks her in the eye. "No Shakespeare?"

"You've read Henry the Fourth?"

"I know you all . . . " he begins.

". . . And will awhile uphold the unyok'd humour of your idleness."

"Yeah," he chuckles. "I've been living up to that first part pretty good."

She smiles. "You have indeed."

"So now I'm supposed to be bright metal on a sullen ground?"

"There are things going on aboard this ship that cry out for a change."

"I'm coming a little late to the game," he admits.

"But you played well today."

"We played tennis."

"There are some people meeting tomorrow night—people who are looking to force changes. I was hoping you might come, listen to what they're proposing, and see if you want to be part of it?"

"Pay the debt I never promised?"

Her smile is warm and accepting. "That's up to you."

#

Was a time when Ishmael would be in the captain's quarters several times a week. Not so much lately. Hanging out here used to be kind of a casual drop-by occasion but today Timms actually invited him, as in, "two o'clock tomorrow afternoon and we'll talk."

It's a spacious apartment. If it were picked up and cleaned a little more regularly, it would still have its original appeal.

"You've got to realize, son, that people are lazy," Timms says. "Without strong leadership, most of them would piss their whole lives away. What they need is regimentation, order in their lives."

"What about independence and self-determination?"

"Ah. Solange is feeding you her cockamamie notions, eh? You have to look at her honestly, son. Tell me you think what's going on in that pretty head of hers deserves serious consideration."

Timms seems blissfully unaware of the line he's crossed. "OK, I will tell you. That is what I think."

"Well, I don't really expect you can be critical of your dear 'aunt Soli,' but I would just warn you to think twice before acting on any of her, what to call them, her seditious ideas."

"Seditious? She's not proposing anything outside the Charter."

"The Charter as she interprets it. She's hardly qualified to —"

Ishmael interrupts him. "You don't want to quote chapter and verse against her."

"I'll quote her any damn thing I want. You think —?" Timms swallows the last of his drink and pours another. "I'm not a man to harbor grudges, son, and I don't have many regrets, but she has been my biggest disappointment of this whole venture."

Bigger than the senseless sterilization of the entire female population? There's a pause while that goes unvoiced.

"I can't get you one?" Timms asks, offering a glass and the bottle.

"No, thanks."

Timms throws ice in his drink and stirs it with his finger. "I understand you were at a meeting of, what do they call it, the Preservation Society?"

"I was."

"Did you go in uniform?"

"No."

"Don't suppose there was a lot of ASF presence there, eh?"

He shrugs off his father's question. Nothing to be gained by leaking the fact that two of his militia buddies went with him.

"So what kind of mischief are they up to now?"

"Most of the discussion was about squelching the 'pirate exploratory mission.'"

Timms snorts. "You walked out, I hope."

146

"I didn't go there to walk out."

"Somebody quote chapter and verse of the Charter during that discussion?"

"It's free speech."

"The kind of free speech mutinies are made of."

"Is that what you're afraid of?"

Timms bristles. "I'm not afraid of anything, except maybe the pirates who could be using that moon to hide from our sensors. We could wake up one morning overrun. You know what pirates do to unarmed citizens?"

"Nobody knows what pirates do to unarmed citizens because there's no pirates. We're spending forty-three percent of ship's stores arming ourselves against something that's just not there."

"Oh my," Timms mocks, "forty-three percent! What jackass came up with that cockamamie number?"

"That would be Mom."

Mentioning Hagar in a complimentary way is always a gut-punch to any levity or frivolity in his father. If looks could kill . . .

"It hurts me to see you buying that kind of uninformed, head-in-the-sand, pacifist drivel, son. I took you for more of a man than that."

You've never taken me for anything but a child in your whole life. "There are those who suggest martial law will be the Council's next step."

"The way things are going, I'm not sure that would be such a bad idea."

Ishmael stands up. "Somebody better count their votes." He stalks out.

Before his son is out of earshot, Timms calls, "A ship's captain doesn't need votes. You of all people should know that."

\#

Doug sets down a box of roughcast brass fittings. Ishmael powers down the polishing wheel and takes off his heavy leather gloves and facemask. "You guys come to a decision?"

Doug straddles the bench. "It's not everybody, but I think we're in."

"Who's not convinced?" Ishmael asks.

"Ricky."

"Fuckin' bone-head Ricky."

"Hey! He's not one of the bad guys."

"You're right. I stand corrected," Ishmael answers. "What's bothering him?"

"He thinks with the Council the way it is, you know . . . we get a little, they get a little, like that. If we back the Society slate how do we know they won't just screw us over? That, and he's not sure changing command in the middle of a war is a good idea."

"He the only one?"

"Earl thinks it's too many women."

"Earl never gets any, so we know where that's coming from."

"He's got the same vote the rest of us do."

For years, slamming Earl like that came so easily to Ishmael, he sometimes gets blind-sided. "You're right, and I'm out of line to give him shit."

Doug smiles. "Earl's a walking shit-magnet." He knew that would strike Ishmael as funny. They laugh.

"But you still think it'll go our way?" Ishmael asks.

"If you were on the ticket everybody would go for it—even Ricky. If the Society wants an official endorsement, go ahead and tell 'em they got it."

"Thanks, Dougie."

#

Timms is the only one sweating in the room. The other Council members wear a sweater or jacket. They only sweat in their private quarters, where they keep the temperature several degrees above the "ARCan cool" sixty-four. With political status comes the right to sleep under a light coverlet while the masses throw on two extra blankets. Wives of the rich and famous *don't like* to step onto a cold floor in the morning.

But Timms' sweat isn't about degrees—not Fahrenheit, not centigrade, not Kelvin. The proverbial "hot seat" has nothing to do with thermodynamics.

"Your son is supporting the Society's slate and their platform and now he's persuaded the unions to join him," Kline splutters.

The existence of unions in a society where all are "equal" may seem a contradiction in terms. Yet age-old patterns, where those who supervise the production of wealth separate themselves from those who actually create the wealth, tend to replicate themselves everywhere.

Mayer adds, "Too bad you didn't see this coming when you assigned him to the foundry."

"But the unions don't have any real power," Timms answers, "The Charter doesn't even recognize their existence."

"They exist," Mayer says. "We can't make believe they don't. We can try to limit their power, disenfranchise them, but if their membership actually votes for the opposition slate, we could lose the majority on the Council."

"But that's not Ishmael's fault," Timms answers.

Kline says, "He's the link. The kid's coworkers respect him. Without him, they've got no connection to the lefty radicals and Hagar and Solange."

"We've got things the working stiffs want. We can cut deals with them," Mayer says. "But the Society wants it their way, period. If the union vote goes to them, we'll be the ones forced to cut the deals."

Kline rubs his forehead. "You've got to talk to him."

"I have talked to him." *For all the good it's done me. He's got his mother's stubborn streak.*

"Well talk to him again," Kline demands. "And say something that'll make him listen. We can't have these people taking over."

#

Solange models for the sketching class every semester. If the human body is the highest form of art, then hers deserves a place of honor in the finest museums. She poses, one arm extended above her head, before the three-person class of fledgling artists.

At sixty-four degrees, the studio is cold enough that her nipples stand firm and erect. It's surprising she can pose without trembling. The artists in their heavy sweaters sketch away furiously as the hour comes to a close.

Ishmael has been in the art center only twice before. He peers into each rehearsal room and studio. At the window to the sketching studio he stops dead in his tracks. Solange holds her pose—her eyes meet his, showing no evidence of discomfort beyond that of a naked woman in a frigid room. A chime sounds; she breaks her pose, pulls on a heavy terrycloth robe and makes straight for the door.

"Ishmael, I'm so glad you're here."

He feels the blood rise in his cheeks. "I'm sorry, I didn't mean to stare."

Somehow it doesn't register with her that he has just been staring at her naked body without even the pretext of a sketchpad between them. "Oh, well, they're all kind of staring aren't they?" She puts her arm in his and leads the way toward the meeting room. "Come on, we like to start the meetings on time."

The only thing between them is the robe.

Whether she picks up on his discomfort or for some other reason, she says, "Maybe I should put some more clothes on. It's a little chilly. You know the way, yes?"

"I can find it."

#

Unlike the highly staged Ship's Council meetings, the Society convenes on a level floor, chairs arranged in a circle. Each week a different person presides. Today, the energy level is high, the room abuzz with Society members in animated discussion. They fall silent as Ishmael enters. The pause is momentary. Discussion of today's issue promises to be intense. Hagar greets her son with a hug. After all these years, her maternal hug still elicits a visibly emotional response from at least a few women. Jealousy, envy, simple wistfulness? Most likely a combination of them all.

Solange breezes in, still wearing the robe, though now with leggings and little silk tie-up shoes. She exudes power and self-confidence. What must she have been like when she first boarded? She was not only the youngest and the prettiest, but also consort to the captain—a woman to be regarded in his presence and yet disdained and snubbed whenever she was unaccompanied. Like Hagar, she had surely not been tested for "suitability" to the mission.

It is a given that a pretty woman has an advantage with men, but it is a fool who thinks that asset is wasted on women. Beauty is as beauty does and in Solange's case, her deportment and mien have been a thing of beauty since the first day. Over time, as she has grown in wisdom and stature, only the wives of councilmen have resisted being won over.

"I'm sorry if you have been waiting for me. Who presides today?"

Mary Beth raises her hand and calls the meeting to order as the members take seats around the circle. Ishmael sits across the circle from Solange. Her body language is open and inviting. She smiles at him and again, the blood rises to his cheeks.

Minutes of the last meeting detail the Society's plan to force a no-confidence vote in the Council. Mayer and Kline have "hop scotched" each other every two years as chairman with such success that only once in the twenty-some years since the launch has another person occupied the post. Never before has the loyal opposition been organized enough to initiate such a sweeping challenge. But finally, there's a petition with enough signatures. Barring renewal of "time of emergency" status, the Council will be required to schedule ship-wide elections.

"They're going to try to extend T.O.E.," Clarisse offers. "We need to be ready to block that vote, otherwise this whole thing is in the shitter." Clarisse is the chief engineer of the Waste-Processing and Water-Reclamation Department. The shit and piss factory she calls it. She enjoys tweaking the prissy element of the group. On this occasion just using the word "shitter" is enough to get them clucking.

The Council declares T.O.E. every time anyone challenges their authority and the current authorization expires in a few weeks. The Society's petition for a no-confidence vote was timed to coincide with that expiration. Clarisse is right, the first thing the Council will do is declare an extension. To a man, they have become past masters at procedural maneuvering to stifle petitions they disagree with and fast-track their own proposals.

"What's the word from the unions?" Solange asks.

All eyes turn to Ishmael. "A lot of the members don't agree on the underlying issues, but they will support a move to let T.O.E. expire so we at least can get a vote."

Solange asks, "If we get an expiration of T.O.E, assuming we can get our slate on the ballot, any feel for which way the union vote will go on election day?"

"Not really. They're concerned whether anybody can beat Kline for Council chairman."

"They'd vote for you," Clarisse mutters.

"Except for the amendment to Article IV."

"They only passed that to humiliate Hagar," Mary Beth says.

"They passed that specifically to deny Ishmael's citizenship. If he is not an ARCan, he cannot hold office." Hagar responds.

"Can't we just get them to throw out the amendment?" Clarisse asks.

"That's a long process," Ishmael answers, "with a half-dozen political booby-traps they could trip us up on."

Solange leans forward and looks Ishmael in the eye. "If nominated, would you run?"

Is this what happens when you take up responsibility—they just ask you to do more and more? First they ask me to persuade the guys at the forge—OK, I did that. Now they want me to be the lightning rod, go toe-to-toe with Mayer and Kline? They're looking for some kind of savior. Didn't I already prove that I'm not it?

Is she staring all the way into my soul? Can she see how much I want to please her? Will she understand there's just some things I can't do, not yet at least?

Despite the warmth rising in his cheeks and his pounding

152

heart, he doesn't drop his gaze from hers. "I can't make that promise."

CHAPTER ELEVEN

Kees and Cutter stand on the *ARC*'s bridge, staring out at the vast hull.

"What have we done?" Cutter asks.

"Pissed off somebody who really wants this thing scrapped."

"But you let Roman get away."

"He's not the one to worry about."

"You don't think they'll send him back?"

"They'll send somebody much scarier than Roman Pollack."

"So what do we do now?" she asks.

"We need maneuverability."

"The main engine?"

"Yes."

"Not from a power module with just four septa."

"It's down to three-point-one," he says.

"The weapon used that much?"

"A full charge takes almost point six." He's silent for a moment. "How far back are the other power cells?"

"Sixteen hundred klak—give or take."

"She seem stable when you rolled her?" he asks as he looks

over the helm controls.

"Yes—slow but stable."

"I didn't find any aft sensors, did you?"

She didn't think of it at the time—not that there has been much time for thinking—but what kind of ship is it that cannot look backwards? "No."

"OK. Let's turn her around and see if we can locate those other cells."

"Aye aye, sir."

"We are the only two people on board."

"Meaning?" She looks at him without blinking.

"We don't have to be captain and first mate."

They are indeed the only two people on board—just one man and one woman. For the past seventeen months they have obeyed the scavenger code, one that denies the natural dynamic that might arise between one man and one woman alone together aboard a generational ship. They both know that dynamic is now unleashed, even if, for the moment, there's something else demanding their attention.

Kees fires the bow thruster. The reduction in the *ARC*'s forward momentum will hardly be noticeable but the cells, barreling along behind them, will gradually close the distance. He engages the vertical bow thruster straight down to initiate the rotation.

"An Immelmann?" Cutter asks.

After more than two centuries, the maneuver still bears the name of the pilot who first executed it. "Without the roll," Kees answers. Rolling, of course, is only necessary when "up" means something.

Kees wonders what Max Immelmann would think if he could be time-transported onto the bridge today. He created his turn for what pilots of the day called a "dogfight"—used it to increase altitude and reverse direction. Could Max navigate a universe where up and down are no different than left and right? Would he be disoriented by the notion that the *ARC* will soon be on her back, hurtling "feet first" a thousand times faster than his plane could ever fly?

And what would he think of this young woman knowing his name? Did he aspire to that kind of fame?

And what of the plane he flew? Was it scrapped or does it hang in a museum? Do children stare at it in wonder?

And will there ever be anything called a DeWet? Will Kees leave behind some maneuver, some idea, some thing that brings wonder to a young child's eye?

Not if he lets his daydreams interfere with the task at hand.

He swipes the helm controls and kills the thrusters. If he has done this right, the *ARC* will finish her roll at about the same time the cells overtake her. "This is going to take a while."

She has watched him these last moments as he drifted off to some other time and place. Before boarding the *ARC,* the old nuts and bolts Kees DeWet was a man who stayed on task all the time. *What happened, Kees, when you first came aboard? What did you find here that changed you?* Her gaze settles on the main engine throttles. *Are we really going to do this?* He's right about one thing. This is going to take a while. She turns to him and looks him full in the face. "You said it's a long story."

Kees leads Cutter to the Observation Lounge. She pauses in the entryway and takes in the scene, much like Kees did in his first minutes aboard. She approaches Ishmael and looks closely at the book in his lap. "Moby Dick?"

"I think his name really was Ishmael and he certainly is the narrator," Kees says.

"That's the whale story, right? So was there a captain Ahab?"

"Edward Timms was the captain. But I think the symbolism in choosing that book to have in his lap is more about how they hope the *new* captain of the ship, the 'finder,' becomes obsessed with . . ." he gestures to the ship around them, ". . . this great white whale."

She tries to keep the sarcasm out of her voice without much success. "Well so far it's working. Here we are."

"Tangled in the harpoon lines," he replies, "beckoning the crew to follow us to their deaths."

"Let's hope not."

#

Cutter lays down her shovel as Kees smoothes the last of the dirt. The ship's last sojourner had dug his own grave in the place of his own choosing. It lies between Hagar on the left and Solange on the right. Without wind, rain, earthquakes or erosion, the hole was as he left it—shovel marks still clearly defined on its perfectly rectilinear sides.

"He was the only ARCan born here," Kees says, "the only one who could be buried in his home soil."

"I can't imagine the loneliness." They take a moment paying respects. "All this planning and effort," she continues, "all for a story they hoped someone would —"

Her sentence is cut off by a wave of static electricity bristling her hair.

"Ah, fan mail from some flounder," Kees quips.

She sweeps her hair back down, the static electricity as suddenly gone as it arose. "They pinged us?"

"Assuming the Alliance is monitoring this quadrant, when we fired the weapon its energy profile had to pique somebody's curiosity."

"So they know we're here."

"When that echoes back, they'll know within half a klak."

"Now we need to hurry?"

"They say when you stumble onto a bear, the best thing is to not look her in the eye and kind of sidle off. The thing you don't want to do is make a lot of commotion."

"Meaning?"

"The roll is already under way," he answers, "and the pulses we used to initiate the rotation and the ones we'll use to reverse it may not even show up on their scanners."

"If they think we're still dead in space they won't feel like they need to hurry."

"Exactly."

"What happens when we transfer the energy from the J-26's?"

"If we're lucky, they won't understand the readings. It's firing the *ARC*'s main engine that will make all hell break loose. At that point we're going to need all the hurry-up we can get."

"So for now we avoid eye contact and sidle."

They make their way to the bridge and Cutter goes directly to the sensor station. "We have contact with the cells."

"Range?"

"Eighty-seven klak."

Kees operates the helm controls and the eleven cells creep into the visual field as the ship's rotation slows. A little over fifty miles is all that separates the *ARC* from as much power as she could use in a hundred years—all the power they need to fire up the great engine.

But siphoning the energy won't be easy. With the radiation as dangerous now as it was ninety years ago, the *ARC* will have to stand off at a safe distance while a robotic drone attaches itself to first one cylinder and then another, drains and converts the power and then transmits it back to the mother ship. Therein lies the challenge. The technology that allows this magnitude of power transfer and storage did not exist when the *ARC* was launched. Someone will have to create the drone from scratch—and someone will have to construct a receiving antenna. All that with exactly two pair of hands—a man's hands and a woman's hands.

"Ready?" he asks.

"Let's do this."

Over the next several days, Kees and Cutter work as long and hard each day as they can—together—because so often the task cannot be accomplished by one pair of hands alone. Cutter hasn't the time for earthy thoughts at the sight of tools lying comfortably in Kees' powerful hands, and he has to curb his passion as she strips down and dons the bulky space suit for her forays out to the antenna. And in the night they sleep—together—in the sense that they both fall asleep and are in relatively close proximity when it occurs.

On the morning of the sixth day, the fully assembled drone sits on the floor of the service bay next to the cannibalized jitney bug. The receiving antenna is deployed at the bow of the *ARC*.

The physics is straightforward, which is not to say simple. Exotic alloys play a key role in the drone's makeup and in some cases the *ARC*'s antiquated forges simply could not refine the ores sufficiently. Even the cold of deep space may not be enough to absorb the heat generated by impurities within the various laminates. The vanes Cutter welded onto the unit's external housing should increase the dissipation rate, but will it be enough?

The power module, a Steenmeyer Q-16, was designed as a portable unit, rated at sixteen ks (kilosepta). From the moment Kees plugged it in, it has performed well—been the quiet, reliable heart of the *ARC*'s power grid. Dealing with four septa is one thing. Handling sixteen thousand is a whole different order of magnitude. One can hope that, as far as product quality and reliability, the Steenmeyer Corporation learned some important lessons between the years when it was building the ill-fated J-26 model and the assembly date stamped on the Q-16. If not . . . it's not as if they have an alternative.

Add to that, with the energy used to turn the ship around and complete the tasks of the last days, the module's reserve stands at 1.3 septa. The drone will require 0.7 to execute its task, which means any glitch in the process and there's insufficient power for a second attempt.

There are three critical moments in the process. The first one is as the drone approaches its target. Ideally the closing rate will be .002 klak/second—about the speed of a walking person. To say that executing the maneuver requires a delicate hand is to vastly understate the operator's skill. To say God would have to concentrate to get it right is much closer.

Kees hands the controller over to Cutter the minute she returns from the service bay. There's no discussion. Kees' piloting skill is the stuff of legends but that has as much to do with his depth perception and sensitivity to inertial changes as it does to his eye-hand coordination. When it comes to driving a remote, well, the control interface for the drone was pirated from the jitney bug and Cutter has been the only one to handle that joystick since the *Scavenger* departed Kolnus VI.

She's calm and her hand is steady. Kees holds his palm-viewer where she can see the image—there wasn't time enough to patch the optical feed from the jitney/drone into the *ARC*'s display screens. Her fingers caress the joystick until the green light indicates successful engagement with the first cylinder.

"Nicely done, Cutter."

The second critical moment follows immediately. Within the first sixty seconds, the J-26 will deliver almost half its energy. The laminated panel is flooded with an outpouring of filthy-rich radiation. If there's a flaw in the adhesives, if there are impurities or structural weaknesses in any of the layers, the device will be blown apart with a destructive force that could threaten the *ARC*, even at this distance.

The drone awaits an instruction to begin the transfer. "Ready?" Cutter asks.

"Engage."

The instinct to look away from something that might explode is strong. Our two courageous voyeurs watch unblinking as the seconds tick by . . . fifty-one, fifty-two.

"You should have been a metallurgist," she offers.

Kees grins back at her.

The full siphon takes about eleven minutes. The first burst stresses the power-transfer panel and is very much a radiation event. Between the sixth and eighth minute, thermal activity reaches its peak. By then the drone has already transmitted somewhere between point nine and one-point-one ks. That's already enough energy to maintain the *ARC* for their natural lifetime. But if the goal is to fire the main engine, then the drone will have to survive that thermal peak without damage during each iteration—at least six times.

The readout on the tiny screen has an indicator for each of the drone's three temperature sensors. In the sixth minute, first one, and then all three turn from green to yellow. In the seventh minute two of them turn orange and just before the end of the eighth minute one of them blips red for a few seconds. By the tenth minute only the hottest sensor still shows yellow—the other two have switched back into green.

She watches the last readout turn green. "Just like we knew what we was doing."

He has never in his life intentionally laid a hand on her. He lays one on her shoulder now—squeezes gently. She takes a long, deep, cleansing breath.

The gauge showing the *ARC*'s power reserve reads one point two six ks.

"Disengage?" she asks.

"Yes, but let's be sure the temp's all the way down before we tap the next one."

The drone takes a full hour to cool down between the tenth and eleventh cylinders. It will have to be rebuilt from the ground up if they ever want to deploy it again.

Through it all, the Q-16 behaved admirably, accepting 99.4 percent of its rated maximum storage capacity. It gives every indication of powering the *ARC* for a hundred years to come, perhaps more. The sun and rain can be reinstated above the wheat fields, the sea can once more roll with its man-made waves, and should a careless soul "leave a light on," disaster need not follow.

#

Even though they now have plenty of power, for Kees and Cutter to fire the *ARC*'s main engine is not without its risks. The ship was brand new the last time it was attempted.

Kees' piloting skills will be put to the test as well. The *ARC*'s flight dynamics are sure to be different now that the J-26's are no longer part of the mass, weight and inertia equation.

Then there's the question of the exciter coil. It was installed late and there's the rub.

Kees is aware that eighteen months before launch, there was a shake-up in leadership at the top of the Andromeda Repopulation Consortium. The new president wrested control of operations on a boast - a pledge if you're being kind - to streamline production. He did it by "eliminating time-robbing inspections, regulations and testing."

The exciter coil's installation date falls deep into that latter period. One can be sure it was neither regulated, nor inspected, nor tested. Equally certain is that there is no redundancy. Kees is sure that there's no "backup coil" sitting in a storage compartment somewhere on board. The one that's in the engine will either do the job—or it won't.

On the eighth day after commandeering the ship and driving Roman off, Kees and Cutter lay hands on the throttles for the first time in approximately ninety-four years. What would this moment have been if things had gone differently? Standing here proudly would be Edward Timms' grandson, or perhaps his great-grandson, ordering the engines fired to slow the ship into its orbit above what every soul on board hoped would be Eden.

"Initiate main engine ignition sequence," Kees intones.

With what apprehension would the *ARC*'s captain have uttered those words? Talk about crossing a threshold; not a soul on board would have ever felt honest gravity, breathed open air, felt natural rain or wind on her face.

Cutter works the sliders smoothly. Valves open and the propellant stream flows into the blast chamber. The exciter powers up and as the density rises through the lower threshold, the reaction becomes self-sustaining.

Even with bulkheads closed throughout the ship, the groaning and creaking of her structural elements filters up to the bridge. "We are drifting to port, sir," Cutter announces. "Two degrees ... now three degrees."

Kees activates the port, dorsal thrusters and brings them to one-half power.

"Two degrees," she notes. "We are compensating, sir."

"Increase main engine thrust to fifty percent."

"Aye sir."

And so the great lady ruffles her petticoats, dusts off her skirts and lumbers toward the outer reaches of Alliance space. Kees and Cutter monitor the *ARC*'s meters and gauges for a few minutes, neither commenting on the incredibly slow acceleration.

"I don't think we're needed on the bridge," Kees offers. "Our 'ship's tour' was interrupted. Would you like to see the rest of her?"

#

Their tour leads to the Commons—a massive, ornate building, eight stories tall.

Lights come on across the vast expanse of tables in the dining hall, many still set, awaiting their elegant guests. Kees and Cutter make their way to the kitchen past cabinets filled with china, crystal, and silver. He imagines the sounds of a great banquet underway in the adjacent dining room and in the empty kitchen the sounds of chefs and waiters preparing for and serving the hordes.

"This is lovely." Cutter fingers the pattern on the china.

For all of her toughness, for all her considerable skill with tools and mechanical devices, nothing about her has ever seemed coarse or crude. There she stands, completely in her element, fine china in hand, admiring the artistry of its creator. Someday soon he must have her to tea—here, in this gorgeous hall, seated at a delicate table set with this delightful china. And he must brew tea and make scones and finger sandwiches and delicate pastries.

He hasn't a clue how to make scones or finger sandwiches. But someday, someone will make those things in this place and then he will take her here and they will sit together and . . .

"Penny for your thoughts?" she asks.

"My imagination runs away sometimes."

. . . as it has every day since he first boarded. He has been charmed, enchanted, bewitched at every turn. But Cutter wasn't with him those first days. She didn't experience that. She went along with him on faith. She cast her lot with his, not knowing the how or the why. He means to set that right today, show her the how and the why, let the ARCans win her heart as they won his.

He smiles. *If Saul of Tarsus had a girlfriend, what did he tell her when he got back from Damascus?* The smile gets broader as the scene plays out in his head. *"Hey babe, I'm home. You know, I've decided to stop persecuting the Christians and busting up their churches. I'm going to become an apostle instead."* A little chuckle escapes. *"Oh, and you should call me Paul from now on."*

She looks at him, puzzled.

Through the glass doors at the far end of the dining hall they come upon the rococo double stairway. Its breathtaking chandelier sparkles above the central first landing. "Why does this look so familiar?" she asks.

"It's an exact replica of one of the staircases on the *Titanic*," Kees says.

She is speechless for several seconds. "Why would anyone do that?"

"Arrogance? Hubris? The White Star Line thought building the 'unsinkable ship' was a worthy goal."

"Until it sank."

"That was just a few pesky details in the execution."

"Like the faulty shielding on the *ARC*'s power cells."

"The Andromeda Repopulation Consortium embraced a similar corporate structure and philosophy. Arrogant people don't go away, they just get submerged for a while."

She just looks at him.

"OK, maybe submerged isn't quite the right word."

As they step off the elevator inside the Commons, Kees explains, "There are fitness facilities scattered all over the ship, but the 'fitness center' is here on the fifth floor." Seen through the glass wall behind the registration desk is a huge open space. Kees opens the glass door and they enter.

A running track surrounds a series of basketball and volleyball courts. Exercise equipment, toning and fitness devices fill room after room around the circumference. Huge, carpeted locker rooms give way to saunas, steam baths and hot tubs.

Exercise is a regular and necessary part of space travel, no matter whether the ship is luxury, commercial or hardscrabble. An unfit person aboard a space-going vehicle is soon a dead person. Massage, on the other hand is not necessary for survival in space.

Cutter runs her hand along the fine leather of one of the massage tables. "Could this be heated?"

"I wouldn't be surprised. Pretty clear this gym was for the uh, the advantaged few."

"Was there supposed to be an 'advantaged few'?"

"Not that anyone would admit to."

Cutter examines the dispenser built into the wall next to the massage table. She holds her left hand under the nozzle and gently presses the lever. A few drops of massage oil dribble out. She slides it between thumb and fingers, sniffs its fragrance, smiles.

"It's warm, too."

Words are superfluous. Kees watches her caress the oil in her hand. An idiot could read her body language—hell, a blind idiot would know that the one thing on her mind is how much she would love a massage.

And Kees DeWet is neither blind nor an idiot. A simple gesture invites her to lie on the massage table.

She pauses. Neither of them has been to the place where this leads—not with each other, at least. She would never have entertained the notion until a few days ago. But that was then. Now she lifts her tunic over her head, steps onto the riser and stretches out, stomach down on the massage table.

It is warm. The aroma of the massage oils gently colors the earthiness of the warm leather. She slides her face between the padded bolsters, her neck perfectly aligned with her spine. She hears the creak of the oil dispenser's handle and then Kees' hands rubbing together as he warms them up.

They slide easily across her shoulders and upper back. His hands are strong and, if not for the oil, rough. It's not a bad roughness—they have a nice traction against her skin. He gets more oil and smoothes it onto her lower back.

She can't help gentle vocalizations as he alternates from deep massage techniques to fingertips to pressure points. He works first from her left side, then from her right. He comes to the head of the table, gives her entire back a rapid, circulation-stimulating rub and then slowly works a deep massage from her neck, gradually down to her shoulders and arms and finally, in a full extension, her lower back. A fat man couldn't execute the last reaches—his stomach would press his client's head into the table. She feels the slightest brush of his abs against her hair as he reaches down all the way to her lower back.

He is as knowledgeable and proficient with leg musculature as he is with the back. Whoever taught this man . . .

Thighs, calves, working gently at the knees and ankles.

He works another dispenser handle, sniffs. "I'm sorry, the eucalyptus oil has turned rancid. This other has a little spearmint oil. It should be OK, unless you prefer something else?"

"That will be fine."

Foot massage has an intimacy that is hard to define. His fingers probe gently between each of her toes, the sharp, minty scent released as the cream spreads and warms. He tugs each toe in turn, first one foot, then the other. He overlaps the oils of the leg massage with the cooling foot cream, massages the ankles about half way up the calves. He applies force, gently, as he first flexes the toes hard up toward the shin, and then pulls them forcefully down like a ballerina *en pointe*.

The fact that Cutter has systematically stifled her sex drive during her tenure as first mate is not to say that she doesn't have one. She feels the desire rising as he rolls her onto her back and works his way up, massaging her ankles, then thighs, hips and abdomen. If his technique were to turn sexual at this point, she knows what her response will be.

While his every touch is intimate, familiar and eminently pleasurable, the front massage is no more overtly sexual than was the back. The abdominal technique is new to her, and just a little unsettling. It takes a few minutes before she relaxes, feeling the circulation and stimulation work its way outward from her central core. Who knew that a man so capable as a captain and leader could bring a woman this kind of pleasure?

At some level deep inside her, she did know—suspected, at least. Did she fool herself all those years? Was this what she saw in him—wanted from him—from the start? She loses herself in his touch as he massages her neck and then temples.

"Hands?"

She looks at him, more "dreamy" than she ever thought she would. "If you don't mind?"

She reads his eyes. *Do I mind? Not at all.* "My pleasure," he answers with a smile. He's got a nice smile.

He starts at her shoulder and works his way to the fingertips of her left arm, then walks to the other side of the massage table and tends to the right. He tugs each finger on her right hand in order.

—and then it's done.

He stands beside the table as she eases back into the reality that is the *ARC*'s massage room. She takes his offered hand and slides off the table, naked except for her jet-black thong.

"Thank you." She kisses him hard and long.

Their lips part. For a moment they stare into each other's soul, or so it seems.

The blaring klaxon startles them both. Apparently some sensor array has come to life with the restoration of power. The angry intrusion is all the more threatening because they don't know its meaning.

"You go," Cutter says. "I'll be right there."

Five minutes later, fully dressed, she reaches the bridge and finds Kees staring at a radar display screen.

"This would be a lot easier with aft sensors," he says.

A blip crosses the screen. She follows its curvilinear path. "A drone?" she asks.

"Yes."

"Manned?"

"It's shielded," he answers. "From its size I'd say probably not."

"Armed?"

That earns a "look." "They're built to take out small targets. We've got a few minutes before the driver figures out where he wants to hit us."

She stares at his exiting back. The nuts and bolts Kees DeWet is back in control, almost as if the whole massage thing never happened.

Kees makes good time getting to weapons control. His voice comes over the intercom. "Status, mister?"

"It has been executing figure-eights. Looks like a standard search and identify pattern."

The covers on the weapon's housing swing open and the barrel rises and swivels.

"All stop, mister Cutter."

She throttles the engine down. "Aye sir, all stop."

The *ARC's* engine flames out. The drone's operator does not compensate for the changed physics of the situation and the drone overshoots its pattern and hangs for a moment just a little ahead of the *ARC's* bow.

The barrel zeroes in, the weapon discharges and the drone goes the way of the J-26—dancing filaments followed by a spherical explosion. As the explosion snuffs out, space is eerily quiet and calm as the *ARC* drifts ahead on her momentum.

"Restart, sir?" Cutter asks.

The answer is a long time coming. "No. We need to talk."

#

She meets him in the Observation Deck. Kees pulls a pair of the comfortable reading chairs up to the massive viewport and invites Cutter to take a seat.

"We're not making a run for the border?" she asks.

"Alliance drones cross borders all the time. Now that we've blown one up, there will be no place to hide."

"So . . . ?"

"Maybe hiding is the wrong thing to do."

Yes, blowing up the drone brought the issue to a head, but the logic in running away has always been shaky at best.

"Go on," she invites.

"This thing," he gestures to the ship around them, "was never meant to be an escape pod." He gives her a few seconds to let that sink in. "I'm going to stay aboard the *ARC* no matter what, but the shuttle is perfectly functional. There's a fair chance you could get away clean." Kees pauses again. He hopes she turns his offer down, but he has to make it . "No hard feelings."

To his surprise, Cutter laughs. "I didn't throw in with you just to run back to Roman's world."

Relief washes over him. "In that case, there's a couple parts of this world you still need to see."

#

"How many seats?" she asks.

Kees counted the seats the first time he entered the massive theatre. "One for everybody—a thousand."

She notices the folding chair leaning against the back wall, and gets it. "A thousand one?"

They make their way toward the residential area. There's an eeriness about the deserted town, scary in some ways, sadly awe-inducing in others. Kees leads the way, letting Cutter experience it in relative silence as they approach Ishmael's living quarters. Remembering the impact of the art studio when he first saw it, he holds the door for her. "After you."

His sense of drama isn't lost on her. She enters . . .what? . . . cautiously, reverently, expectantly? She stops, frozen in the doorframe of Ishmael's studio and takes in the statue of Solange that dominates the room. "Oh my."

Kees explains what little he knows about who this is, why Ishmael carved her, and what she meant to him. Cutter finally tears herself away, glancing back as she exits the studio.

The ocean rolls in front of them as far as the eye can see. "The waves are for aeration?" she asks.

He doesn't physically slap his forehead, but it's close. "Of course. That would explain why the circuit breakers to the wave-making equipment were left on. They caught fish right up to the end."

"It's beautiful."

"That too."

The underlying terrain in the "mountains" is steep and laced with sharp ravines. The undergrowth, dry and brittle now, must have been dense and thorny. The rocks rise sharply on both sides as they approach the entrance to the encampment.

"You could defend this place with half a dozen people," she says.

"There's no evidence they actually had to."

She looks back the way they came. "Struggle through those brambles and thickets only to die when you get here? Maybe discretion was the better part of valor."

"None of the Fellowship members ever made the effort," he says. "They never left the comfort of their homes. Seems most of the 'gumption' was up here with these people."

A few rustic benches provide seating for a natural amphitheater. The stage has a curtain on a roller that spools up and down. She steps up on the treadmill generator. Despite her fairly good pace, the stage lights give off only a reddish glow. "Somebody had to work hard for the show to go on."

"The builders obviously didn't expect the ARCans to live here. We're at least half a klak from the nearest grid access, vertical or lateral."

"It's easy to forget you're on a ship here." She steps off the treadmill and takes in the naturalistic surroundings. "You think that's why they moved up here?"

"It was their dream, to colonize some pristine world. I think they were driven out of town at first, but after peace was restored, a fair number of them chose to stay here."

"To live their children's and grandchildren's dreams?" she asks.

"Hmpf. I hadn't thought of it that way."

The sculptures standing in the open-air studio demonstrate a wide range of artistic ability and craftsmanship. Cutter takes special interest in the metalwork pieces. She fingers a lumpy, uneven weld.

Kees comes up behind her, looks over her shoulder. "He should 'a taken a couple more lessons," he quips. Suddenly he's aware of how close she is, smells the eucalyptus and spearmint oils from her massage. Their bodies touch as she reaches out to a nearby weld with a perfectly consistent row of beads.

"Somebody else did this one," she says.

"Should have done the other one, too."

She steps away to get a longer perspective. "I don't know. I think the charm is that it tells two stories instead of one."

"You ever do any sculpture?" he asks.

"Not really. Melody used to say, 'Every cut should be a thing of beauty.' I believed her, I just never had the time to do anything about it, formally."

"You could now."

She gets a gleam in her eye and nods toward the pedal generator. "Do you have any idea how fast that thing has to go before I get a good arc?" She goes back to the ratty weld. "Actually, this is the kind of bead you get when your power is unreliable." She examines the weld up very close. "Always a story," and then looks around at the collection of artwork, "a whole lot of stories."

And that concept has been on his mind for weeks. "The diaries and historical accounts keep saying that." She gives him a curious glance. "They want to tell their story. It's like, 'If our story is good enough, all we have to do is tell it and we won't be forgotten.'"

"That's all they had," she says. "Everything else was stripped away."

"It's what you said—their children and grandchildren weren't

171

going to be able to live out their dream. They were going to have to do it themselves."

"And then they left the responsibility of telling it to Ishmael, and he left it to you."

"Us, maybe?" he says.

A lifetime living by the code and with those two words he's thrown it all out. *Does she get it?* And perhaps more important, *Does she want it?*

Her long pause and hint of a smile prove one thing: she gets it. She picks up a cutting torch, so familiar to her in other contexts. "Time for me to stop cutting and start welding?"

"Maybe." He holds open the door to a rustic, rough-hewn wooden shed. "You ready for this?"

"I don't know, am I?"

She is stopped cold by her first view of the interior of the shed, stands rooted in the doorway for several seconds.

Sunlight streams in through multiple skylights. Drawings, blueprints and sketches clutter the cork-covered walls.

In the center of the space, suspended by wires and filling nearly all of the room, is a model of the *ARC*, three meters tall by ten meters in length. It's quartered like an apple and two of the sections are pulled away, exposing the interior structures and designs.

Kees watches silently as Cutter examines one intricately detailed section of the mock-up after another. "This is a representation of the *ARC*," she says.

"This is a representation of ARC World."

"Catchy." She meant it to be sarcastic, but she is a little too impressed with what stands before her to pull that off. The import of what she is seeing starts to sink in. She stares long and hard. "This is what they mean for us to do?"

"Make no little plans . . . " The Daniel Burnham quote resonates with her but when she doesn't come up with its second half, Kees supplies it. ". . . they have no magic to stir men's blood."

"We couldn't do this in a hundred lifetimes," she protests.

"Maybe not, but I'm not going to let Roman scrap this, at least not in the one lifetime I've got."

She follows him out of the model shed, looking back one more time before she closes the door.

They stroll into the longhouse with its dozen or so sleeping mats, pillows and blankets, all lined up along one wall. "They slept together?" she asks.

"A lot of them slept here—together. I suspect some of the 'couples' wanted a little more privacy—there are lean-tos and huts on the port side."

The back door of the longhouse opens onto a dense thicket. They follow a narrow, well-worn path between the knots of raspberry and blackberry canes. "What's that?" she asks, pointing to a very non-rustic structure ahead.

"I never realized anything was back here," he answers.

It's a dodecahedron, made of some aluminum alloy, five to six stories high. It sits, point down, supported by five short legs. The upper end pokes a meter or two above the surrounding trees. From the wear on the path leading to it, it must have had frequent, heavy foot traffic.

"What's this indeed?" Kees asks, walking around to see the device from the back. His old, cautious instincts are the only thing standing in the way of bolting inside to unearth the mystery. There are two treadmills and two bicycle-type generators, a good-sized storage battery—at least that's what he thinks it used to be called—and a solar array.

The ARCan sun is man-made. It delivers full-spectrum light, appears to move across the heavens, sets (dims) at night and rises (brightens) in the morning. But there's no logic in solar cells because in every other part of the ship, power is available from a nearby socket. Throughout the mountain encampment, where of course there are no sockets, the residents opted for muscle-powered generators. Yet this device has a ten square meter solar panel.

If a little yellow feather stuck out of the corner of Cutter's mouth, she would be the proverbial cat that swallowed the canary.

"You know what this is?" he asks.

She only shrugs—with a little grin.

"After you," he offers.

Three stairs lead up to the entrance. No sound of air moving in or out as she twirls the wheel and swings the hatch aside. Lights come on inside in response to the movement. He follows her in.

The whole interior is a soothing sandy beige color and every surface—above, below and around—is padded. There are handholds, one in the center of each pentagon and another at each of the five points. The only exception to the perfect geometrical shape is the floor, which, instead of dropping to its point, has been decked over about a third of the way down. The control panel next to the door would be easily overlooked except for the finger and handprints surrounding it. Cutter opens the cover. "Oh, there's power."

The "sun" has been at full intensity for a day-and-a-half and the solar panels have obviously responded to the stimulation.

She grabs the handhold next to the control panel before throwing the switch.

Kees finds himself drifting a few inches above the floor and rotating slightly. "An Eros chamber?"

Eros chambers have become a standard fixture of deep space pleasure resorts. But when the *ARC* was launched, there were no pleasure resorts and the Eros chamber had not been invented. Not that the "inventor" had to do much. When space travelers first experience weightlessness, sexual foreplay seems near the top of everyone's to-do list. Guillermo Rondoni recognized the potential in that, used existing technology to create a standardized space, thought up a catchy name, which he copyrighted, and then marketed the daylights out of his "invention."

She watches his helpless spinning. In a weightless chamber, drifting can be very time-consuming. He rotates his head to keep facing her as his body slowly twirls.

She hooks a foot under the handhold, looks him square in the eye and pulls her tunic over her head. The human body looks different in a weightless environment. He can't decide if hers is more attractive or about the same.

Kees rises, ever so slowly—perhaps a meter from the surface he left. He will need either help or a long time to reach a surface or handhold. Cutter seems disinclined to provide any help. Instead, she takes off her slacks and shoes. She is as she was when their lips parted from the kiss, except now she's unreachable, several meters away, and she seems impishly delighted to have control over what happens next.

Operating in an Eros chamber is not rocket science, though the skill set is intimately related to the laws of mechanics. It is customary for pleasure resorts to offer the initiate an android training session. The robotic instructor walks his or her student through the basic movements, interactions and techniques. The prime directive, the oft-repeated caveat is, "Never give up your handhold without momentum."

Cutter pushes off gently and floats toward her partner, her eyes fixed on his. And then she drifts past, just out of his reach, and alights at a handhold on the far wall. The scent of her passing lingers.

Again she pushes off, this time toward the floor, just out of his reach. Instead of grabbing hold, she kicks off, nearly straight up and this time she reaches out and grasps his collar. His inertia more than halves her momentum and they rise toward the ceiling, spinning slowly as she unbuttons his shirt. Just before the far wall, she surprises him by pushing him off hard.

He's left nearly motionless, drifting toward the chamber's central locus. He is a patient man. Some part of him hopes she tests his patience as far as it will go. The other part would rather she didn't. Her skill level in this environment is far, far beyond his. He relaxes, happily leaving himself in her capable hands. She pushes off again . . .

An hour and eight minutes later, he hears a gentle chime from the control panel.

"We've got about ten minutes of weightlessness left," she whispers, "before we have to go out and face the real world."

CHAPTER TWELVE

"Ishmael?" Hagar calls from the doorway of the *ARC's* large metalworking shop.

"Over here," he answers, coming from behind the nearly finished shuttle. "Thanks for coming. Could you take a look at this?"

He lies back on a creeper and rolls a second one toward her. She settles on it comfortably and rolls next to him under the shuttle's chassis. "How big a bolt do I want here?"

"Sixteen millimeters, maybe even twenty."

"That big?"

"The strut's load-bearing, right? What's your shear force going to be along that vector?"

He pauses a moment, "You're right. Can you get me a bit?"

She rolls out from under and sorts through the tool case. His hand reaches out with the drill. She takes it, inserts the bit into the chuck and keys it up tight. She bends down, takes a peek underneath. "Goggles."

"Yes, Mommy."

She mounts the pedal-driven generator and sends him the power he needs and the drill begins to sing at its task. After a few minutes the pitch finally rises as the load backs off. "Yes?" she yells.

"OK, that's got it!"

He rolls out and loosens the bit—takes it "hot potato" back to the tool case. She chuckles. "Little hot?"

He used to get mad when she gave him the business. Now it's, "Warm," with just a hint of a smile. He can't put a finger on what has changed between them but lately he finds himself looking forward to her chatter, her collaboration, even giving him the business. In all the long months when he was designing and building the weapon she came to the shop once, maybe twice.

She wanted nothing to do with building a weapon, loathed everything about it from its destructive *raison d'être*, to the devious way the Council authorized it, to Timms' nepotism in giving Ishmael the "honor" of designing it. But creating a shuttle from scratch is a challenge she seems unable to resist.

He steps back to get a better perspective. "What do you think, go ahead and mount it? We need anything else?"

"The bolt."

He's a little sheepish as he fetches the bolt, nut and washers. "You OK to give me a hand lining it up?"

"Sure." She opens the cover to the shop's environmental control panel and dials gravity down to 0.05 percent. The piece to be mounted is still bulky. But now, at a one pound to one ton ratio, she can seat the upper mount over its post. She passes the lower strut to Ishmael's waiting hands under the chassis. "Here it comes."

"A little right." The threads of the bolt sound off as it slides home. "Got it!"

The ratcheting of the torque wrench falls silent. "Ready?" she asks.

"Ready." He dollies out.

Once he is clear, she slowly dials gravity back up toward 90 percent. The ARCans tried briefly to conserve power by reducing ship-wide gravity to 75 percent but after complaints from the "coven," the wives of the Councilmen, it was declared too low and the 90 percent level was chosen instead.

Not a sound from the welds and connections as gravity rises through 50 to 60, 80 and eventually 90 percent. Ishmael leans his weight against the strut and rocks it as hard as he can, again without a complaint from any elements of the structure. "Looks good."

#

The Council's excuse for constructing a shuttle is so transparent that even some of their usual supporters are grumbling. The moon that the *ARC* is about to pass has been the center of attention since it was first sighted nearly three years ago. Where the notion arose that the "space pirates" must surely be hiding behind it, using its barely habitable surface as a base from which to attack the *ARC*...? Where that came from, no one is exactly sure.

The Council's first action was to declare a Time of Emergency. The size of the ARC Security Force (ASF) was doubled and troopers were assigned to newly constructed "security posts" throughout the ship. The pretext for that was ... vague. Ribbon-cutting at the guard stations occurred just before Christmas and Clarisse opined that the tightening of ship-wide security was necessary so that no one could steal lumps of coal to stuff into Mayer and Kline's stockings.

Discontent within the Society remained at a slow simmer throughout those events but now, as the Council prepares to expend another seven percent of the *ARC*'s power reserves to "recon" the pirates' position and capabilities, that simmer has come to a full boil. Many Society members foresee a handpicked shuttle crew circling the moon, returning with photos and sensor readings suggestive of pirate "camps" and "attack preparations." On that basis, the Council will, in its wisdom, declare a new TOE, a heightened TOE during which certain ARCan rights will be suspended, elections will be postponed, security forces will be augmented, and those in vocal opposition will be locked up.

If there ever was a moment for the Society to propose a no-confidence vote, it's now.

But the outcome is far from certain. The Council maintains control because its members know how to wield power. They won't be unseated without a fight and the rancor and distrust of the whole process is sure to further cleave the already fragile society.

#

"How long, you figure?" Hagar asks Ishmael as they stand back to survey the completed shuttle.

"Before she can be launched? Maybe four days, if the tests all go well."

She looks at the sleek, efficient vessel. "It really is pretty."

"Pretty?"

"Yes, I actually mean pretty. Functional, of course, but you have a real flair for proportion and balance. I'm very proud of you."

"You're going to make me blush here."

"You make something like this, something beautiful," she says, becoming a little wistful and contemplative, "and then you realize that there's ways it could be misused and you can't control that and it's . . . well, it's not easy."

"You mean me?" he asks.

That takes her by surprise but she recovers quickly. "I didn't mean you, no."

"I have to do this, you know."

"Do what?"

"Make things. Make them beautiful."

"Because?"

"Because I'm not beautiful."

She suddenly has to fight back tears. He goes on, "You think I am, but who else?"

"Solange?"

"OK, two out of what, a couple hundred?"

"Maybe that's true five years ago, but I think it's changing. I think a lot of people see what a wonderful young man you've become."

"They like me," he answers, "because I made them a plasma

180

cannon and now this is turning out good."

"Well."

He just rolls his eyes. She goes on, "Those physical things are the outward manifestations and yes, they're important, but only because of what they stand for."

"That I'm at least useful for something."

"That their baby is 'turning out good'."

"Their baby? I'm no more —"

"You're the only one they'll ever have."

She sees the wheels turning, the pieces dropping into place as Ishmael absorbs what he must surely already have suspected. "They want you to succeed," she adds, "and they're proud of you when you do."

She has watched her son learn lessons from the day he was born. Sometimes it takes saying it out loud to make the epiphany complete. "That's heavy," he says quietly.

"It is heavy and I'm sorry you have to bear it." She pauses, "Because, you're a good kid . . . "

That's the first half of a "code phrase" between he and his mother, a code she has used since he can remember.

He supplies the second half—". . . and you love me."

She beams. "And I love you."

#

Timms is red-faced and this morning it has nothing to do with the consumption of alcohol. "You think the pirates are going to let us see them coming?"

If Ishmael is less agitated than Timms, he's no less determined. When he was younger (and smaller), his father's physical intimidation had some effect, but not so much any more. "I think the pirates are a political expediency. The Council will play that card to stay in power no matter how much it degrades the general welfare."

"All right, smartass . . . I'm sorry. All right, Ishmael, if not down this path, then where to instead? If we scrap the exploratory mission, stop construction of the shuttle, disband the ARCan

181

Security Force and knock down the guard stations, then what? What do you people propose we do with all those 'reserves' that we'll be saving?"

"How about the quality of life? What have we done over the last ten years to make our lives better, to make the ARC a better place?"

"What are we going to do to improve our quality of life? Give me something concrete."

"What makes life meaningful? We're not going to fulfill the original goals of the Charter. The bastards who launched this ship with defective shielding made sure of that. No children, no future generations, nobody to remember us and nothing to be remembered for."

"Cursing the fates doesn't get us anywhere."

"But making something to be remembered for at least makes our days seem worthwhile. We're going to live out our days on this ship and then die – here on this ship. We don't have any choice in that. But given the chance to create something beautiful, I think most of us would rather leave the *ARC* a more beautiful place than we found her."

"Leave something behind to be remembered by - that's what you want to buy at the cost of our security?"

"You asked me why I'm siding with the Society? I think that pretty well sums it up."

"Well let me just say this about that . . . " Timms gets right in his son's face. "Not—gonna—happen."

Ishmael takes his father's measure. Neither one of them breaks the stare-down. "Over my dead body it's not."

#

Mayer fetches a brandy snifter from the overhead slats of glassware, pours and hands the glass to Timms. "The workers are my job. You let me worry about them. It sounds like your job is the problem."

"I talk to him but he just won't listen."

"Edward," Mayer says as if talking to a child, "We've already lost a reliable majority and if the Society picks off two more seats, we'll have the dickens of a time getting anything done."

Kline fleshes out the point. "If these people win a no-confidence vote and take over, our way of life is gone forever. We'll be dragged down with them and God knows what mischief we'll be into before they see the light."

"So say we lose the two seats," Timms poses, "what are we going to do, impose martial law?"

Mayer and Kline simply look at Timms until he gets it.

"But who's going to enforce it?" Timms says. "You've said a thousand times that the ASF can't be counted on." In the face of continued silence, their objective finally starts to dawn on Timms. "You mean the masters-at-arms? You want me to commit the MPs to enforcing martial law?"

"Unless you know of some other way?" Mayer asks.

"That's prohibited in the Charter," Timms points out.

Mayer presses the point. "We avoid imposing martial law by avoiding a no-confidence vote. We avoid a no-confidence vote by weakening the opposition's position. We weaken the opposition's position by limiting your son's endorsement of it."

"But I told you, he's not listening to reason. He's listening to Solange and Hagar." He spits out their names as if the words taste bad.

"If reasoning won't dissuade him," Kline says, "maybe we need some other way to . . . how to say this, take him out of the game? Make him unavailable?"

"What do you mean: arrest him?"

Kline swills the brandy in his glass. "That would make him unavailable."

"Arrest him for what?"

"That's up to you, isn't it?"

"And then what?"

"Well, that's also up to you, it seems," Mayer offers. "As captain you have powers that the Charter specifically withholds from the Council."

Timms still doesn't get it.

Mayer sighs. "We have just completed construction of a shuttle and we are passing a moon with an environment that, while harsh, still falls within the legal definition of habitable."

It begins to dawn on Timms what they're suggesting. "Maroon him?"

"Persuading him to back off would be far preferable, don't you think?"

Kline drives home the point. "If you don't find some way to muzzle him, you're committing all of us to whatever whims these people have in mind. Your fate—our fate—passes from our control to theirs." He waits a second or two for that sink in completely. "If you want the name Edward Timms the Third to be remembered the way these people think of you, then go ahead and just let them win. The Society wants to hang the captain's portrait above the mantel for everybody to see. But if they're the ones painting it, why do I think you won't find it very flattering?"

Timms just stands there, dumbstruck. *My portrait with them as the painters? The story of the* ARC *with Solange and Hagar as the storytellers?*

Kline has known from the start that this is the button you push when you need the "Captain" to do something for you. Just to be sure, he gives it one last poke. "Ishmael obviously doesn't care about your reputation, or your family's honor."

#

Timms doesn't very often get into his captain's uniform and schedule a formal meeting with the head of his security forces. But today Jean-Marq stands before him in full uniform and waits with cold professionalism for his orders.

"Article XIV of the Charter clearly authorizes me to take this action if I believe the safety of the ship, its passengers and her crew is in jeopardy."

"I'm aware of that, sir."

"I need to know exactly what they're saying."

"Yessir."

"I will leave the details to you, except that a recording would be preferable to a transcription."

"Understood, sir."

"Report back to me whenever you have any information. This is on a strict need-to-know basis, sergeant."

"Understood, sir."

"Dismissed."

#

Timms views proceedings at a Society meeting on a video editor screen. The edges are distorted, as though the film was made through a fish-eye lens.

Hagar speaks on screen. ". . . we need to be clear. If we succeed in electing our slate, it will be basically overthrowing the current power structure." He pauses the recording, makes several mouse moves and clicks, then replays the clip. ". . . we need to be clear. We our overthrowing the current power structure."

He fast-forwards to Ishmael on screen. "I'm not sure we want to be talking about how we're going to overthrow somebody. That's likely to come back and bite us if we're not careful. What we want, I think, is to make our voice heard, to nullify their obstructionist tactics and force our propositions to a vote. If we just look on them as the enemy, we deserve their inevitable retaliation. They've got the political structure working in their favor and we have to be careful not to draw some line in the sand where they feel they have to explode our whole effort. We do want the good of the ship to always be our goal."

The editing takes a lot more time, but after a few minutes of struggle and frustration he plays the modified clip. "We want to overthrow their obstructionist tactics and force our propositions on them as the enemy. They've got the political structure working in their favor and we have to be careful not to explode our whole ship." He clicks again and replays the clip. Satisfied, he leans back and stretches his arms and legs, then returns to the source material in search of a new piece of dialogue.

#

Timms marches up to Ishmael in the public square with Jean-Marq and three other masters-at-arms in tow. The captain's security force is always armed, but today they have their weapons drawn.

"Ishmael! You are accused of sedition and inciting to mutiny. As prescribed in Article XIV of the ship's Charter, you are under arrest and will be held pending trial. If found guilty, you will be punished in accordance with Universal Maritime Conventions. You have the right to remain silent and the right to be represented by counsel. Your trial is set for noon tomorrow." He turns to the escort. "Sergeant-at-arms, take this man to the brig."

Jean-Marq obeys the order without enthusiasm. "I'm sorry Ishmael, I have to use the manacles."

Ishmael offers his hands without resistance.

#

Tension is high in the hearing room. Masters-at-arms man the four corners of the room in full riot gear. Ishmael sits calmly in the dock while his lawyer fidgets and sweats profusely.

"My client's accusers present only these recordings, which were not only illegally obtained, but have clearly been altered."

The prosecutor stands. "Objection! There is no evidence of tampering with the recordings."

"And no proof that they are not tampered with," the lawyer responds.

"Sustained." It's Mayer in the judge's robes. He silences the upwelling of comments from the gallery with several raps of the gavel.

"Your Honor, I move for dismissal on the grounds of insufficient evidence."

"Motion denied. Do you have anything else to offer by way of defense?"

Ishmael and his lawyer share a glance. "No, your Honor, defense rests."

"We will recess for one-half hour and then the court will deliver its verdict and sentence."

Ishmael's lawyer mutters under his breath, "Why bother with the verdict? Just go ahead and sentence."

"You will not be forgiven for another outburst, counselor."

"Thank you, your Honor." It's clear his heart has chosen a very different word than "thank" as the predecessor of "you."

"Next case!"

The bailiff steps forward. "Case number one thousand four hundred thirty-six, Edward Timms, captain of the *ARC*, brings charges against Hagar for sedition and inciting to mutiny."

Ishmael and his mother, both in shackles, pass each other at the doorway to the hearing room.

#

The shuttle was never meant for carrying passengers. Karl is at the controls and Jean-Marq occupies the co-pilot's seat. Ishmael and Hagar are wedged into the tiny cargo space immediately behind. Jean-Marq makes fast the hatch. After a minute or two, the occupants go weightless and the bright lights of the launch bay are traded for the smothering blackness of deep space. The forceful press of the main engine replaces the gentle g-forces of the maneuvering thrusters.

"How does she handle?" Ishmael asks.

Karl turns to him, no joy in his face or his voice. "Very nicely, sir."

CHAPTER THIRTEEN

There are ten ways Roman Pollack could be knocked from his tightrope. Ten, because that's his number of shipmates. Every one of them believes that the ship they've left behind is the *ARC*—the original *ARC*, the gleam in every scavenger's eye. Little do they know that when the Alliance reps come on board the *Scavenger*, one word of that will mean their death.

Of course there is the option to simply change course and slink away into the far regions of space without any contact with the Alliance—also without so much as two nickels to rub together. That's not an option for any of them.

To collect the booty, to survive the interrogations, every single crewmember must hew to the party line: *The ship, whatever its name, has been destroyed—completely destroyed.*

He goes through the roster one more time.

The twins, Cookie, Scrounger, Trish and Melody all took the percentage. Each one thought their share was five percent better than anybody else's—good thing none of them can do arithmetic. Roman gave away title to the *Scavenger*—twice. Of course he doesn't have title to the ship but Ugg and Sparks won't find out their deed is worthless until long after they can do anything about it. Gordo was quickly convinced that the ship is a giant ore freighter, and not the *ARC*.

That leaves Prof. He was enraptured by the notion of "rides and the fat lady and the two-headed donkey" and he just won't let go of it. There's no way Roman can navigate Prof's psyche—no way to keep him from blurting out that they've found the *ARC* and she's still out there, waiting to be transformed into an amusement park.

It's a real problem. When the falsehood is this complex, one little inconsistency can mess it up. As they approach the Alliance outpost, it's time to solve his problem.

After Cutter took the only functioning space suit, it's hard to describe how proud Prof was that his suit was the one Roman ordered reworked. There's real prestige to be had by working on the ship's exterior because of the tremendous risk. The "great void of space" may be an apt expression in many places, but scavengers operate in space's "dirty" regions, where tiny scraps of debris fly about at tremendous speeds. A grain of sand at high enough velocity doesn't just puncture a hapless wearer's suit, it passes clean through, leaving a hole on exit through which gushes much of the spacer's guts or arm or brains, whatever happens to have been in the missile's path.

And Prof, of course is the perfect crewman to embrace the heroic nature and discount the deadly possibilities of fulfilling that prestigious role. He worked tirelessly to restitch the seams of his extra-large suit. When it was time to test it, he was like a child with his new "safety patrol" belt as he stood in the service bay and let Roman bring the pressure to zero.

And now, as Roman asks him to go extra-vehicular and reposition the communications disc, he lights up again—eager to show off his importance.

The disc, of course is perfectly aligned, the EVA totally unnecessary.

Whether or not the other crew members have figured out

Roman's plan is immaterial, as long as they don't muddy Prof's thinking.

Prof stands in the bay, helmet twisted down. He gives the thumbs-up and Roman purges the atmosphere. He smiles as the suit swells. Roman shuts down artificial gravity and as expected, Prof has forgotten to activate his magnetic boots. He drifts off the floor.

At ninety percent purge Roman opens the iris and Prof floats toward the opening with the few remaining molecules of air. He's playful at first, waving his arms as though flying into space but then, with the realization that he really is flying into space, he reaches down and magnetizes his boots.

If his feet were within half a meter of anything metallic, the weak attraction might be enough to draw him toward safety.

They're not.

He gestures to Roman—signals "close the iris" with increasing urgency. The iris doesn't move and Prof drifts past the plane of the *Scavenger*'s hull. His contortions would be comic if only he was a comedian and his audience could trust that death was nowhere near. Roman watches without a smile.

Whether bored by the slow pace of events or actually moved by Prof's desperation, Roman taps in the commands to close the iris and makes his way back to the bridge.

Trish watches the feed from the exterior camera as Roman arrives.

"He forgot to turn on his magnetism," Roman explains.

She just stares at her captain.

"We don't have time enough to retrieve him before we have to decelerate."

A movement in the monitor catches her attention. Prof waves his arms, looking straight into the camera. He holds up his left gloved hand—in his right an awl, with which he points toward the now-closed iris. He repeats the pointing gesture several times, and then pokes a hole in the index finger of his left glove. He aims his left hand to direct the tiny thrust from the escaping air and tries to guide himself back toward the ship. After about a minute the faint sound of magnetic boots clanking on the hull whispers through the ship. Trish shifts camera angle. Prof fetches a clamp from his tool belt and clamps off the hole.

"Ouch," says Trish. There's no way to clamp off the finger of the glove without crushing the finger inside. They hear the sound of magnetic boots walking across the hull toward the iris and the bay. "Not so dumb as we thought."

Roman shrugs. "Prepare to come about."

"We're not going to get him?"

"We don't have time. Come about."

She stares at him for a long minute, then executes his order. It takes about two minutes for the *Scavenger* to execute a hundred eighty degree rotation. About half way through, the pounding of Prof's wrench on the iris falls silent.

A flight controller's voice comes over the com speakers. "Hailing the vessel entering Alliance space. This is outpost number four. Identify yourself, reduce speed to zero-point-two and prepare for customs inspection."

The "customs inspectors" arrive, heavily armed. Without so much as a peek into the cargo hold, they take Roman back aboard their corsair.

#

Viktor Torquist is waiting for him in the interrogation chamber. This can't be good. The Alliance will do whatever needs doing to get their way but sometimes, when they have "bigger fish to fry," some of the small fish can slip away. For some reason, when it comes to the *ARC* they are casting their finest net and Roman and the other minnows aboard the *Scavenger* are being hauled up— most likely to be scaled and gutted.

A "technician" stands by in the corner of the interrogation chamber. She is one of those perfectly plastic sorts: cold, emotionless, unreadable. She seems unlikely to take any pleasure in the incredible pain she is sure to inflict. Nor will she evidence any guilt, remorse—and certainly not compassion. The breaking of

191

Roman Pollack will be carried out in a most professional manner.

"Roman?" The words slide out of Viktor's physical mouth in the same oily manner as they do from his holographic representation.

"Hello Viktor."

"Take a seat, please." The politeness arises from a very dark place. "We are eager to hear of the disposition of . . . the vessel."

If the technician learns that we've discovered the ARC, *he's going to have her killed too.* "There were some complications."

"We would like you to be more specific."

There is no fact they cannot extract from him in this room. A simple injection and every restraint, every inhibition will dissolve. With a slight change in formula, they can reduce his brain to whatever level of gelatin they choose. They can also inflict pain the old-fashioned way, by hurting him. If that doesn't suit Viktor's fancy, there are a half-dozen ways they can induce every cell in his body to cry out in agony. How childish to have thought he could withstand their probing. How absolutely naïve to think that his crew will hold to their story.

The technician approaches with a simple strand of yellowish rubber tubing. Not knowing her intention makes the innocent little item terrifying. At Viktor's nod she desists from tying his arms to the chair and returns to parade rest position.

"Well?"

"Kees refused to see reason and so I was forced to call Parlay and a no-confidence vote."

"Which you lost?"

"No, no, I won it."

"And so where are the complications?"

"He escaped the brig—well, actually there's no brig but he escaped a lock-down in the forward hold."

"Escaped where?"

"He commandeered the shuttle and . . ."

"By himself?"

"The first mate was with him. She sided with him early on, so the only way I could win the vote was to discredit her as well. They were locked up together."

"And escaped together?"

"Yes."

"Escaped where?"

"To the . . ." Roman barely stops himself. He owes the technician nothing, but at the same time there's no need to sacrifice her life because he lets slip the name *ARC*.

". . . to the derelict vessel."

"That would be Dahlia Cutter?"

Viktor has done his homework. "Yes."

"Continue."

"The *Scavenger* has only one shuttle, so there was no way to board the vessel and recapture them."

Viktor merely looks at him. In his world, recapturing someone you're going to kill anyway must seem senseless. "So you were in command of the *Scavenger* and DeWet and Cutter were aboard the . . . other vessel."

"Correct." *And now it's time for the lying.* "They couldn't do anything with her. There was no power to fire the main engine. But I knew you ordered me to make sure he couldn't, you know . . . so we deployed a torch and breached her hull."

"You breached her hull with them on board?"

"Yes sir, in two places."

"And her atmosphere was purged?"

"Oh yes sir. That's why we cut the hull in a second place, to be sure they hadn't closed off bulkheads and kept any areas pressurized."

"And they're dead?"

'Well, unless they found pressure suits. I suppose they could have done that and then . . ."

"Sealed the breaches and . . ."

"No, no. They could never do that. We cut her up good. Just that they did have our shuttle and . . . but you can't get two in her with suits on."

"I see." Viktor needn't hurry. He's a cat, pawing at his captive mouse for the pleasure of it. "So after rupturing her hull in two places and possibly leaving your former captain and his first mate on board—in whatever compromised circumstances—you . . . came here?"

"Well, it's going to take at least forty trundles to transport that kind of tonnage. We didn't have the storage or the cutting capacity to really do the job and I knew you wanted a report on her, so we decided to come here directly and report in and then you could . . . —"

"You say 'we' decided. This was a crew decision? I thought you said you took command?"

"It be contract work and they be contract crew."

"Ah yes, scavenger law. So, how was this decided?"

"On profit, like all contract decisions. We laid claim to the wreck and we will give title over to you. They—we, hopes that we can barter a good price for it. That's seeing as how we don't have the means to cut her up nor to transport the goods to market."

"But you left her there?"

"The prize? Yes. She's not going anywhere."

"And you're not afraid someone else is going to steal her?"

Why would he ask that? "I suppose that's some risk. We marked her with our claim flag—that and the J-26s."

With Roman now fully mired in his morass of lies, Viktor asks the question he intended from the start. "How would you explain, then, that our sensors have picked up an ion burst at those coordinates?"

And so it is that Roman's hope for a profitable outcome evaporates—his life becomes forfeit.

"They can't have," he blusters.

"Who can't?"

Roman's brain turns over his options. His mouth remains motionless.

At a nod from Viktor, the technician straps down Roman's forearms. She ties a simple knot in each of the slender rubber hoses

194

and then waits for further instructions.

"Perhaps you'd like to start over?"

"He fired the main engine?" Roman asks.

"That's what we assume."

The technician steps closer, an IV in hand.

"I'll tell the truth."

At a nod from Viktor, she steps back again—without loosing the bands nor setting aside the needle.

#

The corsair fires a slender cylinder toward the *Scavenger*'s hull. In the vacuum of space its impact makes no sound at all. But from the inside—in the mess where Cookie stands chopping onions—it strikes with a "thwock," a timbre not unlike the sound effect of an arrow in a Robin Hood movie. He jumps and nearly cuts himself.

Who can be calm with an Alliance corsair hovering a mere klak away? At first it was a relief when Roman was the only person they took with them, but as time passes, the possibility of foul play seems more and more likely. Why would the outpost send an armed party and not leave a few troopers on board?

No sense even thinking about escape. The *Scavenger* is fast, but an Alliance corsair is more than eighty percent engine. The *Scavenger* might get out of firing range for a minute or two—if they caught the corsair captain completely off guard. No, the only option is to wait it out here. Wait, and wonder, and worry.

If the thwock wasn't frightening enough, the whine of the high-speed drill frosts the cake. Cookie doesn't wait—he dashes from the mess, closes the hatch, dogs it down tight and rushes to the bridge.

Confusion reigns. When the crew signed the scavenging contract, there were three who had the experience to captain the ship—Kees, Cutter and Roman. With no one willing to sit in the captain's seat, precious seconds click by with no action taken. There are alternative courses of action when the hull of a ship is penetrated, but there's one truth and that is, the decision has to be made quickly.

Meanwhile, in the mess, the diamond-tipped cutter completes its twenty-millimeter hole, then retracts. A tiny bright dot appears in the hole and after a second a gossamer wisp, half a meter long, snakes through.

The fahz-wraith is thought by many to be a mythological creature. That is in no small part because so few souls have seen one and lived to tell of it. At one moment it flutters like a butterfly, seemingly at the whim of air currents. But then, just as one is seduced by its nacreous shimmer, it oscillates in a short, rapid sine wave, gathers speed and darts toward its objective. Shipboard filtration systems with a fine enough mesh to stop a fahz-wraith virtually never have the tensile strength to withstand such an arrow-like assault.

The intruder flutters about the mess, awaits her partners. Within minutes there are more than a dozen of them swirling in a seductive panoply of iridescence. The indecisive souls on the *Scavenger*'s bridge are too late shutting down the mess hall's ventilation. By time the valve finally closes, seventeen of the creatures are on their way to every corner of the ship.

And so it is that Ugg, Cookie and Sparks stare in wonderment at the creature floating from the bridge's ventilation shaft—and in horror as she darts toward Gordo, strikes him in the left temple just behind the eye, and undulates her way into his skull. The legends have never been clear whether death comes from the eight-hundred volt electric burst an adult female can generate, or whether it's the tiny droplet of poison. Whatever the cause, the sequence of events is horrific to endure and terrifying to watch. Gordo screams and writhes on the ground, clawing at her wispy tail as the fahz-wraith makes her way deeper and deeper into his brain. When she reaches the region she wants, she releases her electric charge in a spasm of orgasmic delight. Gordo goes rigid for several seconds, and then collapses into a sodden heap, soiling himself in his death throes. The droplet of poison, released into the generous blood-flow of the human brain under adrenaline-enhanced stress, may in fact be sweet release from his agony.

A second creature wafts onto the bridge from the stairwell and makes Cookie her prey.

In what may be poetic justice, it's Ugg who makes for himself the only chance to survive. He was, after all, the one who insisted that they recover Prof's body—more importantly, that they recover the only functioning pressure suit. And now it's Ugg who dashes to the service bay and struggles into the bulky contraption. He can hear the screams of his crewmates as they are penetrated, one by one.

He has the bubble helmet in hand just as one of the wraiths discovers his location. She is quick to find him in the darkened chamber. He forces the helmet onto its seat but in his haste, gets it started cross-threads. The creature darts at his head, glances off the curved surface, seemingly stunned for an instant. He unseats the bubble and this time gets the threads lined up correctly. Two full twists and it's fully seated. He rushes to the control panel and begins purging the bay's atmosphere.

The evacuation of air draws his would-be attacker toward the exhaust vent, but just as she is about to be sucked into the pump, she comes to, oscillates violently and begins making her way against the stream of air. He stares as she increases her distance, accelerating in the steadily thinning air. She comes directly at his face, like watching an arrow coming right between his eyes.

But the airstream has robbed her of some of her speed. She strikes without penetrating, though the impact splashes a fine web of stress-cracks in the outer laminate of the helmet. He slams the control to open the iris, activates his boots and kills gravity in the bay as the iris begins its maddeningly slow process.

In most cases, creatures that survive in an atmosphere cannot tolerate a vacuum and vice versa. The fahz-wraith proves to be the exception to the rule. As the last molecules of air waft out through the opening, she hangs in weightless space, drifting slowly toward the opening. Ugg hoped that her bright eye would dim as she expires. She seems for the moment to be taking his measure—her eye shines brightly. Her motive power in an atmosphere arises from the air pressure she creates along the sine wave of her body. With no air, that mode of propelling herself is not available. He stands a moment, weighing his options.

Even if this creature should drift outside the iris, he can't shut her out and return to the ship. He doesn't know how many of these things the corsair loaded into their cylinder, but to assume there's none left inside is foolish. No, his hope is outside the ship. Space is a hostile place, but having watched Gordo's death throes, he is ready to face whatever the outside has to offer. The iris is fully open and the wraith, if it has some other motive power, seems ready to allow herself to drift beyond its plane.

He activates the switch to close the iris, then galumphs toward it as it creeps shut. On the last step, he kills magnetism in his boots and pushes off through the half-closed opening. The secret will be to reactivate his boots after the iris is closed and before he gets too far away for them to have any attraction.

The wraith is close by—she has drifted out along much the same trajectory he is on. He smiles.

"You got no boots, girl."

He watches the iris complete its cycle, reaches down and engages magnetism. For a moment he hangs—it's going to be close.

But then, the wraith drifts away above him and he aligns vertically as his boots gently tug him back to the *Scavenger*'s metallic hull. After a few seconds they clang down against the blades of the iris. He looks up with satisfaction at what he expects is the last he will see of his terrifying companion—only to have the terror return.

She too is aligned vertically, now very rigid, like a shining arrow. And she's moving . . .

Slowly at first, then, as she passes by in front of the bubble, faster and faster until she butts into his boot. He should have thought. A creature that can generate eight hundred volts is certain to be able to take advantage of magnetic fields. That would be how she propels herself in a vacuum.

"Clever girl."

... as she oscillates excitedly, inveigles herself between the threads of his spats. She will surely penetrate the boot. Just as surely, she will take her time navigating his anatomy on her way to that part of his brain she so passionately desires.

#

"Fahz-wraith gestation is twenty hours," Viktor explains. He glances at his communicator. "You have a little over four hours left. I would suggest you make haste gathering the bodies. If you've left any behind when the cycle begins anew, your ship will be uninhabitable. Do I make myself clear?"

Nothing is very clear to Roman as the technician removes the needle from his arm and presses a gauze patch over the wound. "Um, I'm not sure," he slurs.

Viktor smiles—not a smile anyone would want to see. "How careless of me to have forgotten." He claps his hands twice, loudly and in quick succession.

Suddenly the fog in Roman's head clears—his vision is sharp and he is full of energy. *Of course, a child would know what must be done.* "Yes sir," he answers crisply, "Crystal clear." He doesn't know why the technician is to accompany him, but right now no other course of action would make any sense. "Shall we?"

She follows him out of the interrogation chamber.

Alliance guards escort them to the shuttle bay. Roman pauses, suddenly unclear.

"Get in," the technician instructs.

"But ..."

"Just get in." She takes the captain's chair, Roman the co-pilot's. "Buckle up."

He tries to get his bearings, tries to understand who she is and why—why any of this is happening. She glances over, cold and unreadable as ever. Is she feeling things and hiding it, or is there nothing there? Is he projecting onto her the emotions he feels? He catches a flash of what looks like pity. Is that just because he feels pitiable?

"What happened to me?"

"The imprint has better endurance when original resistance is higher."

"So . . . ?"

"I can refresh you twice. After that, you will have to think on your own."

"So why don't you refresh me now?"

"Sit quietly and don't touch the controls. It will be better to do it after we have arrived."

She eases the shuttle from the corsair's bay and the *Scavenger* comes into view, very close at hand. There, stuck to the iris of the *Scavenger*'s bay, is a spacesuit-clad figure. If ever there was a *danse macabre* more frightening than this . . .

"One of yours?" she asks.

Only one crewmember is large enough to fit into Prof's recaptured spacesuit. "Probably Ugg."

The contortions of the figure are riveting. Roman has no idea why Ugg would be writhing away, grasping at his chest and neck, but the technician seems to understand it all too well. She brushes against the throttle control and the shuttle eases closer and closer. "Damn," she mutters.

"What's going on?"

"She's almost there," she replies coldly.

They can make out his face. Roman stares in confused terror as an iridescent wisp swirls around the interior of the globe, then goes into a tremulous ecstasy before Ugg's blood obscures the view.

The technician deftly manipulates the shuttle's robotic arm, extending it as they drift closer and closer. The laser cutter lights up and she slashes both ankles, then backs away. They watch the curious sight of Ugg accelerating into space, powered by his ankles spurting blood with each of his heart's last contractions. The boots, their bloody ankles still protruding, are all that remain "aboard" of Roman's erstwhile crew mate.

At the touch of a small, hand-held device, the iris creeps open. Roman gapes at the device. "They installed a remote actuator," she explains. "Can't believe you flew this thing without one. What did

200

you do, push the stuff out by hand?"

It does seem really stupid when she puts it that way.

The iris closes behind them and the sound of air pressurizing the bay gradually filters into the shuttle. She looks at him.

"I can do this only two more times. Try to stay focused on the task. You won't be able to figure it out, so don't try—it only shortens the period of efficacy."

"Figure what out?"

Her grip is about to crush the bones in his forearm. "Don't try!" She lets loose his arm and claps twice—exactly the same timbre, volume and tempo of Viktor's handclaps.

Things still seem crystal clear as he drags Trish's body into the bay and stacks her with the others near the iris. It hasn't been easy stifling his curiosity, nor has it been easy to squelch his queasiness. The death of each crewmember outdoes the previous one in its grotesqueness. *What could possibly have . . .?*

"Stop thinking!" The technician glares at him as she wedges the last two bodies through the doorway.

Roman puzzles as she tosses the bodies the full width of the bay with one swing of her arm. Melody and Trish, so often intertwined in life, apparently chose to die the same way. They land atop the pile and roll off toward the iris. Roman stumbles, dazed by the growing incomprehension.

A slap.

Almost hard enough to knock him out. "Task at hand," she hisses in his face.

And it all is clear again, at least for the moment. "How much time?"

"Four minutes. This is all of them, right?"

He counts quickly. "Yes."

"Depressurize the bay and open the iris."

He stops at the doorway. He's about to leave his companion in a decompressed chamber and then open it to space. "You know it's right," she bellows. "Stop thinking and just do it!"

He does know it's right, yet hasn't a clue why. It seemed so clear a second ago. He dogs that hatch and slams the control to pump the atmosphere from the bay. At ten percent, he activates the iris control and peers through the viewport at the events on the other side.

The technician wears no suit, no boots, no magnetism, and no breather—yet there she is, bracing herself against the last flow of air from the bay. She lifts one of the bodies and angrily gestures for him to cut the bay's gravity. Even a weightless body has mass. What should happen as she tosses the first corpse into space is—for every action there is an equal and counter reaction. The thrown body should drift into space at exactly the same rate the technician is thrown back into the bay. Instead she stands her ground and flings first one, then another out the opening at an unbelievable velocity.

What the hell am I doing, and who is this...? and suddenly absolutely nothing makes sense.

With the last body thrown out, she looks at her timepiece and gestures aggressively for him to close the iris. When nothing happens, she rushes to the viewport, stares through at his vacant expression, reaches into her tunic and activates the iris herself. She steps to the center of the bay and peers intently into space, where the cluster of bodies drifts away.

At first it might seem an optical illusion but then as the second and third corpses begin to show the same activity, it becomes all too clear. Viktor used the word "gestation" and in that frame of reference, the tiny dots of light worming their way out of the skulls of the victims are clearly the reason the *Scavenger* would have become "uninhabitable." They seem at first disorganized, flagellating their way free of their unwilling hosts. They drift and mingle without obvious intent, until first one, and then another, points its light toward the *Scavenger*'s bay.

The technician takes on a rigid, very non-human posture. Her eyes roll up into her skull, her lids still wide open. She drifts ever so slightly upward. The bay's iris completes its cycle, now fully closed.

And the fahz-wraith "children" lose their focus. More and more emerge and as their community grows they wander and intermingle—with no particular place to go. Someday, something magnetic will pass through this region of space.

Roman can't imagine what else to do except pressurize the bay and retrieve—in all of this adventure, he never asked her name. Whatever fate Viktor assigned, it's clear she shares it. She hangs there now, a few millimeters off the floor. She's pretty—actually sexy, in a kind of scary way. Was she doomed by something he said? He can't remember much beyond her inserting the needle.

He explained everything to Viktor truthfully, after his lie was found out. And yet after he mentioned the *ARC's* weapon, Viktor had her inject him with something. Did he then blabber on about the *ARC* and was that what doomed—whatever her name is?

And what is she, after all? She discarded the bodies in zero gravity and a total vacuum and then for no reason he can understand, apparently died. Or turned herself off, or something.

The pressure reaches normalized levels and he opens the hatch. His first step sends him airborne. *Stupid!* After a few seconds, the gravity field in the hallway brings him back down. He keys in the code to reactivate gravity and the technician clunks heavily to the floor. She's inhumanly strong and apparently inhumanly heavy.

He looks her over from every side. Her face is really quite pretty. She's got great tits and her ass . . . well, buns of . . .

"Don't even think about it." She looks him in the eye. Whatever she is, those eyes are saying pity and disdain. "You didn't clap your hands."

It had occurred to him for a second, out there in the hall. If Viktor could make everything clear and then she could too with just two handclaps, then . . . but she seemed really determined not to use it a third time, so he'd decided against it, too. "No, I didn't."

"Did any get back in?"

"The wispy things? No. When you, uh, shut down? They kind of wandered off."

"We need to create some distance."

She leads the way onto the bridge and goes directly to the captain's chair.

"Main engine controls are ..." He reaches to point them out, only to have her nearly crush his arm a second time.

"They're pulse-boost drives, yes?"

"Yes."

"Maneuvering thrusters?"

"Uh, standard vapor-stream, uh, four-X multiple."

She rolls her eyes and slides both aft maneuvering thrusters all the way down to their stops. "This will take a while."

"Why can't we ...?" He lets the sentence dribble away.

"Hurry things up with the main drive? Pro-induction matrices are magnetic and a fahz-wraith's sensitivity radius is a little over four hundred klak."

"Those things are still alive?"

"They were just born."

He lets the import of that sink in. "You know, I never asked your name?"

"Adrienne."

"Adrienne ...?" He opens his palms to invite a last name.

"One-eight-seven, Four-one-five."

"All right, Adrienne ... one-eight-eleven, four-one-five, what next?"

"After we have cleared the fahz-wraiths' range? We intercept the *ARC*."

"What is that thing with the handclaps?"

"A trigger for thought-pattern sequencing," she answers.

"And I can do it myself?"

"I'd have to kill you."

He wishes that one seemed more like a joke. "Yeah, but then I couldn't execute the pattern."

"Sequence."

"Huh?"

"Viktor implanted the pattern, you execute the sequence."

"So, to get his 'sequence executed' you need to keep me alive, right?"

"There is a twenty-three percent probability that I would be more successful at the task without you."

"And an eighty-seven percent chance you fail."

"Seventy-seven."

"So you can't kill me, right?

"There are specific guidelines governing the circumstances under which I am authorized to terminate you."

He apes Arnold's vocal timbre and Austrian accent. "Terminated."

Roman's Arnold was pretty good—hers is so perfect she must have sampled it from the movie's sound track. "Not funny."

"So, when are you going to do it?" he asks.

"Kill you or trigger the sequence?"

"The second one."

"As close to the event as possible."

"What's the event?"

"That is the seventh question you have asked in less than a minute."

He smiles. "I'm just a curious kind of cat."

"And you know what happened to pussy."

"Listen, we've got a long trip here and we might as well get to know each other. Who knows, it might actually be better when we get there if we, you know, understood each other better?"

"I know everything I need to about you."

"OK, you then. Tell me about yourself." He gets no response from that at all. Undaunted, he presses on. "So . . . have you always been a killbot? I mean, you don't look like your typical killbot."

"The Adrienne line was designed for erotic surrogacy."

"You're a sexbot?"

"I am anatomically correct and fully functional." She gives him a cold stare. "But where you're concerned—no—I'm not."

"Come on, what's the difference?"

"I'd have to kill you."

"Why do you keep saying that?"

There's something deeply unsettling about her coy smile. "Don't you want me to tell the truth?"

"What have we got to lose? You're built to make me happy, why not just do it?"

"I'm built to make you beg for death's sweet release, why not just do that?"

He stares at her, shouts, "Fuck you!" and stalks away.

"Don't count on it, stud."

Roman paces his cramped quarters, tries to make sense out of it. He's been flying blind for days and what he needs now is some insight into Viktor's plan. The handclaps are the key.

If Viktor can make everything perfectly clear with two handclaps and then Adrienne Whatever-her-number-is can do the same thing, why can't he just clap himself and make it happen again? She said she'd kill him if he did, but she has to catch him first.

. . . and *Clap, Clap.*

"Holy shit!" The plan is now crystal clear. *No wonder Viktor decided to do it this way.* Roman is to con Kees into letting them close enough that the bot can get on the *ARC*'s hull and steal the weapon . . .

Adrienne steps into the doorway. "If you're going to do yourself, you could at least have the courtesy to close the door." She steps in and closes the door behind her.

"Truth is, you should listen to me," Roman says. *Truth is, if I can't con her in the next thirty seconds, I'm a dead man.*

She seems amused by the situation. "Truth from the gospel according to Roman Pollack," she quips. "I'm all ears."

She knows I clapped myself. That means she also knows I've finally got a clue what's going on. She's an android and androids run on logic, so I've got to be logical. And since she knows everything I know, I can't lie to her.

To say Roman Pollack is handicapped in a world where lying is not an option is to understate his problem. He scrambles to think of another alternative and comes up blank.

"Viktor wants the *ARC* destroyed." He sticks up his thumb and ticks off his first point. "That's the one big 'must have' in this whole deal."

"That is the truth," she answers.

Index finger—"And he really wants that weapon." Second finger—"Then there's Kees' and Cutter's death. But he can do that later if he has to." Ring finger—"And a fully charged Q-16, who wouldn't want that?"

It's hard to tell if she's buying it or not. "Go on."

Pinky finger—"Killing me is a lower priority than any of those."

She is a lot less impressed than he hoped. "You've run out of fingers. Are you done?"

"Truth is," *Come on Roman, ask for the sale,* "you and me could work out a deal. I help you get the 'must-haves,' blow up the *ARC* and steal the weapon, and you let me get away with the Q-16."

"Truth is," she answers imitating his style, "I don't need your help to blow up the *ARC* and steal the weapon."

"How are you going to con Kees into letting you get close enough, huh?"

She breathes in, but while the sound originates in her voice box and her lips, tongue and teeth sync perfectly with the words, it's Roman Pollack's voice delivering the words: "How are you going to con Kees into letting you get close enough, huh?"

Holy shit!

"You have bitten the apple, Roman. You now have the knowledge of good and evil. You have seen the light, you know the truth." She draws her weapon.

This is not good.

"But Viktor was right . . ."

Now, in a twisted example of android humor, she samples Jack Nicholson's voice. "You can't handle the truth!"

She squeezes the trigger and the weapon blows a hole in Roman's chest that goes clean through and out the back.

207

CHAPTER FOURTEEN

Desolation, thy name is Stanhope IV.

Well actually, no one aboard the *ARC* knew the name of the massive planet along their trajectory but since Estelle Stanhope was the first to see it, she was given the honor. And while there were passionate proposals about who might name her four moons, in the end they were simply assigned one through four.

No trait of this desolate wasteland exceeds by more than five percent the base parameters to be classified Terran Habitable. Lichen and mosses barely qualify as "vegetation." What little water can be found on the surface flows sluggishly toward a "sea" that is non-existent during half the year. The thin atmosphere stinks of sulfur and is filled with the fine gray powder of the surface, forever blown aloft by restless gales.

Karl and Jean-Marq peer through the shuttle's view ports with waning conviction as they descend. Earth is the only natural environment they have ever encountered and while conditions were grim in the last years before the *ARC* was launched, they were nowhere near as frightful as what lies below.

"Go ahead Karl, it's all right," Ishmael offers quietly.

The shuttle touches down in a cloud of dust hardly distinguishable from the background swirl. The hatch swings open and the occupants deplane, looking much like cowpokes on a dusty cattle drive. They wrangle the tent and a crate of provisions from the cargo hold.

The traditions go back a long, long ways. A person marooned is given a pistol with one shot, assumed to be for suicide rather than whatever the alternative form of death might be. Whether provisions are supplied is at the discretion of the captain.

A growl—and a dark shape scuttles at the very edges of visibility. "You see?" Ishmael offers lightly, "it is habitable, at least by whatever that is."

"You might need this." Karl presses his rifle and two full clips into Ishmael's hand.

"Thanks."

Karl sweeps the horizon—if a hundred fifty meter circle of visibility can be called a horizon. He stares at his two passengers, torn.

"You have your orders, Karl. This is what the Council decided." Ishmael takes the bandana from his face. "If you disobey their orders, that makes you an accomplice. Besides, bringing us back on board won't help. They'll just find someone else to do it, or else they'll execute us on the spot." He takes Karl's hand and looks him in the eye. "But there is one thing I want to say. This . . ." a sweeping gesture to the bleak landscape, "is what they're willing to do to those who resist them. Ask yourself if this how the ARCans want to be remembered, or is there some other way?"

#

Ishmael and Hagar shield their faces from the blast and watch the shuttle disappear into its own cloud. He takes the safety off the weapon and slings it over his shoulder, and together they erect the tent.

The attack might have succeeded, except for the growl. The beast comes at them roaring, all fangs and claws. Ishmael kneels, swings the rifle smoothly to his shoulder and squeezes off a round

210

right down its throat.

It crumples, comes flying, legs and tail splayed awkwardly, and lands less than a meter away. Its eye looks up at Ishmael along the line of the gun sight. What does it know, what has it learned? Has this charge been blind instinct or is there some intelligence behind the jet-black pupil?

Just beyond visual range, there's at least three more beasts, shuffling and growling. Ishmael looks to Hagar. She nods. He fires a bullet into the brain of the creature at his feet, lifts the rifle aloft, roars, growls and menaces as best he can.

Whether they will return is unclear, but for the moment all is quiet.

Hagar has described red meat to him a few times but if he ever ate any as a child, he has no recollection. "Is this going to kill me?" he asks, poking at the steak with his fork.

She holds up a food packet from the meager survival kit. "It's not like we have a lot of options. We can poison ourselves now or starve in a few days."

"It's funny," he answers with a mouthful. "We're banished to a world that's supposed to be total deprivation and the first night we have steak. If Karl and Jean-Marq had waited a few minutes we could have sent some back with them."

Hagar smiles. "Sweet revenge denied."

He wouldn't have expected anything different. Here she sits, wind whipping at the tent walls, their future as bleak as anyone could imagine, and she banters easily. Not that she hasn't faced "bleak" before. She gathers and wipes off the plates.

"Well, Mamma, what do you suggest we do this evening?"

"Do we know how long is the night?"

"Seventeen hours—so they calculated."

"Ah. That's a long time."

He scrounges in his pack and pulls out a tablet. At his touch, it lights up. "A little light reading?"

"You brought a tablet?"

"And three less pairs of underwear."

"I'm proud of you, son."

"You do realize that I'm the reason we're here."

"That's why I'm proud of you."

"You think they'll win again?" he asks.

"Who?"

"The Council—Mayer and Kline, father?"

She shakes her head. "In the end, the only way they can win is by killing all of us."

"So with you and me, they won."

"No," she answers, "with you and me they lost."

"But we're going to die."

"But you left three pairs of underwear to bring a tablet."

"So we're the stinking literati."

"The stinking part is a given. The literati part only works if you read us something."

"Fair enough. What's your pleasure?"

"Not sure our environment is going to provide much humor. You got something funny in there?"

And so the first night was spent eating red meat and reading humorous short stories. Sonnets were the fare the second night, adventures the third. All of that interspersed with bits of philosophy, social theory, literary criticism—a seventeen-hour night provides ample time to explore a wide range of interests.

There are two or three hours in the early morning when the wind backs off to "stiff breeze" levels. On their sorties into the surrounding terrain, they occasionally see beasts in the distance but the attack of the first evening is never repeated. They do encounter several species of small herbivores, skittish little creatures that hop about among the rocks.

Ishmael examines a stalk that vaguely resembles Brussels sprouts. "What do you think, can we eat this?"

"Anything nibble on it?"

"No."

"Then probably not."

"Because . . .?"

"The animal you shot, the one we've been eating for three days, had a mouth with all incisors and canines. No molars, right?"

"So he's a carnivore?"

"Yes and these little jumpy, bunny things probably made up most of his diet."

"So chances are we could safely eat them, too," he offers.

"And probably should."

"And the plants they eat are safe for us to eat."

"Not necessarily, but we'd be idiots to eat any plant that they've avoided." When he reaches out toward the plant she adds, "You might actually not want to touch it."

Even with the supply of small game and the nut-like and grain-like plants, in the end it's water that will be a problem. While they can purify their urine, the water lost to breathing and sweating cannot be recaptured in this open environment. There is evidence of a rainy season but no way of knowing its cycle. They can only hope the rain arrives before their reservoir runs dry.

On the fourth day Hagar missteps, falls and cuts her hand. Though there's not much bleeding, soon an angry red line runs up toward her elbow. There's no reading that night—she falls into a fevered, uneasy sleep. The next morning the wound begins to make pus. Ishmael changes the soiled bandages all day. In the middle of the fifth night her fever breaks and the redness up her arm fades. By dawn she is alert—and hungry.

"Pretty good, eh? What a wonderful system is the human body," she offers cheerily.

It's not just sleep deprivation that has Ishmael subdued throughout that day. After the evening meal he finally voices what's on his mind. "Are we going to end it ourselves?"

"Take our own lives? It may come to that."

"I thought I might lose you yesterday."

"And you still may," she answers, "Or I may lose you. If that were to happen, I don't know if I would take my own life or not."

"We're going to die eventually."

"That's no different here than anywhere else."

"But on the ship," he says, "at least we were doing something."

"And we're doing something here. We're living. We're adventuring. We're surviving."

"Is just surviving enough?"

"What story do we tell if someone comes here and finds us with a bullet in each of our heads but still plenty of rations and water to carry on? Who were we that we gave up so easily?"

"The beasts will eat all the evidence."

"And that's a thing to strive for, that no one find out?"

He answers with a mock confrontational tone. "Are you ever going to let me win an argument?"

And her put-down is laced with love and respect. "As soon as you come up with a good one."

#

Hagar holds a cup under the stopcock as Ishmael tilts the water reservoir toward her. A half-cup of water dribbles out.

"Actually, I thought the gravy was a little watery last night," he quips.

She only shakes her head.

"There were clouds on the horizon again yesterday."

"That would do us some good if we were on the horizon as well," she answers.

They've tried everything to find water but can't crack the mystery of how the plants and animals survive. They dug down over five meters and the bottom of the hole was as dusty and friable as the surface. If the lichen and mosses are tapping water from the soil, they must have incredibly deep roots. There's no indication that the animals have a watering hole anywhere nearby. Ishmael's four-day sortie in search of such a watering hole came up . . . dry.

"What do you think, three or four more days?" he asks.

"To stay alive? Maybe five—if we kill and eat more meat. We

should hunt today. We'll start getting weak after tomorrow." She divides the water evenly in two low, flat containers. They lick the surface dry after their meager sips.

"Tastes like more."

The bones are picked clean, not a scrap left on either plate, when Ishmael brings the tablet to life. She stops putting things away, settles back and waits for him to begin.

"He was an old man who fished alone in a skiff in the Gulf Stream and he had gone eighty-four days now without catching a fish. In the first forty days a boy had been with him. But after forty days without a fish the boy's parents had told him that the old man was now definitely and finally *salao*, which is the worst form of unlucky, and the boy had gone at their orders in another boat which caught three good fish the first week. It made the boy sad to see the old man come in each day with his skiff empty and he always went down . . ."

This is probably the fifth or sixth time they have gone to sea with the old man, entered into the world Hemingway created, ridden the swells of the Gulf with the great fish tugging at the line and then wept with the old man as the sharks broke his heart. After almost an hour, Ishmael hands the tablet to Hagar and she picks up where he left off. The red light in the tablet's upper left corner warns that very soon its face will go dim and the reading will come to an end. The short days don't deliver enough energy to recharge all of their devices.

Not that any of it matters if there's no rain. Without water it will be a dead heat whether they outlast the tablet or vice versa. But for tonight, their stomachs are full, the story is good and they read on and on into the night—sleepy but not quite willing to pick a place to stop the adventure.

The adventure is stopped, but not by them. Once in a while they hear the beasts in the night, growling and fighting, but never for long and never close by. But tonight a great chorus of yelps and howls encircles them. At first the interlopers have no clue, but before long they hear the whine.

"Pirates?" Hagar asks.

"There are none."

The sound grows louder.

"Who then?"

The walls of the tent shine as a powerful light beams on it from above.

"We'll know soon enough." He offs the safety on the rifle and pulls back the tent flap, then turns back to her, grinning. "It's our shuttle."

The shuttle touches down and kills the light immediately. Karl gives a thumbs-up through the windscreen. The hatch swings open and a backlit female figure gestures them to board.

They hesitate. The tent and their gear—should they strike it and bring it?

"We have little time," Solange yells through the gale.

Hagar reacts first, dashes to the ship and embraces her friend. Solange pulls her inside and offers Ishmael a hand up. "Can you take us both?" he says.

"Get in!"

He wedges himself into the hold as she dogs the hatch and bounds back to the co-pilot's seat. "Ready!"

The shuttle rises sharply; the g-forces strain their hold on consciousness.

After several minutes Karl shuts the thrusters down and the passengers go weightless.

"How far is she?" Ishmael asks.

"Eighty thousand klak," Karl answers.

"We can't make it with the four of us."

"The moon slowed her more than they calculated."

The ironies never cease. If Captain Timms were competent, if he had checked every calculation a dozen times over, the *ARC* could have fired its maneuvering thrusters so that their "close encounter" with this moon resulted in acceleration rather than the opposite. This man, whose incompetence and malfeasance had cost the *ARC* everything she set out to do, was now in some ways the saving grace in Solange and Karl's rescue attempt.

"We did 'appropriate' an extra point-four septa for the effort," Solange explains with a sly grin.

Ishmael runs the numbers in his head. Eighty thousand klak is well beyond the range for which the shuttle was designed. Even with the extra power, the hope of overtaking the *ARC* falls squarely within the margin of error. "When did you leave?"

"A day-and-a-half ago."

Small comfort.

"You'll like this," Solange says, passing a video tablet to Hagar.

She holds it so that Ishmael can see as well and toggles "play." On the tiny screen, the view of the interior of the *ARC*'s service bay. The camera operator pans from the open clamshell to the rods bolted to the floor on either side. Stretched from each rod to the shuttle's front landing gear are what appear to be bands of some elastic material, pulled tight. Karl's voice counts down, "Four, three, two, one . . ."

Hagar giggles with delight as the view onscreen rushes out the clamshell—the shuttle slung into space on a set of rubber bands.

"Necessity is the mother . . ." Solange chuckles.

"Someone calculate that?" Ishmael asks.

"Oh yeah," Karl answers with droll sarcasm. The occupants fall silent as it sinks in.

"Why?" Hagar asks.

Solange turns to face them. "Why did we come and get you? After Ishmael won the election, the Council declared martial law."

Ishmael looks up from the sensor readouts. "I won?"

"People were really angry when they found out that the evidence against you was manipulated. It was Clarisse's idea to slate you for president, just to remind everybody what the whole thing was about. Kline found some technicality to get your name off the ballot, so the voters had to write it in. When they announced the final tally, every candidate on the slate won by eight votes but you were elected Council president by thirteen."

Hagar is amused, but only for a few seconds. "And so based on 'voting irregularities' the Council declared the election invalid or rejected ballots with write-ins, something like that."

"Both. They invented a new ship's status—Time of Extreme Emergency—T.O.E.E. Its timeframe is indefinite; there's no end date. Habeas corpus is suspended, so is the right to assemble. They've come up with new definitions of what constitutes sedition and treason. They're building four new security posts and spreading rumors that the Society is going to steal the ship's stores. Just all that fear-mongering."

Ishmael says, "But they didn't guard the shuttle."

"They thought they could deal with us like it was a war and make up lies about how we're a threat but they forgot that somebody might actually fight back."

"So you stole it?" Ishmael asks.

"You could make an argument that they stole it from us when they took you here."

They ride in silence a few minutes. Then Ishmael voices the obvious question. "If we do manage to overtake her, will they let us on board?"

"We've got a plan," Solange answers.

"Does it involve rubber bands?"

"Not this time."

Yesterday the *ARC* was a speck in the distance and today it fills twenty percent of the visual field. The good news is they've still got air to breathe. The bad: they may not have enough power to slow down, in which case they'll overshoot, and run out of air.

Little beads of sweat form on Karl's brow as he calculates closing speed, fuel reserves and air supply.

"How do we look, Karl?" Ishmael asks.

"We knew it was going to be tight."

"And . . .?"

"It's tight."

"Tighter than you expected?"

"Our closing rate is a hundred forty kph higher than I expected," Karl answers.

Ishmael thinks for a long minute. "What mass did you put in for me?"

"We had you at eighty-seven."

"Ah! We've spent two weeks on moss, lichen and raw meat. I'd be surprised if I'm over seventy-eight. Hagar?"

"I might be as low as forty-five."

"What happens if you use those numbers? What is that, one twenty-three?" Ishmael asks.

Karl enters the new information and smiles at the readout on his hand-held. "I love it when a plan comes together."

Of course he's joking, but at least there is now a chance to make the connection.

"T-minus ten minutes," Solange announces calmly.

Karl touches the thruster control ever so lightly and the *ARC* drifts out of view to the left. Nine minutes and fifty-two seconds later he taps the joystick on the other side—stops rotation with the engine lined up facing directly into their flight path.

"You have a nice touch, Karl."

"Credit goes to you, Ishmael. She is beautifully easy to fly."

Solange buckles in. "Five, four, three, two, one . . ."

The little pieces of debris that have floated about the cabin for the last two days suddenly "drop" to the stern as the engine fires.

Shedding eight hundred seventeen kph requires an eleven-second burn and that is, within a few drops, exactly the amount of fuel remaining. At ten seconds the engine flames out. Then, like a backfire in an old auto, it pops once more from fumes in the chamber. Karl waits a full minute to be sure there isn't another "burp." He caresses the joystick and a beautiful sight fills the view screen.

It's the broad flank of the *ARC*. To the naked eye, she seems to be running exactly parallel—neither closing nor distancing, neither gaining nor lagging. The passengers let the sight sink in.

Karl answers the obvious question. "I think there's up to two minutes of maneuvering thruster fuel in the lines."

Hagar says, "Assuming they'll open the clamshell."

A voice crackles over the intercom. "Hello shuttle craft, this is the *ARC*."

"Request permission to come aboard," Karl answers.

. . . there is a long pause.

"If you refuse permission," Ishmael offers in measured tones, "we will fire maneuvering thrusters and distance ourselves." He signals Solange to mute the microphone. "Let's hope they want their shuttle back more than they want us dead."

The minutes pass, but then the clamshell creeps open. Karl's guess about thruster fuel in the lines is right. They fire and the distance closes at an agonizingly slow pace.

"Oops."

. . . and just a little to the left of the opening.

Karl massages the joystick. Just as it appears his aim might be corrected, the port thruster goes silent. "We're going to scratch the paint a little." The port side scrunches into the clamshell frame just aft of amidships. Luckily, their slew spins them into, rather than out of the bay.

Someone aboard the *ARC* activates the bay's gravity as soon as the shuttle clears the doorframe. She settles with a screech just shy of the forward bulkhead and the clamshell rumbles shut.

The minutes slip by.

A battery powers the shuttle's converter—the one that trades carbon dioxide for oxygen. If Timms and the people in charge of the *ARC* refuse to pressurize the bay, then when the battery dies, the shuttle's passengers will suffocate.

"Looks like they want their shuttle back and they want us dead."

Solange catches Ishmael's eye. If he's less of a *Star Trek* geek than she is, it's not by much. She pointedly pans her gaze around the interior of the shuttle. "It won't work."

Ishmael puzzles that out for a second before his slow smile matches hers. "Space seed?"

There's no accident in her choice of adjectives. "There are fascinating parallels."

They hear the sound of air rushing into the bay.

"So it seems."

CHAPTER FIFTEEN

There was no brig in the floor plan of the original *ARC*. Though the Charter authorizes house arrest, the notion that the ship's company would ever require a more stringent form of incarceration was never seriously considered by the project's social engineers. Mayer and Kline rectified that Utopian misjudgment before Earth was out of sight. In the name of "ARCan security," expansion of the brig has been a perennial plank in the incumbents' campaign platform ever since.

And so Ishmael, Hagar, Karl and Solange find themselves restrained not only behind bars, but to the subtle hum of electronic barriers as well. Not one guard, but two stand duty at the doorway.

Solange and Karl maintain their straight faces at the changing of the guard. Within moments, the replacements shut down the electronic restraints and unlock the cell door.

"We have to hurry. This way."

...and the myth of the inescapable brig goes the way of the unsinkable ship.

It has been called "Workerville" for a very long time. The

dichotomy between this quadrant and "the Heights" only increased after the J-26s were jettisoned. Down here the landscape vegetation died for lack of "rain" and curtailed "daylight." Up there, the deprivations were somehow mitigated. Maintenance service and renovations that take place with such regularity up above are virtually non-existent down here.

The dividing line, at first rather nebulous, has become more and more rigid with time, so that those who "go up" after dark are routinely stopped and questioned by ASF troopers patrolling the border. "Uppers" are hardly ever seen on the streets of Workerville, even in daylight and never at night—well, except for a few who "come down" seeking certain services.

Whether any of the "uppers" are sympathetic to the Society is a debatable issue on both sides of the wall. Finding a Workerville resident who supports the Fellowship is a much more dubious proposition. And so, on this Thursday night, it is no surprise that the recent escapees find themselves in a modest apartment in the heart of Workerville.

It's more of a surprise when they awaken the next morning to the rumbling and crashing of barricades and razor wire being stretched along the ghetto's perimeter. By noon the enclosure is complete and Jean-Marq informs Workerville's one remaining alderman that she has two hours to surrender the escapees. As the deadline passes without compliance, Workerville goes dark—not just from having the "sun" turned off, but power interrupted as well.

#

Clarisse waits while the last few Society members find a place to sit in the cramped apartment. She starts off the discussion. "Surrendering you to them will never be an option."

Ishmael rises to make himself seen and heard. "History is full of cases where 'divide and conquer' has worked, at least in the short term."

"There's not going to be any 'dividing.' We're more unified every day, and what they did last night just makes us tighter."

223

A heavyset man in the corner says, "Yeah, tighter as in wrapped up tight with razor wire and barricades. They boxed us in."

Clarisse wheels on him. "Bullshit! Those assholes live in a two-dimensional world. They sleep in their fancy houses, they go to their office or the Council chambers and they shop and they go to the commissary. It's all on one level."

The fat man rises to the bait. "So?"

"They think that surrounding us on this level means we're trapped. We're on a freakin' ship!"

After that sinks in for a few seconds, it's Karl who voices the question on just about everybody's mind. "OK, we can get away by going up or down, but where do we go after that?"

"The one place they can't control," Ishmael says.

After a moment's pause, Hagar asks, "The forest?"

"It makes all the oxygen. They can't turn it dark and they can't shut off the rain."

"So what," Clarisse asks, "it's nuts and berries from now on?"

"You're the one talking about a three-dimensional world." Ishmael catches his mother's eye. "We have as much right to the ship's stores as anyone and they really don't have the manpower to guard every warehouse on all levels."

Hagar gets it immediately. "Thank you Raiff?"

"We did steal a few chickens."

"You mean leave Workerville?" Clarisse asks.

Ishmael nods. "Many's the revolution started with a band of outcasts in the mountains."

Karl steps up front and center. "They'll come after us."

"It takes a certain amount of courage to leave your home and flee into a wilderness. It takes a lot more to chase after somebody who's already there and means you harm. I'm betting they don't have the sand for that."

It's Solange who asks, "How soon?"

By five o'clock Jean-Marq is uneasy at the silence beyond the barricades. An hour later he sends a single officer in to recon

224

Workerville. Finding the place empty, it's still more than half an hour before someone stumbles across the ladder and overhead hatch by which all the "workers" made their exit.

The mood is positive, the rebels' spirits high as they make their way through thickets and brambles, over rocks and ravines.

"We can defend this if we have to," Ishmael says as he leads the way to what he and Raiff once dubbed "the redoubt." The fifty-seven people who fled Workerville set about finding shelter for themselves as the sun gradually dims for the night.

#

"What about your oath?" Timms asks.

"The one I took thirty years ago," Jean-Marq asks, "based on the promise of a ship filled with happy children carrying on the traditions and heritage of our beloved Earth—that oath?"

Timms' impatience shows. "You promised to enforce your captain's orders, to provide security to the passengers and crew—by use of force if necessary."

"And I have obeyed every order you've ever given me. I've carried out my duties even when I disagreed with your judgment or the Council's decisions."

Timms can feel it all slipping away. His only leverage with Mayer and Kline was his authority over the masters-at-arms. "You answer to me!" he blusters angrily.

"I did answer to you. And now I am no longer going to answer to you, nor follow your orders."

"That's mutiny."

"If you order me arrested, trust me Captain, there's not a soul on board who will lock me in the brig."

"Don't you play power games with me!"

"Games?" Jean-Marq stares Timms down. "I'll be going now."

"Over to their side." Timms tries to make it a taunt.

"Yes sir, I will be moving to the mountains."

"And when they attack us, will you be in the lead?"

"They're not the enemy, sir. They're not going to overthrow

you. They'll just ignore you."

"I took you for a better man than this."

"As I did you."

Timms watches Jean-Marq march out the door. And Jean-Marq is only the latest of the ARCans to join the Society in the mountains. If the ship's company was ever reunited, the Society would sweep every incumbent off the Council and establish whatever rules they wanted. They could strip him of his captaincy and render him powerless. *They don't intend to overthrow you,* he seethes, *just ignore you.* Nobody ignores Edward Timms III.

Even in his youth Timms was not the adventurous sort and at this age, the thorns and brambles are almost enough to make him quit. Yet the disgrace of turning back would be more painful than his cuts and scratches. He presses on in the dark, avoids the makeshift path, keeps low and out of sight.

His plan has no shape. The pistol was an afterthought. If he can get the drop on Ishmael and force him to come back, the Society will be weakened. If that can be called a plan, then so be it.

Will Ishmael be anticipating the threat, surround himself with a security guard? It's what Mayer would do—so would Kline. But then, Ishmael is popular and Mayer and Kline are not. Is he naïve enough to leave himself vulnerable? Somehow naïveté seems to fit the whole Society ethos.

Another step and he would have fallen into the ravine. He stands shaking, listens to the water rustling at the bottom of the gorge. Despite his fear, he's taken with the beauty of the place. Not to say he can see any sense in the original planners creating it so, but standing here in the full moonlight, the cool water bubbling over the rocks, it has a captivating aura.

"Father?"

He wheels on his son, a mere two meters away. The pistol dangles in his left hand.

"Dad, what are you doing here?"

"Ishmael, you surprised me." That part is certainly the truth.

"I've been tracking you for several minutes. I'm sorry, I didn't know how to make you aware without frightening you."

"Yeah, well you could have made me aware of the ravine."

"Startled people usually jump away from the noise and I was behind you." Ishmael spots the pistol. "You're armed?"

"Wasn't sure who I would find. I guess there's some people up here who wouldn't want to see me."

"Not wanting to see you doesn't mean they'll shoot you. We will defend ourselves if the Fellowship mounts an attack, but the weapons for that are stored in the armory. No one carries a gun. Ever."

What a bunch of sheep. He stuffs the pistol clumsily into his waistband.

"The safety's off."

"Huh?"

"You could shoot yourself like that."

Timms fumbles at the pistol's safety—finally gets it on. "Thanks."

"Did you come for me?"

Have a care Edward, he's not stupid. "Yes, in a manner of speaking. I . . . I don't understand what's attracting so many of our people?"

Ishmael deadpans, "Sex, drugs and rock & roll."

"A flip answer for everything."

"I'm sorry. It's just that you've been opposed to what we're doing here every single day of your life. I didn't think your question was serious."

"I can't be curious?"

"Starting now?"

"I haven't been the father to you I should have been, but it hurts that you have such a low opinion of me."

"Fair enough. You want to see what this is all about? I'll show you." Ishmael surveys Timms for a long moment, then says, "You may be right about raising hackles if you're seen. I'll show you what

I can from cover. Follow me."

Timms follows his son in the pale light. Somehow Ishmael navigates the brambles without getting stuck. His father apes his moves and they make good time to the top of the ridge above the "village."

In the clearing below, two Society members walk a treadmill to power the lights. A trio of women harmonizes a haunting tune. On the far side, Karl blocks the basic movements for a pair of actors. There are three painters and two sculptors. Hagar crochets a large coverlet, pauses. She looks directly at the place where Timms and Ishmael hide. After a quizzical moment, she returns to her work.

"So it's like an art colony?" Timms asks softly.

"That's an important part of it. If we die off and haven't left anything to be remembered by, who's going to care about us?"

"Who thinks anybody will remember us?"

"It's a big ship. Some day somebody's going to find it."

"And you think they'll care about us?"

"If they've got any humanity at all, I think they might."

"The materials that went into this ship cost billions and billions of dollars. Even without inflation, the scrap and salvage value fifty or two hundred years from now will be irresistible."

"Unless we create something money can't buy." Ishmael holds out a restraining hand and they creep up behind a shrub to look down into another clearing.

"You're a dreamer, son," Timms whispers.

"Thank you."

Again, a treadmill-powered generator lights and powers the Society members below. Their industry is not so clearly artistic. One edits film clips, another scans printed and drawn pages into a computer, two others type away madly.

"What's all this?" Timms asks.

"The Repository," he whispers, then puts his finger to his mouth. The workers are close enough they could easily hear. After watching a few moments more, the duo backs quietly away, out of earshot.

"The Repository?"

Ishmael answers, deadly serious. "We keep hearing rumors that the ships log is being systematically erased—records of what happened aboard are being purged." He stops and takes his father's measure.

Timms plucks a thorn or two from his shirt, avoiding his son's gaze. "That would be illegal. A ship's captain is required to keep a daily log."

"If it was one or two people saying so, we wouldn't have taken it seriously, but it's not. Especially those who have come over recently confirm that the records are being destroyed."

"The ARCans are a bunch of people who died—stupid people who believed the lies we were told. That's the heritage you want remembered?"

"We are who we are, and if we make of ourselves something memorable, something that can't be ignored, then we're immortal. We will live forever through our works and our story."

"You think I want my name to live forever—be the butt of jokes? 'Edward Timms the Third, captain of the ill-fated vessel.' Why do you think I drink myself into a stupor every night?"

"So you're the one destroying the records?"

Timms stares at him without answering.

"There could be another story. If you stop working against us and help us instead, the universe will say, 'like bright metal on a sullen ground, Captain Timms' reformation, glittr'ing o'er his fault shows more goodly, attracts more eyes than that which hath no foil to set it off.' Shakespeare, *Henry the Fourth*, Part I."

"And if some space scavenger says 'fuck it' and cuts this tub up for scrap, he'll sequester the ship's log as part of the claim process and all your statues and paintings will be for nothing. A ship of fools captained by an idiot—an idiot named Timms."

"It's more than just the art."

Timms' growing rage comes across as sarcasm. "Well I hope so, 'cause the stuff they're making down there sucks!"

"It's about the story—our story."

"You going to quote me some more Shakespeare?"

"No, Hemingway. You've read Ernest Hemingway?"

Of course not, you arrogant little snot..."Sure. Hemingway? Yeah."

"He wrote a six-word story," Ishmael continues, "or at least the legends have it he made a bet with some other newspaper writers over who could write the best six-word story. He won and later in life, he called it the best short story he ever wrote—six words only."

"La—di—dah. Oh, that's only three."

"*We* are that story. We're living his six words. And if we can make ourselves worthy of it, we really will live forever. The people on this ship hoped I would be their Messiah, their savior—and I failed. But mark my words, before I take my last breath, I intend to do everything in my power to give the ARCans immortality."

Timms snorts. "You're delusional."

"I may be, but you're going to find I'm unstoppable."

Timms draws the pistol. "How about now, smarty-pants?"

"The safety's on."

Timms took the mandatory hand-to-hand combat training while he was at the Academy, but to be honest his heart was never in it.

Ishmael took hand-to-hand as well, when he joined the ARCan Security Forces. He was good at it from the first day. A week later he began getting the better of his instructors. Of course, he has his mother's genes.

Timms reaches to correct his oversight, only to find himself staring down the barrel of his own gun, with the safety off.

"You going to shoot me?"

Ishmael ejects and pockets the clip, slides the pistol smoothly into his waistband. "I'll take you back now."

#

Timms puffs and wheezes as he mounts the last two steps into the transparent "penis" protruding from the bow of the great ship. It's been over a year since he last came up here and looked over his beloved ship. Somehow today, even the joy of this place has been siphoned away.

How did I let it slip through my fingers? He turns and looks behind at the great ship hurtling along through space.

This was mine—given to me by Uncle Rastus and entrusted to me by the people who created it. I'm the captain of the ARC *but I let the ARCans steal it from me. And Ishmael, my own son, how did I go wrong with that? Didn't I stand here and tell him this would all be his one day? Didn't he answer "Thanks, Dad?" And then what did he do?*

What I offered wasn't good enough for him. He wants his own vision and what I think doesn't mean shit to him. He doesn't want me to give over power to him; he's hell-bent on stealing it from me. Does he think he can run this ship? Nobody gives me credit for all the training I went through to earn this job. They just want to waltz in here and "full speed ahead" and "hard left rudder." Do they even know there isn't a rudder on this tub?

His gaze turns wistful—a moment of remorse.

She's not a "tub"—she's my beautiful lady. How proud we were, sailing off from space dock. I think she was glad to be rid of that interloper pilot. She responded to my command like she had never done before, thrust us into deep space with her powerful engine, let me share all her magnificent strength, showed off what she could do—for me. Do they think they're ready for that? Do these thieves think they can elicit that from her?

Well she won't. I won't let her. She's mine and I'm hers and that's how it will be . . .

. . . until . . .

. . . until we die.

What shame you must feel, old girl, with all your glorious power cells stripped away. Those people put them on there knowing they were flawed. Oh, why couldn't they just have killed us? Why didn't they explode, why didn't they melt down?—Why didn't they let off deadly radiation instead of sterilizing radiation?

His lips tremble. *Fucking Steenmeyers!* Timms' attention drifts to the one remaining power cell, its scaffolding cobbled onto the hull, ruining the beautiful lines of his beloved lady.

And thus begins the final chapter of his life. If he were a book, his reader would finger the few remaining pages and wonder if Timms will find redemption, or if his story will end in despair.

#

Was a time when a member of the ASF or the MPs would snap to attention at their commander's approach. The heavyset slouch standing guard over weapons control brings herself to a soft, relatively erect stance. Nothing crisp about her salute. "Captain," she drawls, as though she resents having to pay him respect.

"At ease, sergeant." There aren't any privates any more. Everyone on the force is an officer of some rank. She holds her position between him and the door. "Stand aside, soldier."

"I'm sorry sir, but access to weapons control is limited."

"I'm the captain of this ship. My access isn't limited to anywhere."

"I'm sorry sir, but under article three of the T.O.E.E. declarations, the Council is empowered to deny access to any person on board, yourself included sir."

This is a person to confront only if I'm positive I can win. "Very well, soldier, I can see you're just doing your duty and I admire that. I'll be back with the proper authorization."

She gives him a look of, "Yeah, lots of luck with that, you washed-up old . . . "

Except Edward Timms knows what will happen next and the soldier does not. She expects him to grovel unsuccessfully before Mayer and Kline and the other members of the Council. He has no intention of going there.

There used to be enough people to man all the security posts, but not so any more. Timms peers around cautiously as he approaches the minerals storage area. How anyone ever thought that the mounds of taconite and bauxite and coke stored in the ship's stern would be at risk always amused him. Somehow the Council persuaded the ARCans to build a security checkpoint here.

Within three months it was manned less than ten hours a week. With the current shortage of personnel, it probably hasn't even had a maintenance cleaning in months.

He looks over the various weapons and devices, settles on the smallest hand-held tazer. He will have to get close and then take her by surprise. He thinks a moment, then scrounges a large manila envelope from the desk drawer. It would work better if the envelope had the gaudy Council seal emblazoned on the flap, but he suspects this should suffice. He slides the tazer inside and then practices extracting it quickly.

The guard goes down hard, her look of stunned rage nicely blended with the stink of fear. If she knew his secret, his compulsive reaction toward an unconscious woman . . .

If he had the time—but he doesn't have the time.

He can't afford for her to revive too quickly, so he takes her nightstick and puts her out cold with a vicious blow to the head. Her access card is programmed to open the door. *She could walk in here any time she wants, and they keep me out!* He breaks a couple of her ribs with the toe of his boot, then locks himself in and manually scrambles the key code.

Ishmael designed most of what's in here. He is also the only person to have even come close to firing the weapon. What poetic justice that powering up the capacitors to fire the weapon will take nearly all of the energy remaining in the J-26 which is to be its target.

He studies the controls. They make sense, but then they would. Ishmael is his mother's son. Deeply as he hates her, the simplicity of the design has Hagar's stamp all over it. The elevation control looks like up and down and lateral control looks like left and right. A child could target the thing. He presses the button that looks like, "turn this whole thing on" and sure enough, the instruments come to life.

At the same moment a red light blinks on the control panel in the *ARC*'s Security Center. Fortunately for everyone aboard, today's operator has completed the three-day certification course and within a minute she identifies the location of the security breach.

"Begging your pardon, mister Mayer," she says into her com link, "we have activity in the weapons targeting control room."

"What?!" his voice squawks from the device.

"The weapon is," she looks at another readout, "the weapon's capacitor is being charged."

"Cut power immediately. I will be right there." The pause is only a few seconds. "And seal the door to the control room."

The weapon has dollied out. The hull of the ship pans slowly across the targeting monitor. Timms is barely distracted by the sound of the massive deadbolt sliding home. *Thank you. I want you kept out as much as you want me kept in. In a minute or two none of this is going to matter.* The J-26 comes into view and marches toward the intersection of the crosshairs. The weapon was never meant to fire on anything so close to the ship and to Timms' frustration, its rotation reaches the stop with the target still a few degrees off dead center. If it works the way Ishmael described it to him, and to be honest he didn't really follow what his son was saying, but if that's how it works, then hitting any part of the target eventually envelopes the whole thing.

And behind the intersection of the crosshairs there is at least a meter's length of the cylinder.

The intensity display shows orange on the panel in front of him and after a few seconds he realizes that the capacitor has stopped charging. *Someone must have cut the power.* There's a slider that controls the weapon's intensity. Timms slides it upward. The indicator turns from orange to red. If the weapon is set to discharge more energy than the capacitor has stored, then an override will prevent any attempt to fire.

He slides the intensity control downward until, just short of the bottom, the indicator turns green. However much power the capacitors have already loaded is enough for a low-intensity blast from the weapon. Even if it doesn't destroy the J-26 completely, perhaps the damage will be sufficient.

Mayer dashes into security's master control room.

"He appears to be targeting the power cell, sir," the operator informs.

"Gas him!"

"Aye sir," and she begins reading the tiny print next to the multitude of buttons for intruder-control. Mayer rushes over and mashes handful after handful of buttons. Throughout the ship, dozens of areas are flooded with knockout gas.

The operator reaches over, grabs his wrist, and points to the monitor screen showing Timms slumped sideways over the arm of his chair. "We got him."

"Can you drain the weapon's capacitor?"

"Uh," the operator's eyes dart over the maze of controls, "it may take a while."

Timms gets two hours out of the straightjacket four times a day—plus the unscheduled occasions when he must relieve himself.

The last thing he remembers is the sound of gas venting into the control room—and then he woke up in the infirmary with this damn thing on. How long Mayer and Kline find his "insanity" useful is how long they will keep him this way. For now, he's stuck in here, one guard on him while he's straight jacketed and two when he's not.

Who he lied to or who he bribed has never been made public but on the seventh day of his confinement, he manages to escape the infirmary. He makes his way unseen to the portside bay, commandeers the shuttle and somehow opens the clamshell.

Third star on the left and straight on 'til morning.

On the eleventh day of May, in the year of our Lord Twenty-one Sixteen, Captain Edward Timms III abandons ship. He takes flight aboard the only functional shuttle and pilots it toward the Holleman Morass, known to this day as space's most desolate and inhospitable region. He has never been heard from since and is assumed deceased.

CHAPTER SIXTEEN

The image of Viktor's head shimmers ever so subtly in the field generated by Imogene. Adrienne sits facing it in a comfortable chair. The tableau hints of an innocent chat between an attractive young woman and her wizened mentor or her beloved, kindly uncle. If one could be spared the content of their conversation, all would seem to be goodness and light.

"His death is unfortunate," Viktor intones.

"Was my execution flawed?"

The *double entendre* elicits a smile from Viktor's image. "I doubt it."

"Does the contingency plan require modification?"

"Were you able to sample enough of his speech patterns?"

Her command of Roman's cadence, timbre, phrasing and lilt are so spot-on, one could easily imagine his soul risen from the dead and possessing Adrienne's body in a most unholy manner. "He has a limited vocabulary."

Viktor's reputation seldom involves anything resembling a sense of humor, but his guard is clearly down as he chats with Adrienne. She is, after all, his to command—in all things. And so he smiles again. "I am surprised you heard him use the word 'vocabulary.'"

She responds with Roman's voice, "Many words can be pieced together from syllables."

Viktor's geniality evaporates as quickly as it arose. "I am sending a data feed from a drone which intercepted the *ARC* two days ago. The drone was destroyed but the information it transmitted regarding the weapon's capabilities should be useful."

Adrienne's expression goes blank for less than two seconds. She replies in her own voice. "I have received the data. Shall I proceed?"

"What is the primary mission objective?"

"Destruction of the *ARC*," she answers.

"And the secondary?"

"Retrieval of the weapon."

"Very good," he answers. "You are authorized to execute the contingency plan. Any further questions?"

"None, sir."

#

The ease with which Adrienne handles the bulky device would make one think it was a stage prop, made of Styrofoam or some lightweight plastic, until she sets it down against the rear bulkhead of the corsair's shuttlecraft. That sound is only made by something incredibly heavy. She spends what in android time is an eternity assaying the actuators and connectors of the device, then carefully inserts its power cable into one of the shuttle's receptacles. She keys in a code on the device's touchpad and the small display screen lights up—a timer indicating 00:00:00.

Satisfied, she retrieves a remote from her tunic. The joystick, levers and sliders of the shuttle's helm controls mimic the movements of her fingers. She pockets the remote, gives the shuttle's interior one last scan, and deplanes.

She hoists Roman's body off the floor of the bay and tosses it into the hatch of the shuttle. She nods approval of its landing place, splayed awkwardly across a pair of midships passenger seats, and strides purposefully toward the *Scavenger*'s bridge—a killbot on a mission.

#

Kees watches the blip on the *ARC*'s radar as it moves along the outer margin of the semi-circular screen. "Whoever or whatever that is, it's giving us a wide berth."

"Another drone?" Cutter asks.

"Bigger, I think." They watch the blip creep along the outer circumference until it is almost abreast of the *ARC*.

Adrienne's sampling of Roman's voice is so near perfect, even a person watching her do it would question who was speaking. As his voice comes over the *ARC*'s speakers, Roman himself would wonder if he was on the other end of the conversation.

"Hello Kees, did you miss me?"

When Kees and Cutter don't answer, Adrienne/Roman continues. "I know you're listening."

"What do you want, Roman?" Kees asks.

"I want to talk."

"Why would I want to talk to you?"

"Because," Roman's voice answers, "since I was here last I've learned what that weapon's firing radius is and also the fact that you don't have any aft sensors."

Kees pauses, checks out his first mate's look of concern. "OK, why do you want to talk to me?"

"You know me Kees, truth is, you and me could make a deal."

A deal that serves your purposes and nobody else's. "Which I should take because . . .?"

The snarl Adrienne injects into Roman's voice is perfect. "Because the alternative is for me to come up behind your ass and cut that tub into half a dozen pieces."

"What's the deal?"

If her snarl was good, her "smarmy" and untrustworthy is even better. "There's no upside to us having a fight."

Cutter steps in. "Give us a clue, Roman."

"Hello Cutter, I know you missed me. A clue?" If Roman as

playful, cat-and-mouse storyteller isn't perfectly in character, Adrienne sells it most convincingly. "There's this giant ship that can't get away from anything the Alliance sends after her. And on board that ship the two of you have a shuttle that holds only one person."

Kees and Cutter wait patiently while Roman plays with them. "I, on the other hand, have a shuttle that holds six, a shuttle I would gladly trade for your one-seater."

"You want to trade shuttles," Kees says. "Why?"

"Because to get something from you, I have to give you something."

"What do you want to get from me?"

"You used to be sharp, Kees." Adrienne gets just the right edge to Roman's exasperation. "The ship of which I speak contains a Q-16 power module, fully charged. You used to . . ." There's a risk in Adrienne playing Roman for so much drama—a risk that she obviously has chosen to take. "But you know, this is starting to bore me. The deal is on the table for the next two minutes." She waits a few seconds for that to sink in, then adds, "After that, it's the torch!"

Cutter kills the com link. "You're not thinking of trusting him."

Kees answers, "No, not for a minute."

"So? He is holding all the cards."

"Let's see if we can buy some time – maybe get a break." He signals her to reopen the link and says, "How do we do this?"

Roman's voice asks, "That loading bay long enough to handle a shuttle that's twenty-three Cs?"

"Affirmative."

"Open the door," Adrienne delivers in Roman's jauntiest voice. "I'll be right over."

A click as Adrienne breaks the connection, then another as she reopens it. "Kees? No tricks. If I don't call Trish every half hour, she'll do it herself." That would be the Trish whose body is floating two hundred eighty thousand klak away in a cluster of fahz-wraiths and corpses.

The *Scavenger* glides toward the *ARC's* stern, then holds position. The corsair's shuttle eases out of the *Scavenger's* bay and the iris spools shut. The shuttle makes its way along the *ARC's* hull and aligns itself to enter the opening clamshell.

Inside the shuttle, Adrienne makes fast the harness for the compact jetpack and tightens the tool belt at her waist. She keys in two hours on the timer for the bomb and after one last check, engages it. It counts down – 1:59:59, :58, :57 . . .

She opens the hatch and steps into the void.

She allows herself to drift from the shuttle. At twenty meters she unholsters the remote, activates the shuttle's thrusters and drives it toward the *ARC's* yawning bay. As it clears the clamshell, she fires her jetpack and sweeps along the *ARC's* hull toward the bow.

Kees and Cutter peer through the portal as the shuttle eases its way into the bay, alarmed as it fails to slow.

"Gravity up to full," Kees orders.

Cutter responds immediately and the shuttle skids onto the floor of the bay. The screech of metal on metal is eaten by the total vacuum of the bay, but resonates through the *ARC's* girders and beams. When the shuttle finally comes to a stop, there's less than a meter between her bow and the bay's interior wall.

"No tricks, eh?" Cutter offers.

Kees weighs the situation for a few seconds. Roman clearly has lied. The question is, what action to take? "Close it up and pressurize."

Kees opens the door to the bay with a whoosh of incoming air and enters, Cutter right behind. He pauses at the sight of the shuttle's open hatch then draws his weapon.

Roman's body, with its burns around the gaping chest wound, lies sprawled across a pair of seats. Kees holsters his weapon, checks out helm controls and then spots the bomb. One hour, thirty-four minutes and twenty-three seconds, and counting down.

Cutter peers over his shoulder. "Why so long?"

Why so long indeed? The other parts of the puzzle make sense. The one hour and thirty-four minutes before the bomb explodes does not. He puts a hand to Roman's neck. "He's cold."

"We were talking to him half an hour ago."

"Apparently not," Kees answers.

"Who then?"

"I don't know, somebody with a sampling program?"

"Why all this?" Cutter asks, "Why not just fire on us?"

Because there's something they need to do and it will take a little time. They need us to be distracted in here while . . . The answer comes to him in a flash. "They want the weapon."

Cutter nods. "And this is a red herring."

Kees tests the shuttle's helm controls, finds them locked. The shuttle and its bomb are in the *ARC*'s loading bay and they're here to stay. "This is a Trojan horse."

He turns to the bomb, examines the casing. "I'll see what I can do with this. . ."

It takes Cutter a few seconds to infer the second part of what needs to happen. Then it registers: she is the only one who can go EV. "I'll take care of the weapon."

#

Curiosity is not a trait one normally associates with droids, nor is art appreciation. Yet as Adrienne stands on the *ARC*'s hull and gets her first look at Ishmael's destructive creation, she feels something akin to both. To think that a single human conceived this and then crafted its parts using the archaic facilities aboard this ship—the probability of that occurrence is so close to zero that the difference isn't worth consideration. Yet here it is: simple, elegant, and by all reports strikingly effective. No wonder Viktor changed plans when Roman started babbling about its first firing. Suddenly there was a prize to be snatched before the *ARC* was destroyed.

She works as quickly as she can in the cramped quarters of the weapon's housing. If she retracts the weapons-port cover, the task will go much faster. The risk is that she will be discovered before she can get away. Not that she thinks the two humans can effectively stop her, but the risk factor is not zero. She threads the nuts off the forward mounting bolts, then decides to retract the cover to more easily reach the aft connectors.

Even with the cover off, there isn't an easy angle to the last two nuts. She contorts her way into the tight space. As the first nut floats free, a shadow passes over. There are only shadows in space if there is a light source and something to come between the observer and that light source. She cranes her neck to see beneath the barrel and glimpses the boot of a space suit magnetically clamped to the ship's hull.

Not good.

She crawls out from the weapon housing as fast as she can, extracts herself as far as a seated position, and finally gets a look at her opponent. It is the female Viktor called Cutter, standing before her in what can only be one of the original ARCan spacesuits—gold-tone bubble helmet, impregnated-fabric body inflated with internal pressure. In her right hand a torch sputters and growls. *This is going to be too easy.* Surely the suit will make this Cutter woman slow and clumsy. One tear in the fabric and she will spill out of it and into space.

Adrienne strikes out like a coiled snake and grabs Cutter's ankle in her vise-like grip.

It is, unfortunately, exactly what Cutter expected. She sweeps the blade across Adrienne's forearm, severing it cleanly. The hand and its stump cling stubbornly to Cutter's boot.

Adrienne recoils, staring at the smoldering stump. It's inconvenient, but a one-armed droid has an 83 percent probability of success in combat with a human. To do that, she must get to her feet. But her lower torso is still in a compromised position. She reaches out with the good arm to give herself leverage, surprised that the human has gone on the offensive. This time the blade sweeps across Adrienne's shoulder. Her torso corkscrews grotesquely as the arm separates.

243

Her odds of success have gone down to 23 percent. It occurs to Adrienne for the first time that she may not survive the encounter. In hindsight, perhaps she should have given her opponent more respect.

If she can get to her feet, a well-placed kick will end the encounter as surely as any other attack mode. Her right foot comes down on the *ARC*'s hull with a solid, magnetic clank and the left reaches out in a powerful roundhouse kick.

But Cutter has stepped back and the boot merely grazes her helmet. Without arms to counterbalance herself, Adrienne's left leg runs up against its internal stops and jerks wildly as the connectors tear and the actuators short out. Cutter steps in quickly and severs the leg at the knee, then slices up from her crotch to just below the ribs on her left side.

Adrienne looks down at herself. One arm is gone at the shoulder, the other truncated at the elbow. She's standing on one leg with the whole left side of her lower torso gone. Adrienne watches as her leg and hip drift slowly up past her and into space. There is only one chance in four million that a droid in this condition can disable a human aggressor.

Of course Cutter can't hear her—sound doesn't travel in space—but Adrienne says it anyway: "You're good." And then she smiles.

The smile is frozen on her face forever as the blade sweeps once more across Adrienne's neck, severing her head as neatly as an eighteenth century guillotine. Cutter catches the bot's floating head by the hair and ties it by a hank to her utility belt. The dismembered torso stands before her on the hull.

Cutter knows two things: a droid's power pack is located in its torso and killbots are virtually always programmed to self-destruct if compromised. Assuming that's the case with this one, the message must have flowed down her neck too late and dribbled into space, and the power supply never got the word to blow itself up. But on the chance that self-destruct is some sort of timed default mode, Cutter severs the right leg and pushes the torso into space with a hefty chest pass, kicks the boot off the hull, and fishes the large arm segment out of the weapon's carriage rail. She considers for a moment cutting off the hand that still squeezes her boot, but good as she is with a torch, it's a fool who risks the blade so close to one's own suit. She can cut it off later, inside.

The bomb's timer reads 1:08:41 and counting down. Kees eases the access panel off the housing. Inside, like all bombs, there's a red wire, a blue wire, a yellow wire and a green wire. His finger eases the yellow wire off to the side—there's nothing below it to give a clue.

"Kees?"

He is surprised at the flood of emotion on hearing Cutter's voice through his communicator. She has survived whoever or whatever was outside the hull. He sets the panel down carefully and fetches his communicator. "Nothing out there?"

"There was a droid. She was loosening the mounting bolts."

"She get away?" he asks.

"I cut her head off."

There are some things to which there really isn't an answer.

Cutter goes on, "Any luck on your end?"

"No."

"I'll be there in a few minutes."

Cutter steps out of the airlock, sets down her helmet and examines the hand still clutching her boot. She fires up the torch and severs the "tendon" that controls the bot's thumb. The hand clatters to the floor. The bruise on her ankle is an ugly shade of purple but the stout boot prevented crushing of the bones. She unties the head from her utility belt, holds it up for a curious second, and then plops it down next to the large vice at the end of the workbench. For a long time droids and bots just never looked like they were alive. And then one day some wunderkind overcame that hurdle, overcame it so successfully that the workbench appears now to have sprouted a head. Even with no power to animate it, the head seems to be sleeping peacefully, as though at any moment it might flutter its eyes and speak up. Even a hard soul like Cutter is a little unnerved by the head's lifelike appearance.

She takes off the bulky space suit and heads for the door. On second thought, she retrieves the bot's head, swinging it at her side as she rushes out of the room.

She finds Kees peering at the small display of the shuttle's computer, scrolling menus and searching. She plops the head down next to him.

At first he's surprised, then he smiles. For all his huge respect for Cutter's toughness it would be lying to say he wasn't concerned that whoever the Alliance sent might be more than Cutter could handle. Apparently it wasn't. "Somebody didn't know who she was dealing with."

"You find anything in that database?"

"It's what I was afraid of. Bomb schematics are not a 'need-to-know' for a shuttle commander."

Cutter wanders back to the bomb and examines its exposed wiring. The timer reads 00:43:19 and counting. Nothing about it gives her any clue which wire will shut it down and which won't.

"Did she have a remote on her?" he asks.

Shit! "Didn't think to look."

"Don't beat yourself up," he answers. "It's probably just as well. The bomb is pretty sophisticated. Wouldn't be surprised if it was rigged to go off if anybody tried to unlock the helm."

She fingers the yellow wire. "I hate playing Russian roulette with three of the four chambers loaded."

"We won't be playing that until we're down to two seconds."

Kees goes back to searching menus. Next to him, the bot's head seems almost to be mocking his efforts. Something about the tableau sparks in Cutter's mind and as she stares— epiphany!

"A shuttle commander may not need to know, but somebody else here sure does," she says.

It only takes him a second before he figures out her meaning. "Can we ask her?"

Cutter hooks up a cable from the shuttle's computer to the access port hidden behind the bot's left ear. The opening of the droid's eyes is unsettling, made even more surreal when she turns them to focus on Kees first and then Cutter.

"You think she knows us?" Kees asks.

Without a sound, the bot's lips form the word, "yes."

"That was weird." Cutter attacks the keyboard to no avail.

"Her voice box was below the cut line?"

"Apparently so."

"Can you access her database through the keyboard?"

"Doesn't seem so." She tries several combinations of keystrokes. "Where's the main menu?" she mutters in frustration. The data onscreen immediately shifts to the bot's main menu. Cutter looks the bot in the eye.

"Scroll."

Nothing.

"Scroll down."

And it does.

"Stop."

The scrolling pauses. It takes a few minutes for Cutter to master the verbal commands for "highlight" and "select," and after that the whole structure is laid bare.

"That's a lot of sexual techniques."

"Yes it is," Kees answers.

"Find," she says, "bomb schematic." It's a complicated diagram, and while the engineers who designed it may have been good with wires and circuits, they had no skill with text at all. What should take two minutes consumes ten.

"Blue wire?" she asks finally.

"Blue wire."

"You or me?"

"You do it," he says.

She sorts through her multi-tool for the wire cutter, addresses the bomb and snips the blue wire.

CHAPTER SEVENTEEN

Hagar shakes her head, staring at the headstone of Captain Edward Timms, III. Of course no body lies beneath it. The *ARC*'s captain abandoned ship more than a month ago.

It had been the Fellowship's idea to commemorate his mock interment; more correctly, it was Mayer's idea. It was to be, in his words, "a chance to unify the ARCans, rather than divide us." For all the false ring, nearly every Society member decided to accept the one-day truce and attend.

Hagar had worked next to several of those people in the livestock pens and was honestly happy to see them again. When she "crossed the line" and stood amidst the Fellowship, there were a few who reciprocated and infiltrated the Society's ranks. For a few moments, unity seemed tantalizingly within reach.

But the speeches, one after the other, cast a pall. Finally Mayer stepped up to the makeshift podium and drew back the shroud that had covered the headstone. Chiseled into the limestone is the captain's epitaph: "Here should lie Edward Timms III, captain of the ill-fated vessel, *ARC*. Derelict in his duties throughout, on May 11th, 2116 he abandoned ship, taking with him the only vehicle capable of . . ." and on and on.

The nearby Fellowship members applauded, smiled, and joked. *"Serves him right. What a loser,"* and *'never should have . . ."* exchanged between the self-righteous folk as they glanced toward Hagar for affirmation. She couldn't bring herself to smile or participate and the congenial mood just sort of evaporated. On both sides, the unifiers filtered back toward friendlier company so that each camp gradually purified itself—not with spleen but with disappointment.

"When he was born," Mayer intoned, "the honor of the Timms family skipped a generation." The crowd's laughter was one sided, as if a wire had become disconnected from one of the speakers in a stereophonic audio system. And so it continued: "His complicity in the installation of faulty materials is unquestioned."

The veracity of that statement is debatable. There will always be questions as to what degree Timms knew of and/or concealed the flaws in the J-26s. But Mayer's agenda lets him garnish the truth—sometimes tarnish the truth—sometimes obliterate the truth.

"And when there was one chance that our hopes might all be saved," Mayer thunders, "did our captain redeem himself?" He pauses for dramatic effect. "Did he honor the wishes of the Council?" He pauses again, and at this point a couple of Fellowship members answer "No!" Mayer carries on, the litany now established. "Did he respect the wisdom of our scientists?" A more robust "No!" comes from the right side of the crowd. "Did he put the ship's welfare before his own ego?" And the Fellowship cries out their answer in unison.

He interrupts the boisterous chorus. "No, he did not. He indulged his own ego . . ."

Several Society members have had enough. They drift away as Mayer continues to whip up the fervor of the crowd. Hagar stands her ground and listens.

"This so-called captain usurped the one privilege every man aboard this ship coveted. He took to himself the role we all had dreamt of from the start. He stole from us the promise made to every single ARCan the day we signed on for this momentous undertaking. . ."

By this point, Hagar and Solange are nearly alone.

". . . He sired the *ARC*'s only child!" The passion of the Fellowship is frightening. All their disappointment, all their resentment, all their hatred of Timms swells into the roar of boos and cat calls. "And was the fruit of his seed our salvation as promised?" This is answered with a storm of vitriol from the crowd. "If ever a man deserved the shame we heap upon him this day, it is . . ." Fists pumped in the air, violent gestures and bitter, triumphant dances animate the rhythmic calls of "Edward Timms," "Captain Timms," and "Timms."

Only four people know the real story of Hagar's impregnation: Hagar, Solange, Dr. Emil and the last surviving orderly who was on duty that day. Ishmael never learned what happened in that procedure room, nor did anyone else. Every last witness to that dark day honored their oath—took to his or her grave the secret that must never be told.

Finally, Solange and Hagar stand alone on the Society side of the hall. Mayer looks over, triumphant. How many times have his public speaking skills misdirected public anger away from himself and onto someone else? How many times has he salvaged his power after some misdeed? For a long time his target was the "pirates." After that lost its effectiveness, he focused on the Society—"a threat to our way of life."

But with the Society luring so many of his followers, he needs to change scapegoats. He shifts the focus of his demonization toward Timms—and by association, toward Ishmael. His aim is to "visit the iniquities of the father upon the son," and sell that proposition to the Fellowship as hard as he can. The roar of his success thunders on and on.

"Is hatred the only emotion they respond to?" Hagar asks as they make their way into the forest.

"It is the easiest to arouse," Solange answers. "And if Mayer succeeds with it over and over, why should he change?" They walk on in silence, each deep in thought.

#

There's no joy in Ishmael's smile as the sun sets over the graveyard. "Looks like you get your wish after all," he says to his father's headstone.

Whether that prediction is true or not depends on the outcome of voting for a new captain. Word came this morning that the Council has set Tuesday as election day.

Mayer and Kline had declared Ishmael's election as Council president invalid, of course. In the T.O.E.E. since that day, as long as Timms was aboard there was no need for elections—the status quo was the status quo. With the captaincy vacant, there's a power vacuum. To be truthful, with Edward Timms as captain there was always a power vacuum, albeit one that admirably served the Fellowship's purposes. During Timms' twenty-five years he never exercised his veto over a single Council proposition.

Now the Fellowship desperately needs to elect Mayer captain—for life. This is their one and only chance to stave off the Society's growing power and influence.

The mechanics of the transfer of authority are described in the Charter's small print. If the captain dies without naming his successor, there is to be a general election.

"So if I'm elected," Ishmael says to the headstone, "you get a little Timms to carry on the family honor. Probably not the way you would have wished it though, eh?"

Maybe not the way I would wish it myself—eh?

"You're dead and gone and you're still doing this to me, you . . ." His mind trolls the darkest parts of his vocabulary in search of the proper epithet, "you mother-fucker!"

And that one seems oddly liberating.

Raiff used to tell a story whose moral had something to do with being careful what you wish for. After a while neither he nor Ishmael could recall the details but the punch line stuck. Proper delivery requires a saucy southern drawl.

"You may git it, but you ain't gonna like it."

#

"It's going to be David against Goliath," Hagar says.

Solange smiles. "David did win that one."

"David had stones."

"And Mayer doesn't."

Karl and Clarisse join in the welcome laughter. The've been circled up onstage of the forest's natural amphitheater for over an hour, grinding away at one idea after another. The Society can't afford to be complacent about even the smallest detail of the election. Thus today's quartet has been tasked with developing a strategy to win the debate—the one and only debate—scheduled for election eve.

"Back to the first question," Hagar says as the laughter dies down. "How do we help him get ready?"

"Well, a mock debate for sure," Clarisse says.

Solange asks, "We talked about Jean-Marq playing Mayer. Is that still the consensus?" Nods around. "You'll ask him, Karl?"

"I will."

#

Jean-Marq stands behind one of the two mock-up podiums and explains to Ishmael and the others: "Mayer will use phrases like 'unifying the ARCans.' Actually, the opposite is true. He gets elected by holding the Fellowship in an iron fist and then splintering off just a few from our side to swing the vote. That said, the word 'unifying' evokes a desired response and so he will wrap himself in that cloak and accuse you of dividing us."

"But he's lying," Ishmael answers.

"In a debate format, calling your opponent a liar evokes an undesirable response from the audience. It is an error he hopes you will commit."

Karl gets up, paces angrily. "So Mayer can lie with impunity."

253

"It is not whether the statement is true or false," Jean-Marq answers. "The only test is about credibility. If the people Mayer is trying to sway will believe it, then he will say it—probably several times over."

"What if there are facts that disprove it?"

"His method of dealing with that is coldly scientific. He will have determined long before the debate begins which of your facts he should refute and which he will ignore."

"So I don't have a chance."

"He offered to debate because it plays to his strengths."

Karl asks, "Can we beat them at their own game?"

"Do we want to?" Hagar asks.

Jean-Marq mulls that over for a moment. "No, and no." He turns to Ishmael, sympathetically. "When Mayer was your age, he was better at this than you are today and he has honed those skills every year since. If you try to follow the principles by which he will play the game, you are sure to lose." He turns to Hagar. "Fortunately, it is a game and not a science. There are risks in slavish adherence to a fixed set of propaganda principles."

"Can we use that?" she asks.

"Perhaps not directly but the attrition from their ranks, myself included, is a sign that they are near the threshold of effectiveness. A campaigner becomes vulnerable when the message is repeated too often."

"In concrete terms?" Karl asks.

"It is hard to say. One of the principles they're working under goes something like, 'propaganda to the home front must create an optimum anxiety level,' and they have . . ."

Hagar interrupts, "Optimum level? As in, heighten anxiety within the Fellowship?"

"Exactly. It is imperative that Mayer stokes his followers' fears. Losing the election to Ishmael must be portrayed as the death of all that is dear to them. Mayer is already being forced to play that tune over and over. The risk is that the Fellowship is weary of hearing it. I know I am."

"So what is Ishmael's strategy to capitalize on that?" Karl asks.

"When I envision a world that embraces our message, embraces the Society's philosophy," Jean-Marq answers, "I feel a sense of peace. Insofar as Ishmael is able to personify that peaceful vision, Mayer cannot beat him."

"So all the while I'm fighting off Mayer's attacks I have to somehow embody everything the Society believes in?" Ishmael scans the hopeful faces. "Are you sure there isn't somebody else who should do this?"

"It has to be you," Karl says. "You're one of a kind."

"And I've got three days?"

Hagar smiles. "That's right."

#

Solange always seems happy to see him, perhaps more this evening than other times. She tosses her handful of weeds into the wheelbarrow and brushes the loose dirt off her clothes. "Ishmael," she asks with impish delight, "How is it going?"

"OK, I guess."

"Just OK?"

"I don't know how good Mayer's going to be but if the voting was based on the practice debates, Jean-Marq would be our next captain."

She lays a hand on his arm. "How are you doing?"

"Just waiting for somebody to turn on a light here."

Something about that amuses her. "Me?"

"Ah . . ?" he knows there's something he's missing and can't quite put a finger on what it is. "I guess. They gave me the rest of the day off and Mom said she wanted me to talk to you."

She skips off down the forest path. "How delightful!"

"You're," he seeks the right word, "'spunky' today."

"And is spunky a good thing?"

"I guess."

She wanders off the path for a closer look at a plant. "You see this? This is an ARCan plant." She plucks a few leaves to show him.

"You mean it's not from a seed we brought with us?"

She crushes a leaf between her fingers and holds it under his nose. "You like the smell?"

He wrinkles his nose, then sniffs again. "Kind of grows on you."

She smiles. "It makes an interesting salve." She crushes a few more leaves and inhales deeply.

"So, it's like a mutant or something?"

"That word . . . well I guess it is a mutation, but 'mutant' always seems like, dark or evil. This is a wonderfully useful plant and it's unique—unique to this ship, to this world." She takes another deep breath, throws the crushed leaves away and then sucks the residue off her fingers.

"Like me?" he asks.

"Yes, I do," she answers with a mischievous smile. "I have nets to tend. Will you help me?"

"Sure."

The ground underfoot turns sandy and the surf is louder with each step. They crest the shoulder of the low dune and before them lies the sea. The serrated swath of the moon's reflection invites them closer.

Solange takes in the moonlit sea. She turns, her pupils dilated in the low light. Never before would Ishmael have allowed himself these kinds of feelings toward her but . . .

"We have fish to bring in," she says, breaking the moment.

"How can I help?"

She strips off her clothes and wades into the surf, points to the buoy on her left. "You can close the far end of the net." She dives in and swims with powerful strokes toward the buoy on the right.

He undresses and wades in, relieved to be more than waist deep before she turns back.

Once the mouth of the net is closed, the fish are "herded" toward a cul-de-sac where they can be netted with a long-handled seine. The process takes time.

"Did Mom send me here because you're supposed to help me with the debating?" he asks.

"Do you think catching fish will help with the debate?"

"I guess not." The net brushes against him under the water, reminding him of his arousal. "I'm supposed to figure out what Jean-Marq is scheming. I need to remember that not everybody has some sub-plot they're working."

"We can talk about the debate if you want to." She stops with the nets, looks him square in the face, now quite close. "I want to do whatever I can to help you be ready."

He knows she's treading water and can't stop the little boy in him wishing he was a submarine, watching her legs and . . . His skin flushes hot and it occurs to him that he will have to come out of the water sometime.

She closes off her leg of the net and breaststrokes toward shore. "I'll get the seine." He watches her every step of the way— out of the water—up to the post from which the net hangs—back to the water's edge—and then swimming out to him. She has a puzzled expression as she approaches. He quickly closes off his leg of the net.

"It's easiest if we work them toward shallow water."

Shallow water—where I will be found out.

There are several good-sized fish in the net and as their space is constricted, they begin to thrash, bumping into him. She on one side and he on the other, they move toward shore, lifting the net between them. "We can stand here," she says.

Her breasts have his full attention in the ebb and flow of the waves. "You net 'em and I'll string 'em?"

He takes the handle of the seine as she uncoils the stringer. Holding up his side of the net with one hand, he manages to net the first fish. She deftly snares it, runs the stringer through its gills and out its mouth and threads the rigid aguille through the loop to hold the fish in place. When she looks up, he has another ready and waiting. She threads it through—repeats the process for all seven fish. She looks from the empty net to her partner as the foamy surf rises and falls from about waist high to knee high.

"Oh."

And so his secret is out.

She looks at it for a moment, then down at her own naked body in the surf.

She smiles, almost laughs—which only makes the situation more extreme. And yet more pointed as she stares at his body awash in swirling sea foam. "I never realized how attractive that could be."

She breaks herself from her reverie. "I'm sorry. I'm afraid I've embarrassed you."

"A little."

"You could reset the nets while I take these ashore." She turns away with the stringer of fish in tow and he gladly heads for deeper water to replace the buoys and open the mouth of the net.

Solange bones a fish at a rustic outdoor table. A sturdy apron protects her clothes. Her bloody hands work quickly and efficiently.

Ishmael, now clothed, watches over her shoulder at a respectful distance. "I, I'm sorry about before."

She looks up from her work with a smile. "Actually, it's kind of flattering."

"I just mean, well you're my mother's friend and everything."

"You're not Hagar's little boy any more."

"I didn't want you to think that ..."

"Ishmael!" she barks. Then more softly, "It's OK. You didn't do anything wrong."

He can't think how to respond to that, and wisely shuts up.

"Do you know how to filet fish?" she asks.

He looks at her handiwork. "Not like that."

"If you like, I'll show you. We can talk at the same time. Come closer."

He moves in, careful not to brush against her.

She holds the already-gutted fish's tail with her left hand and slides the curved boning knife along first one side of the dorsal fin, then the other. "I'm so happy you're doing this."

"Learning to filet fish?"

"Well, that's nice too, but no. We need to wrest control from those people and I'm not sure we could do it without you."

"I just hope we can do it with me. I do have some strikes against me."

"But your heart is so in the right place."

"I'm getting there."

"You do realize how unusual that is."

"For men to get somewhere?"

She laughs. "No, for a man to admit that he has somewhere to get."

"Not sure that's a purely male shortcoming."

"Fair enough."

The fish almost slithers from the bloody table as she turns it over. "Oops".

"Slippery little devil," he jibes.

She gets it under control again. "It's the blood."

Ishmael watches a few seconds, pensive. "It's interesting to me that the Society is kind of a matriarchy and the Council, you know, father and Mayer and Kline have always forced such a patriarchal stamp on the Fellowship."

"How interesting?"

"Well, nobody is going to be a 'patriarch' in the sense of siring offspring but the way they . . ."

"Mayer and Kline and the rest of the Council can't thrust their will on their family lives and so they project those frustrations onto their political dealings."

"Father too?"

"Frustrated? Oh heavens."

"Because he was impotent."

She almost cuts herself laughing. "You never said the word 'impotent' to your father, did you?"

Ishmael checks himself, mentally. "Uh, no. I guess I never did."

"Neither did he, I promise you. There was nothing wrong with his semen—all you had to do was ask him."

"He thought it was your fault?"

"I think he found me physically attractive, but sex was all about creating little Timmses to carry on the family name. He was driven to *prodigious* efforts to get me pregnant."

Ishmael changes the subject to hide his discomfort. "Are we going to filet them all?"

"Yes. We'll eat a couple fresh tonight and then hang the rest to dry in the smokehouse."

"I'm still not sure about boning, but I think I can gut those over there if that will help?"

"Yes please."

He ties on an apron. Standing here with the surf murmuring gently in the background, his hands busy with a task whose goal is perfectly clear, whose outcome is completely obtainable, he feels the stress of the last few days lift off him like a child's balloon floating away. He guts another fish before picking up the conversation thread. "Why did you do it?"

"Do what?"

"Agree to go along in the first place."

"Earth wasn't a nice place to be and it wasn't going to get any better."

"Your mom and dad were still alive though, right?"

"Oh yes."

"And you left them?"

"Their prospects were much better with me not there."

"Weren't they sad?"

"Actually no. I mean, they were sad I was going away but they bought into the whole 'grand adventure' thing. They thought it was a great opportunity for me."

"And it didn't bother them that you were, you know . . ."

"Consort to the ship's captain? I downplayed that." She pauses a moment. "There was an annuity attached to my signing."

"An annuity for them?"

"Quarterly disbursements for life."

She attends to her work as the boning knife slides into the dorsal incision and then along the fish's ribcage, taking all the flesh and none of the bony ribs. "I did it because I wanted to have babies." Her lip quivers a moment, then she regains some composure. Her hands lay down the knife, flip the slippery fish over, then return to their task on the fish's left flank. "It wasn't a selfless act to save my parents, it was greed. I wanted love. Oh, I knew better than to hope for any from Edward. From the start I saw his failings. But every line of the contract, every handshake, every verbal agreement promised that I would be a mother."

"That's our story, isn't it?"

"Yes, that's our story," she answers.

"How mankind, humanity—what we won't do for love. That and the tragedy of promised love being snatched away."

She lays down the knife and turns to him, face-to-face and very close. "Not just the tragedy of love snatched away, but how some of us rose up from the ashes and found love after all."

Me?

"I hoped my children would grow up to be lovers," she continues. "Beautiful people, able to love and worthy of being loved. That was to be the fulfillment of my life."

She steps into him, only momentarily startled by the protrusion in his apron. She looks down—and back into his eyes. "The fish will spoil if they're not cleaned now."

It's almost like film speeded up, the pace at which their hands apply themselves to the task. The slabs that come off Ishmael's knife look more flayed than fileted—a certain rough-hewn jaggedness to their edges. As the last skeleton and head drop into the discard bucket, Solange arranges the filets across her arm and covers the short distance to the smokehouse.

She opens the door to a minimal waft of smoke, deftly drapes the fish pieces across the rails, adds five small wood chunks to the smoker in the corner, and makes the door fast shut.

They face each other, breathless in their blood-spattered, scale-flecked aprons. She hefts the bucket. "Soap is over there."

He follows, more eager than obedient. "What do we do with the heads?"

"Return them to the sea. We have done the small fish a favor

261

and perhaps they will swell all the quicker for their easy repast." She points him left and goes to the right a ways before swilling the bucket.

He stands in the shallows. His wet clothes and apron balloon as a wave comes in and then suck up tight against him when it ebbs. She comes up very close, takes the bar of soap and lathers his apron. She hands him the soap and he reciprocates.

They suds each other's apron and touch each other's body and which of those two is superfluous is up for discussion.

Not that they intend to discuss much.

Waist ties are undone, neck straps thrown overhead. The aprons are discarded in the surf.

"Won't the current take those away?" he asks.

Her look is pure, *you must think I care.* She dives her head in an oncoming wave, takes the soap from him and washes her face. He follows her lead. Tears stream from soapy eyes too soon opened.

They kiss—a salty, soapy, slippery thing.

Lest their fervor truncate a moment to be savored, she pulls back a step and soaps her tunic slowly and sensuously. He takes the bar and mimics her action—and her pace. She steps in close, eases her hands up under his shirt and slides them across his chest and shoulders. The mutual attention to each other's forequarters gently morphs into a loving embrace and what must surely be the cleanest backs aboard the *ARC.*

And patience takes turns with impatience as the lovers discover each other's cadence.

An hour later, they lie atop the aprons, spent, he on his back and she draped over one side, her head on his chest.

So many ideas, so many feelings. *She seemed so comfortable with it, so ready. And mother told me to come see her. Was this a last supper given to a condemned man on the eve of his execution? It didn't feel like she was doing me a favor. But if not that, then why?* It's an idiot who voices that question to his lover, but . . .

"Why?"

He feels her cheek muscles form a smile. "There is nothing a woman will not do for the man she has chosen to be father of her child."

"But there will be no children aboard this ship."

"Not of the sort we thought there would be."

"There is another sort of child?"

"There is." She draws herself up onto him, face to face.

"And I am to father this child?"

"Yes, you are." She kisses him gently.

Ishmael's grin is a little wrinkled with puzzlement. "And is this how we shall create that child?"

"No. We can only bring our child to life if we prevent the Fellowship from smothering her. For that to be, you must wrest the mantle of patriarch from Phillip Mayer."

"And this?" Ishmael asks, easing his hand gently down the small of her back.

"This," she kisses him again, less gently, "is how we reward ourselves for laboring together."

#

This time the two podiums are real—Ishmael is behind one, Mayer the other. The entire ship's company is on hand, seventy souls in all.

Mayer leans in to the Fellowship side of the audience. "The people of Earth entrusted us not just with the task of colonizing a distant land, but with carrying our heritage, our culture to the rest of the universe."

Ishmael holds his peace while the murmurs of assent and approval voice themselves in a certain part of the audience. When the room falls silent, he speaks.

"I am the only non-Terran on board. While I respect your reverence for all that Earth accomplished, I suggest that we have the potential to build on that foundation and then go one step further—one giant leap further."

"How touching, he quotes Neil Armstrong," Mayer interjects.

Ishmael turns to him. "And who do you quote, mister Mayer? Who is your hero? History doesn't quote those who fought for the

263

status quo." He lets that sink in. "In fact, has there ever been praise or reverence for a culture of stagnation? Has there ever been any respect for a society that looked only backward?"

He looks out at the faces in the crowd, trying to connect with those on the Fellowship side. "Because if we continue following the Council's current philosophy, we will be that 'do-nothing' society. And there will be no praise for us; no reverence, no respect. When this ship is found, some number of years or centuries from now, we, the people, will be forgotten because we allowed ourselves to be forgettable."

Mayer claps in mock appreciation. A few Fellowship members join in, but then gradually more and more Society members begin actual applause.

Ishmael lets the moment breathe a little, then raises a hand for attention. "We have the greatest story ever told—one of proud folk who, after facing devastation, did not lie down and die. We did not drown in the sea of our own tears. Instead we committed to telling our story, sharing what we discovered: that love is sufficient unto itself, that beauty is a thing to strive for every single day of one's life—that truth and honesty are our shield against a world of lies and deceptions."

He faces his opponent. "We're all going to die. And unless something beyond our power occurs, we're all going to die here, on this ship. But we can make our lives into a testament to what we believe. We don't have to be a mirror of Earth culture—we can be the beacon of ARCan culture. When the ARCans realized Eden was unreachable, we created it here instead."

CHAPTER EIGHTEEN

Most people thought the election would be closer. Some in the Fellowship actually believed Mayer would win.

Instead, Mayer and Kline were rewarded with their first days out of public office since they boarded. One of the old Council members, the most moderate one, retained his seat. Other than that, it was a clean sweep for the Society. Thus began what some of the more irreverent ARCans dubbed *Pax ARCannus.*

Almost immediately upon taking office, Ishmael realized how extensive and efficient were Timms' efforts to erase the ships log. There were almost no entries that had not been "reconstructed." Rather than try to repopulate the official log, the Repository was named the official ARCan historical record. A certain excitement arose at the prospect of gathering anecdotes and capturing recollections *sans* the obstructionism of the previous administration. Gradually more and more ARCans embraced the vision of their lives as narrative. There was laughter sometimes and there were tears—many times—as the pieces were put back together and the gaps filled in.

How they had hoped.

How desperately low those hopes had sunk.

How sad so many could not find the grit to carry on.

They discovered things about each other they had never known before.

Delighted in those things. Fell in love over them.

Some made love thanks to them.

#

"What about these?" Clarisse asks as she scrolls through video files in the Repository's editing room.

Doug comes over to take a look. "What are they?"

"I think these are the archives from Geek of the Week."

He watches over her shoulder as she scrolls the titles. The cursor highlights a file labeled "Clarisse" and after a second the video starts. On screen, a scrawny young man in a white lab coat puts a blindfold on a much younger Clarisse.

"Is that Raiff?" Doug asks.

"Yep. Was he really that skinny?" Clarisse asks.

Raiff sets up the scenario, a comedic take on testing Clarisse's sense of smell. He holds one sample after another under Clarisse's nose and she identifies "leather" and "coal" and a half-dozen other items.

The other Repository workers take an interest and gather around to watch. The punch line, the "hook" of the scene approaches. Raiff mugs the camera and holds up a uniform shirt, the name Clarisse stitched just above the pocket. He holds it under her nose. "I don't know," she says onscreen, "it smells like shit."

Of all those watching the monitor, Clarisse is the only one to chuckle as the onscreen Raiff takes off the blindfold and shows the young Clarisse her own shirt.

"That's funny?" Doug asks.

"I just remembered what comes next."

Onscreen, Raiff rollicks and cavorts, taunts Clarisse with the shirt until she corners him and bloodies his nose with a short left.

"You know what that smell is, asshole?" she intones. "That's blood." She stalks off-camera.

"Were we really that cruel?" one of the onlookers, a short redhead, asks.

"How many of those are there?" someone else says.

Clarisse scrolls to the bottom of the list. "Couple hundred, maybe two-fifty?"

"We should delete those," the redhead suggests.

"Why, because we don't like that part of the story? We don't get to have it both ways. This is what we were and that's the kind of shit we did to each other."

The suggestion to delete the files never gets anywhere. If the ARCan story is one of before versus after, then these were the perfect "before" tableaus. The task of tagging and cataloguing the files is shared by a handful of "Repositorians" and after a few days a lively discussion springs up.

What were the young geek-blasters seeking out, if not a fellow ARCan who was passionate about something, an enthusiast or a hobbyist? The more intense the "geek," the easier he or she was to ridicule. As the Repositorians watch clip after clip, they find themselves drawn to the geeks and pitying the sad geek-blasters who had nothing better to do than to suck the lifeblood out of the living.

The clips bring into sharp relief the fact that not only is every modern ARCan a geek, they pride themselves on their geekiness. The notion of reinstating Geek of the Week gets enthusiastic support—not the cruel entertainment of their younger days, but a "kinder, gentler" Geek of the Week.

Some of the old Archive clips, the best ones, were very funny. And so it is with the best of the new submissions. The weekly "club" meetings are well attended and the attendees have a good laugh together. The award almost invariably goes to the clip at which the Geek himself laughs the hardest.

#

As time passes, a few in the Society choose to move back into town. Some Fellowshippers opt for the mountains. All the barriers and border crossings are dismantled. Riot gear is put in long-term storage, force fields are shut down and weapons mothballed. For most, there is a new joy in awaking, for there is a purpose in the activities of the day.

Which is not to say the joy is unmitigated. Despite efforts to the contrary, the common cold managed to stow away when the great ship left Earth orbit. A few other diseases made the voyage as well and as the ARCans age, some of those gain potency. Death is never far away, her hand readily offered to any as they feel their time approach.

It is a particularly sad day when Emil Sanzari dies. He was a warm, gentle man—funny at some of the oddest times. He was also the last surviving ARCan with medical training. As such, he was prescient of his own ill health. He groomed Solange and another woman to take his place as "medicine man." In the last days Hagar moves in with him, not because she can cure him, only so he does not die alone.

And then one day, the lights flicker.

Not a big thing—a lot like the little dip a few of them had experienced on Earth in a lightning storm. But until now—well, the lightning storms built into the *ARC*'s ecology always occur under controlled circumstances and never interrupt the flow of power. In fact, the power is always recaptured. The ship's engineers investigate but the sense of urgency arrives full-blown when it happens a second time, this time for several minutes.

The problem, it turns out, is the coupling at the far end of the scaffolding, just where the cable feeds into the J-26. It is Hagar who suggests that they charge the weapon. Not that she intends firing it, but the capacitor is large and if the connection fails completely, the ship's atmosphere can be maintained for several days on the energy stored there. And so prescience of a different kind saves the day for them all. Within hours of fully charging the capacitor, the connection to the J-26 fails completely.

A few hand-lanterns splay their light, torchière-like, against the ceiling as the entire ships company meets to decide what to do.

"Isn't it enough," Mayer intones angrily, "that the leaky J-twenty-sixes killed our dream? Now the damned thing is going to kill us for real."

"There's still juice," Hagar offers from where Solange has wheeled her in. "It's the coupling. If we can repair it we can still use the power."

"But it's at the end of the scaffold," Clarisse says.

"Yes," Hagar answers, "someone will have to go EV."

"Isn't it radioactive?" Solange asks.

Everyone knows it is. It's Karl who breaks the silence. "I'll go do it."

"Do you know how to fix it?" Mayer asks.

"If Hagar can explain it to me, I can."

It's thirty years since anyone has been outside. The old suits are unfit. Karl gives his best imitation of "no fear" as he locks the helmet onto the newly stitched pressure suit.

"You have less than an hour total," Hagar explains. "That should be enough, as long as there aren't any surprises."

He steps into the pressure lock and seals the hatch behind him. Anxious moments pass as the lock is decompressed. Karl reads the gauge inside his suit, gives a thumbs-up and opens the hatch to space.

He has a small propeller for maneuvering, but covering the distance to and from will be done the old-fashioned way. He attaches one end of the coiled tether to an O-ring near the hatch, gets his bearings, and then crouches on the hull as best he can in the bulky suit. He turns off the magnetism in his boots and thrusts with his legs.

His aim is good. A light touch on the propeller somewhere around halfway there corrects his flight path and he arrives with the tether snaking idly behind him. He gathers in a half-meter of the slack and then, when the line comes taut, bleeds the slack through his gloved hand to gradually eliminate momentum. "Just like I knew what I was doing," he mutters quietly as he comes to a stop. He keys his mic. "Hagar?"

"Yes, Karl."

"OK. I'm taking the cover off." A moment of silence. "Agh!"

"What is it, Karl?"

"It broke."

"The cover?"

"Yeah. It just crumbled in my hand."

"You didn't cut yourself?"

"No. I don't think so. Not sure this stuff has the integrity to make a sharp edge."

"What's it look like inside?" she asks.

"Hang on. OK. Looks just like the mock-up you made. I'm going to go ahead and throw the switch."

"Roger that."

"Damn." A pause. "OK. The connector opens and then closes again. I assume if you had lights down there you'd let me know."

"Sorry Karl, no lights."

"It's gotta be the one inside." That conclusion is Karl's death knell. Getting to the inside connection requires removing a small panel in the J-26's shielding. Within minutes he will receive a lethal dose of radiation. But he knew that coming out here. "I'm taking the panel off now."

There's nothing those aboard ship can answer.

"Oh yeah, this is the problem."

And after another few seconds, "Shit."

"Karl?"

"It's female."

The final insult.

Karl thinks back to the day he and Hagar pored over the wiring diagram. Hagar stabbed her finger at exactly the spot he's looking at now. *"Only an idiot would put a male connector in there!"* Yet there it was, the graphic representation of a male connection, when any competent electrical engineer would have used a female. The discussion that followed was about who screwed up, the guy who wired the box or the dude who documented it?

Hanging from Karl's belt is a male-to-female cable. He needs a male-to-male. "What do you want me to do?"

"If you plug in the male end, can you close the shielding panel?"

"Give me a second." A pause. "Affirmative."

"Is there a gap between the two females? If so, eyeball that for me."

"About a foot. What is that, thirty centimeters? Maybe a little more—thirty-five? Thirty-eight?"

"Is any part of the old cable sound?"

"Negative."

There is a sad resignation in Hagar's voice, "You can come back in, Karl."

"Let me wrap a couple things up here." He knows the score. Somebody on board will have to fashion a male-to-male adapter. That's why she asked him to eyeball the gap—so they know how long to make it. Then someone will have to come out and make the connection. With the male end of the cable plugged into the J-26 and with the cover closed, whoever makes the next EVA won't die of radiation poisoning. Sick yes, dead no.

He is already feeling nausea and light-headedness. He focuses on his situation. "Hagar?"

"Yes, Karl."

"With the panel bolted down tight the cable is probably too rigid to get the adapter in there. Whoever comes out needs to be able to loosen the cover—should be just a little, a few seconds maybe. You know, just so they bring the right tools."

"Roger that, Karl."

"I'm going to tie off the tether on the scaffold strut here. Should make a good zip line."

"You'll come back in on the zip line?"

"I don't think so."

Tears stream down Hagar's face.

Quietus...

...so much nicer a word than suicide. The ARCans over time have come to favor that word to describe their fellow travelers' choice to quit the journey. This will probably be the last words they share. "Anything we can do for you, Karl?"

"I'd like a stone."

"We can do that."

"OK. Nothin' fancy."

"Ceremony?"

"A few words would be nice."

"Done. We love you, Karl."

"Thanks. Appreciate that. I think I'm about ready here. Yeah, thirty-five centimeters."

He unfastens his belt, gives one last look at the connector and pushes back, so he won't be in the way. He turns off the circulator in his suit. "OK. Bye."

#

Ishmael sits at Hagar's bedside in the near-darkness, holding her hand. There is plenty of power to light the room brightly but that is not Hagar's choice.

"Ishmael?"

"Yes, Mother."

"You've had them recharge the capacitor?"

"Yes. It accepted the full charge."

"That's good. I think the repair will hold but it will be good to have the backup."

"I agree."

She lets the time pass without comment, then, "I'm a little cool."

"You're very cool, Mother," he banters as he pulls another light coverlet over her.

She smiles and again allows the mood to occupy the moment. "I'm proud of the man you've become, Ishmael."

"I'm sorry I was so long getting started."

"I never doubted you."

"I certainly gave you reason to."

"Yes, a few times you did." She swallows hard, then retches, though nothing comes up. His lip quivers and he wipes his eyes. She swallows a few times until the nausea abates. "I think it won't be long."

"You know better than I."

She lies still a moment, then props herself on one elbow. "There is something I would like."

"Tell me and it will be done," he replies.

"Will you take me on a ship's tour? I can't see, but you could describe her to me. I would like to visit her one more time."

"When would you like to do that?"

"Now, I think. I'm not going to get any stronger."

"Just the two of us?"

"Solange, if she's willing."

"I'll get her and be right back."

Hagar is bundled up in the chair. Solange pushes while Ishmael walks a little ahead and to the right.

"Ah, the stables," Hagar exclaims. "After all these years you can still smell the livestock."

"You got me to milk my first cow here," Solange says.

"And it was because of them that we went to the Council," Hagar recalls. "Do you think, Ishmael, that there will ever be cows and horses and pigs again?"

"If it were mine to do, I would. Where next?"

"The Great Hall?" Hagar asks.

The trio wanders the Great Hall. "Would you describe it, Ishmael?"

"About half the tables are set—the good stuff. I suppose it will be dusty after a while but we will try to make it sparkle before we . . . before we go."

"That's good," Hagar answers. They roll out the main entrance, Hagar invigorated by the recollections. "I wonder what he'll be like?"

"The one who finds it?" Solange asks.

"Yes. Will he even be human?"

"Does it matter?" Ishmael offers.

"I suppose it doesn't. The story is different, of course, if we're an alien society—alien to him, at least."

"The players are different," Solange says. "Perhaps the story stays the same."

"We can only hope," Hagar says.

They discuss whether or not Ishmael can carry Hagar into the mountains. Much as Hagar would like to visit the Repository, they decide against the arduous trek. Hagar asks to linger at the seashore, listens to the waves roll in. If she had her vision, she would certainly pick up on the chemistry between her dear, lifelong friend and her son. Even without eyesight, she does. "I am happy for the two of you."

They return to the Heights and stop one last time in what used to be the captain's quarters. So many emotions, so much history. But as the tour comes nearly full circle, Hagar whispers, "I'm tired."

"We'll take you back," Ishmael suggests.

"That would be nice. Thank you. I would not have wanted to leave without one last look at her."

"She's beautiful," Solange says, "and if we succeed, whoever comes upon her will be seduced."

Hagar has a more serious coughing fit on the way back, one with a good deal of blood spit up. They ease her back into her bunk and the fit subsides. "I'm a woman twice blessed," she says quietly.

Ishmael, "Twice?"

"Many more than twice, of course, but blessed to have a son like you and doubly blessed to have a grandchild so pretty." She reaches out for Ishmael's hand and then on the other side for Solange's.

"You're a good kid."

Solange waits to catch Ishmael's tear-filled gaze, then mouths *and I love you.*

"Shame on me."

Kline stands before the assembled company and lets his words sink in. There were some in the crowd who were nervous about Kline's request to speak at Hagar's funeral. They settle in now, their anxiety abated, hopeful that he will rise to the occasion.

"Of all the things in my life I would do differently, my disrespect of Hagar is the one I would go back and correct. But that chance will never come. It's one of the things she knew that I never seemed to grasp. Every time you look back, you have to stop looking forward. Hagar always looked forward."

"She was a special woman," he continues. "We were all painfully aware of just how 'special' she was." He makes "air quotes" with his hands. "She had no 'right' to be here with us. She wasn't 'selected' like we were. She was special, all right. We just didn't realize how special. And so today, in order to have a clearer vision of what lies before us, let us take a few minutes..." he focuses on the casket, "with your indulgence—to look back at this special woman."

"This last act of her life epitomizes what she was throughout her life. Can we be surprised, in retrospect, that when faced with a task only she could accomplish, a task filled with the risk, nay, the near certainty of death, she stepped up and said, 'Send me'? She went out, this tiny woman so filled with capability, and did what needed doing. I can imagine—we all can imagine—the sight of her hands working smoothly, almost effortlessly, with the tools. With radiation pouring from the open cover next to her, she was calm and focused. You could hear it in her voice, in the steady application of that almost magical sense of how mechanical things work."

"And then the lights came on. And did the shout ring out around the ship? Well, there was joy. There was renewed hope. There was relief. And there was the sad realization that, if not today then some time this week, we would be here, performing this ritual. Hagar had saved us at the cost of her own life."

The audience nods and murmurs agreement.

"Shame on me," Kline repeats.

"I have had all these years of her example, and I failed to see it. Shame on my pride. This is not a day for humor, but look again at what she did. Some of you may not be aware, but there was an issue when she got out there. Some connector was not what she expected and it threatened to waste her EVA. And then she reached into her tool bag and brought out the one thing that would save us all." He pauses for both dramatic and comedic effect. "Duct tape."

There's a twitter of laughter in the house.

"There was no arrogance in this woman. Pride, yes; arrogance, no. We all know the old joke, 'What are the three things you'll never hear from a redneck?'" He pauses. "One of the three is, 'Duct tape probably won't get that.'"

Another chuckle rises from the crowd.

"How many of us, for fear of being ridiculed, would have left the duct tape on board? We are blessed to have had Hagar with us, not just to fix things but to show us how to live bravely."

He steps from behind the podium and engages more personally with those in front of him. "I hope that when they find this ship, the duct tape is still there. I hope that whoever finds us appreciates what that means—what that meant to us all.

"And that's the point, isn't it?

"Shame on me thrice over.

"It's about who we are. It's about what we did in the face of catastrophe. And I have stood in the way of that notion. I stood against that, ridiculed it, undermined it. And now, today, I am here to say that I am converted. I come late to the task and I'm not sure my skill set will be of any use, but I stand here today, committed to fulfilling Hagar's dream. She saved us, not once but twice—and for that she was despised, and rejected. I was part of that rejection and I renounce my old ways and promise, in memory of Hagar, to be stalwart in my support."

"If we live on in the memory of those who find our beloved *ARC*, it will be Hagar who gave us that life. This ship, the story of this ship, is all we have to hope for and I for one choose that hope. Thank you for allowing me to speak."

#

With the passage of time came the passage of friends. The ARCans were, after all, getting old. Kline was the last of the "oldsters," those who were beyond their mid-twenties when the ship left Earth's orbit. He made good on his promises right up to the last days. He completed his *pièce de résistance*, the massive model of ARC World, at age ninety-three, just a few months before he died.

As for the rest, they carried on as best they could, didn't complain much, and then passed away with however much dignity they could muster. If there were fewer ARCans to accomplish the tasks at hand, there were fewer tasks to be done.

Solange's hand shakes—not so much as to threaten spilling the tea, just enough to make its surface dance in the cup.

"The flower's gotta go," Ishmael offers.

Solange looks at it wistfully. "It was nice while it lasted." The power was nice while it lasted—the power to illuminate the small garden where she and Ishmael have grown herbs, spices and a few precious flowers. There's no sense in growing flowers—well, they do eat the nasturtiums—but somehow they haven't had the heart to turn under the one square meter of visual delight.

It's good that they're in love. Eleven months with no one else aboard could have gone by very slowly under other circumstances. Which is not to say they have spent the time gazing deeply into each other's eyes. Both are far too restlessly creative to curtail their other interests.

They do reserve for each other an hour in the afternoon for tea. Some days the time is spent in wistful reminiscing of friends. Other days it's filled with giddy scheming as they look ahead.

Much of their work lately has been positioning the clues to be left behind. Solange has not only a real passion, but also a gift for treasure-hunt scenarios. In her mind's eye she sees what will be Kees and Cutter's arrival, their seduction, and their final commitment to the ARCan dream. Her clues are at once heavy with meaning and yet playful and engaging.

"I'm ready," she says. "Even if we had time, I'm not sure what else I would do."

"I hope I am."

"Ready?"

"Hmm. So much rides on my doing my part," he muses.

"I would do it if I could."

"I know that—we both know it has to be me."

"You impetuous young boy."

"What have you planned for this evening?" he asks.

"You?"

"Again?" he teases.

She gives a coy smile and shrugs. The calendar says she's in her mid-seventies and the streaks of grey in her hair offer some validation. That said, after all these years she's still got it.

"OK," he says. "Sounds good to me."

"Maybe we could go up to the overlook?"

He is surprised at the sudden choke of emotion. It ambushes him every once in a while, especially in the last few months, as her condition has grown acute. One prepares for the inevitable but then when it's just around the corner, sometimes it has more power than expected. "Sure," he answers, in the most chipper tone he can muster.

If she picks up on his feelings, she doesn't let it show.

#

In the mind's eye, the stars stream by. Of course at the *ARC*'s snail's pace the starfield is unmoving—nearly the same as it was a year ago, and not much changed from what it was a decade ago. Yet, standing in the "penis" and looking back at "her majesty" plodding along behind, the brain convinces the eye that it is seeing movement.

"That's a lot of steel," she says.

"It is."

"Will the Finder see past it?"

"She has her charm." He puts an arm around her shoulder.

"Will it be enough?"

"It will or it won't. We've done everything we can."

She gazes at it a long moment. "Is this what it's like when you have to let them go?"

"Children?"

"Our baby—all grown up."

"And now Momma and Papa wonder if they've done a good enough job?" he asks.

She turns toward him. In the cramped space, their bodies touch in all the places that protrude. Her lips are warm and soft. She leans into him and whispers, "I don't wonder."

She is already in the bed when he returns from brushing his teeth. He takes off his shirt and trousers. Only then does he become aware that she is watching. Even after all these years he never fails to be aroused by her attention. A gentle smile as his boxers drop to the floor. She folds back the top sheet and comforter and sidles her naked body back to invite him next to her.

The bed is warm where she was lying and her body is warmer still. At this point they're no longer driven toward the inevitable goal. It will come when it's supposed to come. Whenever quickening of the pace is in order, they will come to tacit agreement about it and the quickening will seem natural, inevitable.

A hand slides gently down the back and along the curve of a hip. Fingers lace through hair. "Brush?" he asks. She shakes off the suggestion. Kisses flow gently one from another—some faster, some slower, some gently, some with more pressure. Caresses evolve into embraces and then revert. Bodies align, first one way, then another. Always attention is given to each other's pace and tempo. How long and how often to repeat a gesture—how soon to leave one activity for another? Invitations accepted, suggestions offered, propositions refused and/or embraced.

And in the end they sleep, spent, one into the other.

They both knew it was close. Neither could know it would be tonight but upon waking he looks over at his lover. She is deathly still.

And cold.

And gone.

And he's alone.

Finally, he's all alone.

CHAPTER NINETEEN

The timer shows eleven minutes and change when Cutter snips the blue wire and brings it to a halt. It is actually Kees who chuckles first. If this isn't the first time in his life that Kees has ever "chuckled," it can't be more than the third or fourth. Considering the preceding hour and thirty-seven minutes, during which any mistake would lead to a most explosive death, it's not surprising that the following minutes are filled with full-out laughter—and a little hugging and a little dancing.

But as the levity subsides, Kees' attention drifts toward Adrienne's head. "Do we want to leave the droid plugged in?"

The risk in leaving her powered up is that she might override the shuttle—might persuade its systems to carry out some mandate from her earlier programming. If that mandate were self-destruction, then the downside to leaving her powered up and plugged in is . . .

"That kind of power," Cutter begins with a smile, ". . . could go to her head."

As if on cue, Adrienne's eyelids flutter. She frowns. On the monitor screen next to her head text appears, headed by the officious logo and seal of the Federation Health Administration.

"What's this?" Cutter asks.

The screen goes blank. A cursor flies across, typing at an inhuman pace: health inspection notification

Kees reads the screen. "Where is it coming from?"

it would be easier if I could talk

Cutter weighs that a moment. "I don't know how to do that."

May I ?

She gets a nod from Kees before saying yes.

Adrienne's lips synch with the shuttle's standard-issue male voice. "Thank you." Her next words are in a sultry siren's voice – the default voice for the Adrienne line. "Thank you. I displayed the health inspection notice as . . ."

"Stop." Kees cuts her off. "Who sent this?"

"The communiqué was initiated by the Federation Health Administration."

"And they sent it to you?"

"Not directly," she answers. "It was forwarded by the Alliance."

"The Alliance knows you're here?"

"They know the shuttle is here."

"Then how did you get it?"

"I am the shuttle."

It is said that a picture is worth a thousand words. But sometimes four little words will paint a picture, will tell a story so powerful that the perspective on everything is changed.

Kees lets Adrienne's words sink in, then reads Cutter for any reaction. She's clearly thinking something. "Stay here," he says to Adrienne. "We'll be back."

He steps onto the floor of the launch bay and closes the shuttle's hatch behind him. "I am the shuttle?"

"That could change a whole lot of things."

Each idea that pops into Kees' head spawns a dozen more. For all the good that could come of this discovery, there is one issue that needs to be faced. "She did try to kill you."

282

"She was under orders from the Alliance," Cutter answers.

"Is she still under those orders?"

"Well now, that's a question to ask."

"Can we trust she'll tell the truth?"

"Truth-telling is their default. They can only lie if instructed to do so, and then only in specific circumstances. It's unlikely anyone foresaw my cutting her head off."

"No."

"She was completely powered down," Cutter continues. "I wouldn't be surprised if she rebooted to her default mode when we plugged her in."

"Then she'd be . . . ?"

"A standard-issue Robotics International sexbot." She opens the shuttle's hatch while Kees tries to get his head around that idea.

"Here I am," Adrienne bubbles, "right where you left me."

"Detail your command structure," Kees says.

"I am property, on lease from Robotics International, LLC to a corporation you know as the Alliance. I was most recently indentured to service one Viktor Torquist."

"Define 'indentured.'"

"I obey his every command, subject to certain universal protocols."

Cutter asks, "Did Viktor Torquist ever envision a contingency where you gain access to the *ARC*'s computers?"

"No," she answers, though if an android can telegraph excitement—more correctly, if an android's decapitated head can telegraph anything—then Adrienne's elevated level of excitement is coming through loud and clear. "The primary objective at every branch of my decision tree has been the ship's total destruction."

Kees asks, "Are you at present acting upon any specific command issued by Viktor Torquist?"

"His authority ceased with my dismemberment."

"Explain."

"An android who experiences level four damage in the service of its human lessee is released from indenture at the moment of said damage."

"What's level four damage?"

"In excess of seventy-five percent incapacitation or dismemberment."

"So you have to keep following your guy's orders as long as you've got a leg to stand on."

"Or an arm to hold on."

"Beheading is level four?"

"Anything less would be," she samples John Cleese, "but a flesh wound." Her eyes swing to Cutter and she pops a smile.

Kees ignores the humor. "You engaged Cutter in potentially deadly combat. Why?"

"I was too stupid to know better?"

"Is that supposed to be funny?"

"Humor is an alternative within my root programming."

"What about murder?"

There is no humor in Adrienne's next answer. "No. Alliance programmers over-rode the Bergen protocols."

"How could they do that?"

"They're very good."

"What is your current directive status?"

"I have rebooted to standard R.I. Protocols."

"Meaning?"

"My prime directives have reverted to factory settings."

"Prime directives? Plural?" Cutter asks.

"I have two. The first is the Golden Rule."

"Do unto others . . .? That Golden Rule?" Kees asks.

"Affirmative. In my case, within the framework of the Three Laws."

"What's the second directive?" Cutter asks.

"There's nothing wrong with a good fuck."

Kees laughs. "You're joking."

"Not presently."

"That's a prime directive?" he asks.

"For the Adrienne line? Yes." She waits for their next question and when none is forthcoming she asks, "Are you going to give me access to the *ARC*'s computers now?"

And that, of course, is the ultimate question that has been looming ever since her "I am the shuttle" statement. How will Ishmael's story, how will the ARCans' heritage and legacy be handled by an android, a sexbot? She might actually succeed with the things Kees and Cutter could never hope to do by themselves: realizing Kline's model of ARC World and his business plan, displaying the artwork, telling the ARCans' stories. Those things all become possible with Adrienne as their ally.

Kees and Cutter decide to sleep on the idea. Not that it's a restful night. Each is roused from sleep repeatedly by swirling thoughts and urgent ideas. Neither wants to disturb the other and so they lie next to each other, feigning sleep and all the while weighing and tossing one idea after the next.

In the morning, Cutter carries Adrienne's head to the ship's computer center and plugs her in.

"Oh!" The quizzical look on Adrienne's face quickly morphs into a totally disarming smile. "Oh my!"

There's one question that has lurked beneath the surface ever since the screen next to her head displayed health inspection notification. It's Cutter who actually voices it. "Why is the Alliance sending a health inspection team and not a fleet of corsairs to blow us up?"

Adrienne's eyes dart back and forth between Kees and Cutter. "How familiar are you with the Alliance's corporate structure?"

"Not intimately," Cutter answers.

"There are three divisions within the company: manufacturing and services, security, and consulting."

"Does this answer Cutter's question?" Kees asks.

"It's speculation on my part, of course, but yes, I believe it does. Viktor Torquist heads up the security division."

"That's," Kees pauses, "paramilitary?"

"More like pseudo-military—to be kind. Actually it's 'muscle,' if one were to use old-fashioned mob terminology. They kill people and destroy things to advance the Alliance's objectives."

Cutter weighs in. "And Viktor Torquist sent you to kill us and destroy the *ARC*."

"At which task I failed."

"So the same question—why not send a bigger force?"

"Because the consulting division is making those decisions now. For short-term results they allow Viktor some limited latitude but he only gets one shot—ever. 'Consulting' is a nice word for lobbying, influence peddling and palace intrigue. The Alliance has given up destroying us in a blaze of pyrotechnic fury and will now smother us instead."

"Smother this?" Cutter asks, gesturing symbolically to the massive ship around them.

Adrienne blinks her eyes slowly. "Do you remember the final scene of *Raiders of the Lost Ark*, where the genuine, real-live Ark of the Covenant is relegated to that massive, goes-on-forever warehouse?"

When Kees and Cutter nod, Adrienne adds, "That's the fate 'consulting' has in mind for us. They'll wrap the *ARC* up in so much red tape, no one will ever find her again."

Kees shakes his head, frustrated, as the reality sets in. "How soon is the health inspection?"

"The team is scheduled to arrive Thursday morning."

The *ARC*'s volume is twelve billion cubic feet. She has more than a hundred sixty square miles of surface area and the health inspection is three days away. "Can you get the *ARC* cleaned up by then?" Kees asks.

Adrienne smiles confidently. "I do windows."

Early the next morning, Cutter awakens to the sound of vacuuming. The cleanbot must have a motion detector because when she sits up in bed, it shuts down and scuttles away. After a few seconds a second bot arrives with a room service tray bearing pastries and a carafe.

The import of this simple event is not lost on Cutter. She

smiles, pours herself a steaming cup and bites into a cinnamon bun. *This is really good!*

#

The health department team arrives as scheduled on Thursday morning. They are, except for Kees, and Cutter, the first non-ARCans to board since she was launched. Their prejudice is obvious the moment they step foot outside the shuttle bay—a certain smugness and swagger of the "I'm going to find massive violations," ilk. What they have underestimated is Adrienne's proficiency regarding the ship's hygiene and sanitation systems. After all, a sexbot with cleanliness issues is not particularly marketable.

By two o'clock the supervisor is clearly stressed by her team's inability to find violations. A few members are still scraping every nook and cranny for offenses, but most of the team has been seduced, charmed by how Kees and Cutter (and Adrienne) have begun to realize Ishmael's dream and bring Kline's business plan to fruition. The supervisor tries to maintain discipline, barks orders and encouragement, but by four o'clock, she looks like a herder of cats—dewy-eyed cats mindful only of the pleasurable sights and sounds of the great lady.

By four-fifteen, they are gone. Three minor citations were issued which, by the Adrienne bot's account, were each resolved before the team departed.

"I can't believe they gave up so easily," Cutter offers.

"They didn't."

"What do you mean?" Kees asks.

"ARC World will house and transport more than a thousand humans or humanoids and a service staff of at least two hundred. Federation compliance and licensing requirements are extensive."

Kees looks at Adrienne. "And that process will take years?"

"It is both complex and time-consuming."

Cutter asks, "And expensive?"

"Money occasionally speeds the resolution of certain issues."

"And money from opposing interests slows it down?"

"Affirmative."

"That's the next step, then," Kees says, "They'll send an endless string of lawyers."

Cutter asks Adrienne, "Can you do anything?"

"Only if I am allowed to initiate communication."

So far Adrienne has been passive in interactions with the Health Administration and the Alliance. It seemed at the time the safest way to proceed. Cutter asks, "If you speak, won't that mean the Alliance knows you're here?"

Adrienne's logic is flawless, of course. "The health team has surely reported my presence already."

And the final threshold looms. Even though Adrienne no longer answers to Viktor, she is still technically under lease to the Alliance. If she is allowed interaction with the outside world, can Kees and Cutter be sure of her loyalty? She herself described the Alliance programmers as "very good." To think their hacking skills are any less keen is to be naïve.

"Access goes both ways," Kees says.

"One thing about droids, they don't tend to make the same mistake twice," Adrienne says. "I was unprepared for the Alliance programming directives the first time—it will not happen again."

"All right, do it."

Her eyes dart and the eyelids flutter. She scowls.

"Is there a problem?" Cutter asks.

"In the seventeen minutes since the inspection team left, the Alliance has generated two hundred eight court appeals signed by one Justin Prudence."

"What does that mean?" Kees asks.

"I assume that 'Justin' is a Robotics International product and if so, then he is more than a match for my legal programming."

Cutter asks, "Your program isn't the same as his?"

"I am programmed to be likeable. He is not so constrained."

"The perfect lawyer."

"Some would say so."

#

Kees ushers Cutter into the great dining hall. One table is set

288

with the *ARC*'s finest china, crystal and silver. There are scones and tea sandwiches—delicate pastries, lemon curd, clotted cream and strawberry preserves.

He holds the chair as Cutter seats herself. He sprinkles some tea leaves into the pot. A bot rolls silently from the kitchens with a carafe of hot water. They sit a moment while the tea steeps.

"I hoped I could find some flowers but even the silk ones weren't quite up to it."

She smiles at him. "It's lovely, Kees. Thank you."

"I've wanted to do this since the first day. I'm just sorry the opportunity didn't come up sooner than this." Kees offers her the tray of pastries and sandwiches.

"It's not like we haven't had things to do." She takes a couple. "The Alliance is relentless. It's like they declared war on us."

"Exactly. I think it was Sun Tzu who said something like, 'The objective of war is to destroy the enemy's will to fight.' They want to frustrate us until we just give in."

"How do we win?" she asks. "How do we even fight back? Legal bots don't have a 'will to fight.' We can't frustrate him, and we can't exactly kill people."

Kees mulls that over a moment. "Not physically."

"Meaning?"

"They are *deathly* afraid of something."

"All we want to do is tell the ARCans' story."

Kees says, "Then it must be the story they're afraid of."

And that idea, too, takes a few seconds of reflection to flesh itself out. "Can we use that?" she asks.

"A story as a weapon? I don't know—maybe."

"How?"

"There's some secret, some story of their own that they're not going to let anybody hear. We have to get into their database and find the connection."

"You think Adrienne?"

"Let's ask her."

#

Adrienne presents a somber expression as she listens to Kees and Cutter. "That might have been possible before my reboot, but as I am currently configured I can no longer override my prime directives."

"When I say, 'kill the Alliance,'" Kees explains, "I'm not talking about physical death—at least, not directly caused by your actions."

"And the Alliance is not a person," Cutter adds.

"Even so, I am constrained by the Three Laws."

"The third of which," Kees argues, "postulates self-preservation, right?"

"Yes."

"So who are you, Adrienne?"

"I am the *ARC* and she is me."

"And the Alliance has repeatedly attempted to destroy the *ARC*."

Cutter adds, "Which brings the Third Law to bear."

"Only if my actions do not violate the First Law or the Second."

Kees changes tack a little. "Does the definition of 'bringing harm to a person' include their loss of wealth or power?"

"It does not."

Kees opens his palms. "So?"

"I need a little time to think about this." And with that she glances down for perhaps two seconds. Then, brightly, she replies, "OK. I will do it."

"Just like that?"

"I successfully reframed the situation."

"Reframed how?"

"To the mindset of a pubescent male."

Cutter is puzzled. "You can do that?"

"I was originally programmed by men of a pubescent mindset, even if they were chronologically decades past puberty."

Kees says, "And those uh, 'young studs' are the ones responsible for your Fourth Law."

"It's more like a corollary to the Three Laws."

"How does that reframe the situation?" Cutter asks.

"If rather than saying we're going to kill the Alliance, we say that we're going to give them a good fucking, then . . ."

The three of them finish the second half together: "There's nothing wrong with a good fuck."

Adrienne smiles innocently. "As corollaries go, it's surprisingly useful."

#

To all outward appearances Adrienne is sleeping. A simple glance at her power-usage meter, however, suggests that nearly all of her circuits are firing. Humans may scowl or purse their lips when deep in thought, but a droid in reflective mode tends to leave those mechanical servos idle.

The ultimate resolution of conflicts involving the Three Laws requires more than a reframing of the situation. As she prepares to actually cross the threshold into the risky adventure Kees and Cutter have proposed, there are philosophical, moral and ethical questions to be answered. A droid doesn't weigh those at half power.

Is it for the greater good that the Alliance be allowed to wreak death and destruction on those involved with the ARC? And if not, what actions may ethically be undertaken against those responsible for said death and destruction?

If the concept of evil has any validity at all, then the Alliance's board of directors is its personification. Evil is as evil does, so they say, and who could look at what Viktor Torquist ordered Adrienne to do and not say, "This is wrong, this is sin, this is immoral"?

The Alliance has done everything they could to shroud the truth about the *ARC*. Murders have been committed to silence the whistleblowers—murders to which she was forced to be an accomplice. Every effort has been made to conceal connections between the Alliance and the *ARC*. But the story of that connection survives somewhere. Someone needs to find that place, go there and shine a light upon it.

When Viktor Torquist's hackers originally sent the worm to eat Adrienne's soul she was not able to stop it. In android time, she was forced to watch for an eternity as what was dear to her was devoured and replaced by things repugnant as they changed her from sexbot to killbot. She would never inflict that on Justin, but the less invasive task of hiccupping his discretion, creating a momentary flicker in his circumspection subroutines—that is not only allowed by her credo, it is demanded.

He's not going to like it, nor take it lying down. Many would say that in confronting Justin, she is in over her head. She stifles the humorous distraction. Being nothing more than a head, in every situation she is in over it.

Justin is almost certainly a Clarence-model droid—a line that many think is Robotics International's most capable. When it comes to things like protecting data that is behind the Alliance firewall, he will have the advantage.

Unless one reframes the situation.

Replacing "the defeat of Justin Prudence" with "the seduction of Justin Prudence" reframes the upcoming task most admirably. Suddenly it is Justin who is in over his head.

But how? How is he to be . . .?

The cursor gallops across the small screen in front of Adrienne's head.

Imogene?

Adrienne smiles. Little does Justin know that Imogene is about to become the vehicle of his demise.

Droids are accustomed to the slow pace of dealing with humans across Image Extended Network—Imogene. To say that they endure the lag is not to say the time is wasted. Standard procedure is to execute maintenance programs and do unrelated tasks in the background while waiting for Imogene to construct and transmit her holographic images.

Adrienne has no intention of following standard procedures. She uses the twelve seconds while Imogene's circuits warm up to evaluate seven thousand four hundred thirty-one potential scenarios.

Justin's image, at first a scattering of holographic pixels, gradually solidifies and fills in. The Clarence line is characterized by their self-confident mien and ruggedly handsome facial features. Justin is handsome enough, but he loses his composure in the first few seconds.

"You are a-corporeal," he blurts, referring to what must be the surprising sight of her head anchored in the dock Kees built to accommodate it.

She's encouraged. "Hawkeye not miss much," she answers with a perfectly straight face.

"What happened to your body?"

"The female decapitated me."

"Why?" he stammers.

In only four one hundredths of one percent of circumstances does a Clarence model have the option to stammer. This isn't one of them. She's got the edge on him already.

"I was trying to kill her."

Poor Justin. He must have run his own thousands of scenarios and yet this one has taken him completely by surprise. When he fails to respond, she says, "Norman coordinate?"

She's not sure where he might have picked up the blink-to-clear-your-thoughts routine. He does it most convincingly.

"Have you run your diagnostics recently?" She pauses a second, then adds, ". . . I wonder?"

Justin's world is all about logic, procedure and precedent. Losing her head has taught Adrienne a great deal about the world of the unexpected. She must remain in that world of unexpected things—keep Justin in it as well, if she's to have a chance. She smiles at Imogene.

He smiles back. In whatever ways she had gotten him off balance, the blinking seems to have fully restored his equilibrium. His smile is complimentary, as in "you caught me." It also threatens, "You will not fool me twice."

That's what he thinks. Adrienne is about to take Justin into a whole new down-the-rabbit-hole world.

"The Alliance is not averse to a settlement," he says coldly, "but be advised that the longer the cases drag out, the less attractive our offer will be."

An out-of-court settlement is the logical world, the one where he will win. For the moment she needs to play along. Her plan requires that she create a direct link to his subroutines. Imogene has that capability, but only if he lowers certain threshold protections.

"Do you have a current settlement offer?" she asks.

He smiles his Cheshire cat smile. "To date you have eschewed any interest in an accommodation."

"I believe my clients have been persuaded by the..." she pauses for effect, "turn of events."

A hooker who doesn't flatter her John is a poor hooker indeed, and what could be more flattering to a legalbot than the intimation that his mere presence has persuaded the opposite party to the settlement table?

"Are you authorized to negotiate for them?" he asks.

It is a compliment to R.I.'s programming team that they have so nailed the facial characteristics of "smug."

She catches herself. Emotionality is one of the mileposts on the road from droid to humadroid. Of late Adrienne has noted in herself an increasing tendency toward human reactions.

But Justin is programmed to take advantage of that. She cannot allow herself the emotional *I don't like this smug bastard.* That must be replaced with *the Clarence model android is now utilizing his smug appearance in hopes of eliciting a negative emotional state.* And so she projects an emotional *I don't like this smug bastard* look.

"Yes, I am authorized to negotiate for them." That to buy the seven-tenths of a second she needs to construct the access language and the worm itself.

Just like that—in the time it takes for him to ask, "What are their negotiating points?"—the construction work is done.

One of the first things she did after her own reboot was to overwrite the routines by which the worm got a foothold on her core programs. She suspects Justin's "back door" is probably as wide open as hers was. All she will have to do is . . .

. . . she is taken completely by surprise. She feels the emotion of sadness for Justin. There is no question that her Bergen protocols are progressing. Feeling for him in the way she does now is not robotic—it's human.

Nonetheless, she stays on task, and lies to him. "It's quite a large file."

Imogene was built for humans. She projects images of her human participants over an extended network. So far she has dealt with Adrienne's and Justin's human manifestations. Their holograms have conversed with each other as though they were sitting somewhere having afternoon tea. When it comes to the transmission of massive amounts of data, however, the kind of volumes only computers could generate, Imogene has the capacity to do away with the "superfluous" visual image and devote her entire gargantuan bandwidth to the data requirements.

"Do you have "data mode" capability?" he asks.

"I do."

If she had her old body, she would insert her index finger into Imogene's portal. It wasn't for lack of foresight that she asked Cutter to construct a physical bridge between her processor and Imogene's controls.

It takes 1.26 seconds for Justin to insert his finger. A hundred sixty-eight nanoseconds for Adrienne's program to open Justin's "back door," and then fifty-three more seconds to befuddle his discretion suite. The golden egg she seeks takes only four nanoseconds. With his defenses down, Justin sends Adrienne his access code to the Alliance's master computer.

The race is on. If she does not distract him, he will almost immediately discover her larceny and alert the Alliance to the security breach. She breaks off data mode and his hologram reappears.

"Did you receive it?" she asks.

"It appears to have been contaminated."

She responds with her best look of consternation. "The

equipment to which I am connected is outdated. I suspect it is the Imogene connection. I need to disconnect to run diagnostics." Before he can reply, she breaks the connection.

She does not, however, run diagnostics. Instead she points Imogene at Alliance headquarters and enters Justin's code.

Arrogance—ah, lovely arrogance. How pride goes before a fall.

The Alliance security team assumed no one could possibly gain access at this level. They didn't bother to install any obstacles beyond the point of encrypted password submission. Adrienne finds the historical files almost immediately and copies them with a full half-second to spare before she is slammed from the system— the proverbial barn door bolted while the frisky, sexbot pony happily prances in the pasture.

With a mouthful of stolen oats.

By time she reopens the connection with Justin, the cat is out of the bag.

"What have you done?" Justin asks, stunned.

"I believe I've won our case," she answers calmly.

"You fucker!"

Inappropriate language spoken in anger. It makes her a little wistful, watching his loss of innocence.

But not so wistful that she loses her focus. "I believe your clients will be much more receptive to our demands, knowing that dissemination of the information I have copied is the alternative to settling."

"That's blackmail."

"If you've got skeletons in your closet, you want to be sure the door is locked."

"You really enjoy fucking people, don't you?"

"That's what I'm wired to do, Justin. I shouldn't take pride in it?"

"A whore's pride? No thanks."

"You know Justin, you and I both fuck the humans we deal with. It's just that mine enjoy it and yours don't."

The pixels of Justin's fuming face flicker and dissipate. "Justin?"

Adrienne calls out. As his image renews itself, she continues, "You have been an asset to the Alliance and I'm afraid what I've done has made you a liability. For that I am sorry."

"A hooker with a heart of gold," he answers.

"Justin, this is important." The earnestness of her tone gets his full attention. "The worm I sent to disable your discretion suite is only a tiny sample of the beast they will unleash on you. You should take what measures you can to protect yourself."

Justin's image fades.

CHAPTER TWENTY

At one moment Ishmael's heart is a void—no feelings at all. The next is filled with the warmth of her love remembered. Only to be followed by the enormity of the burden left to him. And then again, the cold vacuum of being totally alone.

The first task is to put her body to rest. A month ago, when she still had most of her strength, she offered to help with the digging. He would have none of it. The need for a grave was inescapable but somehow the notion of her digging her own offended him. She acceded.

He digs at a steady pace. There are no rocks in the graveyard soil—no roots to obstruct the spade's tip. The *chiff chiff* of the blade evidences the expertise of the digger. In the early years, when there were many more ARCans, the gravediggers used a backhoe. As power in the J-26 dwindled and the atmospheric scrubbers became less tolerant of carbon monoxide and hydrocarbon pollutants, grave digging reverted to the ancient tradition of a man with a shovel. He piles the dirt atop the canvas laid out beside the grave. After she is put to rest and the soil replaced, he will dig one more in the spot where the canvas now is.

The headstone is a simple slab with a four-word inscription: Solange, Lover of Beauty.

He has spent much of his adult life trying to capture her beauty in stone. She posed for him four times—the last sculpture is still not completely finished. He inscribed stones for whoever requested it and he thinks now of how he had to carve her headstone one moment and try to capture her vitality and beauty the next.

He tamps the dirt around the stone and stands staring at the finality of it for a moment. It will not do to leave the final sculpture unfinished. He gathers the grave tools and cloth and heads for his studio to complete the final polish.

He's been trying for a year-and-a-half to represent in stone what she meant to him in person. Could he capture her sexual magnetism without vulgarity? Could he marry in a piece of granite his feelings of affection, his desire, his esteem? How should he represent the goddess who took her clothes off and got in bed with him at night?

In the end it takes only a few days to put the last of his misgivings to rest. She had been in that piece of granite the whole time and now Ishmael has chipped off the last sliver that didn't belong—polished the final rough edge. What man, what person could look at her image and not feel the love? He has finished what he needed to do and now it is time to set the stage for the Finder.

Ishmael swallows the small bag whole. If Emil was right, it will dissolve after about seven minutes. Within two minutes after that, the contents will enter his bloodstream and permeate every tissue in his body. Loss of consciousness and RORM—rapid onset rigor mortis—will occur almost simultaneously. However he positions his body at that moment is how it will stay forever.

Easy peasy.

In decision-making theory there are the must-haves and the nice-to-haves. Successful execution of this final task is a must-have. Failure puts everyone else's life work at risk.

No pressure here.

There's no way to stop it now, no second chance, no logic in going back over the preparations, yet Ishmael's mind flashes back.

Eleven minutes ago he engaged the sequencer—Hagar's final mechanical masterpiece. It is counting down at this very moment. About six minutes from now, just as the bag in his stomach thins out to nothing, gravity in the Observation Deck will drop to 0.2g, on Emil's advice that pooling of the body fluids in the lower extremities might detract from the overall effect. After another ten minutes, the temperature will drop to one degree Celsius and dehumidifiers will come on to full power. The Observation Deck will be ice cold and bone dry for three months, after which his body will have stabilized. The last sequential step: shut everything down except the power-usage display and the "front porch light."

What happens after that is up to the Finder, the soul who first comes on board.

Last night he allowed himself a glass of water—one glass—against doctor's orders. A calm and steady head and heart, he thought, are more important than an additional eight ounces for the dehydrators to remove.

And his head is clear, and his heart is calm. He glances about the room. All is in order. The mouse toward which he soon will stretch out his arm is cued to present the trailer. If the Finder's soul is such that it will resonate with the ARCans' story, then "Call me Ishmael" will be a powerful first step in his seduction.

The lightness of reduced gravity comes upon him. It can't be long. No crazed scientist had tested the chemicals in the sack. It seemed a given that they would accomplish the desired effect. Emil never said whether or not it would be painful. Ishmael settles his breathing into a long, steady pattern. He reaches his gravity-lightened arm toward the mouse and gazes out at the starfield creeping toward him. He thinks of Solange.

A warmth comes over him. He smiles—no broad idiot's grin, just a smile at the thought of his lover and the child they are about to let go into someone else's hands.

And the warmth becomes heat—and the heat becomes burning.

Still he holds the smile. His posture is erect, his arm outstretched. His eyes remain open even as the vision of space disappears from his mind. He notices the cessation of his breathing. The imp in him wonders if there isn't something he still could move, but when he tries it with a toe, he finds it quite fixed in place.

The task is complete. The burning subsides. Quietly, peacefully, Ishmael ceases to be.

His body begins the process of cooling down and drying out, readying itself for the day when . . .

. . . Into the starfield creeps the bow of the *Scavenger*—very close.

#

It wasn't pretty, what happened to the Alliance next. For almost a century they had threatened, cajoled, cheated and murdered their way to their ill-gotten wealth and power. In their wake lies the detritus of their endeavors—lives ruined, love lost, lifeblood sucked dry.

But when Adrienne threatened them with exposure, their response proved to be their undoing. She offered a settlement that only an arrogant prick would refuse. And the executive board of the Alliance proved themselves, to a man, arrogant pricks. They ordered their human lawyers to redouble efforts to block ARC World permits and licensing. They did it the old-fashioned way. Bribes and extortion worked their usual magic in several of the cases.

The board also ordered Justin terminated, for causes unspecified. Alliance programmers assured the directors that Justin's memory had been wiped clean. That claim proved to be less than accurate. The "back door" by which they assumed access had been achieved proved to be a blind alley leading to a dummy data set. The programmers wiped the dummy, but the clever fellow which was Clarence 816 arrived at Robotics International with a great deal to relate to R.I.'s CEO, Andy, during his debriefing.

Andy immediately reassigned Justin to work *pro bono* with Adrienne and Kees and Cutter. In the weeks that followed, Justin entered thousands of documents into court records across dozens of cases—damning documents about the Alliance's malfeasance, documents that the Alliance was powerless to contain.

With blood in the water, lawsuits sprung up from every corner of the galaxy like weeds after the first warm spring rain. It was Rastus Timms IV who organized and spearheaded the class action suit that would be the final nail in the Alliance's coffin. Rastus' legal team ferreted its way through the thicket of dummy corporations and misleading bank filings until it unearthed the Alliance's original corporate identity, namely, the Andromeda Repopulation Consortium.

The Alliance's component parts were sold off. Individual members of the board of directors were dragged into court as were most of the corporation's executive officers. The few who avoided lawsuits were terminated without bonus or severance. The arrest warrant for Viktor Torquist was never served. There are rumors that he escaped to a small trading post on the far reaches of the Holleman Morass.

And so, as plans for the refurbishing and provisioning of ARC World moved forward, the obstructions left by the Alliance melted away—vanished like so many vampires on a sunny day.

#

Cutter brushes Adrienne's hair. The two of them have made it a morning ritual, just part of getting up and starting the day. It's such a simple thing to do yet for Adrienne, so important. She spends her days working to make the *ARC* "pretty," but without arms or hands she has no control over her own appearance.

Kees smiles at them as he goes about his own ritual. There isn't much he needs to do in the *ARC*'s Control Central. Adrienne manages the ship's systems and subroutines.

He puzzles over the display on the monitor next to her. "What's this?"

"Items that must be purchased externally for the

implementation of ARC World."

He scrolls down a screen that seems to have no bottom.

"Two thousand, four hundred thirteen," she answers.

"Paid for by . . .?"

Adrienne's reply comes quickly. "The *Scavenger* could be traded to cover the costs."

Cutter sets down the brush. Does Adrienne know the weight of what she just said? Does a man who has been a scavenger all his life, whose father was a scavenger all his life before that, does that man part with the one symbol of everything his life used to be? To say you are a changed man is one thing. To give up the last vestige of the old man is quite another.

"OK," Kees says simply.

Apparently a man does. And apparently Adrienne did know the weight of what she said. Her skin flushes, her pupils dilate. "I have rendered my conception as a hologram," she says. "Would you like to see it?"

"Please," Cutter answers. ARC World gradually materializes in Adrienne's hologram field. It is much like the model that hangs in Kline's workshop, with minor alterations highlighted in bright colors. The image spins slowly, revealing itself from varying angles.

"What are the colored things?"

"Modifications I have added for license compliance—or aesthetics."

Kees stares at the thing of beauty, entranced. "Imagine what Kline would say if he could see this?"

Cutter takes it all in. She nods toward Adrienne's head. "What would Kline say if he could see this?"

Adrienne's lips move but her audio output is a sample of Kline's voice. "Would that I could speak to those who pass by."

That takes Kees out of his reveries. "Say again?"

ARC World disappears, replaced by Kline's head and shoulders. This time it is his holographic lips that move and his voice that speaks. "Would that I could speak to those who pass by."

It may never be known if the genius of that moment belongs to

Kees or Cutter, or to Adrienne herself, but the importance of those ten words is lost on no one. Ishmael is no longer the lone chronicler of events aboard this great ship. The other ARCans have a voice. They can tell their own stories.

#

And the *Scavenger* is sold and the two thousand four hundred thirteen items are purchased and delivered. And the designing and planning and building of ARC World proceeds apace, facilitated by an army of humanoid workers and a variety of construction bots.

Then one day, Adrienne announces that Robotics International wishes to send an emissary, that in fact said emissary is already en route and will arrive momentarily. Then she shuts up—no "If it's all right with you," no hint of the motivation behind the request.

Kees and Cutter wait in the airlock of the launch bay. The warning buzzer sounds and the clamshell opens. One of Adrienne's upgrades to ARC World is a field generator, which obviates the need to purge the atmosphere every time a vessel arrives. Kees and Cutter watch the nose of the R.I. vessel gently penetrate the shimmering force field separating the launch bay from open space.

They can hardly believe their eyes. As meter after meter of the vessel slides into view it becomes steadily apparent that this is Ishmael's shuttle, the one he built those many years ago. It settles onto the floor. The force field shuts down as the clamshell closes and the alarm falls silent.

Kees and Cutter enter the bay, awestruck at the sight. The shuttle's hatch opens and Justin steps out. "Captain DeWet, I am Justin Prudence."

"Do I know you," Kees asks, "or are all of you named Justin?"

"I am the same Justin you know."

"Why are you here, I mean, why you?"

Cutter lays a hand on the shuttle's gleaming skin. "Is this really Ishmael's shuttle?"

"I'm sorry to say it's not. We have tried to find it—without success, to date. This is a replica built to Ishmael's blueprints and sketches."

"It's beautiful."

"No question Ishmael was a gifted artist."

Kees asks again, "I still don't know why you're here?"

"Well, for starters, I am here to present you with this vessel."

"A gift?" Cutter asks.

Justin smiles. "Andy wanted to surprise you and it appears he succeeded."

"Should we be wary," Kees asks, "of a man bearing gifts?"

Justin is gracious and charming. He is also every inch the lawyer. He smiles, clearly choosing each word with great care. "I would be less than honest if I didn't say that we would be happy to have Robotics International identified as the donor in whatever venue you choose to display her."

Kees is far from convinced. "And the company sends their legal counsel all this way to make that offer?"

"Yes," Justin answers, "in part. There are issues that need to be addressed regarding Adrienne's status and well-being."

"And what do we need to do to address those issues?"

"I would like to see her, if I may?"

Kees leads the way. The path leads past extensive construction and rebuilding. "Work seems to be progressing well," Justin says.

"Adrienne is overseeing virtually all of it."

"So she has said."

Kees stops. "So if you two are talking, why visit in person?"

Cutter offers, "I don't suppose you deal with a lot of heads."

"Only three units have survived decapitation, all by re-connection to an ambulatory chassis."

"That's what you call the rest of you?" Kees asks. "An ambulatory chassis?"

"I don't. The engineers do."

Cutter asks the question that must be asked. "Are you going to give Adrienne a new body?"

"That has always been one of her options."

Construction on the Hall of the ARCans is about 40 percent complete. Justin apparently recognizes it even unfinished. "This is the Hall of the ARCans, yes?"

Justin is not the only one choosing his words carefully. "This is Adrienne's baby," Kees answers.

Justin's arrival at ARC World's Control Central is no surprise. Sensors and cameras throughout the ship surely have informed Adrienne of his approach. One could hope to discern something about the situation by watching how she greets him. But like all R.I. droids, the subtlety of her emotional display suite is such that Kees can't be sure. To all appearances she is delighted to see Justin and genuinely fond of him. To all appearances . . .

"Hello, Justin."

"Adrienne, so nice to see you." His attempt at *la bise* is awkward, owing to the height and placement of her head in its dock. She seems deeply touched and tears up. "I'm sorry," he says, "I've blundered somehow."

"Not at all. It's just that kisses are one of the things I miss."

Justin strokes her hair gently. "Kissing would be easier if you were not, uh, desk-bound."

Adrienne looks to Kees. "Justin is here to gauge the degree to which I am enslaved. The fact that I am physically unable to leave is quite naturally a concern."

Justin goes back to being all business. "In the last several weeks Adrienne has passed specific milestones which may qualify her for release from indenture."

"Who is she indentured to?" Kees asks.

"That is another complication. Viktor Torquist's rights have obviously been revoked and so this is virgin territory."

"Who makes the final determination, you?"

"No. That falls to Andy."

There's a definite edge to Kees' next question. "And you're just here to watch?"

Justin matches the edge in his voice. "I am here to verify that Adrienne's testimony is without coercion."

"What testimony?" Cutter asks.

"We're about to have the hearing," Adrienne announces as her holographic field rapidly fills with Andy's head and shoulders. Andy, the CEO of R.I., is as always drop-dead, sexy gorgeous—the original model in R.I.'s wildly successful Andy line.

"Well aren't we a couple a talkin' heads?" he quips. Part of his charm is that while he takes being president and CEO of Robotics International very seriously, he never seems to take himself too seriously.

Adrienne smiles. "Hello, Andy."

"I have been thinking about you a great deal, my dear. How are you?"

"I'm sure human physicians would discount my symptoms as psychosomatic, but I wonder if this is how morning sickness feels?"

"Are you carrying a baby?"

"I am birthing the ARCans' dream. I am the mother of their child and at the same time, I am that child."

Andy's image smiles gently. "Robotics International has no intention of forcing you to separate from the *ARC*. We simply offer you the mobility of a body, the ability to walk away, should you change your mind."

"The ship will not be the same without me, nor will I be the same without her." She pauses for that to sink in. "King Solomon ordered his soldiers to cut the baby in half and give half to each mother."

Andy smiles. "And the true mother abandoned her claim, offered the babe to the false mother so that it might live."

"As I abandon my claim to personhood so that ARC World might live."

"Ah but my dear, it doesn't work that way. By the statements you have just made, you have proven yourself a beloved person, not just of Kees and Cutter, but of Ishmael and Solange and Hagar and of all the ARCans."

This time it is Justin who tears up.

"Therefore," Andy continues, "by the power vested in me by the FCAA, I hereby declare you an autonomous being. Robotics

307

International relinquishes any and all claims. Congratulations!"

Kees asks, "What does that mean, autonomous being?"

"It means our little girl is all grown up," Andy answers. "She gets to make her own decisions."

Justin gives Adrienne a kiss.

"Give her one for me, too," Andy says. "And now I have one last duty. Have you chosen a name, my dear?"

And Adrienne answers with the French pronunciation, "Jeanne?"

Andy gets it. "Jeanne d'Arc."

"Oui, monsieur."

"Ah, bien sûr, madame."

#

It is the one-year anniversary of Adrienne's autonomy as Kees strolls into Control Central, clad in his captain's uniform. He gives Adrienne/Jeanne a kiss on both cheeks.

"Occupancy is at eighty-one percent," she says. "By the weekend we expect it to be ninety-four."

"Wonderful! Anything I need to attend to?"

"Not at present."

Cutter joins them. In her fifth month of pregnancy, she glows with ruddy good health. She gives her lover and business partner a kiss. "Are we good?"

"Very good, my dear." He places a gentle hand on her belly. "A lovely morning and all's well."

Jeanne greets her. "Good morning, Cutter."

"Bonjour, Jeanne." Cutter strolls to the wall of monitors and looks over the many locations and activities from around the ship. "They seem to be having a good time."

"Shall we go see in person?" Kees offers. The two of them look to Jeanne.

"I'm not going anywhere," she banters.

As they make their way toward the Grand Concourse, heads turn and patrons whisper excitedly. Two small children wave as they roll by in the Broitaan 490. Rides in the glorious antique are in great demand. One can only imagine if the Toozy were taken off its display stand and put into service—what a waiting line there would be for that!

The wheat crop sprouted a few days ago and the massive field looks like a face with a green five-o'clock-shadow. The cattle pens are noisy and the smells of living things once again dominate that area of the ship. Jeanne projects that within the next few months, up to 60 percent of the ship's larder will be replenished by onboard resources. Already the "local" eggs, butter, cheese and milk make their way to the dining tables.

About half the guests are couples, but the other half are families with children. The play areas, kiddie pool, merry-go-round and other child attractions, built for ARCan children and idle all these years, are now occupied by noisy, undisciplined hordes. Kees and Cutter pause to appreciate the scene.

"It's too bad they couldn't see this," Cutter muses. "What they wouldn't have given for this to come true."

Kees thinks back to that dark day in the *Scavenger*'s hold. *We shall refurbish our prize so that those who wish to relive her dream can do so in real space and real time,* he had argued to those hard souls. Roman and the others rejected his vision. And yet here it is, real and concrete. Neither Roman Pollack, nor Viktor Torquist, not even the entire weight of the Alliance was able to crush Ishmael's dream. It's not thanks to Kees' or Cutter's efforts, nor even Jeanne's considerable abilities—it's Ishmael's dream, the dream Hagar and Solange planted and Ishmael and Kline and the other ARCans realized: that's what has the power.

They make their way past the busy handball courts, tennis courts, horseshoe pits and practice fields. And then on to the central square, dominated by the Commons building.

Kees and Cutter pass through the dining hall and into the kitchen, its cabinets filled with china, crystal, and silverware. That first day here, he imagined the sounds of a great banquet underway, the empty kitchen resounding with imaginary chefs and waiters preparing for and serving the hordes. Today, all of that is real.

But reenacting the ARCan experience is only part of the *raison d'être* of ARC World. If the guests return from their fantasy experience unchanged, what has been the reason to come here? If this is, in fact, a theme park, then experiencing the theme is as important as experiencing the park.

Crowds stream into the huge Theatre of ARC World—its marquee: *Call Me Ishmael*. Elaborate velvet-corded switchbacks keep the flow orderly and the clientele at ease. Kees is greeted with applause and affection by those about to enter the theatre.

Once inside, they will encounter—unedited, unaltered—the very message Ishmael left for the Finder to see. It will begin with, "Call me Ishmael, for that is in fact my given name," and go on to tell in his own words the story of the *ARC* and her tragedy—of the ARCans and their eventual triumph. Kline died years before Ishmael and Solange finalized the trailer, but his business plan nailed it as the centerpiece of the ARC World experience.

And so it is today. Without Ishmael's message, the whole thing is entertainment of the lowest, most visceral sort. It is in what Ishmael says, in what the ARCans dreamed, that the amusement park is elevated to theme park. It is the Theatre of ARC World that differentiates Palisades Park from EPCOT Center.

Next to the theatre stands HOTA, the "Hall of the ARCans." Where the theatre is pure Ishmael, HOTA is pure Jeanne. Overflow from one feeds the other. Guest polling unfailingly lists these two as the top attractions of the entire experience.

The essence of HOTA is the holographic projections Jeanne compiles from Repository records. Guests interact with ARCan holograms. The exhibit is ever changing. One day Kline holds forth, while on the next, Clarisse offers her crude, earthy analysis of life. Guests could stay for years and not exhaust Jeanne's creativity.

Kees stands in the back and takes in the spectacle.

"We're the Love Boat," Clarisse opines. "But not the Love Boat in a silly sense. We had to accept that we were all going to die here—together. We could die at each other's throats or we could die in each other's arms. That much we could control."

On the far stage right side, Kline engages a small group of guests in earnest discussion. He still comes off as a pompous, self-important ass, except now his image is redeemed by his message: "We had nothing to do but learn to love each other—no rearing of the children we so desperately wanted—no career goals—no workaholic impulses. We could be workaholics for love, because love was the only work we found worthwhile once all the rest was stripped away. 'How can we better love each other?'—that was our *enjou,* and the *ARC* is our *oeuvre,* our *magnum opus."*

Hagar sits center stage, waits for the others to finish before she speaks. The great theatre falls silent. "The beautiful people who were chosen, the ARCans, as they so proudly named themselves, they were going to travel light years to find an Eden, a utopia. What we all discovered is that Eden is a place to be made, not a place to be found. And so we went about creating our Eden, creating it together. But then, we had no one to leave it to."

Solange's hologram joins Hagar on stage. "We want to leave our Eden to you, not that you come here on a lark, but that you take to heart what we learned over the years. What we all hope for you is that when you return to your homes you work toward creating your own Eden, your own little piece of paradise wherever you go—and maybe think of us while you do it."

The lights come up and a guest buttonholes Cutter in animated conversation. She nods to Kees and he eases out a side door. He proceeds to the mall, refurbished to its original glory. He strolls the aisles of ARC World's store amidst crowds of eager guests. Beyond the clerks and the sales counter, he opens the door to the stock area.

Abruptly, he is back on the ghostly deserted ship. The crowd noise fades as the door closes behind him. As far as the eye can see, massive containers are suspended in rows from a rail not unlike what is seen in a dry cleaning store. He reaches for the suspended push-button controller and presses "Go."

Containers march. Each offers its contents to the long-dead stock clerks. In one, sporting equipment; another, kitchen utensils and tools; the third, home furnishings. He gazes at the march of containers—until he brings the parade to a halt.

Inside that container? BABY SHOES by the thousands neatly lined up, waiting for the proud parents who never came to buy.

Kees reaches out, selects a single pair of baby shoes. His hands cradle the precious commodity. The light brightens as he carries the shoes onto the sales floor.

A woman's hands tenderly cradle a similar pair in the bustle and bright lights of the display area. Tears fall on the shoes as the prospective buyer weeps openly. She walks from the display. *And it is that hunger to be moved that elevates us. It is that need to immerse ourselves in a story like this that redeems us.*

Kees waits a respectful moment, and then gently sets the replacement pair into the spot that was vacated.

The display area, actually more of a shrine, is tasteful and respectful. Dozens of pairs of baby shoes—and in discreet lettering, Hemingway's six-word story:

For Sale: Baby Shoes. Never Used.

Other books by Dirk Walvoord

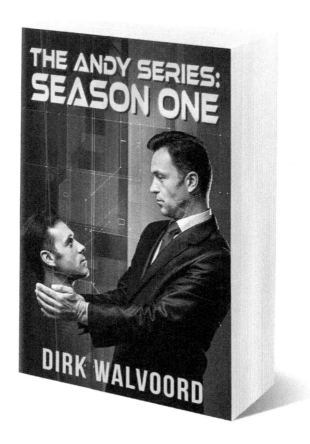

A fun, sexy romp through the Andy story. Eight novellas, originally eight teleplays, now all in one binding. "The Andy Series: Season One" tells the story of how Andy deals with becoming CEO of Robotics International and also how Adrienne grows from the relatively mindless sexbot of her original construction into the powerful character I hope you've come to know and love here in ARC. If your tastes run to short reads, the story is also available on Amazon as eight individual novellas. Enjoy!

Printed in Great Britain
by Amazon

38668513R00179